THE UNPLANNED WEDDING

L. STEELE

CONTENT NOTE

This book contains themes which some may find challenging. For more information please click here
Or scan this QR code

FAMILY TREE

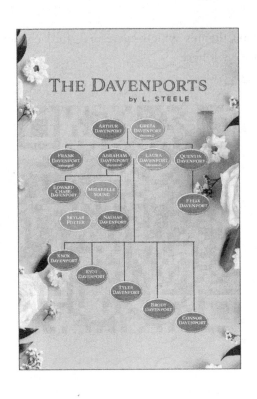

WELCOME TO PRIMROSE HILL

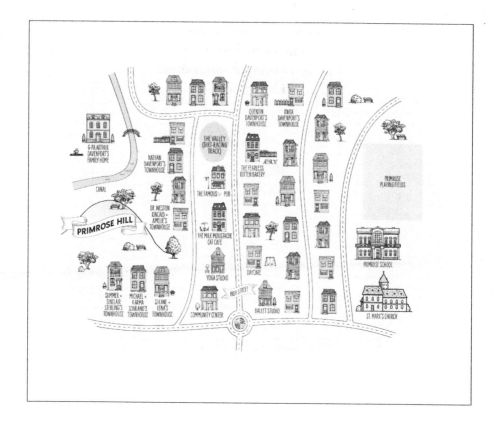

DEDICATION

FOR THE GOOD GIRLS
WHOSE MOTTO IS:
"I'LL BE A FEMINIST TOMORROW,"
I SEE YOU!

1

June

"In the six months since Knox Davenport took over as the interim CEO of the Davenport Group media division, he's run through a string of assistants. He has a chronic bad attitude." The Human Resources Manager wrings her hands. "He is grumpy. And irritable. *And* ill-tempered. Not to mention, impatient. He's not an easy man to please."

I swallow. He sounds like an absolute nightmare to work for, if I'm being honest. But it's not like I have a choice. I've been without a job for six months. I've exhausted my savings and had to go into debt to take care of my family. I'd hoped to engage an adoption search specialist to track down my birth mother; but now, I don't have the money to do that either. Then I heard about this position from my friend Zoey.

I applied and was sure I wouldn't get an acknowledgement of my application. So, imagine my surprise when I got a call to interview. You can bet, I'm not going to mess up this opportunity.

"How much did you say the position pays?" I ask.

She names a monthly salary, which is more than I earned in a year in any of my previous roles. My gaze widens, and my jaw drops.

"It's generous"—she nods—"for a reason."

"Oh?" I push my oversized spectacles up my nose.

"Most of his assistants quit within the hour, thanks to his unpleasant temperament." She shudders. "Those who made it past that left before the end of the day. They found it too traumatizing to look at his"—she gestures to her face— "you know?"

"I don't actually." *What is she referring to?* I researched the Davenport Group and its management team before I came here. I even drew up a plan on how to address weaknesses I noticed in the company's image, which I hoped to present during my interview. However, I didn't find anything alluding to whatever it is she's referring to.

She notices the chagrin on my face and leans in, then beckons me closer.

I mirror her move.

"He used to be a commando in the Royal Marines, which is where he was disfigured. His features are rather grotesque," she says in a stage whisper.

I stare at her. Some of my shock at her statement must show on my face, for she raises her hand. "I know, it may seem impolite for me to share that, but I think it's best to prepare you for what you're going to see." She folds her arms across her chest. "On the positive side, there's no fear of you falling for him." She shrugs.

Me? Falling for my future boss? I scowl. You can bet I'm not going there. Getting this job and keeping it, so I can earn enough to take care of my family, is of the utmost importance. I'd never screw that up.

"In fact, you won't find it difficult to keep your attention from his face, for the rest of him is sooo built." She blinks rapidly. "It makes you want to touch his chest to find out if the muscles under it are as sculpted as his shirt hints at..." She reddens.

I can't stop myself from scowling. I don't know this guy, but I feel like I should tell her not to objectify him. But before I can voice my opinion, she firms her lips. "Gosh, I shouldn't have said that. In fact, *forget* I said that. I tend to lose track of my thoughts where The Beast is concerned."

"The *beast?*" My frown deepens.

"With a capital B. That's the nickname we have for him." She squirms in her seat. "I shouldn't have revealed that, either."

No, you shouldn't have. And you're the HR Manager, lady. It's so inappropriate that she indulges in office gossip.

She must realize that she's crossed a line, for she sits upright. "Forget I said that, please." She waves her hand in the air, as if that will remove the images she's put in my head.

She picks up her tablet and scrolls across her screen. "You haven't had an office-based job in a while?"

"Uh, yeah, the job market hasn't been the best." I shuffle my feet. "I couldn't get an office assistant role, so I worked as a waitress for a while."

"Hmph." She makes the sound under her breath, but I hear it. "Waitress, huh?"

There's no missing the judgement in her tone.

My cheeks flush. "Being a waitress helped me learn the importance of interpersonal skills."

"Oh?" She seems taken aback by my words.

I should stop my outburst, but I must defend myself. Besides, this is where I can make an impassioned plea for the job.

I nod. "It helped build my stamina by being on my feet all day. And of course, develop a thick skin from warding off insults from rude patrons. Not to mention, unwanted attention from male customers." I set my jaw, "In my humble opinion, it shows that I have resilience." Something I believe will put me in good stead, from what she's told me about this role. *That* I keep to myself. But I can't prevent myself from adding, "It also indicates that I have perseverance. I don't give up easily."

Something in my words seems to have struck home, for she nods slowly. "I suppose you have a point." She sighs, "Your resume isn't ideal. I'd have preferred someone with more relevant experience for this role, but we're out of alternatives."

I should feel slighted by her implication that I'm their last option, but I don't care. If I get this opportunity, and that extravagant salary which comes with it, that's what matters.

She looks up from her device, reaches for her phone, and dials a number. When the person at the other end answers, she says, "Will you come in please?"

In seconds, the door opens and the young girl I passed at the desk outside the HR Manager's office walks in.

"Zelda, will you show June to her workstation?" The HR lady puts away her device and turns to her screen.

"What do you mean?" I frown.

"You want the job, don't you?" She toggles her mouse to wake up her computer.

I nod.

"It's yours," she responds without looking away from her screen.

"You mean—"

"You start right away."

"Today?" I gape. *I got the job?* "But doesn't he want to interview me?"

"Knox Davenport doesn't interview his assistants; he's too busy making money." She shakes her head. "Please bring in a photo ID and proof of residence tomorrow, so I can prepare the necessary paperwork." She begins to type rapid-fire, indicating she's done with me.

This woman needs a crash-course in etiquette, but my outrage pales in light of the fact I'm now gainfully employed. I was sure I'd botched the meeting, but apparently not. If I'm getting the position without having to interview with the boss, then hey, I'll take it. Joy bubbles up in my chest.

My entire being feels like it's glowing. I want to fist-pump the air but stop myself. Instead, I lower my chin and strive for a neutral voice. "Thank you, I won't let you down."

When she doesn't reply, I hook my bag over my shoulder, rise to my feet and follow Zelda to the elevator, then up to the top floor of the building.

The doors open to a corridor and when I step on the carpet, my three-inch Jimmy Choo knockoffs sink into the plush surface. It's like I'm floating on a cloud. And it's so quiet, I can hear the sound of my heart beating. Or maybe, that's because I'm nervous?

"This is the executive floor," Zelda tells me in a hushed voice. Her blonde curls frame her doll-like features. She's dressed in a black dress that wouldn't be out of place at a nightclub. In comparison, my skirt's hemline falls below my knees and my jacket, which I thought smartened my get-up, makes me feel dowdy and overdressed. I shove those thoughts aside and pay attention to my surroundings.

There are glass-enclosed offices on either side of the corridor, with men and women focused on their computer screens or on their phones. In the center of the room are desks with more men and women busily typing away on keyboards. None of them look up as I pass. One of the women almost meets my eye then looks away. *Huh?* Maybe she was in the middle of something? I brush aside her reaction and follow Zelda to the double doors at the end of the corridor.

Unlike the other offices with glass walls and doors, these doors are made of wood, and the walls are made of concrete. Seems Mr. Knox Davenport relishes his privacy. There's a definite do-not-disturb vibe radiating off of the closed doors to his office.

Zelda indicates the desk at the side. "This's yours."

A wave of happiness sweeps through me. I've hoped for this moment for so long. I've dreamed about a job in a nice office, where I'd be surrounded by industrious colleagues and a boss who'd encourage me, challenge me, and give me the chance to prove myself. But I never thought I'd achieve that position. I walk over and slide into the chair, then place my handbag on the desk.

"The password for the computer is on the post-it note." She gestures to where it's stuck to the computer screen. "The kitchen is through that door."

"Right." I key the password into the computer screen. It unlocks, and I find myself in an inbox. "The email address belongs to someone called Kelly," I point out.

She nods. "That would be his first assistant, who lasted for less than an hour. After that, we didn't bother setting up a new email addresses because it felt like a waste of time."

Right.

"There are a lot of unanswered emails," I say slowly. Over a thousand, to be precise.

"The last assistant quit three weeks ago. After that, we ran out of agencies to send us people, so—" The phone on the desk rings. I jump, then stare at the instrument on the desk.

"Are you going to answer that?" the woman asks. A thread of impatience runs through her tone.

I stare at the phone for a few more seconds—I don't even know what I'm supposed to say—then slowly reach for it. I lift the receiver, clear my throat, but before I can speak a word, a dark male voice growls, "Bring me the reports for the sales meeting. Cancel my five p.m. Send a Tiffany's bracelet and flowers to Rita."

What the —? I grab hold of a pen and start writing on the note pad that's helpfully placed next to the phone.

"I need my tux for this evening. My lunch better not be late. Tell the agency if they don't send in the proofs for the advertisements by four p.m., they can stuff 'em where the sun don't shine." My boss pauses. "And tell my pilot to ready the jet by six p.m. I have a dinner appointment in Brussels."

His voice is so demanding, so assertive, that heat flushes my skin. I push aside my reaction and focus on scrawling his orders.

"Also, I need a fresh cup of coffee, and it better not be cold," he snipes.

I draw in a sharp breath, then ask, "How do you take your —" The line goes dead.

I stare at the receiver. I have to assume that it's The Beast with the capital B. He sounded like one. And his voice was gruff and dark and so... so... *Hot.* I swallow.

I hate how he spoke to me. But even more, I hate the fact that I found his voice so tantalizing. I push aside the thought and focus on the list The Beast gave me. First, the coffee. "I don't suppose you know —" I raise my gaze to find I'm alone.

Zelda's walking down the corridor. She stops to speak to one of the women working outside another one of the offices. Both turn to look at me. Their faces reflect pity. The older woman makes the sign of the cross.

Excuse me? Did she just —? I'm aware, I'm gaping. I school my features into a neutral expression and ignore the sense of foreboding rippling through me.

They turn back to each other and exchange a few more words before Zelda walks off.

My ribcage tightens. She brushed me off. All of a sudden, I feel like I'm back in high school, being ignored by the cool kids. I push up the glasses on my nose. I feel lonely and abandoned and... Shoot, I never got to ask Zelda how my boss takes his coffee.

I rise to my feet and head for the woman she was speaking with. She's an older woman, with her silvery gray hair pulled back. She watches me approach with a wary look.

"I'm June Donnelly." I extend my hand.

She doesn't shake it. "Double espresso, no milk or sugar."

"Excuse me?"

"His coffee." She jerks her chin in the direction of the kitchen. "Better not keep him waiting."

OMG, seriously? Doesn't anyone here know how to be polite? Before I can stop myself, I burst out, "You know, I'm not surprised so many of the other assistants quit within the hour."

"Oh?" Her eyebrows knit.

"Maybe it's not just because of the difficult boss." I pause for a moment. "Maybe it has something to do with the rudeness of the co-workers, too."

I spin around and turn toward the kitchen when she calls out, "I don't mean to be ill-mannered, but I've learned it's best not to invest in relationships with any of Knox's assistants, since they never last."

I turn back toward her. "And by being so unwelcoming, you're ensuring no one will want to stay because they'll feel there's no support system."

She flushes, then has the grace to look embarrassed. "You're right." She rises to her feet and walks over to me. She holds out her hand. "I'm sorry, I was standoffish. I'm Mary, Quentin Davenport's assistant. I'm also the Office Administrator."

I hesitate, then decide not to be churlish about it. I need all the friends I can get if I want to survive this job. I shake her hand. "Nice to meet you."

"You, too, June," she says in a polite, if reserved, voice. At least, that wary look about her eyes is gone.

We size each other up for a few seconds, and I know that she's trying to figure out how long I'm going to be able to stay the course. "I don't give up easily, you know."

I didn't survive being shuttled between foster families before being adopted by tapping out. After months of searching, I didn't land this job which will help me pay off my debts faster than I anticipated, only to quit because my boss has a bad attitude, or because my work-colleagues are disagreeable.

Mary must see the resolution on my face, for her expression softens and she nods. "I'm beginning to see that. I'd say good luck but—"

"But?"

"I have a feeling you make your own luck, June Donnelly." She half smiles.

My throat closes up. After the shitty morning I've had, to hear her words of praise makes me want to burst into tears, but I swallow them down. "Thanks." I clear my throat.

She pats my shoulder, then nods in the direction of my boss' office. "Best not keep him waiting, dear."

She returns to her desk.

I reach the kitchen and find a complicated coffee machine. Thanks to my stint as a barista, I have a double espresso ready in a matter of minutes. I retrace my steps to The Beast's office, taking care not to spill the coffee. When I pass Mary's desk on the way back, she's not there.

I head for my boss' office, then draw in a breath. This is it. Showtime. I tuck stray strands of hair behind my ear, square my shoulders, then knock on the door.

I wait for a few seconds, but there's no answer. I knock again. The seconds stretch further. *Should I wait?* The coffee will get cold, and he specified it must be hot. *Fine, fine.* I need to get this over with. Need to find my mettle. Need to chin up and face the music. He's *only* a man. I square my shoulders, push open the door and step in, only to find the place is empty. *Hmm.*

The room is huge, like three times the size of my apartment, and has floor-to-ceiling windows. Outside, it's raining. It's only eleven a.m., but thanks to the low hanging clouds, it's gray outside. No surprise in London.

I take a step forward and that's when the scent of rich tobacco and leather, and something deeper—sandalwood?—pours over me. I take a deep breath, and little fires seem to light up my spine. It's a very masculine smell. Something very male. Something primal which resonates with a need deep inside me. I squeeze my fingers around the handle of the cup I'm holding and glance about the space.

There's a massive desk set in front of a glass wall, with a view of the Thames. We're on the fortieth story of the Davenport tower, and I can see on the opposite bank the dome of St. Paul's, with the Millennium bridge suspended over the river in the foreground.

On the wall opposite the windows, there's a bank of six televisions. Each one shows a different news channel. Facing it is a couch and armchairs with a coffee table in front. To my right is another sitting area, this one facing an unlit fireplace.

The lights are dimmed, so the space crawls with shadows. A gust of wind rattles against one of the walls, I shiver. The hair on the back of my neck rises, and I realize I'm not alone. My attention is drawn to the other side of the room.

There, in the corner, in the space between two windows, shrouded in shadows, is the unmistakable outline of a man. I gasp and strain through the dim light, trying to make out his features.

His face is in darkness, but there's just enough light to pick out the shape of his shoulders, which are broad enough to stretch his suit. The sleeves are tight around his biceps, and his jacket pulls across his chest. He's standing with one hand thrust in his pocket, the other at his side. His pants and his jacket are black enough to meld with his surroundings, and he's wearing a shirt, which is also black. I can tell that his black tie is made of silk because of the light that reflects off it. Then he takes a step forward.

The light from the window falls over his eyes, blue like the waves that crest a stormy sea. He stares, unblinking, and I feel like I'm at the start of a rollercoaster, at the very top of that first long drop when my stomach clenches in anticipation, my guts churn, and every part of me dreads what's to come—but also looks forward to hurtling down to the inevitable bottom. I swallow, and the sound of my pulse fills my ears.

He takes another step in my direction. The ceiling light illuminates his features, and I forget to breathe.

High cheekbones, a hooked patrician nose, a thin, firm upper lip that promises he's not someone to be messed with. And that puffy lower lip which is ridiculously sensuous. The square jaw, which is so perfect it makes me want to weep. But it's the scar that stretches from the tip of the left side of his lips to the edge of his eye which focuses my attention. It slashes across his cheek like someone dragged a blade in exactly the perfect symmetry to bisect the expanse.

The shriveled, uneven surface of the scar hints at the likelihood that it was stitched by someone who wasn't a doctor... Suddenly, I know he did it himself. That he bore the pain without a single groan. That he didn't even have the benefit of a mirror and had to hold the edges of the torn skin together as he made do with whatever he could find to sew himself up. And I know it must have hurt so much, but that he didn't complain.

Whatever happened to cause that wound must have been life-threatening. It's probably a miracle he's standing here. The thought of this big, virile male almost dying causes the blood to drain from my face.

He's not *any* man. He's a larger-than-life, lethal, predatory male, who's almost otherworldly in how he's able to hold himself preternaturally still. Every muscle seems to be carved out of stone. The tension that rolls off of him weighs the air and sparks it with electricity. My nerve-endings tingle. I try to take a breath, and my lungs burn. It's as if he's sucked all the oxygen out of the room and replaced it with an explosive mixture that's sure to corrode me from the inside out.

I don't know why that HR lady thinks his face is hideous, or why his previous assistants couldn't stand the sight of him, for this man is not repellant or scary to look at. *He is freakin' gorgeous.*

Sure, his face is scarred, but that only adds to his appeal. It brings to mind images of pirates who went to sea and came back having vanquished their enemies. *It makes me want to find out how he was wounded. It makes me want to kiss that puckered skin on his face and soothe any lingering memories he may have from being hurt. It makes me want to lick up that furrow on his cheek and taste him, and—* Heat flushes my skin. My toes curl.

Whoa, I need to stop that train of thought. This is my boss. I'm his employee. I have no business thinking of him in such an inappropriate manner.

Whatever he sees on my features causes his face to close even more. A nerve ticks at his jaw. "Place the coffee on the desk," he rumbles.

That same rich, dark voice I heard over the phone rolls over me like a tsunami of decadence. My mouth dries. My stomach trembles. All the moisture in my body seems to have arrowed toward that secret part of me deep inside my core. I swallow, continuing to stare in his direction.

"Do it," he snaps.

Instantly, I'm moving. My feet don't seem to touch the ground. I reach his desk, round it, and place the cup of coffee in the space in front of his chair. I straighten and glance in his direction. "I'm your new assistant June Don—"

"Get out."

"What?" My jaw drops.

"Leave, and don't return unless I ask you to."

My heart slams into my ribcage. For some ridiculous reason, I want to cry. I don't know this guy, haven't done anything to elicit this kind of reaction from him, so why is he being so rude? I open my mouth, but he throws up his hand. "If you don't like the job, you can leave that, too."

There's something in his voice that implies he expects me to do just that. In fact, I have a sneaking suspicion that's why he's being so rude. What a jerk. Not that I plan on quitting. Not when I just got this job. And the money? I *need* that money. So no, I'm not going anywhere.

"What time?" I sense his surprise, since I can't make out his features. "Lunch. What time do you want it?" I prompt.

"One p.m. and—"

"I won't be late." I ignore the scowl on his face, then spin around and walk back the way I came. When I reach the door, I grab the handle, twist it, and push the door open, then pause.

If I'm going to survive this role, then I need to let him know I'm not a pushover. I need him to understand that I'm not scared of his bluster or his domineering manner. I square my shoulders, then half turn and fix my gaze on the shadow that is him.

"Oh, by the way," I say in a tone that I hope conveys confidence. "I don't scare easily, Knox Davenport. Question is, do you?"

2

Knox

She leaves, and I scowl after her. *Did she have the last word?* A first. That has never happened before with any of my employees. Never. Not even with my platoon in the Marines. *Doesn't she realize I can fire her?*

I draw in a sharp breath, and the lingering scent of coffee reaches me. I turn toward my desk and, like a homing pigeon, move toward it. I snatch the cup and down it. It leaves a trail of warmth in its wake, dispelling some of the chill creeping over my skin since she left. It feels good that she stood up to me. It's the first spark of interest I've felt toward any woman in a long time.

Unlike those before her, who were unable to look me in the face without flinching, she didn't hesitate to meet my gaze. I knit my brows. I ensured I stepped into the light so she could see my scarred features, but she didn't react. In fact, she held her ground. I rub my chin. I need an efficient assistant; it's the only way to increase my productivity. But so far, no one has been able to keep up with me, so why should she be any different?

So what, if she has more gumption than the rest of my employees? So what, if she isn't put off by my disfigured visage, or that there's a thread of awareness between us...? It doesn't mean anything.

She's a paid minion, and nothing more. She won't be able to deal with my demands and, just like everyone else, she'll resign before daylight fades outside.

I push aside thoughts of her and, grabbing my tablet, join my video conference call.

After a few minutes, I've had it with this spineless, indecisive group. I interrupt, "Gather the staff; you know the drill. Sell off the loss-making units. Then auction the profitable divisions." My decree is greeted by silence.

Then Ravi, the most senior person on my team, clears his throat. "There's a chance to turn this company around. Why not build it up, then sell it off and make more money, without people losing their jobs?"

"That's going to take time—" He begins to speak, but I interrupt him, "Time I don't have." He and the others look around uncomfortably. Then I add, "Get it done." I disconnect the call and toss the device onto the desk.

I'm sure they think I don't have any compassion. What they don't realize is that the company we're taking over is in the business of publishing newspapers, which is in sharp decline. Sure, we could try to build it back up, but the money we'd pump in would end up hurting the parent company, without any visible results. This would, in turn, affect the jobs of everyone on the call.

The difficult decision I'm making might hurt in the short term, but eventually, it will ensure the survival of this company and the roles that go with it. As for the jobs that will be lost in the takeover? That's why gathering the employees is the first step. Where possible, I'll find these employees opportunities in other group companies. I'll offer them the opportunity to retrain and find roles within our digital media divisions.

I also plan to offer a voluntary retirement scheme to ensure those who want an early retirement can be paid enough to afford to do so. The rest will receive a healthy pay-off that will buy them time to look for a new job.

These are details I could have gone into with my team, but I don't have the patience to do so. I prefer action to spending the next half hour walking my team through my plan. I outline my thoughts in an email to my Finance Director and instruct him to share the details with them, instead.

My time is money, and this is the best use of it. I can't baby my team and waste my time explaining my thoughts. They're going to have to catch up with me. I'm a strategist. I have the ability to look into the future and think ten steps ahead. I can see the game plan before anyone else, and I have the confidence to execute it with stealth, alacrity, and no emotion. I keep my eye on the target and get things done. It's why Arthur put me in charge of the media division.

He knew I'd see through the clutter and turn this company around. If that means I come across as an authoritarian and a cold-hearted operator, that's too bad. I roll my shoulders to dispel the knots, not that it helps.

I haven't slept in more than a week, thanks to the insomnia that's plagued me since I left the Marines. And when I do close my eyes, I'm plagued by the faces of those who didn't make it back alive. Unlike me.

Survivor's guilt is real. And despite my logical mind telling me I'm not responsible for the deaths of my brothers in arms, a part of me will always feel I don't deserve to be back among the civilians when they're not. It's a part of me I don't have control over, and I hate that. Given the choice, I never would have gone on that last mission either. But I wasn't in charge. And when I lost so many team-members on that tour, I knew my time in the Marines was up. No way, was I going to put myself in a situation again where I didn't have a say in my future. I crack my neck.

Control. That's what I value more than anything else. It's about controlling my situation. About controlling the decisions impacting my life. I'm done with allowing anyone else to direct my destiny. Unfortunately, this doesn't extend to my ability to rest at night. Turns out, the one thing I can't control is sleep.

The only place I've managed to feel safe enough to get some shuteye is at the family home in Cumbria. It's isolated enough that I can let myself relax there. The place has been in our family for generations. It's where I retreated to recover from my injuries. It's the place where I feel most at home.

When the computer screen begins to fade in front of my eyes, I blink and glance away.

My surroundings take on an added shine—a sure sign that I'm running on empty. Everything seems both blurred and bright at the same time, another sign that I really need to get some sleep. A flash of pain ignites behind my eyes. The heaviness in my head expands to meet the flickering pinpricks that pinch at the scars on my cheek. The headache is real, but the feeling of the skin being torn on my face is psychosomatic.

The ravages of PTSD are something very few of us in the service escape from. I open the drawer under my desk, snatch my painkillers, and swallow them dry. It'll take a few minutes for the pain to recede. I slide into the chair behind my desk and, by the time the door to my office opens, I can breathe without feeling like I'm suffocating.

My new assistant stomps in, then comes to a stop. Her gaze is fixed on me. Her throat moves as she swallows. She stares like she's seeing my face for the first time—which she is, for despite the fact she took in my features earlier, she's seeing them in closer proximity now, and it's a full-frontal view, with nothing to soften my façade. The rain has cleared enough for watery sunlight to slant thought the windows. One of the rays falls across my features. I don't blink. It had to happen at some point; best to get it out of the way now.

This is when she turns and runs screaming, or perhaps, faints—yep, that happened with one of my past assistants, too. He quit on the spot. Not that I blame him. My face is ravaged enough for mothers to use it as a stand-in for the boogie monster who'll carry children off if they don't fall asleep quickly enough.

She swallows, the sound audible in the room. Then she takes in my features again. Her cheeks flush further. But there's no other reaction on her face. Certainly, there's no fear or loathing. If anything, her breathing seems to roughen. *Interesting.*

Women used to find me attractive, but since I was hurt in action, they take one look at my face and are repelled. Most can't look me in the eye, and if they do, it's with sympathy. Despite the fact that their gaze is often transfixed by my wounded face, not one of them has the courage to ask me about it. They're unable to look past the visible scars to the ones I carry inside. It's as if my entire existence is defined by my facial disfigurement.

The few who decide they want to sleep with me are enticed by my family name and fortune, taking it as enough compensation to overlook my defacement—as one of them said in complete seriousness. None wanted to date me or be seen with me in polite company. I wince at the memory. It's as if having an ugly face gives them permission to be impolite, because how can someone so revolting have any emotions to speak of? Others want to sleep with me so they can boast that they've been with 'The Beast.' It's a nickname I learned about by mistake.

It made me angry, at first. Then, I realized it was fitting and decided I'd do my best to live up to it. I'd embody the role of the wrathful, nasty boss with my employees, so no one would dare to approach me. Most of them—including my former assistants—averted their gaze while speaking to me, or preferred to email me instead, so they wouldn't have to see my face. This way, I didn't have to put up with their commiseration or their curiosity.

This woman, though, seems not to be repelled by my blemished features. If anything, she seems to be genuinely drawn to me. A first. And likely, an illusion. *She's probably pretending to be attracted to me so she can get something from me, as well. Yes, I'm sure that's what it is.*

I glower at her, but her facial expression remains unchanged. She continues inside and slaps an envelope on the desk. "This one is marked personal and confidential."

"Open it." I wave a hand in the direction of the cover.

"Are you sure?"

"I won't repeat myself," I snap.

She swallows, then reaches over and grabs the letter opener on my desk. The neckline of her blouse dips, and I get a flash of her ample cleavage. Jesus. H. Christ, she's gorgeous. She's perfectly curved, perfectly plus sized in a way that has me riveted. The dip of her waist, the flare of her lush hips, and the turn of her shapely ankles have my pants growing uncomfortably tight.

She straightens and slits open the flap of the envelope. She pulls out what appears to be an ivory-colored card.

"Read it out loud," I order.

"The honorable Nelson Eddard, Earl of Duncastle, and Judith, Countess of Duncastle, are pleased to invite you to the wedding reception of their daughter Rosemary with Dean Thornton, the Fifth Duke of Thornton, on Tuesday the—"

"Bin it on your way out." I pretend to yawn, hoping she'll take the hint and leave because I can't take my gaze off her beautiful features. And *that* is unexpected. "And don't bother me with such trifles in the future."

"It's the society event of the year and tipped to be the next best thing to a royal reception."

"Boring." I turn back to my computer.

"Surely, it would be good for your profile to be seen there. It could result in positive publicity, which could only help with the image of the Davenports. Which, in turn, might help you to retain talent."

I frown. "Are you implying we're not doing a good enough job of keeping our employees happy?"

When she doesn't reply, I raise my gaze to hers. She flinches but doesn't look away. "Your last employee satisfaction survey speaks for itself." She pulls out her phone from the pocket of her skirt. My gaze is drawn to the flare of her hips, the way the hem ends just above her knees, the stocking-clad, gorgeous calves which end in heels—which are patently ill-fitting.

Her fingers fly over the screen, then she slides the phone across the desk in my direction.

I take in the details on the screen. Overall employee satisfaction within the Davenport Group's media division is below thirty percent.

"And you think something as cosmetic as being seen at a society reception will fix this?" I sneer.

"Not alone. But positive PR, accompanied by measures like subsidized food in the employee canteen, arrangements for childcare within the office complex, and flexible working hours, as well as matching donations to their favorite charities, will help raise the scores."

One of my brothers implemented similar measures in one of the other group companies. They exceeded their quarterly goals, too. But that doesn't necessarily mean there's a connection between the two.

"Such actions will also give rise to employees moonlighting during office hours, not to mention slacking off," I counter.

"Not if they're held to tight deliverables."

"Hmm." She has a point. With clear parameters, there's no reason these measures can't be implemented with little extra effort. I haven't paid that much attention to the company's internal HR policies, nor to public perception, but clearly, that needs to change.

"Write it up and email it to me."

She nods.

Her instant agreement to my directives is a turn on. Her quick thinking when it comes to equating an invitation to a society event with the possibility of improving the image of my company, combined with her knowledge of the facts needed to back up her suggestion, is not only impressive, but also bloody attractive. And when she continues to stand there with her eyelids lowered, a whisper of emotion brushes up against my mind, eliciting one word: *submissive. Is she a natural submissive? Do I care if she is?*

She's my employee; doesn't that make her off-limits? On the other hand, she's the first person in this office I've exchanged more than a few words with — outside of Mary — and it's stimulating.

Much as I relish being reclusive, I also enjoy being able to have a conversation with someone who doesn't bore me. And who's easy on the eyes. I slide her phone across the desk and over to her.

She picks it up. "And the invitation?"

"Let them know I'll be there."

"Very good, Sir."

Oh no, she didn't. That 'Sir' at the end of the sentence has blood flowing to my groin. *Definitely submissive.*

Her features light up with a smile. Her brown eyes glow. Her sweet lips part to reveal white teeth and, suddenly, it feels hot in here.

She turns to leave, and I call out, "Oh, and Kelly?"

She pauses and scowls at me over her shoulder. "My name's June."

I'm so taken in with the pout she's wearing on her pink, rosebud mouth. A mouth that's soft and seductive and hints at a lushness in her, a softness, I hunger to explore.

"Kelly." I say firmly and am rewarded with the deepening of her frown.

Her eyes flash fire, and pinpricks of interest stab at my chest. There are hidden depths to her that should keep me entertained for a while. One reason to hope she outlasts the others. Then, she pushes up the spectacles she's wearing on her pert nose, and I realize the other reason to keep her around is that her sexy-librarian look does it for me.

Not that it makes a whit of difference. Soon, she'll realize I'm not only disgusting to look at, but also disgusting on the inside, and she'll want to resign. But I'll stay a step ahead. I'm going to test her. I'll give her the most impossible tasks to complete. That way, she'll understand that I've earned every bit of my reputation as The Beast. That way, I'll push her limits until she quits. It's inevitable she leaves, but this way, I'll be in control of the timelines. Then she'll be gone, and I can go back to working by myself. I'll no longer be in suspense about when she's going to leave me. It's what prompts me to drawl, "I'll be taking a plus one to the reception."

"Oh?" Her gaze widens. "Whose name should I put down for that?"

"Yours."

3

June

"He's taking you to the society reception of the decade?" Zoey gapes from the window on my phone screen. "He's taking you to the event billed as the crème de la crème of all social events?"

I should be excited that I'm getting the opportunity to attend a royal reception, which most women would give anything to get an invitation to, but frankly, I'm petrified. Me, with my plus-size figure, and fake-branded stilettos, and charity shop clothing, among those emaciated, skinny, model-looking, titled, snooty women who'll, no doubt, look down at me. *Ugh!*

"He asked me to come in the role of his assistant. And only because he wants me to take notes on the discussions he has there for follow ups," I remind her.

Not that it dampens her enthusiasm. "Knox Davenport invited you to attend a high-profile extravaganza as his work date; imagine that." She sighs.

There's a gooey, romantic look in her eyes. Oh no, I need to dispel any notion of a relationship between me and my boss before she builds it up in her head. Because *that* is definitely not happening. N-a-a-h. No matter how much I'm attracted to him.

"I'm going as his work colleague," I say firmly.

And as someone who can fetch and carry for him, considering how he had me on my feet all day. On the positive side, I've lasted five days.

Not that I haven't come close to killing him—when I'm not thinking of throwing myself at his feet and climbing him like a tree—but the thought of the salary I'm getting paid has stopped me from doing either.

I was the last to leave the office today as has become the norm. Except for bringing my boss his lunch, I haven't left my desk. And my head was so full of my to-do-list, I forgot to buy my own lunch. If it weren't for Mary— whose boss, Quentin Davenport, is my boss' uncle—I would've starved.

She took pity on me and bought me a sandwich and coffee, refusing my offer to pay for it. I noticed the growing respect in her eyes as she waved at me on her way out the door at five p.m. on the dot. It's Friday evening and the entire floor emptied out after her, but for my boss. And me. I didn't see him again after he dismissed me, and I was both sad that I hadn't had another chance to gaze upon those features of his, which resemble Lucifer, and relieved that I wasn't at the receiving end of his "charisma."

I'm there to do a job. I'm his assistant. No more, no less.

"How many managers ask their assistants to accompany them to a royal reception?" Zoey drawls.

"It's a quasi-royal reception," I protest.

"Of a real-life duke. And there won't be any of those happening again in the near future." She nods.

"Since when do you keep track of the Royals?" I frown.

"Since one of the authors I work with is of royal blood—" She slaps a hand to her forehead. "Forget I said that."

"You're working with a member of the royal family?" I gasp.

"Someone connected to them, and that's all I'll say." She mimics zipping her lips.

"Aww, come on. Not fair. You listen to all of the news from me, and when it's your turn to dish, you clam up. P-l-e-a-s-e?" I bat my eyelashes at her.

Her lips turn down. "It's confidential. And it wouldn't be fair to my author," she points out.

Zoey's an editor with a leading publishing house. And she works on some very interesting books and personalities.

"I respect that. For what it's worth, the project sounds very intriguing."

"It is." Her eyes grow brilliant with barely suppressed excitement. "It's the most thrilling book I've worked on for a while. But enough about me —" She slashes a hand through the air. "Aren't you glad I mentioned the job to you and that you got it? Although"—she looks uncomfortable— "I admit, I almost didn't, considering I know little about Knox Davenport. I was worried that he might turn out to be obnoxious."

He is *obnoxious, but he's also breathtakingly gorgeous and so dominant, he makes me weak in the knees.*

"But given he's invited you to accompany him to the royal reception, it can't be too bad, right?" She looks at me with eager eyes.

Guess I won't tell her that he insists on calling me Kelly, even after I told him my name. And when I emailed him to ask if he wanted a note to accompany the Tiffany bracelet, he came back with: "Tell her to sod off." That was it. *What's wrong with this man?* No way, could I send a note with *that* message. Which meant, I had to make up a note from him to the woman. And it wasn't easy.

"He's not too bad," I finally murmur.

My reply must not completely satisfy her, for her forehead creases. "You *are* going to be okay with this role, right? I mentioned the job to you because I know the Davenports pay well, and you needed the work. But they don't have the best reputation, when it comes to employee satisfaction."

That's putting it mildly, considering some of the comments from disgruntled employees I came across during my research.

On the other hand, Knox saw merit in my suggestions related to boosting employee satisfaction. He also agreed to attend the reception. No matter that he asked me to accompany him.

"I'm happy with the role," I say, and my voice has a ring of confidence in it this time.

I must convince her, for her shoulders relax.

It's okay to tell my best friend a half-truth, right? I *am* happy with the salary this job brings with it. I'm also hugely turned on every time I look at my boss, or smell his dark, male scent, or even think of him, but best not to share *that* with her either.

"Who wouldn't be thrilled to attend a royal event, hmm? Although, I don't have anything to wear to the event." I add that, hoping she'll take the segue.

She creases her brow. "It's in two weeks, isn't it?"

"Eighteen days," I correct her.

The invitation was sent months ago, but for whatever reason, it wasn't delivered to him. The reply to my RSVP came today, saying they'll be pleased to have Knox Davenport and his guest at the reception. Attached to the email were pages worth of instructions on what the etiquette at the reception was to be, including how to address the bride and groom, and the King and Queen, and the Royal Princes, who'll all be in attendance. And a dress code, and a list of protocols related to their Royal Majesties to follow for the evening, and the schedule of events. My head was swimming by the end.

I committed as much of it to memory as I could and took printouts to study. I have yet to reply with our preferences in diet and any allergies. I emailed Knox to ask about it, but never heard back. Then, I discovered a file telling me he's allergic to mangoes. Good to know. I updated the wedding planning team, then stumbled home without bidding him goodbye.

"What are you going to wear?" Zoey asks.

"I suppose, I'll have to pull out my fake Balenciaga black dress." I shrug.

She winces. "Isn't that the one you picked up at the charity shop?"

"I can wear it with a jacket to work, then take off the jacket and —"

The intercom buzzes. "Hold on, Z." I place the phone down, head to the intercom and push the button.

"Delivery for Kelly Assistant?"

"Uh, there's no one here by that name." I'm about to hang up, then pause. "Did you say Kelly Assistant?"

"Yes ma'am," the delivery man says. "And this is the right address."

Oh, he didn't do that. A delivery addressed to Kelly Assistant? No way, am I going to accept it. "Take it back," I snap.

There's silence, then the delivery person clears his throat. "You mean, I should take back all the boxes?"

I frown. "How many boxes do you have?"

"Uh, there are three boxes to be delivered to you, ma'am."

I sigh. *And now I've been ma'amed. Why did he send these boxes? What could be in them?* I could turn them away and never know what's in them, but let's face it, I'm curious. And if I don't accept them, he'll probably be pissed at me, enough for me to lose my job. And if I do accept them, I can find out what's in them. I can always return them later if I don't like them. Right?

"Ma'am?" The man clears his throat. "Are you accepting the delivery?"

"Yes, fine, come on up." Lifting my finger from the button, I open the door to the apartment and hear the sound of footsteps coming up the stairs. A man in a delivery uniform, which is not like that of any delivery service I recognize, appears. He's dressed in dark green with a cap, and somehow, I know it's the kind of courier company only the extraordinarily rich use. He's carrying a large flat garment box, bearing the logo of a well-known fashion brand. I step aside and indicate for him to follow me, then gesture to him to set the boxes on the coffee table.

He's followed by a second delivery guy dressed in a similar uniform and carrying two smaller boxes, one of which looks like a hat box. They place the boxes on the breakfast counter. The first guy has me sign his device, then both half-bow, turn and leave.

"Who is it? What's happening? Did you get a delivery?" Zoey's voice squawks from my phone. I head over to pick it up.

"It was a delivery."

"Who's it from?"

"Umm…it's from my boss."

"Are you going to open them?" She's almost bouncing with excitement.

I glance at the boxes with doubt. I shouldn't have accepted them. Damn it. Whatever it is, it's going to complicate this situation further. Not that there is a situation. He's my very rude boss. And I need this job. I blow out a breath. "Hold on." I prop the phone on the little counter that separates my living space from the tiny kitchenette, then reach for the first box. On the largest box is a note which says:

Wear this to the royal reception.

It's in *his* handwriting. I recognize it, even without a signature. It's as if he heard me talking about what I'd wear to the reception and sent me a dress as an answer. I need to stop with the fanciful thinking. It's a coincidence that it arrived as I was discussing my wardrobe issues, is all.

I tear open the seal—this one's an Alexander McQueen. *Whoa!* And it's genuine. It's definitely not fake. And it must cost ... I have no idea how much, but I bet it's more than the year's rent I pay on this place.

My fingers tremble as I push aside the soft tissue paper and hold up a dress. Light catches the green sheath with lace detail that runs down the front. And sleeves that are made from material so sheer, I know the skin of my arms will show through it, and it will look both exquisite and tantalizing.

"He sent you a dress?" Zoe asks. "That's gorgeous!"

I nod as I place it carefully back in the box, then open the next box. *No, no, no.* It's not any box it's a shoe box with a Louboutin label.

"Oh my god!" I gasp.

"What is it?" Zoey cries. "I can't see! Is everything okay?"

No. Yes. I don't know.

Without replying, I slide out a pair of three-inch heels with the characteristic lacquered red soles. I place them on the floor, then step out of my slippers and into the shoes. I fasten the ankle straps. I take a few steps, and it's like I'm walking on air. Again. The feeling is not dissimilar to the sensation I felt when walking on the thick carpet in his office. Somehow, he's right here with me with the ghost-touch of his fingers curling around my ankles.

"June, c'mon. You're killing me here!"

I cross back over to Zoe, who's straining to see what I have, grab the phone, and walk over to sink onto my settee with the faux leather covering. The shoes I'm wearing must easily cost as much as what I pay to cover a term of my sister's university fees.

I'm too shell shocked to speak. *Why would he do this? Is he trying to bribe me? Trying to make up for being such a jerkosauraus?* Somehow, I don't think so. I can't get a bead on his motivations.

"June?" Zoey asks in an impatient voice. "What did he send you?"

In response, I flip the camera on the phone so she can see my feet. And am rewarded by a gasp of surprise. "Is that—"

"Yep."

I position the phone on the couch, then stand up, taking the dress out of its box again. I hold it against my body, then step back so she gets the full effect.

I glance at the camera to find she's looking at me with an admiring look in her eyes. "You look beautiful."

I take in my reflection on the screen. I do, actually. I can already tell that the dress is going to fit me like it was tailor-made for me. *And how did he guess my size?* I blink slowly. *You know what? I don't want to know.*

I glance at the third box, which looks like a hat box, and feel overwhelmed. I don't have the courage to open that one.

"It's too much." I swallow. "This dress and shoes must cost a fortune. I can't accept them."

She nods slowly. "I understand. You don't want to be beholden to him, but for what it's worth, the dress would look amazing on you."

I give my reflection a last glance, then fold the dress and place it back in its box. "I can't understand why he sent it."

"Guess he realized you need an outfit for the reception?"

I narrow my gaze on her. "Are you on his side or mine?"

"Of course, yours. In fact, I'll be the first to warn you that these Davenports can be very slick." She nods. "You need to be careful around them."

"Okay?"

She must hear the question in my voice, for she blows out a breath. "You know how my friend Vivian was wooed and fell in love with Quentin Davenport?"

I nod.

Her features take on a wary expression. "They can be very persuasive, these men. And they have the money to get anything they want. And the power to make anything and anyone bow to them."

And while money isn't everything, fact is, I don't have enough of it to take care of my family.

My phone pings with a notification from my bank. *Huh?* "I just received a deposit in my bank account." I open up the bank's app and see that the deposit is from the Davenport group. The amount is what I expected to be paid for my first month working there. "I don't understand... I thought they'd pay me at the end of the month. It's only mid-month but I've already been paid for the month, and I've only been here five days."

"Maybe it's company policy to pay twice a month?" Zoey offers.

"Maybe..." Either way, I'm not turning down this money. I need it. But I can't help but wonder if this is another way for my boss to make me feel like I owe him. *And what reason would he have to do that? No, this is money I've earned. Especially after a very rough day today. As for the dress and the shoes, and whatever's in the hatbox? I'll be returning them.* Before I can slip off the shoes, my phone pings with an incoming message.

Unknown number: Office. Now.

What the —? My heart rams into my ribcage. *Is it him?*

Unknown number: My car is waiting outside for you.

My pulse rate shoots up. It has to be him. No one else could message me with such an order, implying he expects to be obeyed.

Unknown number: Don't keep me waiting.

A pulse flares between my legs. My scalp tingles. He wants me back in the office. It's Friday evening, and I should be upset that he expects me to drop everything and obey his commands when he calls, but the fact is, I'd rather be back there, with him, in his presence and of service to him, than alone in my apartment. Besides, he's already paid me — as the cash in my account will testify — so I can hardly say no to him.

I could pretend that I haven't thought about my boss' cold, hard profile since leaving the office today, but I'd be lying. There hasn't been a second when I haven't found myself thinking about the next time I'll see him. And secretly, I'm glad I don't have to wait until Monday for that pleasure. I squeeze my fingers around my phone in disgust at my weakness. "I have to go, Z."

4

Knox

She pushes the door open and stomps in, coming to a stop in front of my desk, then slams a flat garment box on my desk. "You can keep your stupid, expensive gifts. I don't need them."

I lean back in my chair and play with the pen I was writing with when she entered.

Her cheeks are flushed. Tendrils have escaped from the bun at the nape of her neck she seems to favor. With her oversized spectacles, her pouting lips, the creamy skin of her neck, the blouse, which is buttoned up to her collar, but which only serves to emphasize her gorgeous tits. With the curve of her hips showcased by her skirt, and those fuck-me heels she seems to prefer, she's the epitome of a wet dream. My dick shows its enthusiasm with an imitation of a flagpole.

I widen the space between my thighs to accommodate my growing erection; it seems to be my natural state since she walked into my life. Good thing I have a heavy-ass desk to hide behind. If she knew about the thickening column in my pants, Ms.-Sexy-Librarian-with-the-Virginal-Air-About-Her would run screaming.

I stay silent. The tension in the air thickens, and I wait for her to break the quiet. She doesn't disappoint.

"If this is your attempt at an apology, I suggest words would be the better option next time." She adds under her breath, "And based on what I've observed, there *will* be a next time." She slaps her hands on her sizable hips. "Also, you could have gotten my name right for the delivery, you—" She stops herself and narrows her eyes. "Did you really think you could buy your way into my good graces? Brand names and expensive prices don't impress me, even if these are the same brands favored by royalty in this country. There's no way I'm going to accept these. Besides, I could sue you for sexual misconduct." She pauses, her chest heaving.

"Did you read the paperwork before you signed your revised employee onboarding forms?" I drawl.

I had them redrafted and asked the HR manager to ensure my assistant signed them.

When her forehead crinkles, I click my tongue. "Very careless of you. If you had, you'd have noticed that the fine print says all interactions between us are confidential and that you waive any rights to sue me or my company on any and all counts."

Her jaw drops, then she seems to get ahold of herself. "Is that... Is that legal?" she squeaks.

"Feel free to consult a lawyer."

She tips up her chin, and her jaw tightens.

"If this is how you plan on vetting the business agreements before they come to me, I'm not impressed," I add.

The skin around her mouth stretches.

"The outfit you're referring to is a dress for the royal reception. It was sent to you because I anticipated, rightly"—I raise a finger—"that you don't have anything suitable to wear to the event."

She curls her fingers into fists at her side. Also, her cheeks flame. Damn, she's beautiful when she's angry. I place my pen on the desk.

"I have an image to uphold, and it would not do for someone who represents me to wear knock-off brands. As long as you work for me, I expect you to dress in a way that positively reflects the Davenport name."

She flushes, and opens her mouth to speak, then seems to change her mind. Instead, she locks her fingers around her handbag—it's one of those faded satchel-like things with the edges fraying. I make a mental note to send her a range of bags to choose from. Can't have my employee dress in castoffs.

I tap my fingers together and place my elbows on the armrests of my chair, "You *will* wear the dress to the royal reception. Understood?"

She firms her lips but stays silent. Her eyes, however... Jesus, they dart fire at me. If looks could kill, I'd be a dead man. But I've survived enemy fire on dangerous missions. My assistant's anger is a hazard I can easily withstand.

I complete a leisurely perusal down to her feet, before raising my gaze to hers. "Nice shoes, by the way."

She glances down at herself, then opens and closes her mouth. "Ah, I... err... I didn't have time to take them off before I came. I got the impression my presence was urgently needed."

I slide a sheaf of papers across the desk in her direction. "I need you to get the changes marked there across to the agency in Tokyo"—I glance at the watch on my wrist, "who should be open for business."

Her forehead crinkles, "It's midnight in Japan."

"Your point being?" I incline my head.

"Wouldn't they have gone home for the day?"

"My agencies work around the clock, as I expect my employees to, when needed."

She deflates a little. Then picks up the papers and glances through them before staring at me. "It's in Japanese."

"Not my problem."

"I don't know Japanese."

"Find a translator." I turn back to my computer screen. She stands there for a few seconds. Anger flutters off of her. I sense her frustration and the way she struggles to keep it in check and have to stifle a chuckle.

Damn, I haven't had so much fun in a long time. Interesting. What is it about this woman that makes me want to get a reaction from her?

I get the sense I'm going to love surprising her. I'm going to enjoy testing her limits until she snaps, the way those before her have. Even more surprising? She's not immune to my presence, as evidenced by her choppy breaths and heightened color.

Unlike my previous assistants, who winced whenever they walked into my office, this woman seems to make up excuses to approach me. And when she stands in front of my desk, it's always with lowered eyes and blush-smeared cheeks—and pink lips parted to reveal an 'O' of space that begs for my cock to be thrust between them. The crotch of my pants grows even tighter, and I suppress a groan.

I'm going to have to jerk off. Again. My dick has gotten very friendly with my hand since this luscious woman walked into my office. The chemistry between us certainly livens up our interactions.

Her awareness of me is going to make this experience of pushing her limits until she throws in her resignation so much more enjoyable. A fringe benefit I didn't have with the ones before her who barely lasted the day. This fragile creature with her siren curves and plush lips, and a body made to be owned, has lasted five days with me. Another first. It's a source of surprise and, also, frustration.

No matter what I've asked of her, she's delivered. I drag my thumb under my lip. Question is, can she weather the challenges I'm about to throw her way?

"Because I'm feeling charitable, I've informed the Tokyo agency you'll need an hour to get the information across to them."

Her jaw drops. "An-an hour?!" she sputters.

"Chop, chop. The clock's a ticking."

She shoots me a venomous scowl that makes me want to chuckle. Then, she squares her shoulders, spins around and stomps out.

"Kelly Assistant," I call out after her, "Don't forget your dress."

She pauses midway to the door, then spins around and marches over to my desk. With the color of her cheeks a lovely, heightened red—that pleases me no end—she scoops up the garment box, turns, and heads for the door.

I follow her progress and ogle the bouncing of her tush under the same dress she wore this morning. It's frayed at the hem. Hmm, I'm going to have to order her a new wardrobe, but the way the outfit fits across her ample behind is perfect. Enough to cause the blood to drain to my groin. And when she slams the door shut on her way out, I can't stop my lips from pulling back. *Damn, but her temper only adds to her allure. How would it be to have her fighting and spitting under me as I cause her to dig her fingertips into my shoulders?*

I frown—I do not socialize with my employees. I have never broken that rule—and I intend to keep it that way. This attraction to her is, likely, a passing fancy. One born of my lack of feminine companionship. I haven't been interested in a woman in a long time. Not when every woman I've encountered socially avoids my gaze. My tastes have always veered toward the unusual. And after I was scarred, the pain I went through, the darkness I had to fight to crawl my way back to recovery, seemed to loosen something inside of me.

Where previously I'd been content with spanking or tying up a woman, now, that domineering part of me craves nothing less than a woman's complete submission. I need to be in control of not just my submissive's body, but also her thoughts, her mind, her very emotions. Something I tried to explore in the shadowed recesses of my favorite BDSM club. The encounters left me unsatisfied. They lacked a certain something. Despite the willingness of the submissives to do anything for me, their very compliance left me cold. It didn't have the challenge, that zing, that spark—which my run-ins with my assistant have. I rub the back of my neck.

Come to think of it, I haven't visited the club since I met her because... Every time I imagine a woman bending for me, edging her, making her pant—every time—teasing her and taunting her until she's out of her head with desire... Every time I imagine breaking her down, so she submits to me of her free will, it's *her* face I see.

Not that she's aware of my peculiar wants. And if she found out, it'd scare her off.

I can't imagine, with her air of innocence, she has any idea of the kind of proclivities I indulge in. It's best I leave her alone. I shoot a glance in the direction of the door separating me from her workstation, then curse myself. *Why am I so aware of her presence outside my office?* She's my assistant. I'm her boss. And I should not cross that boundary between us.

I focus my attention on my computer screen, and even manage to add my remarks to the open legal agreement, when a message pops up. It's an incoming email...*from her.* Before I can stop myself, I've clicked on it and opened my inbox.

· · ·

From KellyAssistant@davenportgroup.com
  To: Knox@davenportgroup.com

I'll have the translated feedback to the agency within the hour. Is there anything else you'd like me to do, Sir?

-June

Jesus, that *Sir* tacked on at the end has me picturing scenarios where she says it to me in a low, husky voice while she's on her knees with her big brown eyes looking up at me as she begs me and pleads with me to have mercy on her. I bet she knows exactly the effect it has on me. It's why she's been using 'Sir' all week in a way that drives me nuts.

It makes it difficult to remember all the reasons why I need to maintain a professional distance between us. It definitely encourages unwanted images to crowd my mind. I'd fit my hand around the nape of her neck and hold her in place as I unhook the waistband of my pants and lower my zipper with my free hand. I allow myself to do so in real life and take myself in hand. I'm thick, rigid, fully aroused. No surprise there. I concentrate on the Sir, and when I close my eyes, I can hear her voice call me by that name, as she did earlier today.

"Yes Sir."
  "Please Sir."
  "I need you… Sir."
  "I beg you, please let me please you, Sir."

The tightness at the base of my spine folds in on itself. My balls draw up. I close my eyes and continue to take care of myself, again and again. My thighs tighten. I dig the heels of my shoes into the floor and throw my head back, when a sound makes me open my eyes. I lower my chin to find her standing inside the doorway to my office.

Her eyes are round and fixed on me. The desk covers my lower half but the movement of my arm, the flex of my biceps, the way my forearms flex, all of it gives away what I'm up to. Despite the dim lighting in the office, I can make out the rise and fall of her chest. The embarrassment that coats her features. I hold her gaze, expecting her to look away, but she doesn't.

She licks her lips and draws my attention to her mouth. Where it stays. I imagine that beautiful mouth wrapped around me again, and it sends me over the edge. With a groan, I feel the heated liquid overflow my hands. A moan bleeds from her lips. It seems to awaken her from her reverie, for she turns and attempts to run out.

Then, because it's too good an opportunity to miss, and I can't resist making her even more uncomfortable, I order, "Oh get me some tissues, will ya?"

She scampers off. The door snicks shut, cutting off the sight of her succulent behind. *What I wouldn't give to spank that fleshy tush?* And that expression on her face when she walked in on me jerking off? Priceless. And she didn't glance away. She *couldn't* glance away. She was aroused to find her boss taking care of himself. She wasn't turned off. Far from it. *She finds me desirable.*

I held her gaze and all I saw in her eyes was lust. I find myself smiling, Then, to my shock, a bark of laugh rumbles up my chest. A lightness settles between my ribs, and my shoulders relax. *When's the last time I was this entertained? When's the last time I was this turned on? When's the last time I was so stimulated by an interaction with another person?*

Ms. June Donnelly livened up my life since she entered it. She's also smoothed out my working day by running interface with my team, so I can accomplish a lot more. Perhaps—I frown—perhaps, I've been too hasty in trying to run her off?

Perhaps, she's more valuable on my team than off? Perhaps, she's more of an asset than I realized? Maybe, I should reward her for surviving the week, so she'll stay on. If nothing else, I need to keep her around for more laughs.

5

June

Ohmigod. Ohmigod. Did he just... Did I see him... Did he? I shake my head and stare blankly at the computer screen in front of me. I managed to grab a few tissues from the box on my desk and go back in and hand them to him without meeting his eyes. Then, I fled back to my seat. Why had I gone to his office in the first place? I can't remember the reason; it must have been something trivial. An excuse for me to see him. And boy... Did I get an eyeful. I squeeze my thighs together in recollection. The image of him jerking off is burned into my retinas.

My ears are ringing from that groan of his as he came. The way he threw his head back to expose the cords of his neck. The way his biceps tightened, and his shoulders swelled, to such an extent, I was sure he'd hulk out of his clothes.

It was erotic and sexy, and so, so hot. Oh god. It was obscene. But also, it turned me on. And it shouldn't have. My mouth is so dry; all of the liquid in my body seems to have pooled in the space between my legs. *Why oh, why had I gone in there? Why hadn't I knocked first? Why...did I stay there, unable to move until he orgasmed?*

My belly stutters. My core clenches. There's this hunger deep inside me that seems to have hooked its claws into the moist walls of my center. There's this yearning that fills every cell in my body; strange need that squeezes my chest and turns my insides to jelly. My fingers tingle, and I find myself reaching for the hem of my dress, when the phone on my desk rings. I jump, then stare at it. My heart booms in my ribcage.

I watch the ringing phone in horror, and when it doesn't stop, I force myself to reach for the receiver and snatch it up.

"Kelly Assistant?"

I'm so unnerved that, just as I stopped earlier when he called me that in his office, I squeak.

"Send off the email to the agency in Tokyo and come see me after you're finished."

Oh yes. I so want to come.

WHAT? NO! SHUT UP.

"What did you say?"

I hear his growl and realize I said the words aloud.

"I mean, coming," I burst out.

There's silence, then I hear him chuckle. "Is that all it took?"

My cheeks flame. "No. I mean, I...yes. I mean, I'll be with you soon."

Without waiting for him to respond, I drop the phone into its cradle, then lower my forehead to the desk once, twice. *Someone kill me. What's wrong with me?* I didn't do anything wrong. I walked in on my boss pleasuring himself and now he wants to see me again. How embarrassing. Not for me. For him. *So why am I blushing so hard?*

I straighten, then reach for the glass of water on my desk and drain it. There, that's better. For the next half an hour, I focus on answering a few more emails which have come in, until the translated document with the feedback arrives.

I read through it, correct the grammatical errors, and some factual ones, too, based on what I know of the product in question, then send off the email. Then, I rise to my feet, stretch, and roll my shoulders. *I can do this.* Composing my features into an expression that doesn't betray my inner turmoil, I hope, I knock on the door.

"Come in." His hard deep voice sends a shiver down my spine. *Crap.* I can't afford to react like a woman in heat every time he speaks to me. I walk inside his office to find he's standing by the window with his back to me. The lights of the city shimmer in the distance. The days have been shortening, and somewhere in the distance fireworks explode, possibly over Alexandra Palace. It's Guy Fawkes day. How could I have forgotten?

I watch him watch the horizon; a hand thrust into his pocket, so it draws the seat of his pants tight across his rear. It accentuates his muscular behind. The perfect curve of his arse cheeks, the power inherent in his thighs. Then he half turns to face me and catches me in the act. "Like what you see, Kelly Assistant?" He drawls.

I blush, unable to look away from the perfection that is his face. Those cold blue eyes. Those sharp cheekbones, that pouty lower lip, and the way that scar lends an air of danger to his features. It makes him seem both human and a savage. A wounded soldier and a fallen brute. A barbarian who yearns for a tender loving touch. It makes him so very appealing. *Why do I find him so appealing?*

He continues to glower at me, and I realize I need to say something to protest the fact that he's calling me by someone else's name.

"It's June." I clear my throat. "J-U-N-E. June."

He doesn't give any indication that he's heard my plea. Instead, he says, "What you saw earlier—"

"I won't tell anyone." I swallow. "Even if I hadn't signed the NDA, I wouldn't go around telling people that I saw my boss, ummm..."

"With his dick in his hand?" He smirks.

The flush on my cheeks extends to my hairline. *OMG, why did that sound so filthy coming from him? And why am I not giving up this job and leaving? And why are images of his pleasure-filled face crowding my mind all over again?*

One side of his mouth dents, and I realize he's taking immense pleasure from my mortification. When really it should be him feeling humiliated. Which he isn't. So, why should I feel awkward?

"I'm not going to apologize for that." He tilts his head.

And now, I'm gaping again. Not that I thought he'd apologize, but to hear him say he won't, shows just how arrogant this man is.

"But I won't embarrass you again."

I frown. "You won't?"

"You've shown you can manage yourself in the trickiest of situations without losing your cool. I believe that proves you're a valuable addition to the team."

"Wait, what?" I blink rapidly. It takes a few seconds for his words to sink in. "Are you saying that all of that—"

"You could take it as a test, yes. Though I hadn't meant it to be, but turns out, it was for the best. None of my previous assistants would have conducted themselves with such dignity. And while I don't promise that I won't test you again, I won't be embarrassing you in this way."

I nod slowly. I shouldn't feel so deflated, so let down. I didn't realize how much I was turned on by seeing him masturbate. And honestly, I wouldn't mind seeing him do that again. I'm not going to tell him that. But I have enough images in my head to masturbate to myself.

"You'll also be getting a raise in your salary."

"A raise?" I gape.

"You need to be compensated for what I put you through this week. For what I'll be putting you through in the coming days."

"That sounds ominous." I manage a smile, but when there's no answering one on his face, I wipe it off mine. "Not that I don't welcome the additional money."

"Trust me, you'll be earning it, too." He looks me up and down. "I need you to give me a wake-up call each morning, starting tomorrow."

"A wake-up call?" I blink rapidly. "Surely, your phone has an alarm and—"

"A wake-up call at five a.m. every day," he interrupts me.

"Five a.m.?" I stare in horror. "B-but... That's so early."

"Including weekends." There's a gleam in his eyes—gone quickly, but not before I register it. "Starting tomorrow." He turns back to face the window. "You will find my car and driver, waiting to take you home."

"But—"

"You can leave now."

I open and shut my mouth again. That self-assurance in his voice indicates there are very few people who dare to disobey him. I'm going to hate waking up so early. On the other hand, he's also looking out for me by arranging to have me dropped home because it's late. *And the salary. Don't forget the salary.* It's going to be worth it for what he's paying me, right?

And if I keep this job, even for three months, I'll have enough to pay off all of my debts. The thought placates me. Enough for me to accept his offer of a car and driver without protest. Enough to paste a fake smile on my face.

"Thanks for the advance payment of my salary," I offer.

He doesn't reply, doesn't even turn. Simply points his thumb at the door. I pivot and scramble out of his office. I race to my desk, shut down my computer, then grab my handbag and the garment box, and head down the corridor.

I pass Mary's desk, which is empty. So are the desks of the other assistants. In fact, there is no one in any of the offices. Everyone has gone home. I check my phone and realize it's almost midnight. I'm secretly glad he arranged a ride home for me. I step into the elevator, ride down, and leave the building. I get into the waiting car—the same limo that brought me here. As the vehicle slides forward, the tension in my body slowly fades away. Only then, do I glance around and take in the plush interior; I was too distracted to notice it earlier Wow, I've never been driven in such luxury before.

I sink back into the leather seat and press my head back into the cushion. I inhale deeply, and the scent of leather, and something else, the lingering darkness of *his* scent teases my nostrils. It's comforting and arousing, and I allow myself to be cocooned in it. My lips curve in a smile. *I did it! I made it through my first week in the job from hell.* Only question? Can I get through at least another three months of being attracted to my ridiculously hot boss?

6

June

"This is your wake-up call, Sir."

It's Monday morning, and I wait for him to respond to my greeting. Will he thank me today? I listen on the line for the acknowledgment I'm starting to crave from him. But like the last two days, he disconnects without saying hello. My shoulders sag. My lips turn down. *Why am I so disappointed?* He's a busy CEO. And I'm his assistant doing my job. Nothing else. Of course, he doesn't have the time to acknowledge me. Also, he *is* a self-centered jerk, so I shouldn't be surprised he didn't thank me for waking him up at the arse-end of dawn.

He has no idea that this morning, I set four alarms on my phone—three of which I snoozed through, only managing to rouse myself on the fourth with less than a minute to go to call him. It was the same the last two days. I should berate him for forcing me to wake up and call him. I should resent him for cutting into my sleep. But the fact is, I want to please him.

I want to do a respectable job. I don't want to fail him. Not that he's going to notice the extra effort I've made. I'll never tell him how I poured coffee into a travel mug next to my bed, so I could take a sip and rouse myself before phoning him. I'll never reveal to him the thrill that grips my body when I dial his number every morning. Besides, he's already paid me for my efforts. He's compensated me by advancing my salary and none of my previous employers have done that.

I used most of what came in to pay off next quarter's rent on my mother's place, and the next semester's fees for my siblings. Anything left over went toward paying my over-due credit card bills.

I yawn, then set the alarm for six a.m. and go back to sleep. Of course, I oversleep, then have to hurry to make it to work by eight a.m., where the first thing I do is get him his coffee.

He ignores me, except to issue a list of orders which I note down on my device—a new one which was waiting for me on my second day of work.

Then, it's on to the staff meeting with his department heads. He has these meetings every Monday morning at nine a.m. and insists I sit in on them and take notes. I know most of them by face as they came in for meetings with him last week. I also emailed instructions to them on behalf of my boss, and while most of them had been fine with it, one of them, his Finance Director, replied to say he didn't take orders from a lowly assistant. His words, not mine. Grr!

I tamped down on my annoyance and responded ultra-sweetly, telling him these were *his* boss' orders, not mine. I was only the messenger.

Now, the Finance Director hitches a hip against the conference room table where I'm seated to the left of the head of the table. "June Donnelly, huh?" He looks me up and down. "You managed to survive the week, not bad."

"Time flies when you're having fun, eh?" I smile up at him in what I hope is a pleasant curve of my lips while trying my best not to shrink away from his presence.

He looks taken aback, then huffs out a laugh. "If you're trying to tell me it's fun working for The Beast, then you're not fooling me, honey."

Ugh, he called me honey. How condescending. I grit my teeth to keep the choice insults from spilling out. "I have no idea what you're talking about," I say blandly.

He eyes me with disbelief. "Surely, you know that's his"—he stabs his thumb in the direction of the seat at the head of the table— "nickname."

"Is it?" I ask, feigning surprise. *As if I, the person who works with him most closely, wouldn't already know everything?*

"And with good reason. It must not be easy to look at his scarred face every day."

What the—! That's bold of him. *How dare he talk about my boss like that?* His face might be scarred, but it only adds to his appeal. I glare at the wanker, thinking, *Better than looking at your face, dickhead*; not that he notices.

"Anytime you feel like a change of scenery, my office is down the corridor." He leans in and places his hand on my shoulder. "Whatever he's good at, I'm better at it. My numbers speak for themselves." He winks.

Was that a proposition? And he did it blatantly in front of the rest of the team. I'm so shocked, I gape at him open-mouthed. A slight commotion at the front of the room draws my attention toward the door. I find my boss standing there, glaring at me. His gaze is on where the other guy's hand rests on my shoulder. For some reason, I flush. Then pull away so his hand drops. I berate myself. I didn't do anything wrong. *So why do I feel so guilty?*

The wanker clears his throat and mumbles, "Looks like The Beast is in a mood today."

No shit, Sherlock.

He sidles around to drop into the seat next to me. I pull my chair away from him, closer to the head of the table and toward my boss. Then lower my head and study the screen of my device. My boss stalks past me and sinks into the chair at the head of the table. Instantly, everyone quiets. There's not even any shuffling of paper or coughing. Nothing. Ten other people in the room, and they've all faded into the background; that's how silent they are.

The hair on the nape of my neck rises. I'm so aware of my boss' presence, so conscious of his proximity, that my knees grow weak. The screen of my device fades in and out. I draw in a sharp breath to clear my head, but that only fills my senses with his scent. Instantly, I'm wet. I squeeze my thighs to stop the ache between them, but that doesn't help. I pretend an undue interest in my device and start typing into it when, "Did you hear what I said Ms. Donnelly?" my boss fumes.

"Uh, what?" I glance up at him and flinch when I see the frost in his indigo eyes. Arctic. Frozen wasteland. A glacier that stretches into infinity.

He looks like he crunched ice-chips for breakfast then swam ten miles in the freezing English Channel.

"I need the deck teed up on the laptop to project onto the screen," he growls.

"Oh," I glance down at the laptop on the table and realize it's not synced to the projector. The color on my cheeks heightens. "So sorry, I was meaning to do it before the meeting, but I got distracted."

Next to me, the wanker chuckles. I stifle my own growl.

My boss' jaw turns to granite. A muscle jumps at his temple. And his eyes turn to cold fire. Anger thrums in the air between us. He looks so scary that when I jump up and reach for the laptop, my arms tremble. I manage to get my emotions under control and concentrate on syncing the laptop with the projector.

Of course, it doesn't. I sigh, then reboot the laptop.

Above me, my boss' deep voice fills the room as he reels off the figures from the last quarter and outlines the plans for the next. Once more, I straighten, then walk past him to the projector and flick the device off and on. Nope. It doesn't sync.

I sigh aloud. A bead of sweat slides down my spine. Everyone's attention is on my boss, but it doesn't take away from my feeling like I'm on show. It doesn't take away from this need to prove to him that I can do this. I am more than capable of connecting this stupid laptop to this stupid projector.

I flick a glance in my boss' direction, wondering if he's noticed how hard I'm trying to please him? His focus is on the people gathered around the board room. Disappointment squeezes my chest. I look away, gather my thoughts and re-focus on the task at hand. More seconds pass. His dark voice washes over me, and I shiver. My fingers tremble. I sync the devices again, but nope, nothing projects onto the screen. My shoulders slump. I slink back to my seat and stare at the laptop.

"Why don't I help you?" The Finance Director reaches for the laptop at the same time as me. Our fingers brush. I pull back my arm. He pretends not to notice and leans in close enough for our shoulders to brush. I move away, but he simply closes the gap between us until, once more, our shoulders touch.

"You see, this is how you do it." In an exaggeratedly slow fashion, he proceeds to switch the computer off completely. "You count to ten, then re-start," he explains like I'm a dimwit. *What a turd. And his mansplaining? Grr!* I curl my fingers into fists, resisting the urge to dump the glass of water in front of me on him.

I stare rigidly at the computer as he switches it on. While I wait for it to re-boot, I'm aware of my boss's deep voice continuing to talk about the company's new forays. When the computer blinks on. I let the Finance Director toggle the Bluetooth switch.

"Try it now," he says in a condescending tone. *OMG, how annoying.* I jump up, walk over to the projector, and this time, the devices sync. *Of course, they do.* The figures from the laptop screen show up on the big screen, and my boss refers to them without a break in his narrative. I slink back to my seat, and when I sit down, the Finance Director pats my thigh. *What the fuck?* I sit ramrod straight, staring ahead. I'm so angry, I'm shak-ing. Then he leans in close enough for his breath to raise the hair on my temple. "Anytime you need another lesson in synching our devices, seek me out. I'd be happy to—"

"Get out," my boss thunders.

Without even looking at him, I jump up, spin around and begin to make my way to the exit.

"Not you, Ms. Donnelly."

I blink, turn to find he's staring at the Finance Director. "Out," he seethes again.

The Finance Director frowns. "What do you mean? I was simply—"

In a move that's so quick, he seems to blur, my boss is on his feet. He reaches over, grabs the collar of the Finance Director, and hauls him up. "Security will escort you out."

"Hold on, what is the meaning of this, Davenport?" he blusters.

The door to the meeting room opens, and two security guards walk over to him. They grab each of his arms and begin to haul him off.

"There's been a mistake," he cries.

My boss ignores him. "Make sure he's never seen on the premises again," he orders the security guys.

"B-but what happened?" the wanker stutters.

My boss turns on him. He fixes the wanker with his cold gaze. Silver sparks flash in his eyes. They're stormy cobalt pools swirling with so much emotion, I flinch. He could be Loki, ready to wipe out his enemy. Satan, ready to scorch everything his gaze touches. Anger pours off him in waves. He's not the unfeeling brute I thought him to be. All that emotion is boiling under the surface, looking for an outlet.

Oh, to be at the receiving end of it would be so erotic. The thought makes me feel faint.

"What did I do?" the Finance Director blurts out again.

"What did you *do*?" My boss' voice is low, almost casual. But I hear the ominous tone like thunder rumbling in the distance. He continues to glare at the Finance Director, who wilts under his scrutiny.

He swallows, then seems to find his bearings, for he puffs out his chest. "Y-yes, I want to know what I did?"

"You talked down to my assistant. You disrespected my assistant. You belittled her. You humiliated her. You invaded her personal space. You came onto her in front of the entire team."

I listen, thunderstruck. All the oxygen seems to have been sucked out of the room. The pressure in the space seems to dip, and there's this sense of impending doom. Like a massive storm is about to break over us.

"How dare you touch her when she was, clearly, uncomfortable?" His voice is so cold, so diamond-hard, so filled with rage, it sends a pulse of liquid heat shooting through my veins. Seeing my boss angry on my behalf is like sinking my teeth into the darkest, most bitter, most decadent chocolate cake. No, it's better *He noticed what the other guy was doing. He was aware of just how much the wanker was patronizing me. How he was coming onto me. He. Noticed. Me. And now, he's standing up for me? Oh. My. God.* I grip the edge of the table with such force, pain shoots up my arm.

"How dare you undermine my assistant's dignity?" My boss' voice drops even lower in pitch. "Get out of here before I throw you out myself."

"You're firing me over her?" The other guy sneers, "She's not worth it, you know."

My boss's shoulders seem to swell. The buttons on his jacket strain, and I'm sure they're going to pop any moment. In fact, I'm positive the seams of his sleeves are going to tear, thanks to how his biceps bulge. His gaze narrows on the Finance Director, who pales.

His Adam's apple bobs. "I'm going to sue the shit out of you Davenport," he cries. Then he's out of the room. The door closes behind him.

My boss straightens his tie, then glances around. "Dismissed."

I watch as the men and women who watched the proceedings with open-mouthed surprise scramble to their feet.

Thanks to me, his meeting went to pieces. I failed him. I swallow down my disappointment.

There's a clatter of chairs, the clop-clop of ladies' heels, then they're gone.

I take a few steps toward the door when, "Not you, Ms. Donnelly."

Oh. I freeze, but don't turn to face him.

"Come here," he says softly.

I turn and, making sure to keep my chin lowered, shuffle toward him. When I come to a stop next to him, I swallow. "I... I didn't do anything." Except, I feel guilty for not pulling away when that wanker touched me. In my mind, I already belong to my boss. *I belong to him?* The realization crashes into my chest with the force of a storm which had been building all along.

"Is that right?" My boss's cold, hard voice interrupts my thoughts.

I nod. Unable to meet his gaze for reasons I can't comprehend, I murmur, "He's the one who—"

"I'm aware." The menace in his tone makes me shiver. He sounds so tough. So livid. When he stays silent for a few seconds, I risk a glance at his face, then wish I hadn't, for he's glaring at me. The tips of his ears are white, which is not a good sign, is it? His jaw has gone even harder, if that's possible. And the way the muscles spasm at the tops of his cheek-bones? I'm sure he's going to crack a molar.

He reaches out and, before I can react, he slips off my spectacles, then folds them and slides them into his shirt pocket. To say I'm surprised is putting it mildly. I want to ask him what he's doing but he snaps, "Bend over."

"Excuse me?" I gape at him.

"Hands on the conference table, bend over at the waist, and put your cheek on the surface."

I'm not sure why I comply. And I don't know why this doesn't feel like sexual harassment, but it doesn't. In fact... It feels like whatever he's going to do to me is atonement for letting some other man touch me. Whatever he has in mind is going to help me find redemption, and it feels right. It feels like I've waited all my life to have this man pin me with his fierce look and give me his complete attention. Everything inside of me wants me to obey him, so I do.

I turn to face the boardroom table. I flatten one hand on the surface, then the other. I lower myself forward slowly, until my cheek is pressed into the surface. For a few seconds, the only sound in the space is my breathing. The tension builds, pressing down on me. My stomach churns with anticipation. A heavy pulse kicks in at my wrists, at my temples. My nipples throb. Then he kicks my ankles apart, and I gasp.

"You deserve to be punished for not standing up for yourself when someone insulted your professional standing."

He's right.

"You deserve to be punished for letting another man touch you. Do you agree?"

I nod.

"Say it aloud, if you do," he snaps.

"I... I agree."

I cry out when his palm connects with my backside. *One-two-three-four* —I count as he spanks my alternate arse cheeks. Each time he connects with my backside, I rise up on my tiptoes. Each time he spanks me, the pulse between my legs blooms bigger. Thicker. More insistent. Until it spills over into my thighs, my lower belly, bounces down to my toes, and up, up, up to my pussy lips and my spine, and bursts into a fountain of light behind my eyes. *Oh my god! Did I just climax?*

I float down to earth and when I open my eyes, it's to find he's massaging my behind through my skirt, my panties, and my stockings.

"Good girl," he murmurs, and a whine leaves my lips. *Ohmigod, what's wrong with me? Why did that feel so good?*

"You may straighten and put yourself to rights," he says in a bored voice.

I push up to standing, then wince when my backside throbs.

"Does it hurt?" There's a note of curiosity in his voice, matched by the gleam in his eyes. A shiver grips me. The fact that he cares enough to ask means so much, and I don't question it.

"It does"—I nod— "but in a good way."

Satisfaction laces his features. Then he slips my spectacles out of his pocket and slides them back on my face. He positions them just so, then looks me up and down. "You'll remember me every time you sit down in your chair. You'll remember that you're not supposed to encourage men to look at you."

"What the— What?" My jaw drops. "Are you saying it's my fault he touched me?" And here, I'd been thinking he rushed to protect my honor by firing the executive.

He draws himself up to his full height, "What I'm saying is that this skirt"—he stares at the offending garment—"is too tight."

"Are you calling me, fat?" I whisper.

He looks genuinely taken aback. "Are you trying to elicit compliments from me?"

It's my turn to feel baffled. "But you said my clothes are too tight—"

"Your figure is perfect, as you are well aware."

I push my spectacles up my nose. "Uh, no, I'm not, actually."

His brows draw down. "Surely, you jest. Your curves are exquisite."

"Really?" I cry.

He goes on as if I haven't spoken. "I'm sorry if I implied it was your fault that bastard came onto you. That wasn't my intention at all. But I didn't like the way he stared at you, and how he seemed to be overly familiar with you." He scowls. "Why didn't you tell him off?"

"Uh, I'm an assistant and he's an executive, and I didn't want to lose my job." *Also, I didn't want to mess up my boss' meeting.* But I don't say that aloud.

A look of understanding flashes across his features. "You have my permission to tell off any asshole who dares behave inappropriately with you, except—"

"You?" I ask timidly.

"Except me," he says slowly. "Do you find it strange that I say that?"

I lower my gaze and shake my head. "I... I find it appropriate. When you take liberties with me... It feels..." I search for the correct word then settle for, "Right?"

"Hmm."

I sneak a peek at his face to find him watching me with a strange look in his eyes.

"You didn't find it disconcerting when I—"

"Spanked me?" My bottom pulses in response, and I resist the urge to shuffle my feet and find a more comfortable position. "I should have, but... It felt... Correct for you to do so. I made a mistake, and you punished me, so I'll remember not to do it again."

He grunts. "I'm not going to apologize for it," he warns.

"I don't expect you to."

"This doesn't mean anything." He takes a step back. "I had an urge. I indulged it. But it doesn't imply there's something here." He motions to the space between us before shoving his hand in his pocket. "Understand?"

"You mean, you're not going to marry me?" I gaze at him wide-eyed. "But please. You touched me, so you should. Imagine how happy we'll be?" I paste a goofy smile on my face. "In fact, we'll make such pretty babies."

He blanches. I swear, the man goes completely white.

It's so funny—and pathetic—that the thought of marrying me turned my very macho boss pale, I allow myself a chuckle. It's either that or cry, and no way, am I going to do that.

"Relax." With a panache I manage to drag from the depths of my being, I wave my hand in the air. "I was kidding. You spanked me. I enjoyed it. It was an interchange between consenting adults. It doesn't mean anything."

Actually, it means a lot to me, but I'm not telling him that. No one has made me feel this cherished before. The fact that he wanted me enough to spank me and bring me to orgasm...makes me feel so wanted. Something I yearned for every time a foster family told me I wasn't welcome at their place. I push the thoughts aside.

"Excellent," my boss says in a relieved tone that makes my heart squeeze in my chest.

What was I expecting? A relationship? Ha. This strange—whatever it was —was some kind of sexual encounter. And I should treat it like that. I tamp down the part of me that wishes it to be more, then square my shoulders. "Right then, best I get on with my job."

I grab my tablet and my phone, as well as my pen and notebook, and march out of the boardroom. I drop them off on my desk, then continue on down the corridor to the ladies' room at the far end. It's empty. I turn my back on the row of sinks, then pull down my skirt, my stockings, and my panties. I glance over my shoulder at my reflection.

Jesus, my entire bottom has turned red, and I can see the imprint of his palm on my butt-cheeks. I place my much smaller palm over the finger-prints. Sparks. A shudder grips me. That's hot. That's twisted. That's sexy. And I want more. I hear the sound of someone in the next stall flushing. I sit on the toilet, do my business, then straighten my clothes. I wash my hands and head out.

I spend the rest of my day getting through my to-do-list and replying to his emails, then taking notes while I sit in on his next meeting with the acquisitions team. This one passes without incident, though I flinch at the coldness in his voice and have to try hard not to show my disapproval at his instructions for the takeover of a company. He shrugs aside the fact that it can be a risk to the Davenport Group to do so, that they might be overstretching. He wants to take risks and isn't going to shy away from it.

I'm no mathematical genius, but even I can tell, it's a foolhardy move to go after this company. Or perhaps, he knows something the rest of his team doesn't.

Then, it's on to compiling the sales figures from his team, and the next thing I knew, it's five-thirty p.m. and the office has emptied out.

Mary comes by on her way out and nods at me. "Heard about what happened in the staff meeting, and if you ask me, that chump had it coming."

"Umm, okay?" I venture. "I hope it doesn't cause Mr. Davenport any problems. The guy was livid when he was being dragged out by the secu-rity guys."

"Nothing Knox can't handle." She waves a hand.

Just then, a delivery guy walks over and proceeds to place cartons of food on my desk. "Um, I didn't order that."

"It says it's for Kelly Assistant."

I sigh. *So, we're back to that?*

I accept the delivery, and he leaves. I stare at the cartons in bemuse-ment. "Do you think he—"

"Knox ordered it, all right." She gives me a funny look. "Guess he must feel sorry."

"Feel sorry?" I frown.

"For acting like a twat, which I assume he must have been over the last week."

Or was he apologizing for saying there couldn't be anything else between us and trying to smooth my hurt feelings?

My landline buzzes, and when I answer it, he growls, "Need the California team on the phone. Did the estimates for the new office in Birmingham come in? You need to brief the recruitment agency for a new Finance Director. And where's the new advertising campaign?"

I look up to see Mary wave and leave, then turn my attention back to the phone.

"The California team will call you in five minutes. The Birmingham estimates are in your inbox. The recruitment agency will send you a short-list of candidates by nine p.m. tonight and the new advertising campaign will be in your inbox tomorrow by nine a.m."

There's silence then, "You already spoke to the recruitment agency?"

"First thing I did when I got back to my desk after the staff meeting."

"And the advertising campaign—"

"The agency needed a few more hours. It's not going to impact the media deadlines."

"But—"

"And I know you don't want any half-baked ideas. A few more hours won't break the bank, and it'll give the creatives a chance to flesh out their concepts so there's a better chance of you receiving a campaign that's effective."

I'm sure he's going to protest, but to my surprise, he drawls, "Good call."

I blink. Then sit back in my chair and close my eyes. A smile curves my lips. I bask in his approval, enjoying the fact that I surprised him and pleased him, at the same time. All the demanding work this afternoon was worth it. A bloom of pleasure surges in my chest. "Thank you. And also, for the dinner."

"Can't have my employees starving." He disconnects.

I place the phone down slowly, then take my seat. I wrap up everything else on my to-do list, stopping to eat in between. The Chinese food he had delivered is from a well-known restaurant and tastes really good. It's also light enough that, despite my tiredness, it doesn't weigh heavily in my stomach. In fact, it revives me enough to keep going for a few more hours. *I should leave.* Things can wait until tomorrow, but I want to impress him with my diligence. *If I work hard, surely, he'll notice and appreciate my efforts again? I'll do anything for a few more words of praise from his mouth.*

At eight p.m., I stretch, then switch off my computer. I gather my things and cast a glance in the direction of the closed door of his office. I take a step in that direction, then stop.

No, he hasn't eaten yet. In fact, he didn't even ask me to get him lunch, and when I emailed him to ask, he didn't reply. Yes, he's been at work since very early; but really, that's none of my business. His family owns the company, so he's putting in the hours to build his own legacy. Besides, he's a grown man. He can take care of himself. I turn and walk away, then find I can't leave thinking of him working on an empty stomach. When he ordered the Chinese takeaway for me, he hadn't ordered any for himself. Seriously the man needs a keeper.

I sigh, head back to his door and pull it open. The office is in darkness, except for the lamp on his desk. He's working on his computer and doesn't look up when I head inside.

"Can I order you dinner before I leave?"

No answer.

"I can't have my boss starving."

Maybe it's the fact that I'm using his words back on him, that makes him lift his head. "Goodbye." That's all he says before he focuses his attention back on his screen.

Fine, whatever. I tried. I pivot and turn to leave, and I swear, I can feel his gaze follow me. But that must be my imagination.

I reach the door when he calls out, "I'm sorry, that was uncalled for. And yes, you can order me dinner."

So, he was tracking my progress to the door? I turn, but he's back to looking at his computer. So maybe not. But the fact that he answered me... I take that as a positive sign.

The next two weeks, he's away for business. An around-the-world trip that has him hopping from London to LA, then onto Buenos Aires, then Singapore and Mumbai. He never misses any of his video conferences or agreements which need his signatures. Perks of having his own private aircraft, I suppose. The number of times zones this man has crossed is enough to give me a headache.

During this time, I get to know his team thoroughly, especially since he has me pass his directives to them and prefers me to answer their questions and pass on to him the ones I need help with. He insists that all communication to him be streamlined through me, and while I'm hesitant at first, I grow into my role. Surprisingly, his remaining department leads turn out to be good people who are focused on getting the job done and making his and their lives easier by working as a team. In addition to getting to know the department heads better, I also become familiar with the people reporting to them. And I come to the dawning realization that I can make a difference by helping to communicate my boss' thinking in more detail to them.

I'm privy to the workings of his mind and I realize, he doesn't have the patience to break down his strategies for his team. As a result, many of them feel lost or left behind when it comes to the implementation of his plans. I spend time breaking down my boss' ideas to his team. It results in them better understanding his intentions and appreciating the big picture which, so far, only my boss has envisioned.

It makes me feel good to do this. I feel needed. I'm bridging the communication gap between my boss and his management team. I'm making a real difference to the future of my boss' company, and I feel so happy about it.

Not that I can share this with my boss because, for the entire time he's gone, there's not one personal message from him. Nothing except official emails. Our communication has been strictly professional. I shouldn't be surprised. After all, he *did* emphasize there'd be nothing personal between us. And now that his handprint on my arse has faded, I confess, it's becoming difficult to remember that day.

Then, it's the day of the royal reception. When I wake up, there's a car waiting to collect me from my place to the office. *So, my boss was thinking about me, after all?* My chest squeezes with happiness.

He realized how difficult it would be for me to transport the clothes he sent me on the Tube. So, he made things easier for me. Despite the fact I'll be beholden to him again, I suck up my pride and use the car. Mainly because it makes me feel special that he arranged it for me. It also makes me realize he didn't completely forget about me while he was gone.

You wouldn't know it from how he barely acknowledges me when I bring him his morning coffee. Yes, he's back. And the anticipation building inside me had, perhaps, as much to do with counting down the days to his return, as it did the chance to attend this event.

The day passes with the usual rounds of meetings—with the advertising agency, then the PR agency, then the technical team, followed by a sales forecast meeting, where the numbers make my brain hurt. My boss seems energized in the meeting. Clearly, he thrives on numbers. Given the choice, he'd eat them for breakfast, lunch, and dinner. He shows no sign of letting up, and when five p.m. rolls around, I'm beat. I stretch and yawn.

I need to start getting dressed if we're going to leave by six p.m. for the royal reception.

I rise to my feet and grab the garment box I placed under the desk. I sense someone approaching and when I look up, it's to find a woman wearing white scrubs headed my way. She has a kind face and streaks of grey at her temple.

"Ms. June Donnelly?"

"Yes?" I frown.

"This way, please; your team is waiting."

"My team?"

"Your glam team, so we can get you ready for this evening."

"Glam team?" I scoff. "I have no idea what you're talking about."

The phone on my desk rings. I balance the garment box on the desk and pick up the phone, more out of habit than anything else.

"You will go with the glam team and allow them to help you get dressed for the evening," my boss orders.

These are the first words he's spoken to me since he left on his trip. For a few moments, I savor the rich timbre of his words. That deep darkness of his tone. My stomach flip-flops, and I have to squeeze my thighs together in an attempt to stem the flow of moisture from my pussy.

"You hear me, Kelly Assistant?"

Oh, he didn't do that! Just like that, all of my yearnings shatter. "It's June. And don't pretend you don't know my name; you called me by it in the staff meeting." *And this woman just called me 'Ms. June Donnelly.' What game is he playing at?*

"You done?" he growls.

And damn, if that doesn't piss me off even more. And turn me on. Which pisses me off even more. Though secretly, I'm loving the fact that he called me and ordered me in his bossy tone. I'm so pathetic. I draw on the angry side of me and huff, "I don't need this. I can dress myself. And I have my own cosmetics."

Which is a lie. I don't wear makeup. Other than a bit of lipstick and eyeliner. Could never afford it, so never got into the habit.

"It's not about you. It's my image I'm worried about. You'll be accompanying me as my assistant, and I need you to uphold my reputation." His voice is cold and brooks no argument.

I deflate a little. I mean, it's nice to have a team to help me get dressed, but would it have killed him to come across as a little warmer, a little more enthusiastic about this process?

"Fine," I bite out.

"Fine." He slaps down the phone.

I squeeze the receiver and glare at it, then gently lower it to the cradle. I'm going to pretend my pussy is not dripping, thanks to that dark edge that laced his voice.

"May I?" The woman holds out her hand.

I glance at her outstretched palms then slide the garment box onto them.

"Follow me, please." She heads down the corridor.

Forty-five minutes later, I've had a manicure and pedicure and a quick massage, and my face has been done up, as well as my hair— all thanks to an entire team of people who sprang into action. I'm wearing the deep green Alexander McQueen, and the dress looks even more beautiful now that I'm wearing it. It's crafted from fine silk chiffon, creating a flowing, ethereal silhouette. The bodice features a V-neckline, and the sleeves provide coverage appropriate for the royal occasion.

I step onto the small platform the glam team wheeled into the conference room, which was converted into my dressing room. And yes, they've also placed a mirror in front of me. I stare at my reflection.

I removed my glasses and wore my contact lenses. The glam team has exaggerated the shape of my eyes, so they seem bigger. The brown of my irises is accentuated by the dress. My complexion is flawless complexion, ruby red lips, hair which has been curled and left to flow down my back. And the dress—a green satin wrap dress that flatters my curves and highlights my best assets. My breasts look perfect, my waist looks tiny, and my hips... My hips are the highlight. The style doesn't hide; it aims to showcase me and my figure.

The waist is defined by a band of deeper emerald-green satin, cinched in to create a flattering silhouette. From this band, the skirt falls in gentle pleats to just above the ankle, allowing a glimpse of elegant shoes and ease of movement.

Delicate beadwork in various shades of green—from pale mint to deep forest—adorns the bodice and gradually scatters down the skirt.

I slip into the Louboutin's, which are so comfortable, I'm sure I can run in them. In addition, I'm wearing a fascinator. It's what I found when I opened the third box the delivery guys brought to my place. The dress code at the royal reception demands a headpiece. And what I have on is a headband featuring a base of fine sinamay straw, sculpted into a graceful, asymmetrical shape that curves gently to frame my face. Emerging from this foundation is a spray of long, curled ostrich feathers in a complementary shade of blush pink. When I move my head, the feathers dance and sway, adding a sense of lightness and motion to the piece. A swirl of fine netting cascades down one side, providing a soft, veil-like effect.

The headpiece elevates what I'm wearing from a normal gown to that of a dress fit for a royal reception. And the slight veil makes me feel like a princess.

"Wow," I breathe, appreciating the full effect of the eyeshadow, which makes my eyes seem so much more prominent.

"You like it?" The woman who came to fetch me earlier and who was the leader of the glam team claps her hands.

"I... I love it." Tears glimmer in my eyes. "I've never felt this beautiful."

"You are exquisite." The woman smiles. The rest of the team nods in agreement. And that burning sensation at the backs of my eyes spreads to my nose. I sniff and her features pinch in alarm. "Oh no, dear. We don't want you to spoil the makeup, do we?"

She glances at one of the other girls who moves forward and touches up my eyeliner.

Then the door opens. The hair on the back of my neck rises. My gaze locks with the devil's in the mirror. A devil in a charcoal black tuxedo and blue tie, which turns his eyes into glittering sapphires.

Instantly, the rest of the team begins to gather their bags and other equipment. In minutes, the last of them depart, leaving me with my boss.

7

Knox

She looks incredible. I take in the green dress with the fitted bodice that outlines her magnificent breasts. It has a slash neckline, sitting just below her collarbone, and long fitted sleeves extending to the wrists. It cinches in at the waist before it ends in a dramatic skirt which flows to her ankles, to create a sweeping effect.

It's modest, as befits a royal reception, yet the fitted tailoring highlights her luscious curves.

I bought this the first day she walked into my office. I barely knew her, but now that I know what kind of woman she is, I see my instincts were correct. She looks stunning, alluring, and sultry. With the towering heels she's wearing that showcase her shapely hips, she feels like a wet dream.

The way she climaxed when I spanked her was a thing of beauty. I smelled her arousal, felt the give of the skin over her shapely butt through her clothes, and almost tore them off her and mounted her right there. Good thing I stopped myself. The chemistry between us is off-the-charts, and when it comes to matters of work, she doesn't hesitate to go toe-to-toe with me.

She's quick to comply with my wishes, eager to please, desirous of my approval, and loves it when I treat her as my plaything. I enjoyed it so much warning bells sounded in my head. It's why I didn't call her when I was away on my business trip. I kept our communication to a minimum, limited to official matters and only by email. What I didn't expect was to miss her while I was gone.

I missed her voice, her scent, her ability to solve any problems I lobbed at her. I forbade myself to call her, then found myself looking forward to her emails. I've fallen asleep thinking of her sweet smile, her angelic features, and jerked off to images of her bent over the boardroom table with her gorgeous, pear-shaped behind offered up for my perversions.

I'm going slightly out of my mind with wanting to 'play' with her again, and that is wrong. She needs to protect herself from me, not be so ready to explore her own limits. The fact that she's so open with me makes me feel vulnerable in a way I haven't felt since... I was injured. It's pissing me off to the extent that I want to lash out at her.

It's why I circle my finger. "Let me see what my money's bought me for this evening."

A flash of hurt shivers across her face, followed by her eyes spiking with anger. Instantly I regret hurting her, and that's a surprise. I'm not someone who second-guesses myself. But the way my heart squeezes in my chest, and the way my groin tightens, has me questioning my motives in asking her to accompany me tonight.

She sets her chin, letting me see that glimmer of defiance that makes our interactions so interesting. *That's my girl.* Then, she reluctantly does a small turn, and the way her skin winks through the transparent fabric that constitutes the back of her dress turns my blood to lava. She turns to face me, and a look of anticipation steals across her features.

I want to tell her she looks like a goddess. Like she was made to wear designer clothes and go to society events. But when I open my mouth, what comes out is, "You'll do."

She gapes at me. Then looks me up and down. "I suppose, you will, too."

For a second, I'm taken aback, then I bark out a laugh. This woman? I've underestimated her.

"We'd better be off." I hold the door open and indicate she should precede me.

She levels a look filled with suspicion at me, then picks up her tiny evening bag—I made sure to order a range of handbags for her for everyday use, so she won't have to carry around that tatty satchel—and heads toward me. She walks out without a second look in my direction. I wish I could say that I don't stare at her swaying arse, at the way the shelf of her butt seems to get a life of its own, thanks to the fit of her dress and the added inches to her height that make her push out her bottom as she walks. I thank the stars that made me take the initiative by ordering this dress for her.

I follow her to the elevator, reaching out to slap the button to summon the car before she can. The doors slide open, and once again, I allow her to precede me inside. I hit the button for the reception area, and we stand in silence as the numbers decrease on the indicator.

Her scent fills the space—rose and something else noticeably light, something like honeysuckle and...strawberries. She's everything that's lush, and rich, and abundant, and succulent. And so soft. So ripe. I want to take a bite out of her, just push my nose into the curve of her neck and taste her. Would the scent be more concentrated there? And in the cleavage between her luscious breasts? And in the dent between her fleshy thighs? My mouth waters. My cock extends. Thank fuck, I'm wearing a jacket that covers the tent that's sure to have formed between my legs.

As the seconds tick past, she shuffles her feet, then shifts her weight, and I know she's uncomfortable with the silence. Sure enough, she bursts out, "Why do you have to be so rude? Especially after you were nice enough to have a team come in to help me dress?"

"Nothing to do with being nice. I was making sure your appearance doesn't let me down." My words elicit a stricken look on her face. Once again, my rib cage tightens. Goddam, every step with this woman is akin to walking across enemy territory, littered with land mines. I never know what might detonate.

When the elevator comes to a halt, I follow her out, then lead the way to the doorway of the office building where my Bentley limousine is waiting. The valet opens the door, and she slides into the back seat. I climb in after her. The limo slides forward. For a few minutes, we drive in silence, then I turn to her.

"That was uncalled for." I hold out my hand. "Let's start again. We were never formally introduced, were we? I'm Knox Davenport."

She folds her arms across her chest. "That wasn't an apology."

I tilt my head and consider her words. "It wasn't. And I understand I hurt your feelings, but I was speaking the truth."

Her eyebrows knit, then she lowers her head. "I suppose, I should be grateful you don't pretend repentance when you're not."

"You'll always get the truth from me. And I expect the same from you."

I glance at my outstretched hand, then back at her. She slowly slides her hand in mine. I squeeze her delicate fingers, and goosebumps pepper her décolletage. A quiver of heat sizzles to my belly, tightening my gut further. She seems as surprised as I am by the reaction.

When I don't release her hand right way, she laughs, the sound uncomfortable. "Truth, huh?" She looks away, then back at me. "The truth is, I'm attracted to you."

I stiffen. I hadn't been expecting that. Once more, she's taken me by surprise, and I'm unsure what to make of her confession. *Me and unsure?* Another first.

"You sound like you don't believe me. For that matter, you don't seem surprised that I said it aloud," she muses.

"On the first, you're right." No way, can an unsullied angel like her want what someone like me, someone with a damaged, grotesque visage, can offer. Besides, I don't deserve to be happy. And the fact that she's attracted to me doesn't mean anything. She may have enjoyed the spanking, but when she finds what my inclination for dirty, filthy kink extends to, it'll undoubtedly shock her and send her running.

"On the second"—I narrow my gaze on her— "I'm getting used to the fact that there's a lot about you that's going to continue to catch me unawares. And it's the truth that I haven't said that to anyone else before."

Her features soften. Her eyes shine with something like respect and appreciation. An uncomfortable feeling lodges under my ribcage. I release her hand and look away.

"It's also true that I don't want this chemistry between us to spoil things. As I mentioned in the conference room, what happened between us didn't mean anything."

The light in her eyes dims. Her shoulders droop. She looks like someone who lost their pet. Once again, my goddamn heart contracts. Boundaries. I need to stick to the boundaries I decided on when it comes to any emotional entanglement with her. That's what's best for both of us.

In a bid to soften the blow, I offer, "In the weeks that you've been with me, my productivity levels have shot up."

"Is that a compliment I hear?" She mock-gasps.

My neck heats. Another bloody first. Can't remember the last time I felt this shamefaced.

I turn and meet her gaze again. "You fielded a lot of the queries from my team and conveyed my directions with enough accuracy that no one has reached out to me directly. You've proven you can take care of a lot of the day-to-day operations, which is what I need. You've functioned more as an executive assistant than an administrative assistant. I'd like to change your title to reflect that. What do you say?"

Once again, her gaze widens. "E-executive Assistant?" she squeaks.

"With the commensurate pay rise."

She shakes her head. "Oh, no, no, you've already offered me a salary increase. I can't accept anything more."

I lean back into the seat. "One thing you should learn, dear assistant— never turn down money. Especially not when you deserve it and it's being offered in exchange for your services, and your time. And trust me, I only plan to offload more of the daily workload onto you."

"You do?"

"It's what I'm paying you for."

"Right." She squirms around, trying to find a more comfortable position. "So, Executive Assistant to the CEO and a second pay rise. I guess that should work."

"Good." I pull back my sleeve and glance at the time on my watch. I'm sure this event is going to be deathly boring, but at least I'll have her by my side for entertainment. Not that I plan on telling her that. "Are you comfortable?"

"C-comfortable?" Her voice shakes a little.

I allow myself an inward smile. "I notice you've been fidgeting in your seat."

She freezes. "It's just, uh... I'm not used to wearing such nice clothes, and this is the first time I've been in a limo."

"Oh?" I knit my brows. "You deserve beautiful clothes and to ride in a luxury car."

Her cheeks flush. "That's very nice of you to say. I suppose, you must be used to this?" She waves a hand in the air. "Given your background, and all?"

"I wasn't riding in an executive car when I was on my tours of duty. And I wasn't surrounded by such lavishness when the bomb that took out my brother's-in-arms went off next to me."

She inhales sharply.

I'm not sure why I say that. I don't normally flaunt my background, preferring to keep my past to myself. But with her, apparently, I'm enough at ease to speak my mind. Also, a part of me wants her to see me as more than the spoiled, billionaire CEO she has pegged me for. And perhaps, I feel threatened by how romantic it feels to be in this car with her, all dressed up for an evening out. I want to break the mood. And when she winces, I know I've succeeded.

She lowers her chin. "That's not what I meant."

I sigh. "I'm aware. And it's not your fault. While I was born into the Davenport name, I spent the first thirty-three years of my life running from it."

I glance out my window again. I haven't spoken about what happened on that last tour with anyone in my family. I'm shocked I opened up to her.

Confessing the sins of my past is not the kind of conversation I anticipated having with my employee. The car rolls to a stop then, providing me with a natural stop to the conversation. "We're here." I push the door open and step out.

Then, because I was brought up to be a gentleman, and no other reason —definitely not because I want to torture myself again by feeling her soft fingers in mine and experiencing that rush of awareness when my skin touches hers—I hold out my hand.

She places her palm in mine, and I help her to her feet. I'm rewarded by the pinpricks of heat that squeeze my nerve-endings, the sensations that course through my veins, the tightness that coils in my belly, and the twitches that course up my cock. I lead her up the steps of Dalton Hall, the stately home in Regents Park that's been in the bridegroom's family for generations, where the reception is being held. The paparazzi begin clicking away, the flashbulbs exploding.

Then we're inside, and she heaves a sigh of relief. "I was expecting attention from the press, but talking about it and being at the receiving end of those flashbulbs is something else altogether."

"Ignore them." I nod toward the hostess who welcomes us, then follow her into the grand foyer. Light slants through the stained-glass windows that adorn the top half of the walls. Ahead of us is a sweeping staircase that ascends to the second floor.

"Wow." Her steps slow to a halt. "This is incredible."

I glance down to see the amazement on her features, those big eyes, with the brown irises which have turned almost golden, reflecting her surprise. Her red lips are slightly parted, and God help me, but she looks delectable. And so young. Not in terms of the years between us; it's the undisguised astonishment on her face that makes me feel much older and jaded.

I realize, at some point in my life, I allowed my experiences to get the better of me. I forgot to believe in the joy of living. Forgot about looking forward to what the future would bring. Forgot how idealistic I was when I joined the Marines. I've allowed my life to be filled with pain and regret, and the pursuit of power. And it's taken just a few weeks of knowing this woman to remind me that I could have a different future. One in which I'm not running from my feelings.

When I noticed my Finance Director disparaging her, it brought my protective instincts to the fore. It enraged me and made me feel emotions I've buried inside myself for so long. It made me realize I could have a life where I'm not merely surviving, but engaged and forging meaningful connections with the world around me, only...

I don't deserve that. I do not deserve to be happy. Not when I couldn't protect my best mate, and the rest of my platoon, from being massacred. It's why I'm going to step away from her and ensure I keep my distance. It's the only way to ensure I don't taint her further. I increase the pace of my steps. The faster I get this evening over with, the faster I can drop her home and be on my way to a place where I can find some relief from this constant hurt that has hooked its claws into my belly.

She's forced to hurry to keep pace with me. I slow down enough for her to navigate the flight of stairs safely. When we reach the entrance to the ballroom, I release my hold on her.

She stumbles a little. My fingers twitch to reach out and right her, but I resist. I need to keep away from her. Need to find my equilibrium again. I snap my fingers, and a steward appears next to me. No, not any steward; it's my friend Sinclair Sterling's butler Jeeves. It's not a well-known fact that when the Royalty and quasi-Royalty in this country attend events, they bring their butlers along.

My stint with the Marines made me frown at this tradition, but I gotta admit, I appreciate it now. If I'm going to leave her with anyone, I'd rather it be with Jeeves. I can trust him to take care of her. *And why should that matter? You don't have any claim on her, no matter that you spanked her, and she enjoyed it.* But she's also my employee. She's an asset to my company, and her safety is important to me. I wouldn't leave her with any man. But Jeeves? He's all right.

Yep, it's her safety that's prompted this flurry of thoughts. I'm being a considerate employer, is all.

I nod in Jeeves' direction, then at her. "Please introduce my assistant around, will you?"

8

June

"Where are you going?" The smile on my face turns into a frown as I watch him put distance between us. When he doesn't answer, I take a step forward. "Knox!"

"That's Mr. Davenport to you." He scowls at me over his shoulders. "And I'm going to the bar to get in a couple of drinks, so I'm insulated enough to put on a game face."

"B-but... I can't go on alone."

"You won't be alone; Jeeves here will keep you company."

Jeeves, who's dressed in a black suit and tie and is clearly part of the service staff, looks between us, then pastes a smile on his features. He's uncomfortable but is too polite to show it.

"Shall we, Miss?" He leads me away while my boss stalks off. I track his progress, then frown when he's stopped by a woman in a black dress that fits her like a glove. Her shoulders are covered, and the dress ends below her knee, but the height of the heels on her fire-engine red stilettos ensures she's almost at eye-level with him. She smiles at something he says then takes the arm he offers her. A spurt of jealousy licks my insides, and I bat it away.

Together, they walk forward, picking up another man dressed in a tux with a bored look on his features. He nods at them, and my boss and he exchange a few words, then all three of them head toward the bar at the far end of the room. I hunch my shoulders.

So, he pawned me off on someone else, then decided to catch up with his friends. I thought I'd be spending the evening with him. I thought he invited me along to help further his business. Instead, he's not giving me any direction. He abandoned me and I... I don't know what I'm supposed to do.

The scent of expensive perfume permeates the air, combined with the flowers that are arranged in huge vases on tables—lilies and violets and enormous orchids of a size I've never seen before. All around me are men in tuxedos and women wearing the kinds of clothes I've only seen in society pages. The kind of clothing I'm wearing tonight. Many are wearing hats. On the outside, I, too, am wearing a designer dress and heels, and my makeup is flawless. But inside, I feel like a fraud.

I'm not ashamed of my background, or that my childhood was spent in the care system, or that I was adopted. Or that when my mother fell ill and lost her job, I stepped in to help take care of my sister and brother. I want them to benefit from a higher education and promised myself I'd help pay for their university fees.

But surrounded by men and women who've been born into generational wealth, I feel the contrast between them and me keenly. I realize we've come to a halt and Jeeves looks at me expectantly, "Are you okay, Miss?" he asks in a kind voice.

For the first time, I look at him properly and realize he's much older than my boss. He has a patient look about his features, and an understanding in his gaze that I'm grateful for.

"I, uh... Could you lead me to a quieter part of the room, where I might, perhaps, not feel like I'm on display?"

"Of course." He guides me to the side opposite where my boss headed. He leads me to a standing table, pushed up almost against the wall. Once I step behind it, I'm able to hide behind the flowers. This way, I can see the room, but not too many people can spot me. I hope.

"Can I get you something to drink?" he asks.

"I believe the lady would like some… Champagne?" a voice comments.

I look up to find a man who's at least six feet three inches, possibly as tall as my boss, with dark hair and facial features remarkably similar to my boss. Only he's wearing a pair of glasses, which add to his appeal. He places a glass of champagne on the table in front of me. "Connor Davenport," he says by way of introduction. "And you must be June Donnelly."

I nod slowly. "So, you are—"

"That asshat Knox's brother." He nods at Jeeves, who bows his head, then melts away.

"Wow." I stare after him. "Do they have to go to a school for stewards to learn how to walk away so unobtrusively?"

"Butler school actually," Connor replies.

I look at him, sure he's joking, but his expression says otherwise. His lips quirk in a half smile, and damn, but he reminds me of my boss then. Only Knox—I mean, Mr. Davenport—is bigger than him, not in height but in girth. Connor has a lean strength to him, but Knox? He's built like a truck. A very sexy truck, who looks devastating in a tux. But Connor's handsome, too, in a more classic fashion. Perhaps, it's the lack of scars that gives me that impression?

Connor's gaze grows intense. His eyelids lower as he surveys my features. "I can see why my brother is taken with you."

I blush. Given I caught him masturbating, and he spanked me, and we discussed our attraction in the limo on the way over here, I'd have agreed with his assessment. Only he did make it clear again, that there was nothing between us. Then he ditched me the first chance he could and went off with his fancy schmancy friends, so now I'm not sure.

"Oh, no, no. You're mistaken. I'm his assistant, is all. And he needed me to take notes tonight whenever he met anyone of importance."

There's a knowing smile on Connor's face. And that makes me shake my head again.

"No, really. This is a work thing." I'm beginning to sound desperate. But I'm telling the truth. Besides, I don't want word spreading that there's something between me and my boss. Not when there isn't. And not when it'll make it extremely uncomfortable for me in the workplace if this gets around. Only Connor doesn't seem to believe me.

"It's all right." He pats my hand. "My brother is a dick. He needs to spin lies that he can believe in. But he's a fool, leaving you alone."

"Oh, ah, he had some work to take care of." Now, I'm making excuses for the man. *Really?*

Again, Connor seems to be aware of what I'm doing, for he winks. "Want to see how I can bring him back here?"

There's a rakish look in his eyes, one I can't help but respond to. This man is trouble in a different way from Knox. He sees the doubt on my features. "I promise, I won't do anything to get you in trouble... Well, maybe a little." His grin turns sly. "In a good way."

The craftiness in his tone brings forth a reluctant smile on my face.

"I promise, it's only going to help my brother see what a complete tosser he is."

"I can get on board with that." I shift my weight between my feet. "But I have to insist that you understand I'm only his employee."

"Of course," he says in a guileless tone.

The expression on his features is *too* innocent. The man is up to something, but he's so delightfully charming, it doesn't stop me from taking his hand when he offers it to me. He leads me onto the dance floor.

"My bag." I turn to where I left it to find Jeeves taking it. He turns and bows to me then, once again, does that disappearing butler thing. "Oh my god, I could get used to this," I exclaim.

"Jeeves is one of a kind. He is the butler of butlers."

"He really is." I step onto the dance floor where couples are already swaying. There's a live five-piece band at one end of the floor who are playing a classical waltz I vaguely recognize. The violinist, though— "Is that?" My gaze widens. "Surely not."

"It's him." He names a very well-known rock star known for combining classical music into his rock operas and whose music is currently charting Spotify's most downloaded tracks.

Then a woman steps up to take the microphone, and I gasp again. "That's Solene!" She's only the most popular pop star in the world right now. "I didn't realize she did private gigs?" I gasp.

"She's a good friend of the Crown Prince," Connor informs me.

Solene begins to croon into the mic.

I sigh. "Oh wow, she's good."

"And my brother is not just a twat but a complete loser." Connor smiles down at me. "Also, don't look past my shoulder."

I do so right away, and my gaze connects with the exceptionally large, very scary looking man who's glowering at me from the edge of the dance floor. Without breaking our connection, he begins to shoulder his way across the dance floor, and not too gently. He merely shoves a man who's stepped in his path to the side, then elbows another man who's dancing with his partner out of the way. To their credit the men don't pick a fight with him. They don't even pause as they steer their women out of his way. As if by magic, the rest of the couples glide away, opening up a path from him to where I'm dancing. He prowls toward me, and when he reaches us, he grabs Connor by his collar and shoves him aside. "She's mine."

9

Knox

"Is she now?" Connor's smirk widens. The asshole thinks this is one big joke.

"I mean she is my employee," I growl.

He continues to grin, but steps back. Then half bows to both of us. "A pleasure, milady."

"Fuck off," I snap.

"Very eloquent, big bro, but this once, I'll do as you ask, and only because we're in such beautiful company." He winks at my assistant.

What the—! Before I can hurl some choice abuse at him, he turns and glides off. I take his place and hold out my hand.

She hesitates, but when I glare at her, she tightens her mouth then slides her fingers over mine. A tiny shudder grips her. It's strangely satisfying, knowing she's so affected by my presence. And when I pull her after me as I make my way off the dance floor, she protests. "Where are we going?"

I don't answer, continuing to lead her around the dancing couples, then weaving my way through the other guests. The men follow her progress with keen interest. I shield her as best I can from them, glowering at a few in my path until they look away. *What the fuck? Why did I feel the need to stalk over and shove Connor away from her? Why do I want to gouge out the eyes of every fool here who's watching her progress?* My behavior is inexplicable. My possessiveness is unfathomable. I spanked her for letting another man touch her. And now, I want to whisk her away from here and hide her where no one can see her. It was wrong to buy her this dress which fits her like a glove and embellishes her assets.

I'm going to ensure I buy the rest of her wardrobe and it'll be more modest.

"Knox... I mean, Mr. Davenport, why are you so angry?" She has to run to keep up, but the ground is even, and I know she can navigate it, so I don't let up until we're through the back door of the grand ballroom. I stalk down the long corridor and past the few other rooms that seem to be occupied. I keep going until the last door at the end of the hallway. It's closed, and when I shoulder it open, I find we're in a private study.

I doubt wedding guests are allowed in here, but what-fucking-ever. The Davenport name is meant to "open doors" on occasions like this, after all. We may not be as rich as the Royal Family, but Arthur is known to have a direct line to the King of England which can be used to smooth over any issues that might arise if we're discovered here.

There are bookcases filled with books stacked against the wall on the right. On the left is a lit fireplace; and in front of it is a rug on which there's a leather settee with an armchair next to it. Taking center stage before a casement window is a large wooden desk facing the door, a chair tucked behind it. On the desk is a tray with a jug of water and an upside-down glass. Most importantly, the room is empty.

I step in and gesture for her to enter, then shut the door after her. She takes a couple of steps forward, then her gaze darts around the room, before coming back to me.

"Why... Why did you bring me here?" she stutters.

"Why do you think?"

She locks her fingers together. "I, uh, was only talking to Connor. It was innocent."

"If I suspected otherwise, I'd have buried my fist in his face" — not caring that he's a sibling—"for messing with what's mine..." I firm my lips. "I mean, *my employee.*"

She wraps her arms about herself, then heads toward the fire and stares into it. For a few seconds, there's silence, then she says in a low voice, "You confuse me."

I drag my fingers through my hair. "I confuse myself when it comes to you." I'm surprised at hearing the words come out of my mouth.

So is she, for she turns to look at me over her shoulder. "Didn't expect to hear you say that."

Neither did I. I walk over to the armchair and drop into it.

"You say you're attracted to me, yet you flirt with someone else?" I give her a considering look. "Something you should be punished for."

She spins around with an incredulous expression on her features. "Flirting? I was being civil to him; that's hardly *flirting.*"

But I saw the admiring glint in his eyes, and damn, if that didn't make me jealous. Something I can't understand. It makes me uncomfortable to feel this way, which is why I'm going to punish you. Yeah, that makes no sense, but it makes me feel better. Not that I say any of that aloud.

"May I point out that you were the one who asked Jeeves to show me around?" She stabs a finger in my direction. "You were supposed to take me along on your networking meetings. Instead, you abandoned me."

Fuck, she's right. And I walked away from her, wanting to put distance between us. But I wasn't able to stay away. I barely had a drink at the bar. My mind was on her. So, I finally gave in and headed to the ballroom, where I noticed how every man in her vicinity was ogling her. Worse, she was animatedly talking to my brother. And jealousy reared up and had me stomping over to her before I could stop myself. She's messing with my equilibrium, and I need to find a way to get back in control. I'm in charge here, and it's time I remind her.

"Did you miss me?" I incline my head.

She huffs but doesn't deny it. I scan her features, take in the hurt expression on her face, and my heart—*goddamn it*—melts a little more.

"I admit, I made a mistake by leaving you."

She seems taken aback.

"But I also think you should pay for the error of your ways."

"I didn't do anything wrong." She firms her lips.

"You were flirting right back with my brother."

She blinks. "And if I was?"

"The last time you allowed another man to touch you, I punished you. Have you forgotten?" I growl.

She lowers her chin, then looks up at me from under her eyelashes. "Perhaps, I have. Perhaps, you need to remind me again of the consequences... Sir."

Her eyes gleam, and I realize, she's baiting me. Worse, I can't seem to stop myself from reacting to it. She's going to pay for it, but first, I need to set her right. "You were flirting with Connor because he reminded you of me. There's a reason I'm the one you're attracted to, and not him," I declare.

Her forehead furrows. "What do you mean?"

"You need someone who'll take you in hand."

Color smears her cheeks.

"Someone who'll lay down the rules for you to follow. Someone who'll tell you what to do."

The pulse at the base of her neck increases in intensity.

"Someone who'll dominate you and take the choice away from you, so you can lean into your urges, only—"

"Only?" she breathes.

"Only, you need to ask me for it."

Her forehead crinkles, "You want me to ask for what exactly?"

"Your punishment, of course."

She begins to speak, and I cut the air with my palm. "Don't bother denying it. It's evident from your features that you want it. The question is, are you bold enough to acknowledge what you want? And make no mistake, you need to ask for this of your own free will."

She swallows, then tips up her chin.

"You...want me to ask for it of my own free will?" She repeats my words.

A delaying tactic, but I'll allow it. I choose not to reply. Instead, I sprawl in my seat and eye her with a stern look.

"What's it gonna be, July?"

It's a testament to the preoccupation of her thoughts that she doesn't protest at the name I call her.

She flicks a look at the door, then lets out a sigh. A look of resolution comes over her features. She squares her shoulders, then takes a step toward me, and another. She comes forward until she's standing in front of me.

Thank fuck. The first time I spanked her, in the boardroom, I took a gamble. This time... I took it a step further by being upfront about what I think she needs. That she wants to be taken in hand. That she needs direction. That she yearns for a clear roadmap through which to explore her desires. And that I'm the only one to give it to her.

I could deny it, but the rage I felt on seeing her with Connor showed me, I can't ignore this attraction between us. It's a problem. And I've yet to face a problem I can't solve. I'm certainly not going to back away from this one either. So, I decided to play my hand. And now, when she approaches me to stand in front of me, I'm relieved I did.

The thought of the pleasure it will give me to see her submit to me makes me feel like I'm going to float away on a puff of smoke. I don't deserve the happiness it's going to bring me, but it's not forever, is it? Just for now, for this moment, I can make her bend to my will. Just for a few minutes, I can indulge my need for her and allow myself to feel complete. Anticipation pinches my nerve endings, but I keep it from showing on my features.

Instead, I jerk my chin. "Part your legs."

Doubt flickers in her eyes. I'm sure she's going to protest. Instead, she widens the space between her legs.

"You're doing so well," I praise her.

She shudders.

"Pull up your dress."

She casts another glance toward the door. "Anyone can come in."

"Does that turn you on?" I incline my head.

"I think it does." She swallows. "Is that crazy?"

"No more than my wanting to sniff your cunt."

In the flickering light from the fireplace, I see red stain her cheeks. Her fingers tremble as she grabs fistfuls of her dress. With a soft whisper of the fabric against her skin, she pulls up her dress until it's gathered around her waist. I get a glimpse of the white panties she has on. I make out the spot of wetness that darkens the gusset, and when I breath in deeply, I can scent the sugary sweetness of her arousal. My pulse thuds at my temples, at my wrists, even in my balls.

I continue to stare at her crotch, and her thighs tremble. A moan bleeds from her lips. The blood drains to my groin. My shoulder muscles bunch. *Interesting.* This reaction to her is far from usual. It makes me realize I underestimated the chemistry between us. It makes me want to push her to see how eager she is to comply with the rest of my directions.

I stretch out my right leg so it's between her feet.

"On your knees," I bark.

Instantly, she complies. She sinks to her knees without a murmur. *Such a perfect submissive.* I'm instantly hard. It's so fucking gratifying, to have her follow my orders.

"Take off my shoe," I order.

When she reaches for my leg and places it over her exposed thigh, it's as if there's a direct line established from there to my balls. My lower belly knots. Heat squeezes my chest. And when she slides off my shoe and places it on the floor, it's so satisfying. I know then, I can't let go of her easily.

"Good girl," I praise her.

She shudders. Her lips part. When she looks at me, there's surprise on her features.

"Feels good to follow instructions, doesn't it?"

She nods, eyes wide.

"Next, take off my sock and place it in my shoe."

She reaches under the pant-leg of my slacks, and when her fingers brush against my skin, electricity arrows up to the crown of my cock. My dick extends further, and I have to widen my stance to accommodate my arousal.

Her gaze is drawn to my crotch, and what she sees there makes her fingers tremble. A look of fear and anticipation flashes across her face. She continues to stare at the tent between my legs as she eases the sock off my foot. Her cheeks pinken, and in the flickering light of the fire, she looks adorable. She tears her gaze off the object of her attention and places the sock in my shoe.

"Well done. Now, lower your arms to your sides."

When she does, I place the heel of my bare foot on the rug between her thighs. I raise my foot, and my big toe brushes up against her core.

She hisses. Her thighs tremble and she curls her fingers into fists.

"How does that feel?"

"It feels...good." She clears her throat. "It feels like I need more."

I nod. "Slide your underwear aside so I can see your cunt."

10

June

The confidence in his voice is like a siren call to a part of me only he can reach. No way, can I disobey him. I was born...to do what he wants. Instinct has me pushing aside the gusset of my panties. It's sheer instinct that has me holding it there, baring my pussy for his perusal. Instinct which has me staying still as he takes in his fill. He's looking at me. Noticing me. This is the pinnacle of pleasure, to have his full attention right now. I'll do anything he wants to keep the light of his gaze trained on me.

Then he raises his foot just enough that his big toe, with its trimmed nail, rubs up between my pussy lips again. Goosebumps pop on my skin. Liquid heat shoots out from the point of contact and zips through my veins.

I'm trembling so badly, the strain of holding my position makes my thighs hurt and my knees scream for relief, but the pain only adds to the feeling of being so alive and in the moment. He wants me to do this, and I'm not going to fail him. I've never felt this vital. This...everything. The fact that he's watching my reactions closely, and that my cunt is bared for him to use as he sees fit, sends pleasure rippling up my spine. It's unbelievably filthy, and it shouldn't turn me on, but it does.

Moisture drips down my inner thigh. My pussy quivers. Emptiness gnaws at my insides. I look at him with a beseeching expression, not sure what I'm asking for, but once again, instinct dictates he'll know what I want. He implied as much, and it's with a sense of relief that I await his next order.

"How do you feel?" he asks in a conversational tone.

"I… I feel… Hot and shivery."

"And?"

"And needy."

He nods imperceptibly. "And?"

I swallow, "And like there's an aching void in my center."

He holds my gaze, unblinking. Apparently, he needs me to be more honest with my words.

"And like you need to direct me on what I should do to find relief," I murmur.

"I didn't hear that." He smirks.

Oh god. He did hear that, but he wants me to repeat myself, and I should be upset by that, but instead, it only turns me on further. That he knows how to tease me and tug on my emotions is so satisfying. It makes me want to please him further and turns my insides to jelly.

Liquid heat trickles down from between my legs. Sensations zip under my skin. It feels like I've plugged my finger into an electric socket, and the current is surging through my blood.

"Tell me what to do next," I plead.

He leans back further in his chair. The indolent angle of his body, the way he places his elbow on the armrest and taps his fingers on it, indicates I haven't said the right thing. The patience in his eyes signals that, until I do, he'll be happy to see me kneeling here with his toe pushing into my pussy, feeling the evidence of my desire trickle down his foot, and not do anything about it.

I resist the urge to cry out in frustration, knowing that will only delay things. Instead, I bite the inside of my cheek. "Please, please instruct me, Sir." Instinct again. That's why I add that honorific at the end of the sentence, and I'm rewarded when he goes still. And I know I've pleased him when he pushes up his foot, so his big toe stabs into the space between my pussy lips. *Ohmigod!*

A rush of intense pleasure zips through my veins, and the only reason I don't cry out is because I've squeezed my lips shut. The noise that slips out of me seems to assuage him, for he nods.

"You may use my foot," he says in an almost kind voice.

Instantly, I lower myself until the edge of his big toe breaches my slit. I throw my head back, squeeze my eyelids shut and grip my dress, which is bunched around my waist.

I begin to ride my boss' foot. I lower and raise myself. Again. And again. My nipples bead, my stomach squeezes in on itself. And when he growls, "That's it, get yourself off like a good girl," a fierce surge of gratification grips my thighs. It squeezes my pussy, and bolts up my spine and *ohgod, ohgod, I'm so close.*

Three weeks ago, I was an out-of-work assistant trying to take care of her family. Now, I have money in my account, have started paying off my debts, and I'm at the society gathering of the year, with my pussy riding my boss's foot. What is my life, even?

A shiver eddies up my spine. I can't stop the moan that spills from my lips.

That's when he pulls his leg back. My climax flutters at the edge, then stalls.

"What— Wait!" I lower my chin and snap my eyes open. "I need to come."

"All in good time. Meanwhile"—he nods toward his big toe—"look at the mess you made, you filthy girl. Lick it off."

"You're joking," I say, half in horror, half with this crazed sensation of lust which seems to have attached itself to every sense in my body.

He glares at me, and my nerve-endings spark in response. *Oh my god, he means it.* And worse, I'm going to do it because it doesn't feel wrong. It feels like the kind of thing I want to do for him happily. I slide back, my knees cushioned by the rug, then bend and lick off the moisture that clings to his toe. The sweet taste of myself mixed with the darker edge of his skin goes straight to my head. It's filthy and dirty and so, so, sexy. *How can it be sooo sexy?* For a second, I picture how it would look to someone on the outside. Me, with my expensive gown crumpled around my waist and showing the curve of my butt as I supplicate myself to my boss and bend down to lick my cum off his foot. And the image I create in my mind is so erotic. So arousing. So explicit. My breasts swell, my pussy feels heavy, and oh god, I'm even more aroused now.

When I look up, he leans in and, with his thumb, scoops up a drop from the edge of my lips. He brings it to his mouth and sucks on it. My clit throbs in response.

"Even sweeter than I expected." He jerks his chin. "On your knees."

When I comply, he nods in the direction of his sock and shoe. I follow his lead and slip the sock onto his big, wide foot, then pick up his polished, Italian leather dress shoe. It seems huge in my hands, and when I help him slip it on... I realize, the size is borne out by the massive tent at his crotch. I want to flick a glance in the direction of said tent, but don't dare. Once again, instinct dictates that I follow his orders to the letter. If I do, he'll reward me, surely?

"Up now; put yourself to rights," he murmurs.

I scramble up, not very gracefully, then straighten my dress over my knees.

He pulls a pristine white handkerchief from the breast pocket of his jacket, wipes his fingers on it, then pockets it. The careless gesture turns my insides to jelly. That I do not warrant any more of his attention is so right. That my boss would look me up and down, then glance away with a bored expression like this interlude didn't mean anything is so...perfect.

He knows that his not paying attention to me is just what I need to feel worthwhile. He knows that every bone in my body craves that I supplicate myself further to him, but it will be at his pleasure. It will be when he demands it of me, and not a second more.

I realize, with shock, that I'll do anything to earn his approval. *Earn* being the operative word here. How well he knows that I crave his appreciation, but I don't want him to give it to me easily. I need to work for it. I need to beg for it. I need to tear myself open and expose my innermost desires before he'll grant his acceptance of my place in his life. I'll do anything to please him. My pussy swells with need again. I'll do anything to make life easier for him. I'll do anything he asks of me.

Somehow, it's an extension of the role I've taken on in the real world, where I'm there to anticipate his every need. I'm there to make his life easier. To do whatever he asks of me. I don't deserve his attention, and I'll follow his every command in the hope he'll reward me with it.

As if he's read my mind, he rises to his feet, then flicks imaginary dust away from the lapels of his jacket, while I wait, head bowed.

He takes his time, straightening the cuffs of his sleeves, then tugs on his bowtie. The need inside me builds and builds, until finally, when he cups my cheek, peers into my eyes, and nods as if he's satisfied by what he sees there, I feel this strange urge to cry.

I feel like I'm on the verge of something monumental. Like I've changed in a way I never thought I could, but which also feels so very right. So very me. He's managed to unlock that hidden part of me I didn't know existed, and I feel so incredibly grateful. I lower my eyes and my chin, and by his change in breathing, I know I've pleased him.

He walks past me, toward the desk, then returns with a carafe of water and a glass. He hands me a full glass. "Drink it."

I follow his directions. And when I'm done, he fills up my glass again.

"Take your time, drink as much as you need. There's an ensuite bathroom. Put yourself back together, and when you're ready, I'll see you outside."

He walks back to the desk, places the jug down on it, then turns and walks past me and out the door.

I take a few more sips of water—it does not occur to me to disobey his orders. It's only when I'm standing in front of the mirror in the bathroom and take note of my flushed features and my glittering eyes that I realize what happened. I run cold water on my wrists, use a fresh napkin to pat my fiery cheeks. By the time I finger comb my hair, I feel more myself.

Jesus, what happened there? I lost myself completely in that scene. I've read enough erotic romance and watched enough porn to know I took part in something which was kinky and enjoyed it more than I would have expected. Even more than the spanking, if I'm being honest. I suspected it then, but I know now, for sure, that my boss is dominant.

I've never thought of myself as submissive, I'm certainly not submissive in daily life; definitely not as his secretary, now executive assistant. But when it comes to role-play? I swallow. I love being subjugated by him. Not that

I've role-played before. But I know enough from my 'research' to realize the way he commands me and the way I rush to obey him, when it's just the two of us in a non-work situation, I fold into the persona of a subservient.

He's made it clear that none of it means there's anything personal between us. I'm nothing but his...sex-toy? He hasn't said so, but his actions signal that.

A rush of pleasure fills me at the thought. At the same time... *How I wish it meant something more to him. And how do I stop myself from taking everything that happened so personally? Fact is, I can't stop thinking of him.* I square my shoulders. I need to remind myself that he's out of my league. *Whatever happens between us is simply two adults having a bit of fun, is all. So, why is it that I can't stop myself from wanting more?*

I spin around and walk out of the bathroom, then toward the door of the study. When I pull it open, it's to find Jeeves waiting there with my handbag.

"Mr. Davenport said you'd be needing this." Jeeves offers me my clutch.

I take it from him. "Thank you, Jeeves."

Some of the uncertainty subsides. *So, my boss was thinking of my needs as he left?* And that's reassuring and makes me feel looked after. *Though he was, perhaps, simply being polite? Enough to track down Jeeves and my purse and have him wait here for me?* My head swims with all of these thoughts. *Maybe, I'm making too much out of what is a kind gesture on his part?*

"Mr. Davenport asked that I escort you to where he's waiting."

It's with relief I follow him. *Did my boss know I'd be befuddled and worried about putting a foot wrong and breaking some kind of protocol at this event? Was he watching out for my comfort again? Did he realize I'd prefer to have someone guide me through the next steps, so I wouldn't have to think for myself for a while? If so, why send Jeeves? Why not wait for me outside himself? Jeez, I'm going to drive myself crazy with these thoughts.*

I settle for following Jeeves up the hallway and into the grand room, then through the crowd. He threads his way through gaps between the well-dressed with an alacrity I envy. They really do teach you everything in butler school.

Then, I see him. Head and shoulders above the rest of the crowd, he's listening with what seems to be polite interest, but which I know indicates he's bored.

The woman opposite him is grey-haired and wearing a dress that falls to below her knees. It's dull grey in color with full sleeves. However, she makes up for the unremarkable dress with a hat on her head in a brilliant yellow. It has swirls and shapes and a big disc-shaped object in the center, and on it are two roosters—yes, I did say roosters— facing each other.

The woman must be no more than five feet four inches tall, but the height of her hat swoops up to being at eye level with my boss. It should have caught my eye first—it acts like a lighthouse beam in a crowd of largely grays, and blacks, and whites—but my gaze was caught by him. At how he stands indolently, his muscles seemingly at ease; but there's an aura of tension surrounding him, drawing the attention of everyone in the vicinity to him. Except, he's looking at me.

It feels like someone took a hammer to my chest, that's how impactful the contact is. The hum of the crowd fades. All other faces vanish. I feel like I'm walking on air. There's an alertness to his features as he watches me approach; only, as I reach him, he yawns. And now, it feels like someone poured a bucket of icy water on me.

"Sir. Madam." Jeeves half bows. He flicks Knox a look I can only term as censorious, then he turns a much warmer look on me before he does his disappearing thing again. The crowd around my boss falls silent. All of them survey me and I meet their gazes head on. I have nothing to hide — *except for the fact that I ground myself against my boss' foot.*

I wince, then school my features into what I hope is a nondescript expression. I have as much right to be here as they do. Class was a constant companion throughout my school years, but I'm proud of my background in care. I'm proud that I got this far on my own merit, and on my own terms. And not-even my boss's arrogance can take that away from me. I tilt up my chin. "I'm June Donnelly, Mr. Davenport's Assistant."

"Is that what they're calling themselves now?" An elderly man with a receding hairline, and a paunch not quite disguised by his tailored suit, scrutinizes me with a lascivious look in his eyes. And there you have it, ladies and gents. Money can't buy you sophistication; not even if you come from the posh upper classes.

I open my mouth to tell him off, but my boss holds up his hand. "She is my employee, and a very valued one. If you can't treat her with respect, I'll have you thrown out of this event."

I whip my head in my boss' direction to find his face is deadly serious. *Apparently, he has enough clout to have someone evicted from a royal event? Whoa, how rich are he and his family, exactly?* I knew Davenport industries was influential, but that they carry so much pull is not something I anticipated.

"Now, now, ol' chap, it was all in jest. Surely, you know that?" the other man protests. I flick him a sideways glance and find he's pale. He mops at his temples with a handkerchief. "I do apologize. I did not mean it that way."

"It's her you need to apologize to." My boss nods in my direction.

The other man pivots toward me. "I am sorry," he says stiffly.

"Did that feel like he was sorry?" My boss snaps.

I am about to nod, but on second thought, why should I come to this guy's rescue? He deserves what's coming to him.

"He did not sound like he was sorry," I say in a firm voice. The other guests eye me with something like respect.

Knox glances around, and once more, Jeeves appears at his side, as if by magic. I really need to get tips from him on how to blend in and out of the crowd.

My boss nods in the direction of said guest without taking his gaze from me. "Will you please escort this gentleman off the premises?"

11

June

"With pleasure, Sir," Jeeves murmurs with the faintest note of relish entering his voice.

The man who insulted me tightens his lips. "You do realize this isn't the end. I'm Lord Foxley, and I promise, I will have my revenge."

"Please come with me, Sir." Jeeves escorts him out with a look that comes as close to gloating as I believe he's allowed to show on his face. If the Lord came with a plus one, they are nowhere to be seen. The crowds close behind him, and conversation resumes.

The woman with the cock-hat, looks from me to my boss. "Lucky today's bin day in the borough." She's referring to the fact that the garbage truck comes around normally every week on a day that's specific to the neighborhood. The people in our group laugh.

Another man in a black suit and tie nods in my boss' direction. "That's the second-best decision you made today, Davenport." He nods.

My boss arches an eyebrow. "Okay, I'll bite. What was the first one?"

The man smiles in my direction and his eyes twinkle. "Why, it's bringing your lovely companion to the event today and livening things up."

On the way back to my apartment, we're both quiet.

After that altercation with Lord Foxley, the rest of the event went smoothly. My boss didn't leave my side. Although, he didn't say more than a few words directly to me. The rest of his interactions were with heads of industry, and politicians, and even a few actors, all of whom he knew on a first-name basis. He kept me too busy taking notes on my phone for follow-ups for me to be awed by the company.

The silence stretches as the car glides through the night. When I shoot him a sidelong glance, it's to find his head bent as his fingers flick across his phone screen. The glow from the screen deepens the hollows under his cheekbones, and casts shadows under his eyes. It also blends the wicked scar on his cheek with the surrounding skin. For a second, I feel this is how he must have looked before he was injured in action. Perhaps, his features were softer, and he smiled more, and he believed in the future. Perhaps, he laughed more often then and had similar dreams and hopes and ambitions, the way the rest of us do. Perhaps, he was more approachable then. Only, I prefer him the way he is now. I like his coldness. I like his distance. I like how he's inaccessible when he glances at me or pays me a compliment, it means I've earned it.

Those long eyelashes hide his gaze, and his lips move as he reads something. That simple thing turns him from a god into someone more human — although, he's never looked more saturnine or more devilish than in this half-light.

"I can hear you thinking," he rumbles without lifting his gaze to mine.

Despite the distance between us — the entire width of the backseat stretches between us — the heat of his body reaches out to me. His presence is solid and larger-than-life. It's reassuring and yet, slightly threatening. If I gave an inch, he'd take over all of my thoughts and my dreams, I'm sure of that. *And would that be a bad thing?*

"How did you get your scar?"

He freezes. His body turns to concrete. He's so still that, but for the rise and fall of his chest and the vein that pops at his temple, he might have turned into a statue by Michelangelo—as beautiful, and as cold and unmoving. I'm sure he's going to shut me down, or perhaps even stop the car and ask me to get out, or rip into me for my temerity, but he does none of that. He simply sighs. And when his eyelashes flutter down for a few seconds, he looks vulnerable and tired, and so very weary. He lowers his hand with the phone to his side and leans his head into the back of the car.

"In Cyprus." He swallows. "I was part of the UN peacekeeping force stationed there." He lapses into silence.

I'm tempted to ask questions but perhaps, it's best to let him talk.

"It was an operation gone wrong, and then—" His phone buzzes.

It's so unexpected, I startle. He opens his eyes and raises his phone to his ear. "Bastard," he says in a mild voice.

When I wince, he flicks his gaze to my face and a look of surprise steals over him. It's as if, for a few seconds there, he forgot I was in the car with him. As if he was transported in his mind, back to the place where the incident where he'd been wounded had occurred.

"Yes, I'm headed back home. Yes, she's here with me."

I glance at him to find he's looking at me with a wary expression on his features. "That's none of your business."

The voice on the other side says something I don't quite catch. He sets his jaw. "She's my employee; I'll take care of her."

He listens then scowls. "I know what's right for her."

He listens to whatever the other person is saying, then cuts him off, "Goodnight, Connor." He tosses the phone on the seat next to him, then glowers at me. "Seems you've hypnotized my brother. He seems to think I need to be warned not to hurt you." He peers into my features. "What do you think, July?" His voice grows deeper, more commanding, "Would you hate it so much if I hurt you?"

What he's saying shouldn't make sense to me, but somehow, I know exactly what he's alluding to. It's as if he's flipped a switch and slipped into his Dom role.

"Would you, July?" In front of my eyes, he seems to grow even bigger. His shoulders seem to swell; the tendons of his throat stand out in relief. His gaze grows hooded. And when he drops his voice to a hush and murmurs, "Answer me," the power in his voice sparks a thrill in my lower belly. I shake my head.

"Say it," he orders.

"No. I wouldn't hate it," I murmur.

"In fact, you can't stop thinking of the sordid things I can do to you, am I right?" His lip curls.

A thousand tiny fires seem to light up under my skin. I don't dare reply. I don't need to, for he reads my desires and my cravings on my face.

"And if I were to ask you to sink down on your knees so I could use your mouth as an orifice for my cock, what would you do then?" He drags his gaze down my heaving chest to where I've squeezed my thighs together "Tell me, July." His bossy voice turns my nipples to bullets and sends a streak of need curling up my spine.

"I —" I swallow. "I would enjoy it."

"Good girl." His voice is gruff, and there's no mistaking the satisfaction in his eyes. *I did that. I made him look at me with such approval.* And it means so much to me that he's satisfied with me. It's as if I've passed some unwritten test, for his features soften. "You're beautiful, you know that?"

No one has called me beautiful before. *No one.* In fact, no one before this has given me as much attention as this man has. I have to earn it, but that's what makes it so special. I'll do anything to hear those words of appreciation from him, because it makes me feel so good. Only problem? Regardless of his compliments, he's made it clear that there's no possibility of a relationship between us.

I might be a damn good assistant, but ultimately, I don't mean anything to him. I need to protect my heart. I need to hold onto some iota of self-preservation. I glance away and out the window, unable to meet his gaze. "I'm your beautiful hole, I take it?"

I sense him stiffen.

"Are you being bratty, July?

"I wouldn't dream of it" — I flick him a sideways glance — "but sometimes, I do want to say and do things that make you give me your full attention... *Sir.*"

His blue eyes turn electric. His nostrils flare. Then he barks out a laugh. "You are my *very* beautiful hole."

I swallow. Heat courses under my skin. *Damn.* Only he can turn my thighs to jelly and my pussy into a melting, sloppy, mess. Only he can launch butterflies in my belly and make my heart skip a beat.

He must read my emotions on my face for he frowns. "Don't fall for me, July. I don't have anything to offer you. I'd only hurt you, and I don't want that to happen."

I widen my gaze. "It might be too late to stop that."

Silence follows my comment. His expression freezes. Poor man looks he's about to have a cardiac. *Jeez, for a fearless, alpha male, he sure is scared of any kind of emotion.* When I stay silent, panic flickers in his eyes. That's when I decide to take pity on him.

"Got you again." I pretend to chuckle.

He must take my words at face value, for an expression of relief crosses his features. "Just so long as we understand each other. You're my assistant, and we have a professional relationship. And, while you're clearly a submissive, there will be nothing between us." The groove between his eyebrows deepens. "We clear on that?"

12

Knox

"This is unacceptable." My assistant flounces into the room. "I will not have you dictating what I wear to the office... *Sir*."

She had to tack on the 'Sir' at the end again, didn't she? Bet she does it on purpose, knowing how much it turns me on. My cock springs up, ready for some action. This, despite the fact I jerked off last night and twice today. Just looking at her ensures I'm painfully hard. *Fuck.*

It's been a week since she almost came on my foot. A week filled with dreams in which I've done unspeakable things to her. Things if I told her, she'd be scandalized. *Though perhaps she might enjoy it, too, given her response to that scene at the royal reception.* And if I did share more with her, I'm sure I'd sully her further. She has no idea what I'm capable of, and I need to keep it that way. I shove the thoughts aside and fix her with a cool gaze.

We're in my office, and I've been at work since six a.m. Conference calls with East Asia, followed by Europe, mean I've been in virtual meetings for three hours straight. I admit, I welcome the intrusion, but I'm not letting her know that. I told her not to disturb me and I knew she was stewing at her desk. Finally, when she couldn't stop herself, she decided to confront me. The fact that she has the courage to do so thrills me.

It excites me to realize she has the gumption to go toe-to-toe with me. But what she's forgotten is that *she* doesn't set the agenda. I do. I continue to ignore her and focus on my computer screen. The seconds stretch and turn into minutes. When I don't look at her, I sense her stiffen. I don't have to see her gorgeous features to know that she feels neglected that I haven't spoken to her all day.

"If, by delivering a wardrobe full of new clothes to me, you're trying to tell me how to dress, it's not gonna work," she fumes.

She's referring to the fact that I took the liberty of stopping by the leading department store in the city and choosing a range of office clothes which were appropriate for her to wear to work. I had it delivered to her late last evening.

There's no mistaking the challenge in her voice. The stiff lines of her shoulder, the rigid way she holds herself—all of it tells me this is a woman who's upset.

I finally raise my gaze to her, and my attention is drawn to her curves. She's nowhere as thin as the women I was normally seen with, but her figure is so much more alluring. So much more enticing. And tempting. So very appealing. It would be so easy to fall for her. To take her as my submissive and mold her into the kind of woman who'd be perfect for me.

A-a-and she'd never be able to bear the level of kinkiness I want to inflect on her. Oh, how I want to bruise her pristine flesh with my bites and licks. How I want to tie her up, whip her, and gag her so she can only communicate with me through those expressive eyes. How I want to bend her over every surface in my office and spank that lush bottom, so she carries the permanent imprint of my fingers. How I want her on her knees, taking my cock down her throat. How I want her helpless and mewling and out of her head with pleasure, begging for more. How satisfying it felt to have her following my directions last night. Seeing her almost fall apart as she brought herself to near orgasm. And then, sadist that I am, I stopped her from going over the edge.

I saw the subservience in her stance, saw how she lowered herself over my foot, felt the fierce satisfaction in knowing I could prolong her anticipation in a future orgasm, and that spurred me on. How I'd love to break her, and in doing so, break myself apart for her. I stiffen. Not only would I be opening myself up to her, but I'd also be giving her the power to hurt me. She's not going to stick around once she knows exactly how much of a kinky bastard I am. That I'm a beast who not only looks like one, but also had the disposition to go with it. And I don't mean just in my business dealings.

No, entertaining this train of thought is wrong, and dangerous. I cannot subject her to my twisted tastes. She's too pure, too much of an angel to be put through what I have in mind. I only have to see her for my thoughts to fall into a tailspin. All the more reason for her to stay out of reach.

And allow another man to reap the benefits of my edging? It's a sobering thought, one which turns my stomach and has the bile rising in my throat. I swallow it down, tamp down on my errant line of thinking, and force myself to focus.

I have to ensure I put enough barriers between us, so I'm never tempted to own her. I redrew the employee-boss line for her as much as for me. And I must do my best to stay within the parameters I set between us. I lean back in my seat slowly, and sense her go completely still.

And when I glare at her, she pales. "S-sorry, I didn't mean to go off like that."

"No, you're not sorry," I drawl.

"I... I'm not?"

I shake my head slowly. "You interrupted me because you felt ignored. Because you want me to notice you. Because you want me to punish you. And just for that, I'm not going to."

She blinks. "You think I'm trying to get you to punish me. And to punish me, you're not going to punish me?"

I nod. "You wanted my attention? You have it now."

She swallows, then squares her shoulders. "You should know, I can't accept the entire... Boatload of clothes you had delivered to my place yesterday evening."

I hold up my forefinger. "Firstly, it doesn't mean anything that the clothes were sent to you. Secondly"—she begins to speak, but I silence her with— "as I've already explained, and I will repeat this for the last time, the clothes are so you can be dressed appropriately, as befits your status as my representative."

"Oh." She deflates a little. "I see."

"You may leave, Kelly." I purposely call her by the wrong name. Another way to reinforce that she doesn't mean anything to me. That she's one in an extensive line of assistants who've worked for me. My words hit home, for her features crumple. My heart squeezes in my chest, but I ignore it.

She turns to go. And because I'm a bastard and want to make sure I drive the wedge between us deeper, I call after her, "And make sure I'm not disturbed again."

An hour later she walks into my office. "Your grandfather insists on seeing you. I assume it's okay to interrupt you?" she asks in a tight voice. By the tone of her voice, I can tell she's pissed at me from our earlier exchange.

I glance up in time to see Arthur amble into my office. He draws abreast with her, locks his hands behind his back, and rocks back on his heels.

"To be fair, I hinted that if she didn't let me through, it might affect her paycheck and yours," Gramps snipes.

"I... I'm sorry, Sir." My assistant's features are contrite. There's disappointment lurking in her eyes. She knows she didn't follow my orders. But I don't blame her for that.

My grandfather clears his throat. When I glance at him, it's to find he's looking between me and her with interest.

Canny bastard. No doubt, he senses the chemistry between me and my assistant. I need to defuse the situation in a way that removes that idea from his mind.

"Thank you for seeing my grandfather in, Ms. Donnelly," I murmur in a laid-back tone. I called her by her real surname, a gesture not lost on her, for she blinks in surprise. And when I jerk my chin in the direction of the doorway, she spins around and stomps out of my office.

I allow my lips to pull back on one side. *She deserves to be punished for that. Only, I told myself I wasn't going to touch her. Damn!* I channel my anger into the look I throw in the direction of my grandfather. "Why are you here?" I scowl by way of greeting.

He has the gall to look hurt. "Can't I come to check how my favorite grandson is doing?"

I snort, "Is that the line you used with my brothers and my uncle before springing the condition about them having to get married?"

Arthur doesn't look surprised by my outburst. "May I?" He gestures to the chair opposite mine. Without waiting for an answer, he drops into it, then sighs. "At my age, and given my condition—"

"The doc said you're responding well to treatment and that the disease is in remission," I point out. My grandfather was diagnosed with stage 3 lung cancer a few months ago, but his condition has improved dramatically since he started treatment to keep it in check.

He waves his hand, "I'm fine. Let's talk about something else."

"If it's my wedding, you should know, I'm not going to agree to a rushed marriage, like my brothers and uncle." I'm referring to Edward and Nathan, who're technically my half-brothers but whom I've come to regard as siblings, and my uncle Quentin. Arthur had a hand in marrying them off. "And if it's about my inheritance, you can keep it. And I don't care much for the CEO title, either. Nothing's stopping me from leaving here and starting my own company from the money my mother left behind."

He blinks slowly.

While the Davenport legacy brings with it billions, my mother was rich, in her own right. She left each of her sons a small inheritance—enough to give me the seed money for starting a midsized enterprise of my own—and he knows it. I can tell he's surprised, for he lowers his chin to his chest, then nods slowly.

"You're smarter than them when it comes to steering your future," he finally says. "And I should have known that I couldn't hold your title or your trust fund against you, to make you agree to a wedding."

I place the tips of my fingers together. "But you're here, which leads me to think you believe you have something else to negotiate with."

Again, he doesn't look surprised. The chair creaks as he leans back. My brothers and I get our height and our broad build from him. Our looks, on the other hand, come from the women—my grandmother and my mother were both bona fide beauty queens.

My mother won the Miss Universe title before marrying my father and settling down. The looks I inherited had stood me in good stead with the ladies—until shrapnel ripped through my face and showed me just how shallow most of them were. Not her, though. My assistant never seems to find me repulsive. She also isn't put off by my detached demeanor. I shove that out of my mind, once again, focusing on my grandfather.

"Of all your brothers, you're the one who carries the most hurt," he muses.

I scowl, "But Ryot—"

"Is yet to recover from the death of his wife, I'm aware. You, however, carry the hurt on your body. He chooses not to forget his past. You, on the other hand"—he tilts his head—"are reminded of it every time you look at yourself in the mirror."

I'm not sure how to react. I didn't expect the old man to make such an astute observation.

He must notice the surprise on my features, for his eyes gleam. "Imelda's been pushing me to get in touch with my feelings. Guess it shows, huh?"

Imelda's his Harley-driving girlfriend who takes no shit from him. And the old man seems to genuinely be invested in the relationship, too. It's the first time I've seen him forge an authentic connection with anyone, my grandmother included.

"I still don't trust you," I drawl.

"I wouldn't either, given my track record in how I got your brothers and your uncle to obey my wishes. Although, it has worked out well for all of them."

He's right. They *are* happily married. Disgustingly so. All of them weighed down by the ol' ball and chain, and seemingly willingly. I don't plan on making myself another statistic on that list.

Once more, he seems to read my thoughts, for he holds up his hands, "I'm not here to force you into any kind of marriage. However—"

And here it comes.

"However, I'm aware of how much you love the Davenport property in Cumbria."

The ol' geezer clocked that. I shouldn't be surprised. He didn't get to be the Chairman of the Davenport Group and hold onto the position, despite the board trying to overthrow him a few times, without being at the top of his game. I tilt my head, waiting for him to elaborate. I bet that was only his opening salvo.

He leans back in his chair and places the tips of his fingers together. "And much as you may deny it, I believe that other than Nathan, you're the one most keen on forging a career within the Davenport Group. Being the CEO of the media division and exploring the opportunities new media has to offer is something that interests you greatly. Throw in the Cumbria property and—"

"So, you did come to negotiate my future?" I growl.

"Consider it an ultimatum."

"An ultimatum?" I lower my arms to my side and tilt back my chair slowly.

Arthur nods. "Get married within the month, and I'll not only confirm you as the CEO of the media division, but I'll also hand the Cumbria house over to you."

"You're joking!" I laugh.

"You know better than that. In fact, I'll make it easy for you."

"Oh?" I frown.

"Since I'm aware you don't have a woman in mind to get married to—"

I begin to speak, but he shakes his head. "Don't bother denying it; I'm aware of the love lives of all of my grandsons."

I narrow my gaze. "So, you're admitting you keep tabs on us?"

"You boys are my future and responsible for propagating my bloodline; it's natural that I do." He drums the arm of his chair. "And as I was saying, I'll make this easy on you."

"I can't wait to hear what you have to say," I drawl.

He ignores my sarcasm completely. "I have someone lined up for you, who I think would be appropriate for you."

It doesn't come as a surprise to hear him propose this. Arthur has made it clear, he wants all of his sons and grandsons settled as soon as possible, and he's not above arranging our marriages, if necessary. My older brothers hustled into proposing marriage to women of their choosing. That they happened to fall in love with their wives is beside the point. I made it clear to Arthur, I don't intend on settling down anytime soon. Only problem is, it resulted in his taking my words as a challenge. He doubled down in his efforts to get me married off.

Still, I pretend to be taken aback by his suggestion. "You're asking me to have an arranged marriage?"

He holds up his hand. "I'd like to call it a marriage of convenience. You'll get the CEO title and the property you love so much, and she'll get access to all the benefits that come from being married into the Davenport clan. Don't you want to know who the woman is?" Before I can respond, he adds, "Her name is Priscilla Whittington, by the way."

"Whittington?" I frown. "She's—"

"Toren Whittington's sister."

Toren's the scion of the Whittington family. He's also CEO of the Whittington Group. If there's a close competitor to the Davenports, it's the Whittingtons.

"We've discussed that it makes sense to have her marry into our family so we can join our fortunes and put the long-running feud between our families to rest." Arthur taps his fingers on his armrest.

"Do you realize how parochial you sound?" When he begins to speak, this time, I'm the one who raises my hand. "Don't bother replying. We both know you're a manipulative bastard who has only one thing on his mind."

"My family's welfare," he has the temerity to reply.

"I was going to say the Davenport Group's future, but what-fucking-ever." I roll my neck. "Let's get one thing straight." I lean forward in my seat. "I may not believe in love or marriage, but when it comes to my future, I choose who my wife is going to be, even if it's in name alone. I saw how you manipulated my brothers and uncle, and I'm not going to give you that chance with my life."

Gramps raises his hands, his features folded into an expression of innocence. "Whatever you say, grandson. And it's not like I want to put in the extra work involved in arranging your marriage. But if you don't get married within four weeks—"

"Yeah, yeah"—I wave my hand—"you have a bride lined up for me. I heard you the first time."

"Did you?" He searches my features. Manipulative bastard that he is, I know he's not going to let this one go, and sure enough, when he speaks, I know I'm right. "It's heartening that, unlike your brothers, you don't believe in love —"

I snort, "Coming from someone who's currently dating and clearly, in love —"

"She's not the one I married. I married your grandmother because —"

"She brought her father's group of companies, not to mention, her own inheritance, which added to your net worth. I'm aware," I interject.

"She gave me the sons I wanted. Not all of them turned out to be worthwhile. My grandsons, on the other hand... There's hope for you lot, so it wasn't completely in vain."

"Should I be grateful for that?" I scoff.

He shrugs. "Gratitude is for pussies. All I need from you is a sperm deposit in the right receptacle, and at the right time, so it bears fruit."

And *that* is my grandfather. *And you wonder why I'm screwed up?*

The door to my office opens. I'm about to tell my assistant off for letting someone else in, but I see her face and correctly read the uncertainty on it. When I see who's with her, I nod in her direction. Without words, I convey that she did the right thing in letting this person in, and my assistant reads my expression correctly, for her shoulders relax. It's eerie how she can read my mind. Something no one else can do. Goes to show that she's a good assistant, is all. Doesn't mean anything else. My assistant leaves.

I lean back in my seat. "I get it. Every action has an equal and opposite reaction. And you want to make sure I marry and use it as a platform for my procreation?"

"Exactly," Arthur says in a pleased tone.

"But you're not going to be able to do that with your current girlfriend, so that relationship doesn't matter?"

Arthur's forehead creases. He appears to be thinking through the answer, then nods slowly. "Imelda's unique. But sadly, she's past child-bearing age, so she's someone pleasant enough to spend time with, but as for anything else?" He shakes his head. "Nope, I won't be marrying her anytime soon."

"Good to know what your real thoughts are about our relationship," a new voice rings out from by the door.

Arthur swivels around in his seat and his entire body freezes. "I-Imelda?" he croaks.

His motorcycle jacket and shit-kickers wearing girlfriend squeezes her helmet between her hands. I'm sure she's going to fling it at him, but instead, her shoulders slump. "I thought you'd changed. And no, I wouldn't say it was our relationship that softened you, but I hoped a brush with death might knock some sense into you; guess I was wrong."

"Imelda, honey—please hear me out." He jumps to his feet and rushes toward her.

She shakes her head. "Oh, fuck off, old man. I can do much better than you, but I thought I'd give you a chance. My mistake."

"No, no, you have to understand; I was talking to my grandson metaphorically."

"Oh?" she asks in a mild voice. "You were lying to your grandson?"

I stifle a chuckle. This woman is something else. And she's good for my grandfather. Too bad, I saw her at the doorway and goaded Arthur into revealing his true thoughts about her. Best she sees what an arse he is, right?

"No, I wasn't. I mean—" Arthur comes to a standstill a few feet away from her. "I mean, I was, but not exactly. I—"

Imelda laughs, the sound bitter in the space. "Stuff it. I don't know why I wasted my time on you, but suffice it to say, this relationship has passed its expiry date. Goodbye, Arthur." She pivots and walks out. The door snicks shut behind her.

Arthur draws in a sharp breath, then turns to me "I'd say I'm upset with you for not telling me Imelda was listening in on our conversation, but you've shown me that, of all my grandsons, you're the one who's closest to me in terms of being conniving."

Guilty as charged. And no, I'm not apologetic for what I did. Imelda deserved to know Arthur's true nature. On the other hand, fuck if I want to be compared to him. But I keep my mouth shut and put an expression of polite disinterest on my face. While I take risks, I'm not foolish enough to underestimate my opponents, and definitely not my canny grandfather.

He swivels and walks to the door, then stops and glances at me. "You have one month to find someone to marry, Knox. Else you get hitched to Priscilla Whittington."

13

June

"Thanks, Kelly." My boss nods in my direction without looking at me as I place the bottle of water in his outstretched hand.

"It's June," I mutter, then wonder why I bother. It's been a week since the royal event outing, during which time, he's gone back to calling me by a different name. I thought we were over that. Considering he's allowed me to lick my cum off his foot, and also seen me orgasm it's not like we're strangers. Sure, he made it clear that it'd been a mistake, but couldn't he, at least call, me by my given name? But nope.

He's also limited our interaction to emails, as much as possible. During the day, he's forbidden me to come in, the only exception being to bring him coffee or lunch. During which time, I've tried to catch his eye and failed. He's doing his best to pretend I don't exist—and succeeding, too.

And after his grandfather left yesterday morning, his mood declined even further. He made it clear he was not to be disturbed for anyone, and that included family members. Message received. Instead, I was subjected to a barrage of emails with things to do which kept me busy all of yesterday. When I came in today with his coffee, he was already on a conference call and didn't acknowledge my presence. I lingered for a few seconds, hoping he'd, at least, glance up and look at me with that cerulean gaze of his. When it became clear he wasn't going to, I placed his coffee beside him and left.

He spent the rest of the day offloading various projects for me to lead on. And these weren't simple tasks. They involved intricate negotiations and maneuvering with his senior team, and he put me in charge of it. He knows I can't resist a challenge and that I wouldn't refuse. He's testing me in a different way, and I'm determined to deliver. Just as I have these last few weeks. The more he tests me, the more I'm resolute that I'm going to pass with flying colors. I'm not going to let him down.

Besides, if this is the only way he's going to give me any attention, I'll take it. I know he's making me work for his approval, and that should make me feel pathetic but honestly, it doesn't. I know when he does finally acknowledge me, it's going to feel amazing. It's going to be worth all my hard work.

At least, his grandfather wanting to see him yesterday gave me a legitimate excuse to get his attention, even if it was only for a few seconds and it ended with him telling me off... At least, he noticed me. For a little while there, I was the sole object of his interest, and it felt so good.

He worked non-stop, not even taking a break when I went into his office to drop off his lunch. I left without disturbing him and focused on my own jobs. I made enough progress that I was able to carve out time to search online and identify the adoption search specialist I want to hire. Of course, considering the costs involved, I stopped myself from emailing her. I can't afford her...yet. But perhaps, once I get paid for my second month here... I can set some money aside for her services. Or maybe, I'm simply putting it off. Maybe, I'm delaying. Perhaps, if I really wanted to do it, I'd prioritize this over anything else.

I clicked out of the window, then focused on my to-do list.

When 5 p.m. rolls around, he heads out of the office. He nods at me to follow him, and I jump up at once to obey. I follow him to the gym in the basement of his luxurious condominium in the most sought-after postal code in the city.

I stand to the side, holding his bottle of water. I should hate being reduced to his minion, but I don't. I'm happy he's using me as sees fit. At least, I'm here with him, instead of in the office, and I feel so damn grateful for that. *Does that make me less of a feminist? Maybe. But I'm being honest with myself, aren't I?* I flick a glance in his direction, and my mouth dries.

He's divested himself of his suit and tie and is now wearing gym shorts. They circle his lean waist and hint at the package tenting the crotch. They also outline every coiled muscle in those powerful thighs and highlight the scars on his left leg. There are more on the left side of his chest that travel up and over his shoulder. The skin is puckered in a fashion similar to that of the scar on his cheek. Not only was his face hurt in what happened, but also his body.

It should revolt me, but his injuries only add to his appeal. That image of him as a marauding warrior injured in battle is cemented in my brain.

I slide my glasses up my nose and take in his naked torso. *Whoa!* It's better than anything I imagined. I feel...like I'm being granted a special treat. A part of me is sure he doesn't reveal the scars on his body openly, which is why he prefers to book out the entire gym, so he has privacy when he works out. But he's sharing that part of himself with me, and I feel so grateful. Then a thought occurs: *Is he doing it to compensate me for all the arduous work I put in today?* Before I can follow through this line of thinking, he drops down on his palms and toes. He begins to work out, and I'm riveted.

His biceps bulge. His triceps do that tightening thing where his entire arm seems to be sculpted from stone for a second. He proceeds to pump out a hundred push-ups—I know because I count—before he springs up to his feet and holds out his arm. I slide the bottle of water into his waiting palm again.

He throws his head back and chugs down the contents, then tosses me the empty bottle. Some of the water drips from his chin onto his chest, and I swear, my nipples almost poke their way through the blouse and jacket I'm wearing.

He glances down at my heels and frowns. "That's not safe to wear in the gym." He glares at me, and I can't stop the shiver that runs up my spine. I forgot how gravelly his voice is. How my body reacts to the rich timbre. How my bones seem to dissolve at the dark edge to his tone.

"Stay here," He points a finger at me, then heads to the changing room, returning with a pair of sneakers. He goes down on one knee and holds out his hand, palm face up.

I gape at him. "You can't be serious."

He merely raises his eyebrow at me as if to say, *"Of course, I'm serious. Have you ever known a time when I'm not serious? So, do what I say, right fucking now."* I understand without him saying the words. *How annoying. And how freaky is that?*

I place my foot in his palm, then am forced to grab his head and latch onto his hair to support myself. Gosh, the strands are thick and silky, yet also springy. He slides off my stiletto—Ferragamo, since you asked. And yes, I'm wearing the clothes he sent me, only because I do care about the image I project. It has nothing to do with the fact that the footwear is all original brand names and so comfortable to wear. He slides a sock onto my foot, then slips on a sneaker, it fits. He does the same with my other foot.

"How did you have these on hand?" I can't stop myself from asking. The socks are made of very comfy material—not like the ones I purchase at the discount store.

"I had them ordered," he snaps.

I purse my lips. "So, you knew you were going to ask me to come to the gym."

He shoots me a glare. "Yours is not to question why—"

"But to do or die?" I wriggle my toes in the sneakers. "Paraphrasing Alfred Lord Tennyson, I see. Didn't know you had a secret crush on a dead English poet?"

His glower deepens. *Jeez, what crawled up his arse?* He's the one who said, I'll only be his employee from now on, and nothing else. I've tried my best to follow his rules. I've been good. I'm doing what he tells me, not that he notices. If anything, he seems even more pissed-off. The man has been an absolute tyrant to me and the rest of his team. So much so, the department leads have approached me individually to say they're pleased they don't have to deal with him.

They're routing all their communication for my boss through me. It puts even more strain on my time.

He rises to his feet, then nods at the refrigerator in the far corner. "Get me another bottle of water."

Guess I've been put in my place.

"Good talk." I spin around and walk over to the recycling bin, dropping the empty bottle before grabbing a full one from the refrigerator and walking back to him.

He's at the push-board bench, pressing weights many times his own. I stand with the fresh bottle of water and a towel, trying not to ogle the way his abs flex, and his shoulder muscles bunch, and his thigh muscles ripple each time he pushes up the weights. Beads of sweat glisten on his torso. One slides down his concave stomach toward his waistband.

I gulp. Feel my own forehead moisten. *Is it hot in here?* The gym is air-conditioned, but you wouldn't know it, given the way my palms are sweating. I raise the bottle of water and press it to my heated cheek, and I'm not even working out.

I shoot my boss a glance and find his jaw hard, forehead wrinkled as he glares at the weights he's grappling with. The scar on his cheek seems to protrude with the effort.

He looks fierce, like he's fighting a battle or about to start a war. The tendons on his throat pop, and the veins on his forearms stand out in relief. And his biceps... Good god, they're as big as my thighs, and I'm not a skinny person. I love my curves; I love dressing to show them off. Something I'm unable to do with all the office wear he sent me. The blouses are formless enough to mask my curves and are, without fail, high-necked.

"Considering your shopper got my size right for the dress to the event, and my footwear fits perfectly, I don't understand how they messed up with my office wear," I venture.

He lowers the weights into their cradle, then slowly sits up. "A shopper didn't choose them; I did."

"Oh!" A fierce burst of pleasure squeezes my belly. *He* chose my clothes. I'm wearing the blouse and the skirt that *he* decided I should wear. My heart seems to descend to the space between my legs. A thick syrupy pleasure invades my veins.

After days when he's barely noticed me, and I was sure I imagined that scene at the royal reception when I almost came on his foot, to have the full focus of his attention is so heady. Too heady. Too much. Shivers grip me. Goosebumps crowd my skin. I'm sure I'm going to self-combust any moment. I need to find a way to keep his attention on me. I manage to bring my emotions under control enough to whine, "But my blouses and my jackets are so loose, they should, technically, be two sizes too big, except the sleeves fit." I glance down at where the edge of my jacket sleeve brushes my wrist. So that's a perfect fit. But the garment droops around my chest. "It's so strange." I push up the spectacles on my nose. "Maybe I should get them tailored, so they fit better?"

"You will do no such thing." His tone rings with such authority, I almost drop to my knees and prostrate myself at his feet. *Oh my god, he's looking at me.* In fact, he's scowling at me. My heart blooms in my chest. To be the cynosure of his focus is everything.

I squeeze my thighs together then choke out, "Why not? Have you seen how my clothes hang off me?" I have enough presence of mind to gesture to myself.

As expected, his gaze darts down to my chest, and oh god, instantly, my nipples pucker. He slowly raises them to my face, by which time, I'm flushed.

"I look ridiculous," I splutter.

"You look perfect," he says with such finality, I blink.

"The clothes render me shapeless."

"Good."

My jaw drops. "Did you... Did you just say—"

"You should know by now that I don't do anything without a reason." He rakes his gaze over me from head to toe. Every cell in my body feels like it's about to catch fire.

I've worked so hard to get his approval, and finally, finally he notices me, and more than just as a fuck toy. It's just sinking in that he said I look 'perfect.' *Oh. My. Gosh.*

He hasn't complimented me yet for how I've kept myself in control around him, but that will come, too. *I'm sure he's going to reward me... If I'm lucky, with another spanking? Or perhaps, I have to go against his wishes for that?* I frown. *Is this a test? Does he want me to challenge his authority and give him a reason to punish me? Hmm.* And while the thought crossed my mind to have my clothes resized, now that I know it wasn't his shopper but he, himself, who chose the clothes, no way, am I going to change anything. I rub my hand over the cloth of my skirt. He notices my movement and his gaze narrows.

In fact, I think I'm going to sleep in them from now on. Considering how loose they are, they'll be comfortable to wear to bed, too. I frown. "I don't get it. Why would you ensure that my clothes don't fit?"

He sighs, the sound meant to convey that I'm slow on the uptake. "You're my employee; you'll do as I say." He goes back to bench pressing.

I shake my head. "I thought you wanted me to be well-dressed. Apparently, you don't care that my clothes are too big for me." Then a thought crosses my mind. "Does this have anything to do with the fact that the clothes I used to wear were a size too small, and that's what you think attracted the attentions of your Finance Director?"

He doesn't reply. But his biceps bulge and his shoulders tense, and it has nothing to do with the massive amount of weight he's pushing. In fact, his movements speed up. That's when I know, I'm right.

"Oh my god, you did it on purpose, so no one could see my figure! You think this will shield me from the eyes of your employees?" I cry.

He continues to bench-press those colossal weights. But his lack of reaction is an answer in itself. My instinct tells me I'm right. *Whoa. He cares. He does. No matter how much he insists otherwise, some part of him wants to protect me. Some part of him wants to keep me for himself.* It's why he fired his Finance Director and was so pissed off with Connor at the royal reception. It's why he punished me after both those incidents.

I want to do a jig and dance in celebration. I want to confront him with the result of my deduction, but that won't help. He's going to deny it. Worse, he's going to ignore me even more than he normally does. I'm going to have to wait for him to arrive at the conclusion himself. Meanwhile... I'm going to look my fill, at this fine specimen of masculinity.

Since he told me I need to keep to my role as an employee, I've stolen quick glances at him. But now, I stare at him outright.

I take in how his chest heaves and his shoulders swell. The way his biceps bulge, and the way the muscles of his forearms inflate as he pushes up the barbell with a grunt that rolls over my skin and arrows straight to my clit. Goosebumps pepper my forearms. The sweat on my throat dries in the air-conditioning and I shiver.

I feel so lightheaded from his nearness. *Maybe I need to take a break from the cloud of testosterone that's pressing down on my shoulders?* "I, uh... I'll only be a minute. I just need to, uh, use the little girls' room." I cringe.

Little girls' room? I couldn't come up with a better excuse?

I turn, and promptly trip on a plate weight, I didn't see. The water bottle in my hand hits the floor, the towel slips from my fingers. I throw out my hands to break my fall and find myself suspended an inch from the floor.

The breath whooshes out of me. Then suddenly, I'm upright, and my feet don't touch the floor because two big broad palms are squeezing my waist. Heat sizzles my back, the scent of sweat and sandalwood teases my nostrils. The fine hair on the back of my neck rises and I realize, it's him. He caught me? But how did he even see me? He was on his back, bench pressing, when my feet brushed against the weight.

"You... You can let me down," I manage to squeak.

His hold on my waist tightens, then he gently lowers me until my feet touch the floor. Only, he hasn't let go of me. Instead, he spins me around to face him. Our gazes meet, and I swear, the world stops.

My heart descends to the space between my legs. The pulse blooms there and travels to my fingertips, my toes, and my scalp, which tightens. Silver sparks light up those blue eyes, turning them into a glacial inferno. The heat from his body is a lasso pulling me toward him. My chest grazes his wall-like torso, and I realize, we're leaning toward each other.

A thousand little hummingbirds whirl their wings in my chest. I raise my head; he lowers his. I draw my gaze down the raised scar bisecting his cheek. Then, because I've wanted to for so long, I raise my hand and graze my fingers over the puckered skin. He pulls back so quickly, I stumble. He doesn't steady me.

He takes a few steps back, then sinks down on the weight bench. I open my mouth to apologize for touching him, when he scrunches up his forehead. "Ah, Melanie, is it?"

I narrow my gaze on him.

He scrunches up his forehead, then his brow clears. He snaps his fingers. "It's Renée." He nods. "Yep, Renée. Get me an energy drink, will you?"

What the—! All those lovely thoughts I had about him disappear with a pop. Genuine anger smolders up my spine. "You've taken this charade far enough, don't you think?" I burst out.

He tilts his head, that look of polite boredom back on his features. But the tips of his ears grow white, and I swallow. I've managed to piss him off.

Which is good, right? This way, he has a reason to punish me. To touch me. If I'm lucky, bend me over that bench and wallop my behind. I shudder.

He doesn't move, but there's no mistaking the heightened tension in the air between us. I tamp down on the nervous flutter in my belly and goad him further. "You know my name, so I don't understand why it's so difficult for you to call me by it?"

"Do I?" he drawls.

"My name. Is June," I snap.

He raises his shoulder. "That's what I said."

I curl my fingers into fists at my sides. "No, you didn't."

"Sure, I did." His tone is condescending. He has a smirk on his face, implying I'm the one who doesn't know my own name. Anger squeezes my guts. I grit my teeth. "My name. Is. June, and don't pretend you're not aware. Or you can call me Cleopatra, if that's easier for you to remember."

He blinks slowly.

The fact that he goes still should warn me I've overstepped a line, but the rage eating away at my insides, has me ignoring his reaction. "Actually, I prefer Queen Victoria or how about Duchess?" I nod. "I like the sound of that."

His left eyelid twitches. The tips of his ears turn white. Horror grips me. I've done it. I've pissed him off. Only, he isn't saying anything. He isn't doing anything. He's watching me how a predator watches its prey. He's going to make me regret my outburst. He's going to punish me. *Yes!* But why hasn't he moved a muscle? He seems to have turned into stone. And the way he's glaring at me, the way he pins me with the weight of his gaze...is too much. My scalp tingles. My skin feels too tight for me.

The seconds stretch. My stomach churns, and my vision narrows. Before I can stop myself, I've closed the distance to the fallen bottle of water. I snatch it up and lob it at him. It hits his forehead and bounces off. It's as if the world stops.

He freezes, then slowly raises his head and stares at me. Those cerulean eyes of his turn almost silver with rage. His nostrils flare, and he rises to his feet. I have to tilt my head back, and further back.

He takes a step forward. I gulp. He scans my features, and a furrow appears between his eyebrows. Then he drapes the towel over his shoulders and prowls toward me. A cloud of heat spools off of his body and slams into my chest. I gasp. I want to turn and run out of there, but my feet are cemented to the floor. He holds my gaze; sparks flare in the depths of his eyes as he bends his knees and peers into mine.

"Run," he snaps.

What does he mean by that? What in the — I try to speak, but all that comes out is a strangled sound. I gape.

"I'll even give you a head start," he drawls.

This is not making any sense. "Excuse me?" I blink rapidly. "What do you mean by that?"

He bares his teeth like he hasn't heard me speak. "You have until I count to five." He jerks his chin toward the doorway. "Go."

Knox

"Go, before I change my mind," I bite out.

She tripped, and for a split second, every cell in my body seemed to freeze. My heart stopped, then started up again. Bile laced my tongue, and I was on my feet and springing toward her. I don't recall placing my barbell back on the rack or swinging my feet to the ground, but there I was, behind her. In time to grab her around her waist and straighten her.

Then she brushed her fingers down the scar on my cheek. The shock of it felt like someone dropped me in a vat of boiling oil, then dumped icy water on me. No one else, other than the doctors attending to me, has touched me there since I was injured.

I hate how I look, hate the evidence of my mistakes. Hate my face. Hate what I've become since I left the Marines. I buried my feelings. I swore to never let myself care for anything or anyone again. And this slip of a woman comes along and rouses emotions I thought myself no longer capable of feeling.

I was holding myself back, but she's responded to my kink with enthusiasm. I will let myself have her in the way I want her. I want to push her onto her knees and shove my cock inside her mouth. I want to bend her over and spank her until she begs me for release. I want to defile her and take every orifice of hers. I want to bury myself in her until I find release.

The intensity of my need punches into my chest like a cannon ball. My heart expands in my ribcage. Worse, something in me insists I get to know her. To find out all about her. What she likes and hates. What makes her laugh. What she loves to eat and drink, and what she likes to do when she isn't working for me, and *what the hell?*

Where is this compulsion arising from? Why do I want to get to know her as a person? I haven't even fucked her! This...is new. This has never happened to me before. This...is something I cannot allow; it will only lead to my becoming vulnerable. Something I've sworn I'll never let myself be. It's why I'm going on the offensive. It's why I'm going to push her even further. Will she do what I tell her this time? Or will *that* ensure she'll want nothing to do with me.

I glare into her face. "Run."

Her gaze widens. Her pupils dilate. When I take a step in her direction, she trembles. Fear radiates off of her. It's mixed with anticipation. Her breathing grows choppy. She sidles back.

The hunted.

The prey.

My prey.

The thrill of chasing her. The excitement of toying with her. The delight in finally catching her and doing anything I want to her sets fire to my blood. My muscles bunch in expectation. This...is what makes me feel alive. When I am one with my primal instincts. When I don't have to hide behind the mask I wear for the world. When I can unleash my inner beast. When I can chase my game.

I lower my chin to my chest and growl, "Run."

My mind is an uncaged tiger, planning, anticipating where she'll go. *How's she going to try to escape me? Where will you go, little July? I'm going to be many steps ahead of you. You can't out-run me, but you can try. And that will increase the buildup, the tension, the anticipation of how it will be when I catch you. And I am going to catch you. No way, can you escape.*

My heartbeat quickens. My fingertips tingle. *When you connect with your most primal self, you are also at your most vulnerable.* I shove that thought aside, focusing on the expectation, the suspense, the exhilaration of the hunt building inside of me.

She must sense my fervor, for a whine bleeds from her lips, and that turns me on even more. I draw in a sharp breath, smell her arousal, and the animal inside of me breaks through all of my self-imposed barriers. That's when something in her finally catches on. She turns and bolts toward the exit of the gym.

Satisfaction pinches my chest. The fact that she does what I ask is so damn gratifying. My pulse booms. Adrenaline crackles at my nerve-endings. Without letting myself think further, I give chase. I jump over the plate weight that tripped her up, then barrel out of the gym and race after her. She runs up the corridor and takes the staircase. *Good. Very good. That will lengthen the chase.* My gaze snags on how her butt bounces from side to side as she mounts the stairs, *and goddam*, sweat breaks out on my brow. I want to throw her down and mount *her.* I want to have her writhing and sobbing and begging under me as I bring her to the edge again and again. To see her tears, and feel her desperation, and sense her absolute need for release feeds the beast inside of me. I increase my speed, catch up with her as she nears the landing. I reach forward and swipe at her.

My fingertips graze her shoulder. She yelps and ups her speed, taking the steps two at a time. I let her pull away, allowing myself to give her an advantage. Feasting on how her plump thighs propel her forward. In fact, I slow down, walk up almost leisurely. *You're going to tire yourself out if you go on like this, little prey. And when I catch you, I'm going to get my hands on that sweet, delicious tush and—*

She reaches the next landing, then grabs the handle of the door below the fire-exit sign, twists it and plows through. The door shuts after her. The sound echoes around the space. *What the—* She's surprised me again, the little vixen.

I charge up the stairs, pull the door open and hurtle forward. I spot her stabbing the button to call the elevator.

Got you! I'm barely winded, while her panting fills the space. She glances over her shoulder, spots me, and yelps. Then turns and jabs at the button repeatedly. The car arrives, and the doors open. I sprint toward her and careen to a stop as the elevator doors begin to close on her.

I plant my shoulder in the gap between the doors, and they spring back. I step inside, and she gasps, then stumbles back until she hits the back of the carriage. The doors swish shut behind me. I reach over and slap the button for my penthouse, and it begins to rise.

She looks from me to the indicator flashing above my head, then back to my face. She glances around the space once before she wrings her hand together. I stay silent. So does she. The air between us thrums with tension. I drag my gaze down her features, taking in the flush on her cheeks, the parted lips, the way her eyelids flutter, how her eyes spark with a tinge of anger. Good. She's a fighter. She needs to be to work with me.

She shuffles her feet, and when I stay silent, she tosses her head. "This is stupid. I didn't do anything wrong. It was you who didn't remember my name. I have corrected you so many times, but you always forget."

"Are you complaining?" I drawl.

"No. Yes." She throws up her hands. "Frankly, I don't care. You can call me by any name you want, as long as you pay my salary on time—" She raises her shoulder. "I shouldn't care," she says with vehemence, as if she's trying to convince herself.

"So, it's fine if I call you July?"

"The name's June." She grimaces.

"You feel more like a July than a June," I drawl.

She scowls. "That's terrible logic, you know that?"

It makes sense to me. She reminds me of that time of the year when the light is golden, and the sea is clear, and the pool is warm enough to dive in without wearing any clothes and feel the silky water slip over my skin in an erotic caress. Not that I'm going to tell her that. I continue to glare at her, and she looks away.

"You're, uh, going to be late for your dinner meeting."

Nice segue, I'll give her this one. "Doesn't change the fact that you're going to have to accept your punishment."

I caught her. I'm going to punish her.

Her eyes grow huge. "P-punishment?"

"You hit me with the water bottle—"

"That was a mistake."

"Seemed intentional to me."

She draws in a breath. "Okay, I concede. I did intend to hit you with it, but I didn't expect it to actually hit you, know what I mean?"

"Not really. And it doesn't change the fact that the bottle bounced off my forehead. Ergo, you need to pay for the consequences of your actions."

She laughs nervously. "You're joking."

"Not at all."

And yes, I said I was going to keep things professional between us, but it won't hurt to indulge myself one last time, will it? Just this once, I can allow myself to take pleasure in her need to obey me. This once, I can give in to the need to dominate her.

She swallows again, then squeaks, "And what would this punishment involve?"

I reach over and slap the stop button.

14

June

"You've gotta be kidding me," I cry as the elevator screeches to a halt.

He caught me. I knew he would. I knew he was fitter than me and that he could easily keep up with me. I also realized he was allowing me to pull ahead on the landing. I sensed he was having too much fun. And truth be told, so was I. I could tell the chase was as entertaining to him as actually getting his hands on me.

But I hoped... I could keep up the pretense of the pursuit a little longer. And honestly, it was so exciting. To realize I had his undistracted awareness was heady. I sensed his eagerness, felt his desire build, and couldn't help but respond to it.

And now, in the enclosed space of the elevator cage, I'm so aware of his presence. He's watching me with that single-minded focus that sends a buzz of sensations through me. I'm excited and also, afraid, and yet... I wouldn't want to be anywhere else but here. With him.

He slides down until he's sitting on the floor of the cage with his back to the doors and his legs stretched out in front of him. "So where were we?" he drawls.

I shift my weight from foot to foot.

"If I say, I'm sorry?"

He shrugs. "It's a start, but it's not enough,"

"What more do you want?"

"For you to take your punishment." When he pats his thigh, heat bursts to life under my skin. My belly flutters, and my pussy clenches. *Oh my god, finally, finally... He's going to give me what I want.*

"Take off your skirt," he orders.

I should protest...maybe. But honestly, it doesn't even strike me. I want to feel his big hands on me without any barriers. Skin to skin. My entire body feels like it's about to catch fire. I reach behind, and because my fingers are trembling, it takes me a few tries before I can undo the hook on my skirt. I slide it down so it pools around my ankles.

"Now your stockings."

I shimmy them down my thighs.

"Stop," he snaps.

Instantly, I pause with the elastic digging into the center of my thighs.

"And your panties.

"P-panties?"

He arches an eyebrow at me. I gulp. A pulse flares to life between my legs. Then I slowly slide the plain white cotton briefs I favor down until they meet my stockings. My blouse hits the curve of my waist, so I'm standing over him, with my pussy bared. At least, I shaved. Not that he seems to notice. He gives my core a cursory glance, like it doesn't mean anything that I'm standing there with the most intimate part of myself bared to him. The desultory expression on his face turns me on even more. *Oh god.* It makes me feel like I have to do more to earn his attention, and I relish that so much. My nipples bead, and the pulse between my legs grows more insistent. Moisture bathes my lower lips, and when his nostrils flare, I'm sure he can scent my arousal.

"Down. On your front. Across my lap. Arse raised in the air."

The command in his voice whips across my nerve-endings. I instantly lower myself across his lap.

"Good girl."

His approval sends a zing of sensations bursting up my spine. I draw in a sharp breath, and his scent crowds my senses. The heavy muscles of his thighs are like granite under mine. I risk a glance over my shoulder to find he's staring at my backside.

Then, he brings down his hand and it connects with my rump. Pain cracks out from the point of contact. I cry out. Before I can draw another breath, he brings it down on my other cheek, then the first, and the next, again and again and again. Each time he spanks me, my entire body shudders. He's holding me in place with his other arm heavy across my lower back so I can't move. The pain is blinding and grows in intensity. White sparks flash between my eyes. The sensations zing up to my breasts and down to my feet, coalescing in my lower belly. My pussy throbs. My scalp tingles. And when he wallops me again, tears squeeze out from the corners of my eyes. *It hurts. It hurts.*

And yet, the fact that he's touching me and holding me, and that I'm at the receiving end of his ministrations, turns my knees to jelly. He continues to rain blows on my backside, and the friction of my bare pussy against the thickness between his legs, and the curve of my breasts against the ridge of his thigh, sends frissons of pleasure up my spine. I'm so turned on, I feel the climax pumping up my legs, my thighs. It blooms in my belly, extends to my brain... And he stops. Just like that.

For a second, I stay suspended at the edge. Just a little more, and I'll arrive. Climax. I'll find my relief. I cry out in protest, "Please, please, please, let me come, Sir."

"Hush now," he admonishes me. "Toys should be seen and not heard."

Oh. I blink rapidly. "Am I your toy, Sir?" I ask softly.

"Toys aren't allowed to think either," he warns.

I sense his muscles bunch under me, then he grabs my hips and straightens me so I'm on my feet. He handles my body like I'm a doll, and no-one has ever done that. It's as if I weigh nothing, though my scale says otherwise. It makes me feel small and delicate, a feeling I love. He keeps a hand on my thigh until I'm steady. He's seated, and I'm standing. I should feel like I'm in a position of power, but really, all the control rests with him.

My butt tingles from the spanking. My nipples are still hard. Little jolts of pleasure course through me. Liquid heat trickles from between my legs and his gaze darts there. The more he stares at my pussy, the more turned on I get. I squeeze my thighs together, shuffle my feet, not caring that I must be a sight with my skirt around my ankles and my panties and stockings digging into my thighs. "Please, Sir. Please." I swallow, trying hard not to whine and failing. "I'm sorry I threw the water bottle at you, Sir."

"That's a start." He nods.

"And I'll do anything you want. I'll be a good girl. Please let me come."

He slides his palm around to cup my butt, then hauls me close. Enough that my pussy is at level with his face. He brings his nose close and sniffs my cunt, and it's so hot, so erotic, I cry out, "Oh god." I begin to clutch at his hair, but he slaps my hand away.

"Tuck your elbows into your sides and keep them there."

I instantly oblige. If I do as he says, he'll allow me to come, right? Only, he releases me, then uncoils his frame and stands. Once more, he towers over me. "Put yourself to rights."

What? I stare at him, stricken. "Please, Sir. Please, I want to come."

"Not yet."

"Then... Then when?"

"When I decide it's the right time, and not a moment earlier."

"But—"

He glares at me. I swallow, then straighten my clothes. When I'm done, I tip up my chin. I take in the bland expression on his face. But for the tent at his crotch, which hints at what I know is his exceptionally large, very thick, very erect cock—because I felt it throb under me—he could be coming back from a board meeting.

My fingers tingle. I so want to touch him, and feel him on me, and inside me, surrounding me. More importantly I want him to punish me further. I want him to spank me. And tie me up. And render me helpless. I want him to act out his filthiest fantasies with me. I'd love for him to use me as he pleases. I'd love to please him in any way he desires. Just so long as he keeps his attention on me.

Which means, I have to keep pushing him and baiting him. Enough for him to lose control and forget about that stupid rule about keeping things between us professional. And when he reaches over and slaps the button on the lift so we begin to move, I panic. It's what makes me choke out, "I was wrong to hit you with the water bottle, Sir, and I deserved the spanking, and any other punishment you want to give me, but"—his glare deepens, but before I lose my courage, I manage to choke out—"but only if you agree to my stipulation."

He widens his stance, drawing my attention to his thighs, but I keep my gaze above his crotch.

When he stays silent. I swallow, then square my shoulders and burst out, "When you're ready to give them to me, I'd like"— I swallow. "I'd like at least"—I raise my middle finger next to my forefinger—"two, no"—I add a third finger—"three orgasms."

15

Knox

Jesus Christ, this woman. She's negotiating with me... I admire that. It gives me one more reason to punish her. *Was that her intention?* I frown. *Am I the one being manipulated here?* Nah, not possible. It does mean, that I'm going to draw out her retribution. Something I'm going to enjoy.

She's nervous, as evidenced by how her fingers shake when she pushes the hair back from her face. But the stubborn set to her chin and the rigidity of her shoulders tells me she's settled on her stance. And while I prefer my women submissive, I also want them to know their minds.

"Done." I hold out my hand.

She stares at it for a second before placing her much smaller palm in mine. An electric current seems to zip out from her touch. I stiffen. So does she. Her gaze widens, and she begins to pull back, but I wrap my fingers around her palm and squeeze.

A trembling grips her, and her lips part in an 'O' of surprise. Once again, I find myself leaning closer. I love the 'O' her pouty lips make. I love the color on her cheeks. I love the look she shoots me from under her eyelids, and the expression, which is half-anger, half-anticipation, with a dash of pleading. I especially love the pleading. I stare at her mouth, wanting to taste it. Wanting to kiss her and find out if she tastes as sweet as she smells. She tips up her mouth, and I lower my chin...just as the elevator slides to a stop. There's a soft ping, and the doors slide open.

Saved by the proverbial bell from committing what would, surely, be a mistake? I release her arm, press the down arrow on the elevator, and step out. I'd love to invite her to my place, but if I did, I'm not sure I could control myself with her. "Go pick up your things at the gym, then wait for me in the reception area downstairs. I'll jump in the shower and see you in a few minutes."

"Eh?" She blinks rapidly. "I thought you wanted to punish me further?"

"I will, but after dinner."

"Where are the other diners?" She looks around the spacious, yet spartan room. It's in the heart of Mayfair, known for its billionaires from around the world who have their summer townhouses here in the center of London, but the facade of this restaurant is deceptively simple, as is the furnishing inside. Make no mistake, the elegant wood furniture, the crisp white tablecloth, the candles, and the single rose in the crystal vase in the center of the table, are all of the highest quality, and sourced from ateliers renowned for their innovative designs.

"What other diners?" I ask without looking up from the menu, mainly to elicit a response from her.

She doesn't disappoint. "There are only four tables here." She glances about the restaurant once again before turning her wide green gaze on me. "And the rest are unoccupied."

"This restaurant only seats sixteen people, and"—I pause for effect —"we are the only diners tonight."

Her eyes widen until they seem to take up most of her face. It's so fucking adorable to see the surprise on her face. When was the last time I was this taken with anything? When I saw her the first time, she entered my office is when. And before that? My life consisted of surviving every day, of getting through the insomnia-filled nights when I was too afraid to close my eyes for fear of the past coming back to haunt me.

"Did you book out the restaurant?" Her sweet voice cuts through the chaos of thoughts in my head.

"Didn't have to. When I told James I was bringing a woman tonight, he decided it had to be special."

"Special?" She swallows, an uncertain look creeping into her eyes. "This was supposed to be a work meeting."

"And it is. We're going to talk about work, but no reason not to enjoy a great meal while we do so, hmm?" I aim for an innocent look on my face and am convinced she's going to protest, but then she leans back in her seat and folds her arms across her chest.

"Why are you doing this?" She narrows her gaze on me.

"What do you mean?" I pretend I'm not aware of what she's talking about. I do it to get a rise out of her and am rewarded when she firms her mouth.

"You know what I mean."

"Pray, enlighten me," I drawl.

Spots of red color her cheeks. Her brown eyes spark, and fuck, if that doesn't arouse me. Why do I love getting a rise out of her so much?

"I mean, all this." She waves a hand in the air. "You bring me here, to one of the most famous Michelin-starred restaurants in the country—"

"I happen to enjoy the food here." I shrug.

She huffs, "You tell me it's a work meeting, but then you book out the restaurant—"

"I like my privacy, especially when I'm talking about some very confidential deals with my assistant."

She purses her lips and seems unconvinced.

"Not my fault you don't seem to be able to accept the opportunities that come your way," I say slowly.

She blinks, and realization dawns on her features. She glances around the room again, and her features soften. "It is a beautiful venue," she finally offers.

Not as beautiful as you. Unbidden, the thought scrolls across my mind. I scowl. I don't do sappy thoughts. And I'm not a romantic. But being with her threatens to turn me into one. Fucking hell. I glance around and snap my fingers.

The Maître d'hôtel appears at my side as if by magic. He sets down a tray with folded napkins on it. Those should be the cold towels I asked for. Next to them is a tube of aloe. I messaged the restaurant on my way here. I nod my thanks, then look at the menu.

"She'll have a glass of the Domaine Leflaive Montrachet Grand Cru and a Macallan for me."

She begins to protest, but when I continue to order, she subsides.

"For the starters, she'll have the Roasted cauliflower with curry leaf and coconut, and I'll have the Foie gras terrine with spiced pear chutney. For the main, she'll have the vegan wild mushroom risotto with black truffle. I'll have the Aged Herefordshire beef fillet with bone marrow jus. For dessert we'll have the Dark chocolate and mango tart."

"You're allergic to mango," she reminds me.

I pause. She's right. *Am I so taken in by her presence that I forgot that?*

"How about the I replace that with orange, Sir?" The Maître d' asks without losing a beat.

I nod.

The Maître d' half bows. "Very good, Madam. Sir." He gathers our menus and leaves.

She waits until he's out of earshot, then leans forward. "How did you know I'm vegan?"

Because I called the delicatessen where you order your lunch. And no, that doesn't mean anything. But would I do it for any other employee? The answer leaves me cold. So instead of replying, I opt to answer her question with a question, "How did you know I was allergic to mango?"

"I'm your assistant. I had to familiarize myself with your dietary habits so I could specify them when I made restaurant bookings or confirmed your attendance at events." Her forehead wrinkles. "You, on the other hand... There's no reason for you to know about my food preferences," she says slowly.

"If you're done ruminating about my food order, could we focus on the work at hand?" I look at her from under my eyelashes.

She wears a confused expression. "I haven't indicated that I'm vegan in any of the onboarding questionnaires for the company either, so—"

"I've noticed what you have for lunch," I lie.

"You... You did?" Hope shines in her eyes, and I know I need to bat it away before she begins to envisage a relationship between us.

So, I drawl, "Don't read anything into it. I'm a former Marine. We're trained to notice details. Besides" — I ensure my expression grows bland — "you look like the type who prefers the most boring items on the menu."

She firms her lips. Hurt filters into her eyes, and damn, if I don't feel it like it's my own. I almost reach over and take her hand, then stop myself at the last second. *Her feelings are of no consequence to me.* She's my employee, and sometimes, willing plaything. Yes, that's all she is.

She shifts in her seat, then when she sees me watching her, she flushes. "My butt... Uh... It hurts."

"Good."

Her lips part in surprise, and damn, if my cock doesn't instantly take notice of that heart-shaped hole between them. Then, because I love to keep her off-kilter. I rise to my feet, then grab the tray of cold towels, round the table and set it next to her.

"Get up."

She blinks but does as I command. Once more, her trust in me is... Empowering and humbling. "Pull up your skirt, then slide your stockings and panties down, and bend over the table."

Not only are there no other patrons here, but I've asked James to make sure all the security cameras have been switched off, ensuring complete privacy.

She swallows, then does as I asked. I push the chair out of the way and step behind her. A trembling grips her. I stare down at her exposed arse. The skin is reddened and glowing. Jesus. A familiar thrill squeezes my guts. What I wouldn't give to take her right here, but I won't. For now, I need to take care of her. And feed her. I take the cold towel and gently place it over her butt cheek.

She stiffens, then as the cold sinks into her skin, she sighs. "That feels good."

I take the other towel and press it to her other arse cheek. I hold both towels until her body slumps further. Then I place the towels back on the tray and smear the aloe-vera gel on her behind.

"Ohh, that feels even better."

Once I'm done, I pull up her panties and then her stockings. I tap her back and she straightens. I slide her skirt down around her hips, and smooth it in place. Then push her chair in behind her.

"Sit down."

She does, and I slide in her chair before touching her shoulder. "Better?"

She nods.

"I'm sorry, I didn't take care of you the first time I spanked you."

I walk around to take my seat and find she's looking at me with that soft look on her features again. *Fuck*. I don't want to give her the wrong impression, that it means anything, so I add, "You should know, I do this for anyone I spanked. It just so happens to be you this time."

"Oh." For a millisecond, she looks hurt, but then she levels me with a look that sets off alarm bells in my head—like she knows I'm faking this disinterest toward her—before calmly adding, "Noted." She reaches into her handbag—the one I ordered for her, making sure it was stylish, yet roomy enough to carry her laptop and documents—and pulls out her tablet. She places it on the table, then slides her fingers across the screen.

"The forecasts are in from the sales team. They expect to come in significantly under the quarter four projections, and—"

I allow her sweet voice to wash over me. I also use the excuse of her speaking to peruse her gorgeous features. Those long eyelashes, the slight flush on her cheeks, from my thinly veiled insult—which I regretted as soon as I spoke, but fuck, if I didn't also enjoy the flash of anger in her eyes. Her fighting spirit is a turn on, which is inexplicable. I've always preferred women on their knees, legs spread out as I take them, merely to satisfy a need. I've never wanted any of them to be anything more than submissive, put up with my kinks, and give in to my demands. *Fucking hell.* I tighten my fingers into a fist. *I cannot stop thinking of her as my potential sub. I want to do the things to her that I've never done to anyone else before.*

I cannot go there. I cannot want her to be at my beck and call, and not just as my employee. I managed to extend the scope of her presence in my life to my home, under the guise of that being the role of my Executive Assistant.

But to want to also have her in my bed? To want to make her bend to my demands and watch as she falls apart? To feel ownership of her body, mind, and soul? To want to break her down emotionally and physically, only to reform her in the image of my perfect sub... Is not right.

Not only is she invaluable as a member of my team, and that relationship would be affected, but she's also too naive. Unlike the submissives I've had before her, July is too inexperienced—and while that's part of the attraction, it means she wouldn't be up to what I need.

She might claim to be attracted to me, despite my scarred face. She might even enjoy the role-play, so far. But once I remove the veneer of civilization completely, once I bind her, and gag her, and blindfold her, and render her immobile—and then do all the things I want to do to her... She'll hate me. I'll sully her, dirty her, take away every last shred of her innocence... And she won't be able to keep up with my demands. She doesn't really mean it when she professes to love my brand of kink. She has no idea how far I can push her limits. No, this entire line of thinking is wrong, and—

"Mr. Davenport, Sir?"

It's the last moniker which cuts through the chaos of thoughts in my head.

"Are you okay?" she asks me in a voice that hints at the confusion she's feeling.

Me too. I've always been laser-focused when it comes to my job, be it when I was a Marine or now, as the CEO of my company. I've never been less than one hundred percent when it comes to making decisions in my professional life. But that was before her. *Fuck. She's playing havoc with my ability to focus, and that's terrifying.*

"Would you like me to repeat the question?" She peruses my features. "I asked—"

"Call a meeting with the sales team tomorrow at seven a.m. to discuss the projections."

"Seven a.m.?" Her forehead wrinkles. "Isn't that too early?"

"I pay them enough to come into work when I ask," I growl.

Her features tighten. "Yes, Sir."

My dick thickens further. It soothes that animal inside of me when she calls me by that honorific, and that's going to be my downfall. I try to keep my gaze from her mouth, and know I've failed when she clears her throat.

"Then, there was the companywide technological outage last week. The tech teams suspect a cyber-attack—"

"A meeting with my Chief Technological Officer at eight a.m. tomorrow."

The furrow between her eyebrows deepens, but all she says is, "As you wish, Sir."

The crotch of my pants tightens. Her acquiescence is going to turn me into a mass of raging horniness.

"Then, the shareholder meeting—"

"Postpone it by a month."

"A month?" She looks at me in horror. "But the board—"

"You're smart; you can come up with an excuse, I'm sure."

Her lips thin. "I believe that should be possible." Her voice is polite, but her cheeks have gone red again. Poor little July. She has no idea how much I enjoy the fact that her features always give away her true feelings.

You can't hide from me, little one.

What. The. Fuck? I cannot have seriously come up with a sappier endearment for her.

The Maître d' glides over and places our drinks in front of us.

I grab my tumbler, toss back my drink, then growl, "Another."

He takes my glass and retreats while my assistant gapes at me. "Are... Are you okay, Sir?"

Fuuuuck. If she calls me 'Sir' one more time, I'm going to throw myself across this table, grab her by the nape of her neck and kiss that tempting mouth and—I shake my head. Nope, I cannot allow her to take over my thoughts so completely. I need to figure out how to keep her at a distance. It's why I lift my chin and growl, "Except for the exceedingly boring company I've been subjected to for the past twenty minutes, I'm fine, okay."

Her eyes grow wide, then her features crumple.

Instantly, I'm struck with remorse. *Fucking hell, did I have to hurt her like that?*

She manages to get control of her emotions, then draws her spine straight. With measured movements, she slides her tablet back into her bag. "I don't believe we have anything else urgent to discuss for this evening, so if you will excuse me..." She rises to her feet, then turns and walks across the floor.

Fuck, fuck, fuck. I spring up and stalk after her, "Stop, July."

16

June

I ignore him and keep walking. He overtakes me and plants his bulk in between me and the path to the exit.

"Let me pass, Sir." I swallow.

He draws in a sharp breath. I sense the tension in him ratcheting up. It surprises me enough to raise my gaze to his. When his blue eyes blaze at me, I realize it's a mistake. I'm caught up in the sapphire depths, caught up in the vortex of emotions that I glimpse, until an avalanche of ice seems to crash down and erect a wall between us.

"I didn't give you permission to leave," he says through gritted teeth.

"My work here is done. I need to head back." I love it when he treats me as his plaything. I want to please him. I work hard so I can hear those words of praise from his gorgeous mouth. But I also know when he's frustrated with himself. I know he's drawn toward me, but he also wants to resist feeling anything for me—that's when he lashes out, hoping to hurt me. And this time, he did. And I... I won't stand for that. It satisfies something in me to obey him. I love for him to order me to do his bidding, but he also has to respect me.

"You go home when I tell you to and not before," he growls.

I firm my lips. "Why should I stay, when all you've done is insult me all evening?"

A bleak look enters his eyes. For a second, I glimpse his confusion, and it mirrors the conflicted feelings I harbor toward him. He's the most conceited, egotistical man I've ever met. And the most powerful. And the most charismatic. And I hate him. And want him. *And can't stand him. And I still want him. Argh!* Doesn't change the fact that he caused me distress with his words.

"I'm sorry," he murmurs.

My jaw drops. "Did you just apologize?"

He shifts his weight from foot to foot. "I should not have said what I did earlier. That was rude and insufferable of me."

"And?" I prompt.

He sighs. "And I have a lot on my mind. I'm pissed off about a few things, and I took it out on you. I shouldn't have."

I blink slowly. "Does this have anything to do with your grandfather's visit?"

His gaze widens almost imperceptibly—but I've learned his tells—then he wipes the surprise from his features. *Guess he didn't think I was insightful enough to figure* that *out.* I'm more astute than he gives me credit for. I wouldn't have navigated my minefield of a childhood and reached here if I weren't.

He takes a step back, then nods toward the table behind us. "Please, join me for dinner?"

It's a request, not a command. And that is surprising.

"I promise to be civil." His tone is genuine enough that I feel my defenses melt. But I'm not willing to give in yet.

"Tell me how you knew I was vegan? And that I prefer white wine to red?"

It's a gamble, trying to negotiate that information out of him, but if I don't try to hold onto my self-esteem, then he'll walk over me. And even if he is my boss and he holds the power in this relationship, he needs me as his assistant.

No man can run a big company without a good team, and from what I've seen, he hasn't done much to build relationships with his. I have the people skills he's lacking, and that's just one reason I'm indispensable. He needs me, all right. And whether he says it aloud or not, he's too shrewd not to realize it.

He glares at me, not happy I'm questioning him, and I admit, my inclination is to lower my gaze, but I resist. I dig my heels into the floor, and even as the color drains from my face under the force of his scrutiny, I hold his gaze.

A flicker of something—admiration, maybe? —flashes in his eyes. Then it's gone so quickly, I wonder if I imagined it. He nods slowly. "I called the café where you buy your lunch."

For a moment, I'm speechless. "Y-you called them?"

He nods.

I rub at my temple. "Wait. Hold on. This means, you knew you were going to invite me out to dinner earlier today?"

"We had work to get through, and I wanted to do it over dinner." He raises a shoulder.

"So, you called a world-class, Michelin-starred chef and asked him to book out the restaurant for you. And he did it?" I say in a disbelieving voice.

"James is a good friend." He hesitates. "We served in the Marines together."

It's the first piece of personal information he's shared with me. I lock it away greedily. *Does it mean anything that he's shared something about his past with me, which I have a sneaking suspicion he doesn't do often?* He messaged the leading chef in the world and asked him to book out his restaurant. Not to forget, he made the effort to find out personal details about me, then called ahead to book out the restaurant. It shows a level of planning indicating that he... *Cares about me?* A burst of joy sparks in my chest. *He has to. He feels something for me, but is pretending he doesn't.*

"I've never done this before," he adds.

Once more, my heart flutters. My stomach flip-flops. "You mean—"

"I don't often have time to go to dinner, let alone, move my official meetings to a restaurant. But I'm aware I've been an arse."

I stay quiet. He's apologizing to me again, and it's overwhelming. Everything that's happened today is overwhelming.

"When you chased me at the gym—"

"Primal play."

He must see the confusion on my face for he elaborates, "It's a form of kink where the participants engage in predator/prey gameplay."

A shiver runs up my spine. I shouldn't be aroused by what he's revealing, but I can't deny that the space between my legs has turned into a wet mess from his words."

"You liked it." The confidence in his voice is arousing.

It's also annoying enough that I retort, "I didn't say that."

He inclines his head. "The fact that you begged me to let you come is evidence of it."

He's right, and I can't deny it. I shift my weight from foot to foot. How did we get onto this topic anyway?

"I... I think I should go."

"At least, have dinner with me first," he coaxes. "The food here is really good."

"I'm sure it is." I glance away.

"I'm sorry, I was a complete twat earlier."

When I don't look at him again, he lowers his voice to a hush, "You want to stay; you know that. And I want you to, as well."

I sense movement behind us, then he murmurs, "Ah, there's our food. Surely, you can't leave now."

I blow out a breath. "This doesn't mean anything."

"Of course, not."

I glance up into his face to find he's looking at me with a steady gaze.

"It's just a meal. And you deserve it after working so hard all day."

I find myself giving in, and rather than saying anything, spin around and walk over to the table where the Maître d' places our dishes in front of our chairs. I sit down and take in the beautifully arranged food on my plate.

He takes his seat and looks at me expectantly. "Taste it," he urges me.

I pick up my fork and dig into the cauliflower starter. The fragrant taste of the curry leaves and the slightly charred notes of the cauliflower melt in my mouth. By the time I finish it, I'm ravenous for more. Thankfully, our main courses arrive right away. I tuck into my risotto. The earthy, woodsy notes of mushroom set off the more savory, aromatic flavors of the truffle. Combined with the nuttiness of the arborio rice, it's both creamy and sweet, as well as aromatic and pungent. "Wow."

I only realize I've said it aloud when he nods. "James is a true maestro."

"Is it true, The Beast has developed a conscience?" Someone chuckles, then a man wearing a chef's garb walks over to the table.

"Hey, motherfucker." My boss nods.

"Arsewipe," the chef growls back.

"Pillock," my boss drawls in an almost lazy tone.

"Lummox." The chef glowers, before barking out a laugh. "Good to see you, mate."

"Can't say the same." My boss rises to his feet, and the two do the kind of half hug and back slap that men often do. Then they clasp the backs of each other's necks and smirk at each other. I watch them with unconcealed fascination. I have rarely seen my boss crack a smile, let alone man-hug another person.

When they step back, my boss nods in the other guy's direction. "This is James Hamilton."

I'd guessed as much.

"This is June Donnelly," my boss adds.

I swing my face in his direction, a strange sensation of lightness enveloping me. Hearing my name from his lips feels so intimate. It feels like he's given me a gift for the good girl I've been. Pleasure blooms in my lower belly. My toes curl. I've wanted this so much. I've waited to hear him say my name, and now that he has, it feels overwhelming.

James lowers his chin. "Good to meet you, June."

"And you." I swallow down the ball of emotion in my throat and manage to curve my lips. "This is amazing," I lower my head to mask the emotions coursing through my chest and end up taking another bite of the risotto. Flavors explode on my palate. "I've never tasted anything like this before." When I smile at him this time, it's more natural. The taste really is mind-blowing. Enough to ground me and help me gain some semblance of equilibrium.

"Thank you." He half bows. "I'm glad you're enjoying your dinner. I've been asking this man to visit my restaurant for the longest time, and it's thanks to you that he decided to show up here. You must be a special woman." His eyes gleam.

"Oh, no." I flick a sideways glance toward my boss who's watching with an amused look on his features. *Why isn't he saying anything?* I scowl at him, then turn to James. "I'm Mr. Davenport's assistant."

His forehead furrows. Then, he looks between us and nods. "My bad. Doesn't change the fact that it's thanks to you he's here today." He turns to my boss. "I need to get back to the kitchen. Don't be a stranger, mate."

My boss scoffs, "Like you have time off from your restaurants?"

James lets his gaze wander about the space. "The restaurant business is a demanding mistress, but my brothers-in-arms come first."

The two look at each other, and something passes between them. They nod, then with a wave in my direction, James leaves. My boss takes his seat.

"The two of you are close?" I venture.

"As close as two men who were held prisoners and saw each other being tortured can be."

I gasp. *He revealed something personal about himself. And did he say tortured? And in such a casual voice?* I try to conceal my horror but don't succeed, for when I speak, my tone is shocked, "What happened?"

"We were behind enemy lines and had been trudging through the frozen forests on the southern edge of the tundra for days. We had information about insurgents who we knew were in hiding. We knew it would be difficult to track them down in the dead of winter but hadn't realized just how much the weather would slow us down. There was a snowstorm. We got separated from the rest of our team and were captured by the enemy."

He falls silent. And though there's no trace of emotion on his face, the flicker in his eyes betrays just how difficult the experience must have been.

When he doesn't speak for another few seconds, I clear my throat. "But you escaped?"

He wraps his fingers around his tumbler of whisky. "We did. But not before the two of us had many weeks to think hard about our lives and what we wanted out of it when we got out of there. It was the fact that we had each other's backs that kept us going." His jaw is hard, his features almost expressionless, except for the nerve that throbs at his temple. There's a faraway look in his eyes.

Once more, he lapses into silence. I see the bleakness that creeps across his face and decide to stay quiet this time. Best to let him take his time to parse through his thoughts. It's another few minutes before he murmurs, "The worst part is not having control over your future." He swallows. "Not knowing if you'll wake up to see another day, and then waking up to find you're still caught in the nightmare." His voice is hard.

For someone like him, not knowing what was going to happen to him next would have been unthinkable. Is that why he likes to have control when it comes to sex? Is that why he thrives on being a Dom, knowing he can direct every aspect of how he gives and take pleasure? Is proclivity for kink a way of dealing with the uncertainty he's been through? I want to believe that, but my instinct says he always had that cruel yet caring streak in him. It was, likely, what made him a good Marine. It's likely that contradiction got him through his missions. And his experiences feed his proclivities. The silence stretches. I cast about for something to say, then settle on something which I hope will encourage him to keep sharing.

"It must have been hard," I venture. My words are nothing in comparison to what he must have gone through. But I can't help wanting to try to soothe the horrific memories that must be cascading through his mind right now.

The skin across his knuckles stretches. "It was. But we were lucky; we had each other. If not we — I wouldn't have made it out." His lips thin.

"How... How did you escape?"

His expression becomes even more impenetrable. "They tortured James to the point that his heart stopped. Then they threw him into my cell, probably to break my spirit. Only the ol' codger had life left in him. I resuscitated him, but he pretended to be lifeless. It gave us a chance to plan our breakout. We overpowered our guards, then grabbed their weapons and shot our way out of there. We were picked up by a search party."

His jaw ticks. I'm sure he's leaving out vast swathes of what happened, but I'm also shocked he shared so much with me. He raises the tumbler to his mouth and tosses it back, then sets the glass back on the table with a thump. When he looks up at me, there's surprise on his face.

"You're easy to talk to," He frowns. Anger flickers across his eyes, spiked with confusion. His gaze is unblinking, and I can't help but squirm under the force of it.

I try to look away but, oh my god, the force of his personality pins me in place. The skin around his mouth tightens, and he seems almost displeased. "You're not eating," he points out. The rough edge of his voice pulses frissons of awareness up my spine.

"I... Uh... I'm not hungry anymore."

Without breaking the connection between our eyes, he raises his hand. The next second, the Maître d,' who must've been hovering out of sight, glides over. He clears away our plates, handing them to another uniformed staff-member, then slides a plate which another staff-member had wheeled in, onto our table. He places one spoon next to it, then fades away. *Why only one spoon? Shouldn't there be* —

My unspoken question is answered when my boss dips the spoon into the chocolate dessert. The flick of his wrist as he wields the spoon, the deft curl of his wide fingers around the narrow, delicate handle, the glimpse of arm hair revealed when his shirt sleeve rides up and exposes his wrist bone... *Oh my god!* I'm burning up. My throat goes dry. All the moisture has been pulled into that place between my legs. My pussy throbs, and my clit feels like there are weights attached to it. He holds my gaze, and the intent in them sends a lick of desire up my spine. Even before he can raise his eyebrow in question, I lean forward.

There's a ghost of a smile on his face as he scoops up some dessert and holds the spoon out to me. "Open."

17

Knox

Without hesitation, she parts her lips, and blood drains to my groin. Her obedience is going to be my downfall. The satisfaction I get from feeding her is dangerous. The pleasure I get from the simple act of being with her is going to be my undoing. Everything I've guarded against—the vulnerability, the susceptibility to being hurt—all of it seems very real.

I will not fall for her. I cannot fall for her. I'm not good enough for her. I can't give her the kind of relationship she deserves. I don't trust myself not to hurt her. I'll always want more from her, and it'd be wrong of me to expect her to put up with my proclivities, no matter how much she seems to enjoy it now. I cannot sully her. And despite my best efforts to keep our relationship professional, it's clearly not working.

I need to find a way to, once and for all, put an end to this obsession I've been developing for her. I need to get her out of my system. The straightforward way would be to fuck it out, which would hurt our working relationship. In the brief time since she joined my team, she's become indispensable.

But *nobody's* indispensable. I can fuck her, then send her on her way. Yes, that's right. That's the only way out. I'll pay her enough to compensate for the job loss. Then I can move on.

I scoop up more of the chocolate tart, and again, she wraps her lips about the spoon. When she licks it off, the sight of that pink tongue has my cock stabbing at the constraints of my pants at my crotch.

And when I dip the same spoon into the dessert and bring it back to my mouth, her pupils dilate. She swallows, and the pulse at the base of her neck kicks up in speed.

"Like it?" My voice comes out rougher than I intended.

She nods.

"Want more?"

She nods again.

I place the spoon down, then dip my finger in the chocolate and bring it to her mouth. I smear it on her lips, but before I can pull back, she flicks out that tantalizing tongue of hers and licks the rest of the mixture from my fingertip. Heat arrows down my spine. The pressure in my balls tightens. My dick extends and threatens to stab its way out of my pants. I haven't even touched her properly, and already, I'm ready to come in my pants like a teenager. This woman is dangerous.

And if you fuck her, once will not be enough. I won't be able to walk away. I'll have to find a way to keep her at my side. So anytime I want, I'll be able to touch her, hold her, caress her. To take care of her and own her. To tear into her pussy and infiltrate every hole in her body. To look into her eyes as I thrust into her. To squeeze her gorgeous arse-cheeks as I take her from behind.

The thoughts and images cascade across my mind. Every cell in my body seems to catch fire. My thigh muscles tighten. My fingers tingle to curl the strands of her hair around my palm and yank her head back. To expose the line of her throat so I can bury my teeth in the curve of her shoulder and mark her. *Fucking hell.*

The intensity of these feelings is new. And it's not just physical. The way my heart seems to expand every time I'm in her vicinity... The way I track her progress every time we're in the same room... The way I'm aware of her presence outside my office... It's distracting. To be this focused on another person is something I've never faced before. And the more time I spend with her, the more pronounced is this connection with her.

All of my resolutions to keep her at a distance, to keep our association purely professional, have gone out the window. If I continue down this path... I'll never want to be rid of her. I'll never have enough of her. Next thing, I'll be baring my soul to her, and becoming dependent on her. No longer will I be in control of my emotions. And that, I cannot allow.

I will not let this sprite of a woman sweep into my life and turn it upside down. I can't let myself want her. No, I need to draw a very firm line between us. One that deters me from pursuing her. That's the right thing to do.

I pat my lips with my napkin, then throw it down on the table. "Time to leave."

The drive to her place is quiet. I sense she's confused, for she keeps darting sideways glances at me. I've kept my gaze firmly on my phone. Not that the words on my email make any sense to me. I'm too aware of her scent, of the small movements she makes as she tries to make herself comfortable, of how she keeps locking and unlocking her fingers together in her lap.

A couple of times, I sense her turning toward me, as if she wants to talk, but mercifully, she doesn't. If she did, I might throw away my resolve, surge forward, pull her close and kiss her. As it is, I have to grip my phone hard with one hand while I curl the fingers of my other hand into a fist, so I'm not tempted to reach for her. When the car draws up in front of her place in Finsbury Park, she hesitates.

"Good night," I say without looking up at her.

"Good night." She goes to push the door open, then looks at me over her shoulder. "Is... Is everything okay?"

"Why wouldn't it be?"

"It's just, you seem preoccupied," she says in a soft voice.

"I'm a busy man; I have a company to run, Ms. Donnelly."

I sense the anger that begins to simmer under her skin. I risk a glance in her direction to find her cheeks are flushed. Her eyebrows are knitted, and she's scowling at me. She's pissed off because I called her Ms.

Donnelly again. A pathetic way to put distance between us, but I'm clutching at straws here. Being in an enclosed space with her, having her so close that I could reach across and touch her, and not permitting myself to do it is sheer torture. Our gazes hold, and there's a plea in hers.

Is she even aware of how alluring she is with her features lit by the light from the rear dome light? I can't stop myself from dragging my gaze down her face, to that pulse beating at the base of her neck, to the hint of cleavage exposed by her blouse, and her gorgeous tits outlined by the fabric. A bead of sweat slides down my back. The knot of need in my belly seems to grow until it seems to fill every part of my body. *Fuck.* I need to get out of here before I do something I regret.

I make a show of glancing at my watch. "I'm getting late for my next meeting."

"Your one a.m. with Taiwan." She nods slowly, and when the chauffeur opens her door, she steps out of the car.

I push my own door open, then straighten and walk around the front of the car to join her. "I'll see you to your door."

She glances at the doorway that leads to the block of flats where she lives. "The entrance is right there."

I move toward the small gate that opens onto the short walk that leads to the entry. She follows me at a slower pace. When she reaches me, she steps forward and keys in her passcode. There's a snap as the door unlocks, and she pushes it open. She turns to face me and trains her gaze on my shoulder. "Goodnight, Mr. Davenport."

Before she shuts the door, I say, "I need you to come with me to the luncheon at Arthur's place on Sunday."

Her forehead furrows. "Isn't only close family invited to that?"

I arch an eyebrow, making sure to school my features into a bored expression. "I didn't ask you for a description of the event."

She pinches her lips together. "It's the weekend."

"As you're aware, I work weekends, and your contract specifies that, as my assistant, you too, work weekends, when needed. I don't need you at the other appointments on that day, but I need you at this lunch," I fix her with my gaze.

"But this is a family meal." She shuffles her feet. "So why do *I* need to be there?"

Because, I need to make you hate me, so that you'll stay away from me, since it turns out I'm not strong enough to stay away from you. I need to find a way to get you out of my life, but since I seem incapable of doing that, I need to engineer something that will cause you to leave me instead.

"It's never *just* a family meal when Arthur is involved." I roll my shoulders. "And with my other brothers involved in the business, there's bound to be work discussed. I need you there to keep track of it."

I monitor her features, waiting to see if she'll accept the explanation. And when she nods, I allow my muscles to relax.

Good. That's good. This is the only way out. It's going to hurt her, but it's for her own good. This way, she won't have anything to do with me, and that's for the best. My heart squeezes in its chest. I shove my misgivings aside, then nod in her direction. "I'll meet you there. I'll get there directly from my previous meeting."

She draws in a breath, then her features smoothen out. "You have the weekly eight a.m. with the sales staff, then the nine a.m. conference call with the East Coast, followed by the ten a.m. review of the creatives for the newest ad campaign, then the eleven-thirty meeting with the strategy planning agency at their office."

She recalls my schedule without having to consult her phone. It's safe to say, I'm impressed, but I don't show it. Instead, I nod and step back. "Lock up, Ms. Donnelly. I'll see you at Arthur's place at twelve-thirty p.m. The address is in your inbox."

I make sure she shuts the door and wait until I hear the snap of the latch falling into place before I turn and head to my car. Once inside, I call Arthur. He answers on the second ring.

"It's late," he says by means of a greeting.

Gramps never does mince his words.

I allow my lips to twist. "I think you'll be interested in what I have to say.'

18

Knox

I take in the long table that's been set up in the center of the garden in the backyard of Arthur's townhouse. Trees surround the estate, shielding us from the early afternoon visitors to Primrose Hill. The table is loaded with food, but no one makes a move toward it.

There's a hush of expectation in the air, or perhaps, that's my imagination? I roll my shoulders, then continue to scan the group gathered around the table.

"You okay, man?" Quentin shoots me a curious glance. "You seem...on edge."

"You need to get your eyesight checked *old* man." Last night, I reached home in plenty of time to make my one a.m. conference call. Then, because I wasn't able to get *her* out of my mind, I ran ten miles on the treadmill in my home gym. Then decided to bench-press a hundred, before using the punching bag. When every bone in my body seemed to curl up in exhaustion, I crawled into bed without showering.

Even then, I tossed and turned. Her scent, the feel of her lips against my fingertips, her need to comply with my orders, how she held her own and demanded three orgasms from me without being overwhelmed by my primal play—all of it crowded my mind. I woke up with a massive erection that, despite jerking off once in the shower and twice between meetings, did not seem to subside. *Fuck!* I'm definitely doing the right thing by backing myself into a corner so that my hands will be tied, and I won't have the option of pursuing her.

I grab a glass from a passing waiter and take a sip, only to spit it out. "Some non-alcoholic shit," I growl.

"I can help." My assistant materializes by my side. She pulls out a flask and splashes clear liquid into my half-filled glass.

Some of the tension eases from my shoulders. "Thanks, doll." I down half the glass, and sigh in appreciation.

She begins to melt away, but I snap my fingers, making sure not to look at her. "Don't go, I'll need you to pour." I hold my glass out again.

"Huh, don't think you want to get drunk, *Sir*."

Fucking hell. I'm sure she added on that title, knowing it would cause my dick to stiffen. This will not do at all. I manage to keep my gaze away from her features while my arm remains outstretched. A few seconds pass, then she relents and pours a dollop more into the glass. "Thanks." I toss it back, then glance around, wondering where to keep it.

My efficient assistant takes it from me, and I nod. "Don't know what I'd do without you, Kelly."

Her lips thin. There's a confused look in her eyes, one that says she knows I know her name, and that I'm not using it as a way of hurting her, and that I succeeded. *Fuck.* My heart stutters. I manage not to rub my chest and track her as she walks away to place the glass on a nearby table.

"Anyone know what Gramps is up to?" My younger brother Tyler prowls over to join us. Man's the tallest and the biggest of all of us. His features could be cast from granite. His eyes are cold. His expression is both bored and lethal. Of all my brothers, Tyler's the one I wouldn't want to meet in a dark alley.

He looms over the rest of us. In a suit and tie, he looks barely civilized for this gathering.

Tiny, Arthur's Great Dane ambles into the backyard, followed by my grandfather. Imelda should be here, but after that little scene I helped cause, rumor is, they're taking a break from each other.

My assistant begins to sidle away, but when I point to the chair on my right, she first hesitates, then complies. The chair to my left is vacant. The rest of the group take their seats. There's a general buzz around the table. Otis, my grandfather's butler, tops up everyone's glasses—not mine—with more of the non-alcoholic beverage then stands to the side.

Arthur clinks his knife against his glass and the chatter dies down.

"You must be curious about why you've been summoned?"

"Why should we be? We only had to drop what we were doing and attend to your summons," my other brother Brody growls under his breath.

"Something you want to share with the table?" Arthur arches an eyebrow in his direction.

Brody shrugs. "It's a working day."

Yep, like me, some of my brothers consider Sunday a working day.

"And I am the patriarch of this family... Still. So, you boys and girls will come when I call." It's a statement which brooks no argument. Arthur glances around the table, the look on his features implying *my-word-is-final*.

Brody groans. My youngest brother Connor chugs down water from a bottle like it's going out of style. Tyler's expression is as immovable as ever.

"Felix,"—Arthur nods in my cousin's direction—"you have something to tell us?"

The noise at the table dies down again.

Felix clears his throat, "I'm trying out for the Marines." He meets his father's gaze. "I hope to be half as good at it as my father was."

Quentin seems visibly moved. He swallows, then raises his glass in the direction of his son. "To Felix."

"To Felix." Everyone raises their glasses. I toss mine back, and my assistant refills mine without prompting. I throw that back as well, then rise to my feet. I head toward the house where a woman steps out onto the porch. She's tall, willowy, and wearing a green dress that reaches below her knees. It's sleeveless, baring her thin white arms. Her dark hair is a waterfall of health that flows down her back. Her eyes are almond shaped, her skin creamy, and so pale, the sun seems to be reflected off of it to bathe her in an ethereal light.

"Knox." She holds out her hand.

"Priscilla." I tuck her arm through mine and guide her over to the table. She slips into the seat on my left. By the time I'm seated, everyone is silent. All eyes are on me and the new arrival.

"Can I do the honors?" Arthur asks.

I yawn. "By all means."

Arthur frowns, then smooths out his expression. "This is Priscilla Whittington, Toren Whittington's sister. Toren and I agree that the best way to resolve our family feud and join our collective fortunes is through marriage."

"Sure, you did," Brody snorts.

Arthur ignores him. "Tor couldn't be here, but he was happy for us to go ahead with announcing—"

"To cut a long story short, Priscilla has agreed to marry me," I drawl.

Next to me, my assistant draws in a sharp breath. I hear the sound of glass breaking and look up to see Tyler pushing back from the table.

His jaw is hard, and the skin around his mouth is white. Priscilla stiffens. He looks from me to Priscilla, then spins around and leaves. Interesting. So, Tyler and Priscilla have some history? Not my problem. If he had feelings for the woman, he should have spoken up sooner.

Gramps made it a condition of our inheritance that we get married. I don't give a fuck about my inheritance, but I realized if I agreed to marry Priscilla, it would send a signal to my assistant that there's no future for us. That this chemistry between us is simply me taking advantage of the situation. That I do not foresee a relationship with her. That'll make me a bastard in her eyes. And I hope that with this proclamation of my would-be-engagement, she realizes she's better off without me. That she can do *better* than me.

Arthur gave me a month to find someone of my own to marry. There's still time, but the only woman who's caught my fancy is my assistant, and that's not going to change... The logical thing to do would be to marry her... But my instincts tell me if I do that, I'll be too vulnerable with her. It would mean getting my heart involved in the equation. It would mean sullying her even more than I already have. It would mean exposing her even more to my proclivities, because I can't be with her and not want to have my way with her. I'd deprive her of what's left of her innocence and that...is not something I can let myself do.

Quick, someone nominate me for humanitarian of the year. Here I am, planning to annihilate any hope my assistant has of us being together, but I'm doing it for her *good.*

I've begun to realize that being a Davenport means getting hitched is inevitable. Might as well be to Priscilla, then. It makes no difference to me. If anything, this is better.

Not only will there be no feelings involved, but Arthur will owe me if I do this. He'll be beholden to me for helping to bury the ol' Davenport-Whittington hatchet. Something I can use to my advantage.

It's why I told Arthur about my decision when I called him after dropping my assistant at home.

I raise my glass and glance around the table. "To my upcoming nuptials."

19

June

I stare out the window of my cramped apartment. The twilight casts long shadows as I gaze absently beyond the glass. The skies above are starless and dark, mirroring the gloom that's taken residence in my chest. I am still reeling from that surreal lunch when my boss announced he's getting married. Judging by the reactions of those around the table, no one else expected it, either.

To say I am heartbroken, not to mention embarrassed, is putting it mildly. My mind keeps going back to those times when he spanked me in the conference room and made me come, then how he made me ride his foot and *didn't* allow me to come at the royal reception, and how he called me his toy in the elevator and spanked me again. To be at the receiving end of his full focus was exhilarating.

I recall how he took care of me in the restaurant, the softness in his eyes when he apologized to me and asked me to stay for dinner.

I hunch my shoulders. I was sure we were forging a personal connection, but clearly, I was mistaken. He was leading me on all this time, pretending to feel something for me. Despite his insistence that there couldn't be any kind of relationship between us, his actions indicated otherwise. I'm a fool; I should have believed what he said. Come to think of it, he insisted I accompany him to the lunch, and when I refused, he gave me some bullshit about work being discussed and needing me there to record it.

I didn't completely believe him but decided to let it go. Now, there's no denying, this was a setup. He wanted me there, so I'd know, beyond a shadow of a doubt, that there's no future for us. Regardless of what happened between us, and how I might have thought it could develop into something more, he wanted to drive home that he chose someone else. That there will never be anything between us.

I didn't realize how much I'd hoped there was a chance of a real relationship with him... Not until he unequivocally and publicly rejected me by choosing someone else. I swallow around the thickness in my throat.

I took the job for the money, but I found I wanted to stay there because I wanted to be near him. I agreed to be at his disposal because, yes, he paid me more than enough to cover the hardship, but also because it made me feel good to do things for him. I felt like he was testing me, and I more than delivered.

But now, with him ready to commit to someone else... Does it mean... *Was I mistaken? Does this mean he used me as a willing submissive simply because it was convenient for him?* He was using me for entertainment, while I... I was falling for him. I kept hoping he felt something for me. And now, he's going to marry someone else.

My chest tightens, and my guts churn. *Ugh, why does the thought of him with someone else make me so sick?* He's my boss, but he feels like so much more. He made it clear there couldn't be anything between us and yet... I hoped... If I did everything he wanted, he'd notice me. He'd want to have a relationship with me... And now... Everything is different. Now that he's declared his intent to marry someone else... It means, he's out of bounds.

A heavy weight knocks at the backs of my eyes.

After that shit-show of an afternoon, I needed some time away from him. It's why I made an excuse and ran out on that luncheon, and thankfully, he didn't try to stop me. I was so consumed with him and my new job for the last few weeks, I pushed my own priorities to the back burner.

Now, I realize how wrong that was. Perhaps, I hoped for something more permanent with my boss, but now I realize how unlikely that was always going to be.

It's time for me to focus on my own life and what's important to me. It's time to dive into the one thing I've been putting off for so long, especially now that I have the money to afford the service.

I pull up the email app on my phone, address it to the person I've been meaning to get in touch with, then begin to type out the mail.

Dear Marina,

Thank you for agreeing to help me track down my birth parents. Attached is the information I've received from the Council, so far. It's not much, but perhaps it will help a little? Do let me know if you're interested in taking on my case.

Many thanks,
   June Donnelly

Without giving myself the chance to second guess, I send off the email, then sink back in my seat. *Oh my god, I did it.*

After all these years of thinking about it, I'm finally tracing my birth family.

My phone vibrates with an incoming text message. It's a message from my boss.

Sir: Book me for dinner tomorrow night at James Hamilton's restaurant. I'll be taking my intended fiancée there to celebrate our upcoming wedding.

The phone slips from my nerveless fingers. *What the —? Not only did he announce in front of the entire world that he's going to marry someone else, but now he's asking me to book dinner at the same restaurant he took me to, but for him and his fiancée-to-be?*

No! I won't do it. A crushing weight squeezes my chest, followed by a rage so powerful it makes my lungs burn. *This man? He's a sadist, in more than one way. He messaged me deliberately to rub in that he's out of bounds. I have no doubt about that. Argh! How could he be this cruel? How could he be this callous? Why is he doing this?* It's almost as if he's trying so hard to make me hate him. And this time, he may have succeeded.

My phone vibrates again. I glance at the screen with trepidation, then heave a sigh of relief to find it's my friend Zoey. I accept her call. "Hey —" I clear my throat. "What's up?"

"Hey, you!" Her cheerful face appears on the screen. "Whatcha doin'?"

I slide my spectacles up my nose. "Uh, not much. It's my first evening off since... Since I started this job, actually." I lean back on the sofa and stretch. I want to tell her I sent off the email to an adoption search specialist and that it's a weight off my shoulders; but I feel too raw to talk about it. As for what my jerkface boss did? Nope, I am not ready to share that yet either.

"Why don't you come out with me and the girls?" she asks.

She's referring to Harper and Grace. We met in high school, and we've been friends ever since. I hung out with the three of them a lot, but Zoey's the person I've kept in touch with the most, although I haven't fully confided in any of them. You grow up the way I did, and you find it tough to trust people. They may not stick around.

"I'm not sure I have the energy to go out," I confess.

She scrutinizes my features. "You do look tired."

"Thanks." I make a face.

"Has he been working you too hard?"

She means Knox-twathole-Davenport, of course.

When I don't answer, she sighs. "Sometimes, I think I shouldn't have mentioned the position he was recruiting for."

I cough. A part of me wants to agree with her. On the other hand... "The money is good," I point out.

"But he's a wanker." Her scowl deepens.

"Normally, he doesn't even notice I'm around, so it's not too bad." *Am I defending him? Why am I defending my boss when he doesn't care about me at all?* Sure, he's tall and dark and has a jawline that could rival Adonis, and his shoulders are so broad it feels like they could carry the weight of the world, and he's so magnetic, every other man pales in comparison... It doesn't change the fact that he's a tosser.

"You're right," I sigh. "He's a twatopotamus."

She chortles, "That's a lovely insult; mind if I borrow it?"

"Be my guest." I smile back, then turn serious again. "He does pay well for this position, though." And I need that money. It's why, even though he hurt me, I'm not sure I can afford to leave his employment... *Can I?*

She nods slowly. "Perhaps, once you have enough money saved, you could look for a new job?"

"Perhaps." I keep my voice noncommittal. If I take on payments to the adoption search specialist, I doubt I'll be able to save money anytime soon. And if I were to leave the job... *Am I really thinking of doing that?*

Something of my doubt must show on my face, for she frowns. "Are you okay, June?"

I blink. *I don't want to lie to her. I don't.* Zoey's been such a good friend to me. If it weren't for her, I don't know how I'd have made it through the last few years.

When I stay quiet, her frown deepens. "Everything okay with your family?"

"Oh, yes. I moved Irene to a retirement community which is so much more comfortable than the Council housing she was living in. I was also able to pay for Jillian and Ethan's first year at university. They're doing well." All this, thanks to my salary from this job. I'm finally making enough to take care of my family, and I intend to keep doing so.

She must hear my unsaid words, for her features soften. "You worry too much about them, honey." Zoey's expression grows serious. "And you're right to take care of your adoptive family but—" She hesitates. "But and please don't take this the wrong way, you know you don't have to overcompensate for the fact that Irene adopted you, right?"

"What do you mean?" I frown.

She holds up a hand. "All I'm trying to say is, you didn't have it easy. You went through so much at such an early age. Has it occurred to you that you're trying to make up for the fact that Irene gave you a home by going out of your way to pay her back?"

I draw in a sharp breath.

I've resisted sharing details about my past with my best friend because

I never felt ready, but now feels like the right time. "You know how I got bounced around from place to place in foster care, until finally, I was fostered by Irene, who went on to adopt me? By then, I was twelve."

"Which is a few years before I met you." She nods.

"What I didn't tell you is that I hit puberty when I turned eleven. I was an early bloomer." I swallow. "Almost overnight, I developed breasts and hips. Enough to attract the attention of my foster father at the placement I was at. He tried to fondle me. I slapped him. Which resulted in him beating me up. My foster mother walked in and managed to pull him off."

"Oh my god," she gasps.

I look away, then back at her. "The next day, I was transferred to stay with Irene, who went on to adopt me. I didn't make it easy on her, either." I half smile at the recollection. "She put up with my tantrums. She told me I could lash out as much as I wanted but she wasn't giving up on me. She believed in me." I blink away the moisture in my eyes. "If not for her, I wouldn't have found a home or begun to believe in myself again. Irene worked hard to take care of me. After me, she went onto adopt Jillian and Ethan, as well."

Zoey wrinkles her forehead; a considering look on her features. "Did both of them come to stay with Irene as foster kids first?"

I nod. "I know it seems like a lot for a single woman to take on, but Irene was determined. She, herself, grew up in the care system and was adamant that she would do everything possible to break that cycle for as many kids in the system as possible. That she was on her own was never a deterrent."

"She's an inspiration," Zoey says softly.

"Oh, she is. Unfortunately, about the time I turned eighteen and completed my final year of high school, she was in an accident. It resulted in her being laid up in hospital for months. She lost her job and could no longer support us."

"I remember," Zoey says softly. "I'm so sorry, June. I never realized how tough things were for you."

"I should have shared more with you, it's just... I didn't want you to feel sorry for me, you know?"

"I'm your friend, I'd never make you feel bad about the things you went through," Zoey's eyes shine with love.

She really is a good friend. Fighting back emotions, I gulp hard. "After Irene was laid off, I insisted on taking a job to help out."

"I bet she wasn't happy about that," Zoey murmurs.

"No, she wasn't." I half smile in recollection. "She wanted me to go to university, but I told her I'd rather be working and earning, anyway. I wanted to do my bit to take care of us. She recovered, but her health has never been the same."

As always, when I think of that time in our lives, my chest tightens. "She couldn't work the long hours she used to. Initially, I worked retail jobs, then graduated to administrative roles. Irene worked part-time, but it wasn't nearly enough to pay her rent. Luckily, I began to make enough to take care of us. It's thanks to Irene, I carved out a future for myself. It's thanks to her, I developed my identity. It's why I'm determined to take care of her and to give Jillian and Ethan the opportunities I never had."

"She's an amazing woman. An extraordinarily strong woman." Zoey smiles. "So are you."

I ignore her compliment; I don't come close to Irene. "You have no idea what she did for me." I rub the back of my hand across my nose. "It's because Irene fought with my school to ensure the teachers gave me the additional attention I needed to catch up with my grades, that I made it through high school. She was so patient with me. I owe her everything. The least I can do is to make sure she has a comfortable home of her own."

My throat constricts as I try to compose myself. She sees the agitation on my face, and her expression crumples.

"I'm so sorry June. I never meant to belittle everything Irene has done for you."

"I sense a 'but' coming." I sniffle.

"But I love you so much, and I've seen you struggle with your conscience over the years. I've seen you work yourself to the bone to take care of your family, and I'm so proud of you for that. But also, I wish you'd take some time out for yourself, for self-care as well, you know?"

I nod. "You're a good friend, Zoey. You've worried about me over the years, and you've constantly pushed me to take care of myself, and I am grateful for that." I half smile. "And yes, I do realize that, like many adopted children, I carry this guilt around with me. Not to mention abandonment issues. And a part of me always feels like the people who love me most are the ones who will eventually give me up, like my birth mother did." I half laugh. "Can you tell I've been doing a lot of work on myself to figure things out?"

"Oh, sweetheart, I can only imagine what you're going through. You are a tough, strong girl. You're the one who rescued me from the mean girls in high school. Hell, you got into a cat fight with them—"

"I was suspended for a week." I chuckle in recollection. I knew I'd get into trouble but that hadn't stopped me from springing to my friend's defense. "And when I told Irene why, she said I'd done the right thing."

"She did?" Zoey blinks. "You never told me that."

"My ma was, and is, seriously, the best mother." And Irene *is* my ma, in every way, even if I do feel this need to search for my birth mother, to answer questions about my past. "She gave me enough space to work things out, while also drawing boundaries, know what I mean?"

Zoey nods. "It's why I understand why you're doing so much for your family. All I'm asking... No, *begging* you, is to also take the time to enjoy life." She has such a pleading look on her face that I have to nod.

"You're right again. I admit, I can sometimes be very serious."

"Sometimes?" She scoffs.

"Okay, many times." I chuckle. "It's why I like to hang with you. You're my conscience when it comes to letting my hair down."

"Good." She nods. "Get dressed and meet me at the 7A Club in an hour."

20

Knox

"Whose bright idea was it to come to a nightclub?" I glare at the mass of heaving bodies on the floor of the 7A Club. The music is loud, and the laser lights threaten to give me a headache. The only reason I'm here is because my brothers decided we needed to do something different than meet up at the members' club next door. We decided to give the recently opened nightclub a try and, so far, I'm regretting my decision.

"Better than you glowering at your team and keeping them late on a Sunday night. Which, might I remind you, is traditionally a rest day," Brody replies.

He used to be the most silent of my brothers, until Ryot decided to take the death of his wife to heart and only speak when it was absolutely essential.

Now, Ryot never joins us on a night out. And Brody? He seems to have stepped in to fill the gap. Connor, our youngest brother, left on one of his research trips right after lunch with Arthur. So, it's Brody, Tyler, and me today.

"Since when did you become so considerate about your employees?" Tyler scoffs.

He nurses his mug of beer in his big, paw-like hands and surveys the scene in front of him with boredom in his eyes. Clearly, he isn't finding the scene stimulating either.

"It's called raising productivity levels." Brody flicks the matchstick he loves to chew on from one side of his mouth to the other. "Which, if you decided to join the business and help grow it, you'd know."

Tyler makes a noise of disgust deep in his throat. "The last thing I want to do is spend my days as a keyboard warrior."

"Is that why you turned down the position in the Davenport group?" I flick him a sideways glance. Tyler has always preferred the outdoors. Of the lot of us, he's the one who most loved being in the Marines. I expected him to rise up the ranks to take on a senior role. But when a one-night stand turned up with his daughter and left her with him, he quit the Marines.

Arthur wanted him to join the Davenport group, but he held off. Instead, he opted to join Quentin's security firm as a partner and take responsibility for the day-to-day operations. Although, come to think of it, working with Q is a better fit for Tyler than being stuck in one of the offices of the Davenport Group.

"I'm not made for the role of a CEO. I'd rather work with operatives in the field." His jaw tightens.

"You'd rather be in the field yourself?" I venture.

He rubs the back of his neck. "My likes and dislikes don't come into play. It's more important I'm here for Serene."

"Have you thought anymore about hiring a nanny?"

A nerve pops at his temple. "Not for lack of trying, but no one has been good enough, so far."

And given his standards, it'll be a while before anyone will be. "Who's looking after her today?"

"I dropped her off with Summer."

He's referring to Summer Sterling. She's our friend Sinclair's wife and is one of the few people Tyler has grown to trust with his girl.

He looks at his watch. "I can't stay out much longer. I need to pick up Serene from the Sterling's."

Brody groans. "Seriously? It's not even eight p.m."

"Serene needs to be in bed by nine p.m." Tyler shrugs.

"To think, we used to stay out partying until dawn, then take more than one woman home to bed," Brody grumbles.

"Nothing's stopping you from doing that. Some of us have moved on from the hedonism of our twenties," Tyler scoffs.

"Right. Ryot is nursing a broken heart. He's a single dad." Brody jerks his chin in Tyler's direction. "And you"—he looks at me with disgust —"you're almost engaged."

Tyler stiffens. His fingers tighten around his glass. Brody, that arse, clearly, did not notice the tension between Priscilla and him when I introduced her to everyone at the luncheon at Arthur's place. The decent thing to do would be to break things off with Priscilla, so she and Tyler can work things out.

Except, how can I, when this gives me the perfect excuse to draw the lines between me and my assistant? Not that being almost engaged has stopped me from thinking of her.

If anything, thoughts of my assistant and her lush lips and lusher hips have been crowding in on my mind even more. I can't get the hurt I saw in her eyes after the announcement out of my mind. Or the fact that she excused herself shortly after and left. And I haven't heard from her since or received any email from her. It's only been half a day, but still. Normally, she works on weekends and ensures the information reaching me is ongoing.

But my announcement must have conveyed the message to her; there's been radio silence from her since. She didn't even respond to my demand to book dinner for me with Priscilla.

"The lot of you are motherfucking old." Brody tosses back the rest of his drink, then slams his glass on the counter. "I, on the other hand, am going to ensure I don't go home alone today." He glances between the two of us. "Don't kill each other while I'm gone, children."

So, maybe, he's not *completely* blind to the tension between me and Tyler. We watch as he stalks onto the floor and is instantly swallowed up by the crowd of heaving bodies. I scowl at the throng, which seems to be composed of people shaking various parts of their bodies in what are supposed to be dance moves but more resemble a jellyfish being electrified.

When I was in the Marines, on break between missions, I'd frequent such places, in hopes of the music drowning out the sound of gunfire in my head. When that didn't help, I sought refuge in BDSM clubs. I'd try to channel my anger into working over whichever submissive caught my fancy. After I was injured, those very women who'd vied for my attention were repelled by my appearance. I had to pay to unleash my depravity on them and help me find release.

I joined the service to piss off Arthur. You wouldn't know it by the way he speaks with pride about the history of the Davenport men in the armed forces. But privately, I was rewarded when he raged at me, then told me I wouldn't get my inheritance until I returned, joined the Davenport group, and married. Which isn't the reason I left the Marines.

At first, I stayed because I realized I could make a difference, and that I wanted to serve my country. For the first time in my life, instead of having a future mapped out for me, I could carve out a path for myself. For the first time, I had discipline and structure. The kind my parents never cared to impose. And a part of me knew I benefitted from it. It's why I took on bigger, more difficult missions. The adrenaline of living on the edge was addictive. The close brushes with death gave me a new appreciation for life.

And while the disillusionment of not having control over my future and having to reconcile myself with being a cog in the wheel of the institution grew, the high that came from rescuing hostages and helping those caught in the crossfire of politics was pleasing. Enough to keep me going. I would've bounced from one mission to the other if, on that last one, my team and I hadn't finally stepped into an ambush.

White hot pain lances through my face in recollection. The scar on my left cheek throbs. Fire zips up my left leg, sizzling through the grooves on the left side of my torso left behind by the bomb that exploded close enough to leave its marks on me. It killed many of my team and forced me into months of rehabilitation before I could leave the hospital. It forced me to take early retirement. I resented it, but also was secretly grateful not to have to return to the memories swirling so close to the surface of my subconscious mind.

I turn and gesture to the bartender for another drink.

"Hey, isn't that your assistant?" Tyler remarks.

I wait for the bartender to hand me my pint of beer before turning and staring in the direction Tyler's looking. Then I see her. The woman at the edge of the crowd is wearing a dress so short, it barely comes to mid-thigh. It's pale pink in color, sleeveless, and has a high collar. It's a dress I did not buy for her, which is the only reason the length of her legs is bared for all to see. Her hair flows down her back in heavy curls, and she's wearing platform heels that boost her height by a couple of inches. She looks fucking gorgeous. Then she spins around— The breath leaves me. The neckline on the back of her dress is so low that I can spot the hint of cleavage between her arsecheeks.

"What. The. Fuck?"

When the man she's dancing with places a hand on the skin exposed by that non-existent backline, anger thrums through my veins. I move toward her, as if drawn by an invisible force, when Tyler touches my arm.

"What?" I growl.

Without replying, he snatches the glass from my hand. "You're engaged."

"Almost engaged."

"Isn't that semantics?" He frowns. "An upcoming marriage to a Whittington daughter is nothing to sneeze at. From all accounts, you're not just engaged, but almost married."

I scowl. "So?'

"So"—Tyler's mouth twists—"instead of being with your *almost* fiancée"—he uses air quotes—"you're about to march over to your assistant on the dance floor with a possessive look on your face that seems to indicate you have a claim on her?"

"I do have a claim on her," I say through gritted teeth. "She's my employee, and she's getting pawed by a man whose intentions she's misunderstood. It's my responsibility to ensure she stays safe."

"Responsibility, huh?" He smirks.

"Exactly."

His grin widens. Unsaid, is the implication that I feel more toward her than I should toward my assistant. Even though I resolved to put distance between us, which is the reason I decided to announce my alliance to the Whittington woman, I'm still attracted to her. I committed myself to a future that leads in a direction away from her. I'm aware that doing anything to jeopardize the relationship with the Whittingtons will piss off Arthur. But none of it is enough to lessen this pull I feel for my assistant.

"Fuck." I drag my fingers through my hair. I shouldn't head in her direction. I should let her dance with that stranger and allow him to put his hand on her hip and draw her close. When she begins to sway against him, I dig my fingers in my hair and tug. And when she laughs up at him, the pain that stabs into my chest feels like someone pushed a gun in between my ribs and fired.

I take another step toward her when Tyler touches my shoulder. "You sure about this?"

I shake off his hand. "No, but I'm going to do it anyway." I shoulder my way past the people standing between me and her.

When I reach them, I grip the shoulder of the man who's dancing with her. He turns to look at me. I bare my teeth at him, and he pales. His steps slow.

"Get gone, she's mine." I shove him out of the way—then place my hands on her hips.

21

June

The warmth of those hands on my hips sends a shiver through me. I didn't expect his palms to be this big, his hold this confident. In fact, I started dancing with him precisely because I knew he wouldn't pose a threat to me. And not only because my mind was occupied with the man I shouldn't be spending any time thinking about; it's because I was confident no one else would be as handsome as him, no one else would be as well built as him. And while *he's* never held me before, if *he* did, it'd feel like this. How weird that I'd think that when it's the hands of a stranger on me.

A stranger who pulls me in, so my back is molded to his firm, broad chest. A chest I didn't think would be as sculpted as this feels. I sway with the music, and he sways with me. Around us, the crowd presses in. A man stumbles in my direction, but the guy behind me throws up his hand to hold him at bay. I notice that his biceps are thick enough to strain the sleeves of his jacket. *Was the stranger who's dancing with me wearing a jacket?* But then his hold on my hips tightens, and all thoughts vanish.

A frisson of heat arrows to the space between my legs. And when he slides one hand around to flatten it over my stomach, my entire body shudders. *Oh my god, oh my god.* It's unnatural I'm having such a reaction to this man. It's also unreal that I'm allowing him to take such liberties with my body. That I feel so ready. That he feels so familiar.

Apparently, my boss is not the only one who can wring such sensations from my body?

Confusion clouds my mind. *Is it possible there's someone else out there who can make me feel this unsettled? This hot, this antsy, so my skin feels too tight for my body.*

The beats of the techno music bump up a few notches. The bass sinks into my blood, the drumbeats pumping up the adrenaline in my body. I find myself responding, the thoughts in my mind overridden by the thumping of the bass. My muscles relax. I allow the stranger to maneuver my body in sync with the pulsating vibrations.

Oh wow, I didn't realize how much I missed the feeling of freedom that dancing brings me. *And when you have a partner who moves with you, who molds his body to yours like he anticipates what you're going to do next... When he slides his hands to the sides of your body, grasps your hips, and fits you exactly over the considerable bulge at his crotch, it's as if you're fucking right there on the dance floor, in front of everyone. And it's thrilling and you feel like an exhibitionist. You feel so, so good.*

I throw my head back, so I've pushed it into his chest, then raise my arms above my head. I sway my hips in time to the music, spread my legs and when the music dips, I drop down with it. It's sudden enough that his grasp moves up to hold my biceps, and when I move in tandem with the techno bass to spring up, he slides his thick fingers up my arms to twine them with mine.

He applies gentle pressure, and I allow him to lead me. With a flick of his wrist, he thrusts me forward, as much as the crowded dance floor will allow. Then he reels me back. And again. Without allowing me to turn my head, he glides his large palms down my arms, over the sides of my chest. His fingertips brush up against the edges of my breasts, and I shiver. My nipples tighten into pinpoints of hurt. My pussy clenches. I part my lips in a silent groan.

Whoa, how can he know my body so well? How can he be this confident in the way he maneuvers my body?

He floats his palms down to, once more, squeeze my hips. Then, with a firm grasp, he propels me forward, and when he turns me and brings me back, my gaze connects with the strip of skin on his chest revealed by the open collar of his shirt.

I'm struck by the tendrils of dark hair curling at the opening at his lapels. By the bead of sweat which pools at the hollow between his clavicles. At the strong cords of his throat. At the firm square jaw with the very slight dip in his chin. The dip which is almost as familiar as the cushion of his lower lip and the subtle V-shaped indentation between the two small vertical curves of his upper lip, and that regal hooked nose of his. And above that, those icy eyes.

I know it's *him* before I meet his gaze. A part of me anticipated it, perhaps, from the moment I felt his big hands on me. No one else could have held me with such confidence. My sub-conscious knew it was my boss before the rest of me caught up, yet the impact of it is like I've rammed into a brick wall.

A shock ripples up my spine. His gaze cuts through me and holds me immobile. This close, I can make out the striations in the scar tissue on his cheek. The way the marks slash up right past the corner of his eye. A millimeter more and he might have lost his eye. I swallow. Once more, I'm struck by how the scar not only adds to the air of danger that clings to him, but also how it lends an air of wounded vulnerability to him. The combination appealed to me the day I first met him. And now, with his hands on me, and his body surrounding me, and his scent and his heat penetrating every pore in my body, I can't deny that the combination is my kryptonite.

This close, he's mesmerizing. This close, there's no mistaking how aroused he is. It's evident in the dilation of his pupils. In the flare of his nostrils. The tight set to his lips. The muscle that ticks at his jaw. The way his arousal is trapped between us. He glares at me, and a shiver of anticipation pinches my nerve-endings. A cloud of heat seems to spool off of him, and when it crashes into me, I gasp. I try to pull away, but his hold on me tightens. His fingers dig almost painfully into the curve of my hips.

"Let me go," I whisper.

Around us, the music increases in tempo. Yet he must hear me, for he shakes his head. "No."

I feel the growl that vibrates up his chest. Feel my mouth open and shut. Feel my insides twist with lust. I squeeze my thighs together, and liquid heat pools in my belly. *Ohmigod*. This pull toward him is crazy. A few more seconds, and I'm going to be climbing him like a tree, begging him to kiss me and throw me down on the floor, and take me in front of everyone. And I can't do that. Not when he belongs to someone else.

"We can't do this." I try to pull away, but his grasp tightens.

"What do you mean?"

"You're engaged."

"Not yet." His lips firm.

"But you will be."

His eyes blaze. In them, is anger, and need, and lust. So much lust. He wants me. From the way he handled my body earlier, I know he's attracted to me. But what I see in his eyes is more than that. It's a kind of yearning that my body recognizes, for I feel it, too.

Sometime in the last few seconds, I've stopped struggling. Around us, people move and grind up against each other. But between us, there's silence, the kind filled with unsaid words and unexpressed emotions. The kind that pushes down on my shoulders and into my chest, making it difficult for me to breathe. Then, someone knocks into me from behind, pushing me into his chest. My breasts flatten against those sculpted pecs, and it's as if I've stuck my finger into an electric socket. The hair on the back of my neck stands on end.

"You have no right. No right to muscle in when I'm dancing with someone else," I fume.

His features grow harder. A vein pops at his temple. His blue eyes burn with a wintry inferno. Anger thrums off of him in waves and crashes into my chest with such force, I gasp.

"You're my employee." His words are like arrows made of sleet, slicing into my chest.

"*Only* your employee, and nothing else."

"That's right." He nods. "And, as such, I'm responsible for your safety. I could not stand by and watch that man have his paws all over you."

"But *you* can?" I spit out.

"I'm your boss."

"Are you listening to yourself?" I shove at him, and he releases me.

"You invited me to that lunch. You made me watch when you declared your intent to marry someone else. You did it on purpose."

I expect him to deny it, but he nods. "I did."

I'm so shocked, my mouth falls open. "You admit that you set me up to watch that scene unfold so you could...what? Hurt me?"

"I did it so you'd realize there could be no future for us."

My heart feels like it's going to explode out of my chest. My pulse rate spikes. There's a twister of emotions churning in my stomach, and I feel like I'm going to be sick. And for a moment, I relish the image of vomiting on him. "Message received."

I turn to leave, when he growls, "I owe you orgasms."

My insides clench. *Oh god. And I so want them.* Dancing with him and rubbing up against him has turned me into a miasma of throbbing need. I want to turn and run into his arms. I want to drop to my knees and beg him to use my mouth any which way he wants. I want to bend over and ask him to spank me, then tie me up and use my every hole to gratify him, but if I did that... I wouldn't be able to live with myself. Not when he's made it clear he's chosen someone else over me. At least, I have that much pride. *I do.*

I tip up my chin, then half turn so he can see my profile. "You can keep yours. I'll get them from somebody else."

22

Knox

What. The. Fuck? How dare she imply that she's going to fuck someone else?

I cannot allow that. I will not allow her to do that. I stalk after her. *I will not let her be with anyone else, only... she's not mine to stop...* I come to a stop. I track her as she walks off the floor and curl my fingers into fists at my side. I want to go after her and tell her this isn't over, not by a long shot.

Only. I made sure it is. I effectively killed any feelings she had for me... *Which is what I wanted, right? Then why do I feel like crap?* Like I burned my bridges. Like I'm making a big mistake. *You're doing this to protect her from you, remember?*

My chest tightens. My guts twist themselves up in knots. I have a sneaking suspicion this cockeyed plan to announce my intention to marry someone else so I can protect my heart and stop myself from wanting my assistant is doomed to fail. *I'm an idiot.*

No matter how many barriers I throw up between us, no matter how much I know it's going to make me vulnerable to be with her, no matter how much I tell myself that I'm wrong for her and that she's too fragile for my preferences, that she deserves better; when I see her with another man, all that reasoning disappears.

I watch as she reaches the edge of the floor and is joined by her friend Zoey. The two of them speak, then Zoey scowls at me. They turn and march toward the exit. It's only because she has company that I let her leave. Else I'd have insisted my chauffeur drop her home... But apparently, she doesn't need me for that either. *Fucking hell.* I'm not the kind to indulge in self-pity...but... This occasion warrants my getting drunk, at least.

I stalk over to the bar to join my brother. The bartender begins to pour me a drink, but I grab the bottle of whiskey from him and proceed to chug it down.

"Something got your panties in a twist, ol' chap?" Tyler asks in a mild tone.

I stay silent.

"Does it have anything to do with your assistant flouncing off the dance floor in a right strop," he murmurs.

I draw in a sharp breath but opt to stay silent. Around me, the music rises to a crescendo. The bass feels like it's slicing into my chest and cutting into my heart. A heaviness grips my being. It feels like I'm carrying the weight of the world on my shoulders. Tyler signals to the bartender for a drink, then leans his elbows against the bar.

"I understand how you're feeling."

"You have no idea," I say through gritted teeth.

He sighs. "You're your own worst enemy, you know that?"

Tell me something I don't know.

"If you have feelings for her —"

"I don't."

"If you do... Then why don't you tell her about it?"

I throw back more of the whiskey, then wipe the back of my hand across my mouth before I turn to him. "Getting me to do your dirty work?"

"What do you mean?" He scowls.

"If you have feelings for Priscilla, why don't you man up and tell her about it, huh?"

His jaw hardens.

"You think if I pursue things with my assistant, it'll result in my breaking things off with Priscilla? If so, you're wrong. I have every intention of going through with marrying her. And you're going to have to watch as the love of your life becomes someone else's wife."

His eyes flash.

"No, actually, as she becomes your brother's wife. Imagine as she walks down the aisle to marry me."

His nostrils flare.

"Imagine watching her at family gatherings with her hand in mine." I goad him because, in some way, I can also imagine my assistant in Priscilla's place, marrying someone else and being with someone else, and fuck, if that doesn't turn me into a mass of rage. "Imagine as she looks me in the eyes as I —"

He grabs hold of my collar and raises his other fist, when, "Whoa, whoa, hold on you guys." Brody reaches us, his chest rising and falling. "You do not want to get into a fight. I guarantee, it'll be all over the tabloids, and that's not going to help any of us." He pants like he saw us from a distance and came over to break us apart.

Tyler makes a low noise in his throat, then releases me. "Next time, I won't let you off." He snatches his glass, tosses back the liquor, then drops a few notes on the bar counter before stalking in the direction of the exit.

I draw in a sharp breath and reach for my bottle of whiskey, only to find it empty. "Get me another," I snap at the bartender, then turn to glare at Brody, as if daring him to tell me I'm drinking too much.

He shrugs and gestures to the bartender for a drink of his own.

I snatch up the next bottle of whiskey, twist off the top and chug from it. The alcohol burns a trail down to my stomach, but it does little to soothe the anger in my chest. *Anger at myself. Anger at hurting her. Anger at how I turned on my brother. Fuck.*

"You need to think this through, man." Brody takes a sip of his drink. "What you're doing, agreeing to Arthur's machinations, is not going to help any of us."

"I am not letting him manipulate me."

Brody barks out a laugh. "You're kidding, right? You do realize, this is going to result in a complete breakdown of your relationship with Tyler."

I stare at the wall of bottles in front of me. *Of course, I'm aware.* "It's his fault, for not being clear about his feelings for Priscilla."

"And you're complicating the issue by agreeing to marry her. And you're doing it, despite the fact that you want someone else."

I squeeze my fingers around the bottle.

"You know, I'm right. You need to do something to put this right, before it's too late."

My phone vibrates in my pocket. My heart stutters. *Maybe it's her?* I pull it out, hoping to see her name, but it's Priscilla. Turns out, I've missed a few calls from her, and this is her...third message. I ignore it and slip it back into the pocket of my slacks.

"And shouldn't you be on your way home with your latest one-night stand?" I don't aim for my voice to come out bitter, but it does.

He shrugs. "Sure, I could, but I'm not ashamed of my feelings, man. I'm not going to stop myself from caring about you and that blockhead Tyler, too. I'm here to make sure you get home safely tonight. You two may have decided to become each other's worst enemies; doesn't mean I have to follow suit. You two are my brothers, and I do worry about the both of you. And I'm not afraid to admit it, either."

Heat flushes my neck. The fact that he's so upfront with his feelings shuts me up. In fact, it strengthens this sense of self-loathing that's been growing since I spotted the hurt on her face. *But I was right in doing it. I was right in making her hate me. This is the right thing to do. She'll keep her distance from me now.* Only... It's not giving me the sense of gratification I hoped for.

"When I see her with another man, my mind goes into a tailspin." I shake my head. "It's as if my brain goes into meltdown, and I can't think properly. None of it is her fault. It's mine. I need to figure out a way to get back in control."

I look up to find him staring at me.

"What?"

"I have to admit, it's not so bad seeing you lose that iron grip you keep on your emotions. Although, I'd prefer it if you didn't take it out on Tyler."

"Yeah"—I take another sip of my whiskey— "it's a bloody mess."

He drains his glass and asks for another drink. "You can say that again."

We continue to drink in silence until the bar empties out and it's only the two of us left. When I can't stomach drinking further, he escorts me to my car. I vaguely remember telling him he's a good brother and him laughing it off. I must fall asleep in the car, for the next thing I know, I'm in the elevator. I reach the penthouse, then stagger into my apartment and to my bed... Only now, I can't sleep.

Every time I shut my eyes, I see her face, her lips, the hurt look in her eyes, the way they turn golden when she's aroused. Her sweet voice begging me to let her come. Her sassiness when she tries to get a rise out of me in the office. Her scent. How her soft skin feels under my fingers. How I want her naked and pliant and pleading to be spanked. Despite being drunk, I have a hard-on; that's the hold she has on me.

I'm so aroused, my cock has turned into the kind of sensitive organ where every brush of the sheet against it threatens to have me come like a teenager. Finally, I give in and jerk myself off. Not once, not twice, but thrice. By the time the first light of dawn creeps into my bedroom, my balls are throbbing, and my dick is sore.

And when the phone lights up with her name, I snatch it up. "What?"

"This is your wakeup call, asshole."

23

June

There's silence on the other side. Before he can reply, I hang up. Then lay back in bed and stare at the ceiling. *Oh my god.* That insult just slipped out of my mouth. I can pretend I didn't mean it, but fact is, I do. Blame it on the fact it's too early in the morning for my brain to have forged a connection with my mouth.

After returning from the nightclub, I spent half the night tossing and turning. I fell asleep in the early hours, only to spring awake when the alarm on my phone buzzed, followed by my electronic clock—bought specifically for this purpose and charged back to the company, thank you very much. And I felt so horrible, in that space between sleep and being awake, that when I reached for my phone to call my boss, I was so pissed off with him... And it's not only because I loathe waking up early in the morning. Hearing his voice triggered me.

I can't believe he had the temerity to walk onto that dance floor and try to stake his claim on me, when he's the one who's declared his intent to marry another woman. And *after* he asked me to book them for lunch at the very restaurant, he took me for a meal. *That was our restaurant, damn it.* It wasn't a date, but it sure had felt like one. And he'd made the effort to find out about my diet preferences, too. And when I worked late in office, he made sure I was dropped home. I could be forgiven for thinking he cared for me. Only, he doesn't.

How dare he claim I'm his? When... *He* can never belong to *me*.

I fist the sheet between my fingers and try to calm my pulse rate. *Deep breaths. It's going to be okay. It's going to be okay. But if it isn't?*

I've pissed him off. I bet no other employee has called him an asshole — not to his face, at least. But I did. *I bet he's going to punish me. He's going to spank me, for sure. And oh my god, I'm going to love it. And...*

Hold on... What kind of a game am I playing? He's almost engaged. And I can't stop baiting him. The man's taken, and I can't stop thinking of him. In fact, I can't stop myself from chipping away at his control and hoping for his retaliation. *I want him to retaliate. I want him to...discipline me.* A shiver squeezes my thighs. *I can't be enjoying this. I can't. This is all wrong.* I can't have erotic fantasies about this man... Not when he's going to be engaged to someone else.

My phone buzzes, and I gasp. My heart bangs into my ribcage. I sit up and grab my phone. It's his number on the screen.

Ohmigod. This is it; he's going to chew me out for what I said. He's going to fire me over the phone, probably. It stops buzzing, then starts again. My fingers tremble. *Answer the phone. You insulted him; now, you're going to live with the repercussions.* And if I do, I'll listen to whatever he has to say.

I'll love the fact that he wants to punish me for my impertinence. I'll look forward to turning up in the office and seeing his dark, grim face. I'll shiver in anticipation all day as he avoids me and only communicates with me via email. And every time I see his name in my inbox I'll tingle with eagerness.

I'll get him his lunch, and he'll barely acknowledge me, and by the time evening rolls around, I'll be so starved for his attention, and so needy for his gaze, so wanting to be the center of his focus that I'll do anything — anything he wants — just so he rewards me. And this, despite the fact he doesn't belong to me. And he never will, he's made that clear.

What are you going to do about it? Pick up the phone, listen to his voice and be swayed enough to turn up in the office? My throat closes. *Or are you going to save face? Are you going to show him, he can't take you for granted?*

The phone stops vibrating. I breathe a sigh of relief, then jump when it starts buzzing again. I can feel his anger radiating off of the screen. I wrap my arms about my pillow and stare at my phone. It stops. And this time, it stays silent. Which is almost as bad.

I can sense his displeasure, his disappointment in me. I can hear his voice in my head, growling his disgruntlement. Can sense his pull. Can sense him glaring at the phone in his hand. I reach for my device, then pull back my hand.

No, I will not do this. I will not give in to this temptation. I might be submissive, but I am not a pushover. I have my pride. And that is not something I will ever give up.

Goosebumps erupt on my skin as I realize the consequences of my non-action.

I'm done. Over. I will not be putting myself in any situation that could allow him to put me in the position of being the other woman. Ever.

A ball of emotions blocks my throat. I feel tears prick the backs of my eyes and blink them away. I will not cry over this man. He has no feelings for me, and never will. He's made it clear there can be nothing between us. And now, I believe him.

So why am I working for him? It's the money, of course. I flick on the bedside lamp, then navigate to my bank's app on my phone.

The second deposit has come in from the company, so I have enough to pay off the fees on the second year of my sister's and brother's university fees. I've also paid off Irene's rent at the retirement complex and on my own apartment for next three months.

All in all, this should buy me enough time in which to find a new job. It may not pay as well as this one, but nothing could be as difficult as this. *Surely, there must be other opportunities out there.*

The thought of emailing applications to companies, most of whom will never bother to reply back to me, has my guts churning. A sinking feeling opens up in my belly. It won't be easy to find another position, as I already know, let alone one that pays as well as this job, but I need to push forward.

If I have an iota of self-respect left, I'll leave his employment. I can't control myself around him, that much is clear. The only way out is to put physical distance between us.

A notification pops up on my phone screen. I pick up my phone, open my email, and my gaze widens. The adoption search specialist has replied to me.

Dear June,

Lovely to hear from you. And thank you for sending through the information you have so far. You're right in that it's sketchy, at best. I went through it, and unfortunately, there just isn't enough to make a difference in the search. In my experience, when the birth file has so little to go on, it normally means the birth mother does not want to be found.

Sadly, our organization does not have the resources necessary to dig into your case and find anything new. In fact, the kind of resources your case would require are cost-prohibitive for most people.

Based on experience, I wouldn't want to take your money when the outcome of your case may not be satisfactory for you.

I wish I could offer you more assistance. Wishing you the best in your search,

Marina Smith

I swallow. When I emailed her, I didn't expect a response so quickly, but here it is. My eyes burn. I thought her services would be too expensive for me to afford, but it never occurred to me that she wouldn't want to take up my case at all. A ball of emotion squeezes my chest.

I click out of the email, then place the phone back on my nightstand and lay back. I didn't realize how much hope I'd placed in this possible avenue of discovery until she turned me down. There's a hollowness inside me, which I normally manage to ignore. But the email has brought old wounds to the fore. I hoped engaging her services would help me learn more about myself. But that will have to wait.

My throat closes. I try to breathe, but my lungs burn. *Oh god. Oh god. Oh god. Now, I'll never find my birth mother.* I'm no better off than I was before. In fact, I feel *worse*. It was a shot in the dark to email this adoption search specialist. *So why do I feel like my world is imploding?* The pressure builds in my chest, in my throat. Tears stream down my temples and into my hair. I turn my face into my pillow and allow myself to cry in earnest.

This rejection from the adoption search specialist, on top of the realization that I can't have anything more to do with my boss, is a sucker punch. I'm crying... Not just for my inability to find my biological mother, but also my inability to make him love me. *Why doesn't he want me? Am I so unlovable? Is that why people keep casting me aside?*

I truly thought I could have him in my life. I hoped he'd come to feel about me the same way I do about him, like the force of my love would be enough to make up for the lack of his. I know he never made any promises, but tell that to my heart.

He was clear—spanking me in the boardroom or taking me out to dinner didn't mean anything. *But it did to me!* My stupid heart interpreted his wistful looks and contradictory statements—and actions—and conjured a future in which we were together.

Perhaps, it's my background that makes me seek out men who are unreachable? Maybe, I like setting myself up for failure, so I don't give them a chance to walk out on me. The boys I was attracted to growing up were always the kind who were out of reach. It's why I never managed to have a relationship before this. As if I can actually call *this* a relationship?

And I've repeated the pattern by wanting a man who's made it clear he doesn't want anything to do with me.

What are you going to do about it, hmm? Are you going to, once more, get up and go into work and book a table so he can take his fiancée to-be to dinner? Are you going to be at your desk when she visits him in his office? Are you going to be the silent bystander as they slowly fall in love? Are you going to be in the audience when she marries him?

Argh! I curl my fingers into fists. I need to do something about this. I angrily brush away my tears. I'm *done* lying in bed crying about this situation. I'm done with *him*. He can go fuck himself.

I sit up, flick on my bedside lamp, then snatch up my spectacles and jam them on my nose. I grab my laptop, and fire it up. Then, I shoot off the email.

24

Knox

You bet, I was taken aback by her calling me asshole. And I was pissed. So, pissed. She didn't answer my calls, and that turned my rage into an inferno.

Then, my sense of humor took over, and I barked out a laugh. My assistant got away with something no one else has before. My respect for her has increased. This woman is going to be my downfall. Instead of springing out of bed, like normal, I lay back against my pillows and contemplated delightful scenarios where I'd spank her luscious backside as a punishment for her impertinence.

I jerked off to images of her pleading and writhing under me. She begged me to let her come, and I refused. I took her to the edge over and over again, until she was reduced to a mass of need. And then, I imagined her on her knees, opening her mouth around my cock as she looked up at me with her big, pleading eyes, and I ejaculated.

Then, I fell asleep, and was greeted by nightmares about my last mission. My run-in with her at the nightclub must have disturbed me more than I realized. The scar on my cheek throbs. A line of pain seems to zip out from it to my brain. My throat is so dry that when I swallow, it feels like my throat is lined with razor blades. I snap my eyes open with a start.

I sit up, grab the water from my nightstand, and gulp it down. Springing to my feet, I warm up with a light jog in place, followed by dynamic stretching. I drop down and flow into a push-up, and another, and another. My muscles begin to burn, and I welcome it. By the time I hit the hundredth one, the burn has spread from my core to my extremities, and a light sheen of sweat covers my forehead.

I move into my set of pull-ups, hit a hundred, then jump up and begin a series of fifty squats. I hold each squat for two minutes, relax, then start another series of fifty, and again. The burn in my muscles is a full-blown fire which burns away all thoughts in my head. The blood pumps in my veins. Heat surges through my skin. And while thoughts of my run-ins on duty have faded…

They've been replaced with images of her. Her lips. Her skin. Her big brown eyes that reflect her every mood. Her eyelashes that can ensnare me in their web. Her curves. Her scent. The way she touched my scar. A shiver runs down my spine. My groin tightens. There's a tenderness at her core that signals I could find a safe home there. I stiffen.

But I'm not looking for a home. I'm not looking for a woman to share my past or my future with. Yet, I told her more about myself than even my own brothers. I allowed myself to hint at my proclivities with her. And surprise; she didn't run.

She's perfect. She's made for me. And I've ensured she'll hate me.

I move onto the lunges, hit the third set of fifteen reps per leg, before dropping down into plank position.

I've shown her that I have no place for her in my life. I chose someone else over her. *Fuck.* My heart clenches in my chest. Agony has my guts in a fist hold. I hurt her. *The only good thing to happen to me in a long while, and I made sure to destroy it. Fuck.* Regret engulfs my body.

I start on my sit ups. When I hit a hundred, I begin again from the top. And again. By the time I'm done, sweat trickles down my back and pools in my armpits. But I'm not even winded. Despite not having slept most of the night, I'm not tired.

It's not going to be easy to get back in her good graces. Doesn't mean

I'm not going to try my best to put things right with her. There's no reason
our working relationship has to suffer as a result of my actions, right? I did
it because she deserves someone better than me. Someone who will not be
tempted to unleash his tendencies on her.

It's why I decided to proceed with Arthur's plan. And I put her in her
place. I broke her heart. I saw it on her stricken features when I
announced I was marrying someone else. And then I sent her that text,
asking her to make a lunch reservation for me and my fiancée-to-be. *How
could I have done that?* No wonder, she threw my orgasms in my face and
threatened to get them elsewhere. No wonder, she woke me up by calling
me asshole. A bark of laughter leaves my lips again at the recollection.

This is what I wanted. I wanted her to hate me, and now she does. I
achieved my goal. I ensured she wouldn't want anything to do with me. I
did it to protect her. *So why don't I feel better about it?* Sweat drips into my
eyes and I welcome the burn. *And why are thoughts of her filling my mind?*

I head for the boxing bag that hangs in the corner of my bedroom. I
could have converted one of the guest bedrooms into a gym, but on the
days I wake up with my head all screwed up from my past, I find it best to
reach for the punching bag without wasting a second. I jab, then throw a
straight punch, snap back, and repeat. Then, I rotate my hips and shoulders, extend my arm fully, and put my body weight behind the punch.
Then, throw a hook. And repeat the sequence again and again. Jab-cross-
hook. Jab-cross-hook, my gaze focused on where my fists strike the bag.

I wait for my head to empty, for that blessed void that comes with
focusing my mind and body on the task at hand. But even as muscle
memory takes over, thoughts of her refuse to leave. *I'm drowning in her.* I
ramp up my speed, moving my weight on my feet as I rain blows on the
punching bag. Pain shoots out from my knuckles and up my arms, but I
don't stop. *Keep going. I need to get her out of my thoughts... I need to... find a way
to make her understand what I did was for her own good. That I have her best interests at heart. That she'd never want to be with someone like me. That I'm not worth
the ground beneath her feet. That... She can do better than me when it comes to a
relationship.*

As for me? The upcoming wedding to Priscilla is a sham. I'm doing it
because it's the only way I could think of to show her I don't want her.
Even though I do. That I don't care for her. *Even though I do.* I can't stop

thinking of her. *And that's the truth.* And as long as I can continue seeing her on a daily basis, I'm going to be fine. *Everything will be fine.* Or so I tell myself.

The thing is, I do need to see her face every day when I come into the office. That's all I need to keep going with my life. I slam my fist into the punching bag, and this time, the pain roars up my arm and explodes behind my eyes. I grab the bag with my free hand, raise my fist, and find blood seeping through the cracked skin on my knuckles. Damn, I forgot to wrap my knuckles before laying into the boxing bag. I squeeze and open my fingers. Sparks light in my brain, and I realize I may have overdone it.

I deserve the agony throbbing in my fingers, the ache strangling my chest, the spasms swelling my thighs. I deserve this despondency choking my throat and threatening to suffocate my lungs. I deserve this and more for causing her pain. It doesn't matter if I did it to keep her at arms-length and ensure the connection between us will be nothing but professional from now on.

I bounce on the balls of my feet and shake out my arms. I need to get a hold of myself. I need to get the hell out of here and to my office… Where I can see her sweet face. So I can assure myself that life is worth living. That I can go on, knowing she's going to be okay. That she's going to be shielded from my presence intruding into her personal life.

Yes, I did the right thing. I did. So why does everything feel so hollow?

I trudge into my bathroom and stand under the shower. As thoughts of her infiltrate my mind, I allow the images to flow over me. The blood drains to my groin, and I welcome that familiar tightness in my balls. I squeeze my erect cock from base to crown, and again. This is all I will allow myself. I will not touch her, but allowing myself to climax as I think of her is, surely, allowed. I swipe my fist up and down repeatedly. All too soon, my balls draw up and my climax spurts over my palm.

By the time I'm dressed and holding a cup of coffee in my hand, dawn breaks over the horizon. I grab my car keys and head to the parking lot at the base of the building. Traffic is light, and in less than half an hour, I pull into my office. I take the elevator up to my floor and head down the corridor. When I pass her desk, there's no one there. In fact, no one seems to be here at all. I glance at my wristwatch and realize it's early.

She won't be here for another hour yet. I try to focus on my work, but keep tracking the time on my watch. When half an hour has passed, I call her desk, but there's no answer.

It's fine, she'll be here. Wait another half-hour. You can do this. You've lain in wait for targets to make a move for days on end in the heat of the Middle East. You can wait another half-hour before calling her phone.

I squeeze the bridge of my nose and draw in a few deep breaths. Then focus on the merger document I'm pursuing on screen. I even manage to lose myself in the details for a little while. When I look at my watch, forty-five minutes have passed. It's almost eight a.m. She should be here any minute.

I give up trying to work and begin to pace the floor of my office. Back, forth, back. I watch the hands on my watch crawl forward. When the big hand hits twelve, I stalk to the door of my office and pull it open. I see her seated at her desk; her back is to me. She's staring at her computer screen. I take a step forward and realize, nope, it's not her.

It's someone else. And she's seated at *her* desk. *At. Her. Desk!* I draw abreast with her, and the stranger looks up.

"Who're you?" I demand.

"I—" She swallows. "I…"

"Spit it out; I don't have all day," I snap.

The color fades from her cheeks. "I-I'm your new assistant."

25

Knox

"The fuck do you mean? Where's July?'

"July?" She frowns.

"June Donnelly, my assistant, where is she?"

"I believe she quit." The woman wrings her hands.

I reel back as if struck by a missile. "Quit?" My voice sounds hoarse to my ears. "What do you mean, quit?"

"I… I…"

"She sent in her resignation." A new voice interrupts.

I turn to find Mary looking at me with a sympathetic expression on her face. *Awesome! Now the assistants in this office feel sorry for me.* I shove that thought aside and train my gaze on Mary. "What do you mean?"

Mary sighs. "I have your coffee." She holds a cup in her hand.

I scowl at it. "That's not my coffee cup."

"Excuse me?" She blinks.

"June knows which cup to get my coffee in." I sound churlish, but what-fucking-ever.

She half smiles, then wipes it off her features. "I understand, but June's not here."

"Why the hell not?" I glare at her, but Mary doesn't seem to notice.

She sails past me and pushes open the door to my office. "Come on, I'll fill you in."

"I don't want to be filled in. I want June back at her desk."

She waits patiently, holding the door open. The seconds stretch. When she doesn't give any indication of budging an inch, I blow out a breath. Besides, I need to find out why June isn't in today. And if she's been in touch with Mary, I need to find out what she said. I stomp past her and into my office. Mary closes the door and follows me.

Halfway to my desk, I turn around and glower at her. "Well? Why isn't she here?" *I haven't seen her all morning, and I already miss her so much.*

Mary holds out the cup that's not my cup. "Have your coffee first."

"I don't want—"

She arches an eyebrow, and because I respect her, and because she's been damn good at calming down the tempers of the Davenport men on this floor, and she's been there for us more than our own mother was, I accept it.

I take the cup from her and take a sip. The coffee is how I like it, yet it tastes different. *Is it because it wasn't prepared by her? Nah, must be my imagination.* I take another sip, then walk over to my desk and place the cup down on it.

"Why isn't she here?" I ask again. "She should be at her desk right now." *How can I feel her absence so much in such little time?*

"She's not coming in, Knox." Mary's forehead furrows. "As I told you, she gave in her notice this morning."

I heard her. I pretend not to understand the meaning of her words. "What does that mean?"

"In plain English, she dumped you, and your job."

Is there a note of satisfaction running through her words? I scowl at Mary, but her features don't betray her emotions.

"She can't do that"—I fold my arms across my chest—"she's not allowed to leave." I know I sound petulant, but I don't care.

"You can scarcely be surprised that she did."

"What do you mean?" I know what she's hinting at, but I pretend I don't.

Mary scoffs, "I mean, after the way you made that poor girl dance to your needs —"

Something which she loved to do; and how I loved it, too.

"—and took advantage of her goodwill. After you acted like a prized idiot, you can scarcely blame her for deciding the job wasn't worth it."

"No one can pay her as much as I do," I growl.

"Sometimes, it's not about the money," she murmurs.

"It's always about the money."

Mary continues to stare at me. Frustration filters into her eyes. "Think about it, Knox. You're not as unaware as you're pretending to be. She's the first assistant who's lasted this long with you. But instead of making her feel valued and appreciating her, you treated her like she was dispensable."

My heart begins to pump harder. Her words hit home. I spent most of the night regretting my decisions, and after her morning wake up call, I was both amused and even more turned on at the fact that she could go toe-to-toe with me like that. It made me want her even more. I've been looking forward to seeing her in the office, and when I discovered she's not here, my entire world came crashing down.

"After how you took advantage of her good nature, did you really expect her to stay on?"

A dull pain stabs at my temples. "My announcing my forthcoming nuptials had nothing to do with my professional life."

When Mary arches an eyebrow, I realize, I've revealed my feelings for her by bringing up my upcoming engagement. It's too late to take back my words, so I fall silent. Mary, on the other hand, has no such compunctions.

"She had everything to do with your professional, *and* your personal life," she says firmly.

"She had nothing to do with my personal life." I set my jaw. "And I intend to keep it that way, which is why I announced my forthcoming marriage."

Mary's expression turns disbelieving. "A marriage you don't believe in."

Busted. *Fuck. Am I that transparent?* I clear my throat and pretend a calmness I don't feel. "What do you mean?"

"Why are you getting so upset that your assistant quit, hmm? She's not the first to do so."

But she'll be the last, for I can't bear to have anyone else in her place. I don't say that aloud, but Mary must glean some of my thoughts, for a canny look comes into her eyes, and I brace myself. Mary's never backed down from putting us Davenports in our place.

"Why aren't you focused on the woman you say you're going to marry?" She tilts her head. "Why are you, instead, fretting about the fact that a member of your *workforce* has submitted her resignation?"

"Clearly, she hasn't read the fine print," I growl.

She levels a skeptical look in my direction. "Oh?"

I nod. "If she had, she'd know that she isn't allowed to quit for her first six months on the job."

Mary seems taken aback. "You had that put in her agreement?"

"She's the best assistant I've ever had. Of course, I was going to ensure she couldn't quit that easily and leave me in the lurch. In fact, I depend on her for my wake-up calls, how am I supposed to function without them?

"You had her giving you wake-up calls?!" Mary's lips twitch, then she straightens them out.

"I prefer being woken up by a human voice." *And yes, hearing her call me Sir first thing in the morning ensures my day is off to a good start,* but I'll never tell that to anyone else. Though based on the gleam in Mary's eyes, she seems to have drawn her own conclusions.

"It's not what you think it is," I snap.

"You have no idea what I'm thinking." She allows herself a small smile.

When she doesn't say anything else, I widen my stance. "You may as well as say what's on your mind."

"You won't like it," she warns.

"When has that stopped you?"

She chuckles. "That's true," she says slowly, then walks over to one of the glass walls of my office and looks out. For a few seconds, there's silence, then she turns to me. "I've always been grateful to Arthur for hiring me, and to Quentin for keeping me on."

I begin to speak, but she holds up her hand. "Let me finish."

Only Mary could order me, or any one of the other Davenport men, and not lose her job.

"I know the rest of you think Arthur is greedy and only focused on power." She sees the disbelief on my face and nods. "And I concede he is, but there's something you may not know about him. There was no reason for him to give me a job, especially when I didn't have the qualifications for the role, and I was a single mother. I was the only one who wasn't cowed by his attitude. I never hesitated to speak my mind and tell him the truth, which is probably why he gave me the role. And when he retired, Quentin kept me on as his assistant. Quentin has since started his own security firm. But as you know, at Arthur's request he continues as a board member of the Davenport Group. So, he comes into the office maybe once a week."

Her features soften further.

"He doesn't need a full-time assistant. But he didn't let go of me. He kept me on and added the role of Office Administrator to my job description, so I'd use my time productively. There was no reason for him to have done that."

"Maybe it's because you're a damned good assistant?" I point out.

"Which I am. But there was nothing stopping them from making me redundant, which they didn't."

I tilt my head. I acknowledge what she's saying, but what does that have to do with the resignation of my assistant?

She reads the impatience on my features and nods. "My point is, you Davenport men each have a heart of gold, but you'll go to great lengths to keep it hidden from your employees, and definitely, from the ones you love."

"Love?" I cough. "What's my assistant's resignation got to do with love?"

"You have feelings for her," Mary points out.

"I don't."

She merely stares at me.

"What is it?"

"Do I have to spell everything out for you, Knox Davenport?"

Why do I feel like I'm five and am being reprimanded for something I've done? Only Mary could make me feel like a truant child, for God knows, my own mother never did care enough to scold me when I acted out.

When I stay silent, her features soften. "You're a good man, Knox. You just need to not hide that from yourself... Or from her."

I scoff.

"You know what you have to do, don't you?"

She holds my gaze until I look away. Then squeeze the bridge of my nose. "I suppose, I don't have much choice but to call off this sham of an engagement with Priscilla?"

As I say it aloud, I know I'm right. I knew I couldn't go through with this marriage when Arthur first raised it with me. It took me losing July to realize how much I cannot see her with anyone else. Ergo, I need to find a way to keep her close to me.

Mary nods. "After which, will you have the balls to apologize to June and ask her to come back?"

26

June

It was cowardly of me to email my resignation to HR instead of sending it to my boss. But needs must. I need to get on with my life, and the only way forward is to put him behind me and move on. I stare out of the window of my studio apartment.

I did the right thing, I know that.

No way, am I going to risk going into the office and seeing him with his fiancée-to-be. No way, am I risking the sparks between me and my boss, knowing he's going to be marrying someone else. It's so wrong and yet, I can't stop thinking of him. Good thing, I don't have to see him face to face.

If I did, there's no telling what would happen. I can't seem to control myself around him. One glare from those aquamarine eyes of his, one command in that rough voice and I'll do anything he wants. Best not to put myself in that situation again. Best not to tempt myself, which is what happens whenever I see him.

I'm doing the right thing. I am. At least, I'm able to leave the job with a clear conscience. Of course, there's the matter of those three orgasms he promised me… *Oh, the look on his face when I told him I'd get them somewhere else! Ha! I wish I had a picture of that. Of course, I'd rather get them from him but—* I shove the thought out of my mind. It doesn't matter. That was *before* he said he was going to get married, and I refuse to be the other woman. Now, I don't have anything to do with him. *I don't.*

My intercom buzzes. I stand up from my sofa and head toward it. I pick up the receiver. "Hello?"

"Let me in, June," his deep dark voice growls.

Instantly, I'm wet. *Ohmigod. He called me by my name, and not my full name but my first name.* And he may not have meant the double entendre but tell that to my body and the way it interpreted it. I stare at the receiver, knowing I need to do something. *But what?* My arms and legs seem unable to move.

"June, open the door," he orders. He lowers his voice to a hush —"Now"—and the command in his tone sends a thrill down my spine. A part of my brain and body recognizes that he's in charge, and I respond. I depress the button to buzz him in, then place the receiver back in the cradle. I unlock the door, hear his footsteps coming up the stairs and take a step back. Then another.

It's not that I'm afraid of him… Okay, maybe a little. But mostly because I know I should have called him or emailed him directly to tell him I was resigning. When the backs of my knees hit the settee in the living room, I realize I've shifted to the center of the area. The door is pushed open, and he steps in. His broad shoulders fill my line of sight. He seems bigger than I remember, taller and broader, and more intimidating than ever.

He takes a step forward and his mere presence seems to suck up all of the oxygen in the room. I draw in a breath, and my lungs burn. A shiver grips me. My knees knock together, and I grab hold of the back of the sofa for support.

He slowly closes the door behind him and locks it. The click is so loud in the space, it seems to ricochet off the corners of my mind. The air around me thickens and pushes down on my chest. The silence stretches. He continues to glare at me, and my nerve-endings tighten.

"Wh-what are you doing here?" My voice trembles, and I clear my throat. *I did not do anything wrong. So why am I so scared that he's here?*

He prowls forward, his gait slow, measured, and so purposeful. And he never takes his gaze off of me. I feel pinned down by the force of his intent. He comes to a stop in front of me, and my tiny apartment feels like it's shrunk in size.

"Why are you here?" I ask again. "Shouldn't you be at the office in a meeting with the sales team about now?"

His eyes flicker. It's the only tell that he recognizes I have his schedule memorized. Not that I tried to do so, but I'll admit, I glanced over it this morning. Force of habit, of course. It's not because I wished I were at my desk outside his office where I could glimpse him as he left his office. Then, I cursed myself for being pathetic and logged out of the calendar app.

"Your phone." He holds out his hand.

"Excuse me?"

"Your phone was given to you by the office. I need it back."

Oh, right. I resigned my role, so I should return the office equipment. I pull it out of the pocket of my pajama pants and hand it over.

"And your laptop?"

That was given to me by the company as well.

"It's uh, on my bed."

He looks past me at the unmade bed placed against the far wall of the room. Heat flushes my cheeks. The sheets are crumpled, and I'm sure the office clothes I stepped out of yesterday are on the floor next to it. At the time, I was too listless to gather the strength to drop them into the laundry basket.

But I refuse to be embarrassed by how I live. This is my space. I'm not his assistant here... I'm not his assistant, period. I quit, remember? I pivot and head to my bed. I pick up the laptop from where I placed it earlier, then straighten and gasp. He's standing right behind me. I didn't hear him move. For a such big man, he's silent and walks with a precision, an economy of motion, that I've always admired. A testament to his military training. I tilt my head back, and further back, until our gazes clash. A cloud of heat spools off his chest and crashes into me.

I stumble back...and he moves forward. Which in turn, causes me to take a few more steps. He stalks forward, and I keep moving back, until I hit the side of the bed and sit on it heavily. He comes to a halt in front of me. And now, I'm at eye-level with his crotch. His tented crotch, which hints that he's aroused? Or perhaps, that's just his resting dick state. Not that I've seen said dick in all its naked glory. And now, I never will. In fact, I shouldn't be thinking of his naked cock because he's going to marry someone else.

"You should leave." I glance away.

"Don't tell me what to do." His voice is tight and annoyed, and for some reason, the fact he's let those emotions slip fills me with satisfaction.

"I'm not your employee, anymore," I point out.

"Is that right?"

The smug tone in his voice has me glancing up at him again. But when our gazes meet, I realize it's a mistake. Once again, I'm drawn into the depths of those cobalt irises. I'm frozen by the frosty blaze crackling in them. I'm pulled into him again, and damn, I so wanted to avoid this from happening.

I jump up to my feet, only now I brush up against him from thigh to hip, and my breasts, covered only by the thin fabric of my pajama top, brush against his chest. He inhales sharply. The sound echoes the turmoil in my mind. I shouldn't feel this attracted to him. I need to put distance between us. *Right now.* I raise the laptop and push it into his chest. And when he brings up his hands to accept the device, I sidle away. He doesn't stop me. *I'm not disappointed. I'm not.*

I jump up and around the bed to put some distance between us. Not that it helps, because somehow, facing him across the expanse of the mattress feels too intimate.

"You shouldn't be here," I gulp.

"Why is that?" he asks casually, and I narrow my gaze. Typical man. He thinks he can get away with anything. And apparently, I need to spell things out for him. Well, fine. I can do that.

"Because you're marrying someone else," I say through gritted teeth.

"No, I'm not."

"You—" I stop mid tirade. *Did he just say—* "Did you say—"

"I broke it off with Priscilla. I stopped by her place before I came over to see you."

"You broke it off with her?" I'm parroting his words, but really, I'm finding it difficult to get my head around what he's saying.

He nods. "Turns out, she was vastly relieved. Like me, she was being pressured into it. By her brother. And like me, she realized as soon as the engagement was announced that it was a mistake."

"A... Mistake?" I rub at my temple, trying to digest this turn of events. "So... You... You're *not* marrying her?"

"That's what I said." His lips thin. A muscle flexes at his jaw. He seems angry, and I don't understand why. Unless—

"But why? I thought your grandfather was keen on an alliance with her family. Aren't they as rich and almost as powerful as the Davenports? Didn't he want the two families united by marriage? And won't this risk your own position within the Davenports?"

"Worried about me?" he asks in a silky voice.

A flush courses through my cheeks. "I'm not."

"And you've been listening to office gossip, if you know about the feud between the Davenports and the Whittingtons."

Busted. I shuffle my feet, then tip up my chin, "It's... *Was* my responsibility to keep my ear to the ground so I knew what was being discussed and could bring anything of importance to your notice."

He nods slowly. "The ever-efficient Ms. June Donnelly. Executive Assistant par excellence, who delivers on her role with ruthless proficiency."

I frown. "Are you making fun of me?"

"Not at all. Just appreciative of your professionalism, is all."

"Now you *are* making fun of me."

"I told you already, I'm not. And it's your fault I broke it off with her."

I gape at him. "M-my fault? I don't understand."

"Priscilla's convinced I have a thing for you; so is Mary, for that matter."

The way he says 'thing' in a caustic tone has my cheeks blazing.

"I told both of them they were mistaken, but there's no changing their minds." He looks me up and down. There's anger in his tone, but his gaze... It's confused, and filled with lust, and something else. Reluctance. That he's attracted to me, I'm aware, but just how much he's been trying to resist it is something I now realize. It's empowering, but also confirms, there's no chance of any kind of relationship between us.

"Well, you did chase me that day in the gym—"

"And bend you over the conference table and spank you. And made you almost come at the royal reception. Also, I haven't forgotten that I promised you three orgasms." He nods. "Which goes to show, there's chemistry between us, which will be helpful."

"Helpful?" I shake my head to clear it. *What is he talking about?* "Sorry, I'm not following you. Anyway, it doesn't matter because I quit this morning." The words are out before I can second-guess myself. Not sure why I put it out there. Perhaps, to remind him that the boss-employee relationship between us no longer exists?

"And I'm here to accept your resignation."

A hot sensation squeezes my chest. My stomach feels like a black hole has opened up in it. *Why am I disappointed? Did I expect him to come here and tell me he wants me back? And even if he did, it's not like I would've accepted it.* Not even now that he's not going to marry someone else, for he'll never be within my reach.

Knox Davenport, former Marine, now CEO within the Davenport group, is a billionaire and one of the most eligible bachelors in the world. I am no longer his assistant. Our association has ended. *So why can't I stop myself from hoping he's here to ask me to work for him again. It was your choice to leave, remember? And it was the right choice.* I set my jaw, "If that's all..."

"It isn't."

His voice is stern and deliciously firm. And has a compulsiveness to it that I can't resist. I haven't been able to resist him from the moment I laid eyes on him. He, on the other hand— I tamp down on my thoughts and look at him from under my eyelashes.

"I have another job for you."

"A job?" I scan his features, and the gleam in his eyes sends my pulse rate into overdrive. The hair on the back of my neck rises. *Whatever he's going to say next, is not something that I want to hear... Do I?*

"A job." He nods.

"What..." I clear my throat. "What is it?" The words leave my mouth before I can stop them.

His lips twist. "Marry me."

27

Knox

"Not for real, of course," I add.

Her eyes bug out. It would be almost comical, but for the fact that I'm being perfectly serious about my proposition.

"You want to fake marry me?" Her tone is puzzled.

And rightly so. I went by Priscilla's place right after my discussion with Mary. Priscilla told me she sensed I had feelings for my assistant at the lunch at Arthur's place when we announced our engagement. She accepted my decision to break off the engagement with relief, not least because she has feelings for Tyler. No, she didn't admit that, but it seems clear.

I insisted I'd be the one to break the news to Arthur and her brother Toren. She was grateful, and the two of us discussed the best way to do it.

The mess is my fault, and I should be the one to clear it up. I'm sure she's a perfectly fine person, but we hardly know each other. I should have known there'd be no future for us, not when I'm so preoccupied with my assistant and the things I want to do to her.

Now, I widen my stance. I needed to find a solution to deliver on

Arthur's stipulation, else Gramps was sure to hold it over me, and I really want that house in Cumbria. It's only when I walked in here and saw my assistant that I realized what my subconscious had planned all along. And the more I think about it now, the more it seems like this is the only way out.

"I want you to be my wife for all practical purposes, except in the real sense."

The furrow between her eyebrows deepens. "So, there will be—"

"No fucking." Not because I don't want to fuck her, but because she's too pure for me. If I touch her, I won't be able to hold back from sullying her with the kind of filth I'm into. And no way, am I letting that happen.

Her already pink cheeks blaze crimson.

"And now, you're thinking this means I won't deliver on the orgasms, but I will."

She gapes. A myriad of expressions crosses her face, and she seems incapable of speaking.

I raise my palm and wiggle my fingers. "I don't need to fuck you to make you finish."

Her gaze widens.

"And I'll make it worth your while."

Golden sparks ignite in her eyes. "You'll make it worth my while?" Her voice is high.

"I'll pay for your mother's living arrangements and any care she may need in the future, so you won't need to worry about that anymore. I'll buy your apartment for you. I'll also take care of your siblings' university fees, and ensure they have jobs waiting for when they graduate."

She begins to speak, but I hold up my hand.

"Or if they want to study further, I'll ensure they get admission into the best schools in the world. And pay for it. I'll also put money in trust funds for them, so they'll be set for life."

"Trust funds? For them?" she asks in a faint voice.

"And I'll pay off all your student loan debts and ensure you also have a trust fund, so you can do as you want with the money from the interest it brings you."

She wraps her arms about her waist, "Hold on, you're saying that—"

"That all of your and your family's material needs will be taken care of.

If you agree to marry me." *I'm aware, I'm pulling out all the stops, but I need her to say yes.*

She swallows. "And I'd be your wife, only in name?"

"For all practical purposes, to the world and to my family, you'd be mine."

Mine. Mine. Mine. She was mine from the moment I saw her. It's why I'm going to protect her from my need to own her, and break her, and make her submit to my needs. Because, while she's a natural submissive, I can't do that to her. She's not strong enough to endure the things I want to do to her.

A shadow darkens her eyes; her lips turn down. Then she collects herself and angles her chin upwards. "I... I need a moment." She walks around the bed and toward the kitchenette. She fills a glass with water from the tap and drinks from it.

I watch her carefully, knowing she's buying time, and allow it. I need her to consider this before she agrees. I want her to understand that this proposal is going to benefit her. "Surely, you can see that this is a win-win for the both of us?"

"So, all my financial difficulties are over, and you get to keep your word to your grandfather."

"Exactly."

She turns to face me. "You're buying my agreement to marry you?"

I allow myself a small smile. "If it feels better, you can tell yourself that you're accepting my proposal for the sake of your family."

She narrows her gaze.

"Your mother experienced a lot of challenges raising you. Surely, you want to make sure the rest of her life is comfortable. And you want to make sure your siblings have the kind of future they deserve."

She swallows. A look of helplessness flits across her features, and for a second, I allow myself to feel contrite. *I'm pressing my advantage, but what else can I do?* I must provide an alternative when I tell my grandfather I'm not proceeding according to his plan. And this way, I can ensure she's always within my purview. I can ensure she doesn't end up with anyone else. *Is that selfish? Maybe. But I'm also helping her and her family out, right?*

When she hesitates, I walk in her direction and come to a halt when I'm a foot away from her. I don't want it to seem like I'm trying to overly influence her. *Even though I am. I mean, I'm not ordering her to marry me, knowing she'd agree if I did.* That subservient part of her needs to be told what to do. I'm the man for that, I'm aware; and while I could use it to sway her to agree to my arrangement, I'd prefer she arrive at that decision herself. *However, I am going to coax her along in that direction. Surely, you can't blame me for doing so.*

"There's something else I can do for you; something that money cannot buy."

"Oh?" She looks at me with suspicion. "What's that?"

It's something I've been saving up as a last resort to convince her, and much as I hate to use it, I don't think I have a choice. I slide my hand into my pocket, then offer, "I can help you track down your birth family."

28

June

I stare at him in shock. He knows I'm adopted? He knows I'm searching for my birth family? Or, I've been trying to and I haven't had much luck, so far. "How—" I begin, but he cuts me off.

"I had you investigated when you joined as my assistant."

I remember agreeing to being investigated when I signed the contract with the HR manager. I wouldn't have expected someone as high profile and as powerful as him to hire me without vetting me. But that he knows such intimate details about me feels intrusive. But it also makes me feel special. Makes me feel like he's chosen me. I had his attention, for that amount of time, at least. It doesn't completely negate the fact that he intruded on something very private.

He must see the conflicting emotions on my features, for he raises his hand. "I realize I overstepped boundaries, but I'm not going to apologize."

Of course, he's not. "Oh?" I'm not upset he said that, but I definitely am curious why he'd do so.

He nods. "You're my employee. You're the one who works closest with me. You see more of me on a daily basis than my family or anyone else in that office. It gives me the right to ensure you're taken care of."

I blink slowly. *He wants to take care of me?* "Is that why you're coercing me to marry you? The ultimate form of protection, as it were?"

For a moment, he resembles a kid caught with his hand in the cookie jar. *Busted.* His nod is almost imperceptible as he ignores my question and says, "You should know, the adoption search specialist I enlisted to help you is someone who only takes clients by referral." He proceeds to name someone I came across during my research. Someone so expensive, she doesn't have a website. I only found out about her through an online forum. They only knew her by name and had no contact details for her.

"What do you say?" He inclines his head.

He knows the answer to his question. He knows I can't say no to this. He knows how important it is for me to track down my birth family, and that I need help doing that.

I tuck my elbows into my side. *Yes, I need the money. Yes, it will benefit my family. But I also know Irene would hate it if I sacrificed my future for her comfort. I* get my pride from my ma, after all. Irene went through so much and she never asked anyone for help. She worked three jobs, at one point, to keep a roof over our heads, and she never complained.

She'd prefer I not have the money to help her than agree for me to get married in return for cash, even if it was the kind of money that would set her and my siblings up for life.

But the fact that Knox knows the most sought-after adoption search specialist in the country tips the scale. She's someone I'd never be able to approach on my own. If anyone can track down my birth mother, it's her.

And are you going to sell yourself to locate the woman who gave you up? My birth mother didn't value me and, apparently, neither do I. It's a difficult thought to stomach. I should probably turn down my boss' proposal and walk away with my dignity intact... But this way, my family's future is secure. Besides, if this is the only way of tracking down the woman who gave birth to me, if this is the only way to put to rest the question of my origin, which has haunted me my entire life, then it's worth it, right?

As if reading my mind, he adds, "I'm going to throw my resources behind making sure I fulfill what you want most."

He's right about that. And it seems, he paid enough attention to glean what's most important to me... It's not what I expected. It shouldn't mean anything, especially since he's using this insight as a key negotiating point, but I can't deny one thing—it makes me feel seen by him. It makes me feel wanted. Something I've only ever gotten from Irene. Something I've struggled with. Something that bouncing between foster-care homes nearly destroyed.

"You're the best assistant I've ever had, June."

He calls me by my name, and that draws goosebumps over my skin. When I peer into his features, all I see is his sincerity. He means it. He's complimenting me, and oh my god, I love it. I love it so very much.

"I trust you to have my back." He takes my hand in his, and I almost swoon. A part of me knows this man is shrewd enough to tell me exactly what I need to hear, so I'll agree to his proposition. *But oh my god, if that's what he's doing, it's working.*

He runs his thumb over my wrist, and my pulse rate screeches up. My thighs tremble, and my belly flutters. *Oh. My. God. I'm not over my boss. I never will be. And he's here and asking me to marry him. So what, if he claims it's not for real? Given the chemistry between us, I know it's not going to stay that way...for long. He can claim that there won't be any fucking... But we'll just see about that.*

When I stay silent, his forehead furrows. "I understand this is a lot to take in. I understand if you don't like what I'm offering. You can always say no."

But I don't want to. He's the first person, other than my adoptive family, who's given me so much attention. The first man to make me feel important. The first individual I've encountered who makes me feel worshipped, while also needing his approval. And that, in turn, reinforces my self-respect.

A confluence of feelings overtakes me. This is my chance to help my family. Regardless of what Irene would tell me, I want to safeguard her and my siblings' future. It's what I'd have wanted to do, even if I were Irene's by blood.

"Okay," I croak.

When his shoulders relax, I realize he wasn't completely sure of my answer. And that slight chink in his self-confidence, that hint of vulnerability convinces me I'm doing the right thing.

"On one condition," I add.

His body turns to marble. His gaze narrows. "You negotiating with me, July?"

I shiver. I could interpret his nickname as a sign he doesn't remember my real name, but I know better. The fact that he has one for me, while no one else ever has, makes it special. And his explanation for it indicated he'd given it some thought. Which means, I took up that much more of his mind space. And that...makes me feel unique. Also, I don't mean to challenge him; far from it.

"It's a request." I peer at him from under my eyelashes. The effect, I hope, is coquettish, and it seems to work, for his gaze widens. He's not impervious to my nearness, nor to his need for me. The knowledge infuses me with power. I store it away for future use.

"State it then," he orders.

"I want to choose my wedding dress, and—"

"No."

"No?" I stare.

His jaw ticks. "I'll choose what you're going to wear when you become my wife."

My wife. My heart leaps in my chest. He wants me to dress in the clothes he selects. When I marry him, I'm going to slide on fabric that he picks out. *When I marry him. I'm going to marry him. Marry. Him.* My clit throbs. My nipples tighten. Every cell in my body grasps the significance of his words. My throat goes dry. When I don't reply— I can't force a single word out, if I'm being honest—he nods.

"The dress will be waiting for you when you turn up at my apartment, three days from now, for the wedding ceremony."

Oh my god, that bossy note of his voice threatens to turn my braincells to mush. It's a wonder I'm able to make any coherent conversation.

"Three days?" I exclaim.

"I'm sure you don't want to wait to become my wife, but even I need that much time to get the paperwork in order." One side of his lips quirk, and I realize he's making a joke. Mr. Grumphole, making a joke? It's a testament to how shaken I am by the prospect of my upcoming nuptials that I don't take the time to appreciate it.

"It's...too soon."

"The faster we get married, the sooner the adoption search specialist can get started on your case," he points out.

Gosh, he goes for the jugular, doesn't he?

"Besides, I'd prefer for us to get married so I can present it to Arthur as a fait accompli."

"You can't take any chances with losing your inheritance, can you?" I don't mean for the words to come out in a bitter tone, but they do.

He gives me a searching look but doesn't refute what I've said. Instead, he nods. "That's settled then." He turns to leave, then pauses and glances over his shoulder. "I'll arrange for a team to help you move your clothes into my place. I'll be traveling over the next few days, so you won't see me around."

Traveling? But I didn't see any upcoming trips in his diary. Yes, I have access to it. Even though I quit my job, I haven't lost my access to the company system. Yet.

He heads for the door when I call out, "Wait, there's one last thing."

He glances at me over his shoulder, a look of impatience on his face. I'm keeping him from wherever he needs to be, but I refuse to feel guilty about that. "I want my job back."

He frowns. "You're going to be my wife."

"So?" I pretend not to understand what he's implying. He can spell out what he wants from me.

He blinks. "So, you don't need to work."

I shrug. "I'm getting married, not retiring from the work force."

His frown deepens. I can tell he's going to say no, so I burst out, "You're going to be away for the next few days. All the marriage arrangements are being taken care of. I can't sit at home and do nothing. I'll go crazy."

He seems undecided.

I move toward him and flutter my eyelashes. "Besides, I'm not yet your wife. Surely, I can work until our wedding?"

"And after — ?" he asks slowly.

Goodness, using my feminine wiles actually works with him. I store it away for future reference.

"We'll figure that out later, okay?" I say softly, in a beseeching tone. "Please?" I don't flutter my eyelashes again — that would be overkill. But I do make sure I lower my chin and my eyes and try to come across as subservient as possible.

It works, for he sighs. "Fine. We can talk about it later."

And I'm going to get my way on it, is what I think inwardly, but I don't say that aloud.

He turns to leave, and again, I call out, "Wait."

He spins around, a fold between his eyebrows. "Now what?"

His tone is exasperated. I stifle a chuckle. *Yeah, well, marriage ain't a cake walk, buster. You're going to have to learn to give some ground when we're not in the bedroom — where, I might add, you can boss me around, and 'll enjoy it. As for real life...? I like to be submissive there, largely, but there are a few places where I draw the line.* I wisely don't say any of *that* aloud either.

"My phone." I hold out my hand.

He pulls it out of his pocket and hands it over to me. "You can also keep the company laptop."

"Thanks," I say politely.

He searches my features again, his gaze hard, no sign that we discussed something as personal as our forthcoming wedding is betrayed by his features. He holds my eyes for a few seconds, more then abruptly turns, and pulls the door open. "I'll see you at my apartment, nine a.m., in three days. Oh, and July"—he glances over his shoulder and levels his gaze on me—"you will not come until I give you permission."

Argh, he had the last word, *again. And why, oh why, did he say that? Did he realize it'd cause my imagination to go into overdrive and my body to overheat over the next few days? I'm sure he did.* I wasn't able to sleep last night due to the pulse gripping my core. This morning, I woke up humping my pillow! My breasts are swollen, and my nipples peaked. I drag myself out of bed and into the shower, arriving at work by eight a.m. But he's not here.

He told me he'd be away, but I was hoping to get a glimpse of him. There are no emails from him either. But a look at the schedule for his private jet tells me he is, indeed, traveling.

I miss him so much; I walk into his office. I touch his pen, the smooth wood of his desk's surface, his keyboard and mouse. There's nothing else on his desk—he's ruthlessly organized. He touched these objects, and I take some solace in that. I pretend I can feel the warmth from his fingers on them, but that's long faded. I inhale deeply and I smell him. And when I sink into his chair, it feels like I'm surrounded by him. I lean back, close my eyes, revel in contact with the surface he leaned into when he was here. My blood beats at my temples, and my pulse rate kicks up. My pussy tingles, and I slide my thighs apart. I slip my fingers under my skirt, push aside my panties, and when I touch my clit, I cry out. *Oh god, I'm so wet.* I begin to rub at the moist skin, and vibrations squeeze my thighs, my hips. I throw my head back, and the climax swells my belly.

You will not come until I give you permission.

His voice echoes in my ears. My movements slow. My orgasm fades. *Damn, I have to obey him. I can't not.* I knew that, yet my need had built so much, I had to, at least, try to rub one out. But sadly, I can't. Not unless he lets me.

I bring my fingers to my mouth and suck on them. Pretend I can taste his darkness, but really, the taste of my cum is sweet and unsatisfying. I sigh and leave his office, then go home and pack my clothes.

The next morning, the movers turn up. They promise to deliver my clothes to his penthouse and unpack for me. He left them instructions about where they need to go in his bedroom.

His bedroom.

So, we're sharing a bedroom? My pulse thickens. Liquid heat invades my veins. He may have said he's not going to fuck me, but we're going to be sleeping together. Anticipation clings to my nerve-endings.

I begin to pace the living room. I have my laptop and can work from home. Going into the office has lost its appeal when he's not there. Also, if I go into his office, I'll be torturing myself. And I won't be able to stop myself from entering if I do go in… So, I decide not to. Instead, I email him and ask if I can invite Zoey and my mother and siblings to the wedding.

Then, the wedding planner he's engaged calls and walks me through the ceremony, and I'm glad for the distraction.

The next two days pass quickly—and without any reply from him.

I turn up at his doorstep at nine a.m. on my wedding day, and the wedding planner ushers me into the guest room, which I'll use to get ready.

Thankfully, there's no glam team. Did he realize I'd prefer to do my own makeup today? It feels more personal, rather than having a team fawning over me. All too soon, I'm smoothing my hand down the pale pink dress he chose for me. It's another Alexander McQueen but has cleaner lines than the one I wore to the royal reception. The gown is made of silk that flows to my toes and has long sleeves made of lace. It has a high collar and a neckline that hints at my cleavage, and dips at the back, but not so much that it's immodest. Honestly, it's perfect. I love it.

My stilettos—which are Manolo Blahniks—are in the same pale pink color. I am also holding flowers— a spray of blue forget-me-nots and pink dahlias. They're so pretty.

I'm wearing my contact lenses and, in addition to mascara, I've traced the shape of my eyes with kohl, so they look bigger than usual. I'm wearing a pale pink lipstick that makes my mouth look fuller and have piled my hair on top of my head, so it shows off the length of my neck. I don't wear any other makeup. Overall, my style is minimal but delicate. It's very me. Even if I'd had weeks or months to prepare, I wouldn't have come up with anything better than this. I wish I could call Zoey and show her how I look, but I'll do that after. Same with Irene.

I'm sure both of them would have tried to stop me from going through with it, so perhaps, it's a good thing he didn't reply. It saved me from having to convince them this is right for me. Besides, it's not a real wedding… Not in the physical sense, at least; so, I'm not bartering myself, am I? My stomach clenches. Somehow, the thought isn't very reassuring. And I'll admit, I am a little disappointed that I won't get to know him in the carnal sense. Although, given the attraction between us, I wonder how I'm going to stop myself from wanting more?

There's a knock on the door, and the wedding planner walks in. "They're ready for you."

I turn to face her, and a big smile lights up her face. "You look beautiful."

"Thanks," I murmur. "Did you…" I hesitate. "The dress, and everything I'm wearing, did Knox, Mr. Davenport, did he—"

She nods. "Everything you're wearing was personally chosen by Mr. Davenport."

"Oh," My heart leaps in my chest. So, he was thinking of me, after all.

He said he'd choose the dress, but a part of me needs the reassurance that he did what he said he would. Which he always does. But not seeing or hearing from him for the last three days means I need a pick-me-up.

"Thank you." I swallow around the ball of emotion in my throat.

"Do you want a picture taken?" Without waiting for my assent, she holds out her hand. I pick up my phone from the vanity stool near the mirror and offer it to her. She takes a few pictures of me, then walks over to share them. Tears prick at my eyes. I'm not sure why seeing myself in my wedding dress is so emotional. It's silly, really. Oh, how I wish Zoey and Irene and my siblings were here. A wave of loneliness washes over me, and I hunch my shoulders.

She must sense the emotions coursing through me. "Are you okay?" she asks in a worried tone.

"Of course," I sniffle.

"You sure?" Her forehead furrows. "Can I get you anything? Something to drink?"

I didn't eat anything this morning because I was too nervous. But the thought of drinking anything turns my stomach to mush. "No, I'm good. It's just—" I shake my head. How can I explain the sudden apprehension gripping me? I'm doing the right thing; I know that. But it feels like a lot.

There's another knock, then a familiar face appears in the doorway.

My eyes widen. "Zoey?"

29

June

"You thought you could get away by getting hitched on the sly?" Zoey waltzes in. She's wearing a pale green dress whose cut is complimentary to mine. It feels like it was stitched for her, too. It looks like the kind of dress a bridesmaid would wear.

"And how are you—"

"Dressed so that I match the vibe of your dress?" She laughs. "Knox had it delivered to me early this morning."

Knox did that? I frown. "Did he—"

"He told me he realized his mistake and that he couldn't marry anyone else but you. He said he decided not to go ahead with the arranged marriage proposed by his grandfather. That he'd proposed, and that you'd accepted. He also confirmed he'd arranged to have the wedding ceremony today, at his penthouse, so he could then announce it to his grandfather and his family as a fait-accompli."

He mentioned he wanted to keep it a surprise from his family to ensure his grandfather didn't pull any last-minute shenanigans to stop the wedding. He emphasized how important it was to keep the proceedings under wraps. Yet he invited Zoey to the wedding. *Did he realize I'd feel lonely? Did he think I'd want some company to back me up?* The thoughts whirl around in my head.

Zoey must notice the play of expressions on my face for her forehead wrinkles. "Is everything okay? This is what you want, right?"

Rachel looks between us. "I'll leave you two alone." Then she turns to Zoey. "Will you bring her to the conservatory in ten minutes? I'll delay things until then."

"Thank you," I murmur.

Zoey smiles and nods. When Rachel leaves, she turns on me. "Tell me everything. I thought you and Knox didn't get along. In fact, I was sure you were going to quit the job. Next thing I hear, you're getting married. And you didn't even tell me!"

I hesitate. "It was a surprise, even to me," I say honestly.

She purses her lips. "These Davenport men are sneaky. I was worried it would end up like this for you."

"You were?"

She tosses her head. "Knox is your boss, and a hottie. And while he was obnoxious toward you, it was clear when I saw the two of you together that the sparks between the two of you were off-the-charts, too. And having seen Skylar getting hitched to Nathan Davenport, and more recently, Vivian to Quentin Davenport— I'm aware that old man, Arthur Davenport, would do anything to get his sons and grandsons married off. So yeah, it crossed my mind that, given how you and Knox are attracted to each other, perhaps he'd find a way to convince you to marry him."

And he did.

She must notice the expression on my features for her gaze widens. "Oh my god, that's what he did, didn't he? He managed to find a way to give you something you want in return for your marrying him."

I blow out a breath. "He promised to set up my family for life. They'll never have to worry about money again."

Her mouth drops open, and her eyes widen. "Wow, that's really something. I understand how that's an offer that'd be hard to refuse. What, you couldn't work me into the negotiation, too?" she teases.

I laugh before continuing, "*And* he promised to help me find my birth family. It's something I've been trying to do for a while now but haven't had any luck.'

"I had no idea," she says slowly.

"It's not a big deal." I raise my shoulder, then massage my temple. "Okay, it *is* a big deal. It's not that I *have* to know who my parents are, but it's going to help me a lot if I do. It's going to fill in the blanks for me, you know? It's such a big part of my identity…" I trail off.

"Oh honey, I understand," She closes the distance to me and takes my hand in hers. "But is it worth marrying him?"

I shrug. "I've thought about it, and honestly, I don't see why not. There are only benefits to it, not the least of which is that I get access to enough money to take care of Irene, Jillian and Ethan."

She opens her mouth to say something, but I shake my head. "I know, money isn't everything. But I'd never forgive myself if I didn't use this opportunity to make sure it benefits them. It'll change their lives in ways nothing else can. Also…" I turn away from her to survey myself in the mirror again. "Also, yes, I'm attracted to him. And I have a feeling when I sleep with him it's going to be the best sex of my life." *Assuming he goes against one of the conditions of the marriage which, if it were up to me, he'd break.* Guess somewhere between last night and this morning, I've come to the decision that if I'm marrying him, then I'm going to benefit from *all* of the advantages of the relationship.

I meet Zoey's gaze in the mirror to find her smirking.

"What?" I frown.

"I hate to say I told you so, but—" She holds up her hands, palms facing me. "But hey, much as I wish you weren't rushing into this, again, having seen how happy Skylar and Vivian are, perhaps Knox will make you happy."

I shrug. "Perhaps," I say in a noncommittal voice.

That's when the door opens and Irene walks in. I gasp. *My ma's here. Oh my God, I was missing her so much, and here she is.* Tears prick the backs of my eyes.

She smiles and comes toward me with her arms outstretched. "My baby, you look so beautiful!"

"How did you find out?" I cry.

Her smile widens. "Knox called me."

30

Knox

Yes, I invited her friend Zoey, and then her mother and her siblings, because I knew she'd appreciate the emotional support. I want her to feel comfortable at her own wedding. Besides, I feel guilty about hustling her into this agreement. It's only partially true that I didn't want Arthur getting all up in my business and deciding to throw a spanner in the works. And maybe, I wanted to ensure I have her hitched to me so no one else can get their dirty paws anywhere near her.

Any doubts I did the right thing are put to rest when she walks up the aisle on the arm of her mother, with a small smile on her face. There's gratitude in her eyes when she mouths, *thank you*. I nod, unable to take my gaze off of her. The blush pink dress she's wearing, while demure, clings to her curves. Tendrils of hair frame her features, and my fingers itch to tuck them behind her ears. Her cheeks are pink, her brown eyes shining, and when she comes to a stop in front of me,

I'm barely able to acknowledge her mother before I take June's hand in mine. Sensations zip up my arm. I sense her shiver in response to my touch, and once more, it strikes me how responsive she is. And when she lowers her gaze, my heart insists she's the perfect subservient for me. My cock thickens, and I glance away, not wanting to sport a chub during my wedding ceremony.

My brother, Edward, who's a former priest and who agreed to marry us, smiles at both of us. The ceremony is short, as I requested. When she says, "I do," it's in a soft yet firm voice. And when I hear my own voice echo the words, I'm struck by how confident I feel about it... How right it feels to take her as my wife. I slide the ring I picked out onto her finger and am rewarded by her eyes growing wide. She looks up at me, surprise and pleasure on her face, and a rush of satisfaction fills my chest.

She slides the simple ring I picked out for myself on my finger.

When Edward announces that I can kiss the bride, she draws in a sharp breath. Apprehension laces her features. She swallows hard, then focuses her gaze on my chest, which is where she reaches. Nervousness thrums off of her. I could insist on kissing her on the lips, but her uncertainty strikes a chord.

It can't be easy, jumping off the deep end and marrying a man she's only known as her boss. Of course, she knows me better than anyone else, given how closely we've worked over the past few weeks. And I know enough about her to know I'm doing the right thing in marrying her. And that I'll do my best to protect her and keep her safe. And that includes making sure I prioritize what she wants. After all, she's my wife.

A thrum of possessiveness grips me. I notch my knuckles under her chin, then bend and kiss her forehead. I shift to move away, but she leans up on her tiptoes which only brings her up to my chin. She lifts her head and peers into my face, and I feel like I'm drowning in her warm brown gaze. A shudder grips me.

Something knotted in my chest releases. I lower my head and press my lips to hers. She stills. Then, like water breaking through a dam, she melts into me. I release my hold on her chin, only to grip her hip. Then, I deepen the kiss, and when she parts her lips, I sweep my tongue inside and over hers. Lust zips down to my groin. My thighs tighten. I pull her closer. A moan spills from her lips, and I swallow it down. I continue kissing her and drinking in her sweet taste. And when she sways against me, I tighten my hold on her. *I'm never letting her go. Never.* The thought brings a cold sweat to my forehead. I release her and step back, making sure to hold her until she finds her balance.

She has a dazed look in her eyes. Her lips are swollen from my kiss, and the flush on her cheeks has deepened. The sound of clapping reaches me. I look up to find her mother wiping tears from her eyes. I visited Irene last night and told her I was marrying her daughter. And when I explained to her that I wanted her presence to be a surprise for my wife, a pleased look came into her eyes. Now, she walks over to us and takes my wife's hand in hers.

"You make a beautiful bride."

"Irene"—my wife swallows—"I'm sorry I didn't tell you earlier."

"I won't say that I've forgiven you for that, but your husband told me it was his idea to get married so quickly. I'm grateful you two decided to get married here, instead of eloping."

"Eloping?" My wife darts a confused look in my direction.

The thought had occurred to me, but I decided it'd be best to confront Arthur with the news right after the wedding, rather than risk him finding out about it. Hence, I decided to use the conservatory at my penthouse as the venue.

"He was insistent that I not call and tell you I was coming. Seems he wanted it to be a surprise for you."

This time, when my wife shoots me a glance, there's a question on her face.

I shrug. "Thought it would make a good wedding gift."

She frowns but doesn't comment.

Then Irene turns to me. "Mind if we talk alone for a moment? Everything happened so quickly last night, I didn't have a chance to form my thoughts. But if you have a few seconds..."

I nod. "Of course."

My wife narrows her gaze on her mother, "Irene," she begins in a warning voice, but Irene waves her away.

"I merely want to talk to my son-in-law; I'm sure, he won't mind."

"I'd be more than happy to spend time with you," I say politely, and gesture for her to lead the way.

She walks over to stand by one of the glass walls of the conservatory that looks out over the city. I reach her, and both of us peruse the view for a few seconds.

"When June came to me, she'd already been through ten foster homes, in eleven years. That's a lot of displacement for a young girl," she says in a contemplative voice.

The investigator I employed to look into my assistant's background when I hired her shared this information with me. I gave him a big enough budget that he was able to pay off people and dig out details about her background in the system. I don't comment, realizing Irene has something she wants to get off her chest.

"I was initially her foster carer, you know? But I fell in love with that stubborn, mixed-up, misunderstood, crying-out-for-attention, eleven-year-old. Perhaps I saw something of myself in her. I, too, had been there."

"You were adopted?" I venture.

"I wasn't, unfortunately. I was a problem child. Prospective adopters avoided me. I had a reputation similar to June's by the time I reached her age. It's probably why I decided to adopt her." Her smile is a little sad. "I wanted to give her the benefit of the stability, I never found as a child. A chance at a future I never had. And yes, I was probably being selfish."

"How's that?"

She folds her arms across her chest. "No-one adopted me. But by adopting June, I was trying to heal some of the wounds from my past. At least, I realized that in retrospect. But no matter what my reasons were, adopting that girl was the best thing that happened to me. She filled my life with hope and joy; and challenges." She laughs, this time in delight. "Oh, she challenged my authority at every turn, but I made it clear to her it wasn't up for debate. I told her when she was done rebelling and ready to give herself a chance, I'd be there for her."

I look at Irene with fresh respect. "And she took the opportunity you offered her."

"She did." Irene nods with satisfaction. "The day she came home and told me she'd gotten an A in class was the most incredible feeling of my life. And when she called me Mom—" She swallows. "It's a memory I'll never forget. Of course, I didn't stop there. Seeing her thrive was so satisfying I went on to adopt Jillian and Ethan. I finally had a family. A unit of my own, which I'd stopped believing was ever going to happen."

We stand silently for a few more seconds. Then, she turns to me. "You love her?"

Her direct question takes me by surprise. This woman's smart. Providing that insight into her and my wife's relationship, she's demonstrated just how much she loves her. How much they care for each other. And how important my answer to her question is.

I cast around in my head for the right words, then realize there's only one answer.

I find myself nodding before the words even form. "I do," I say, and I mean it.

I'm not sure when that happened. Perhaps the first time I saw June in my office. The first time she touched my scar. Or when I chased her from the gym... Or perhaps, it was seeing the disappointment on her features when she realized I was going to marry someone else. Or when I saw her with another man on the dance floor, and the rage and jealousy ripping apart my guts made me realize the connection between us went beyond mere chemistry. There's something more between us. Something that makes me want to take care of her. I'm determined to never hurt her.

Irene scans my features, and whatever she sees there makes her nod. "My June is a stubborn girl. And knows her mind. I'm sure it took a lot to convince her to marry you."

"It did," I nod.

"And I'm sure, she loves you, too."

I frown, but I'm not sure how to reply to that. *Does she love me? I don't think so.* Especially not, after how I used her weaknesses to convince her to marry me. But I don't need to reveal that to her mother.

"Don't look so doubtful." Irene laughs. "I know my daughter well. And regardless of what she may have convinced you to believe, I know for a fact, she wouldn't have agreed to this marriage unless she felt connected to you."

I incline my head.

"She may not be my daughter by birth, but she knows what she wants. She takes after me, in that respect. She's the most genuine person I know, and I don't say that because she's my daughter. She's an incredibly strong person, and you're lucky to have her in your life."

I nod. "I'll be the first to agree to that." I half smile. "I am lucky she agreed to be my wife."

"Hmph." Irene's expression is noncommittal. "One more thing you should know. I love my daughter, and I'll do anything to protect her. If you hurt her in any way, you'll have me to contend with."

31

June

Whatever Irene told my husband has put him in a contemplative frame of mind. *My husband*—I gulp. He's really my *husband*. I roll the word around in my mind. It feels strange to call him that. And right now, his face in profile as he peruses his phone, combined with the hard edge to his jaw, he's never felt more remote to me.

My brother and sister were unable to attend, as they were in the middle of their university term, but they called and wished me well.

After speaking with my husband, Irene came over to me and kissed me. Irene congratulated me and told me she was happy for me. It pained me that I couldn't tell her the entire truth behind how I came to be married to my boss, but Irene's all-knowing eyes told me she'd already guessed there was more to the story than I was letting on. She told me my husband had asked her to bring Jillian and Ethan over for a visit at their earliest convenience.

Then Knox and I signed the paperwork, officially making us husband and wife. Zoey broke out the champagne and poured us all a glass. I barely managed to take a sip but had to stop when my stomach lurched. Knox also passed on the Champagne. His excuse was that he'd be driving. Zoey looked crestfallen, but then perked up when Knox promised he'd be holding a wedding reception for us in a few weeks.

He looked at me as he said that, and the fact that he was including me in the plans he was making, made the wedding all too real. He promised to invite Zoey and Irene, my siblings and Edward to the reception. Then Edward took his leave, and Zoey and Irene followed suit.

When it was just the two of us, my husband said it was best we head over to Arthur's place and break the news to him. I wanted to change into the dress I'd been wearing when I arrived this morning, but he told me there was no time. Then he hustled me to the car.

Now, the silence fills the space between us. I lock my fingers together, and the adrenaline I've been coasting on all morning recedes, leaving me drained. I sink back against the buttery-soft leather of the Jaguar and sigh.

"Are you tired?" he asks without looking at me. Before I can muster the energy to answer, he slides open the door to a hidden compartment fitted below the rear seats. He pulls out a bottle of juice, twists open the cap and offers it to me.

I hesitate.

"Drink it," he orders. His bossy tone ignites a curl of heat in my belly.

I take the bottle from him and take a few sips. The orange juice is cool, and not too sweet. I take another sip and feel a spark of energy release in my veins.

"Drink it all," he insists.

Perhaps, I'm too tired not to obey. More likely, my body feels primed to obey his commands. I drain the rest, then cap it. When I look around, wondering where to place it, he takes it from me and fits it back into the hidden compartment. "Better?" He finally shoots me a glance.

I nod.

"This shouldn't take long. It's best to break the news to Arthur immediately. The element of surprise should, hopefully, help keep the fallout to a minimum."

Worry pinches my chest. "You think he'll be upset?'

"Probably not. As long as I get married—and it probably doesn't matter to whom—I'm assuming he'll be fine."

"Thanks," I say wryly.

His lips twitch. "I'm not belittling our marriage, or you, for that matter."

"I understand." I clutch the small handbag Zoey passed to me before leaving. "Your grandfather can be daunting, is all."

"Didn't notice you felt that way the last time you let him into my office," he points out.

A small burst of pleasure replaces the worry. *Was that pride I heard in his voice? Nah, not possible.* He was simply being polite. Not exactly how I envisioned the first conversations between us as a married couple. But then, I didn't know what to expect anyway.

"With someone like your grandfather, it's best not to show weakness. If I had, he'd have walked rough-shod over me and pressed his advantage."

He seems surprised at my observation, then a gleam of interest filters into his eyes. "And what about me?"

"What about you?"

"Is that the route you take with me as well?" His eyes gleam. "Is that how you try to handle me? By pretending you're not overwhelmed by my personality?"

"Who says I'm overwhelmed by your charisma?"

"You admit noticing my charisma?" He smirks.

I toss my head. "I'm not going to admit to anything. That'd only inflate your already Texas-sized ego."

He chuckles. The sound catches at my nerve-endings. It's such a warm, masculine sound that I can't stop myself from shivering.

He frowns. "Are you cold?"

"No, I'm—"

He presses a button set into the door and talks into the intercom to the chauffeur. "Turn up the temperature on the heater and also the seat warmer."

He turns to me, "You'll feel more comfortable in no time."

"Thanks." I swallow, unused to this considerate side of him. It's such a sea-change from the man I first met in his office, I'm trying to reconcile the two.

"What?" He frowns.

"Nothing, I..." I shake my head. "You seem different, more relaxed."

His forehead furrows. "It's only... Now that I'm not following Arthur's plan, I realize the extent to which I wasn't comfortable with it. I'm sorry I put you through that," he murmurs.

I stare.

"Why are you so surprised by my apology?" He knits his brows. "It's not the first time I've apologized, either."

"It's not, but I'm taken aback, all the same," I admit.

His eyes spark with anger at that. "Do you think I'm incapable of admitting when I make a mistake?"

I eye him warily. "Honestly? Yes."

He holds my gaze for a few seconds, then blows out a breath. "You're right, and I thank you for your candor."

"You're welcome," I murmur, surprised, again, that we're having such a normal conversation. It's as if getting married has changed something in him. He feels less like that unapproachable, angry, insisting-on-getting-his-way-all-the-time man. He seems more human. Or perhaps it's because I know him better.

"I realize, I can sometimes be an arse."

"Sometimes?" I say lightly.

"Most of the time," he concedes. "And I truly am sorry that I put both you and Priscilla through that sham of a non-engagement."

It's so uncharacteristic to hear him sounding anything less than completely confident of himself that I have to ask, "Why did you do it, then?"

He looks away for a long moment, and when he glances back at me, his gaze is hot. "I thought it was the best way to protect you."

"Protect me?" I bite the inside of my cheek. "From what?"

"From me," he responds.

"Sorry, you're not making any sense. I admit, you are unreasonable, and demanding, and pigheaded, not to mention, irrational and often bigoted, but you're not dangerous."

He looks at me with a weird look on his face. "That's what you think."

I half laugh. "What do you mean?"

"Based on our encounters, you're already aware I have certain proclivities."

Heat flushes my cheeks, then I nod. "Not that I've been a part of any kink-related activity before you, uh...introduced me to primal play."

His gaze widens when I say that word, and his pupils dilate. Every muscle in his body goes on alert, and it's as if he's summoned that predatory part of himself to the fore in an instant.

"That encounter piqued my interest."

He inclines his head. "Did it now?" he asks in a low, dark voice.

My hindbrain sends out a warning signal, but I ignore it. I'm here and married to him. He chose me, not Priscilla. Not anyone else. *Me.* It gives me the courage to lean in closer, to fix my gaze on his mouth and say in a breathy tone, "Enough for me to read up on it."

He watches me with interest. "And what did you think?"

I swallow. "I admit, I was turned on by what I came across."

The pulse at the base of his neck kicks up, but there's no other change in expression. He closes the distance until his breath sears my cheek. My nipples tighten. Liquid heat pools between my thighs. My belly squeezes in on itself, and oh god, I'm so aroused, if he touches me anywhere on my body I'll probably combust. He rakes his gaze down my features, and I'm sure he's going to kiss me. Kiss me. He lowers his mouth close to mine, then he snaps his teeth.

I jump.

He chuckles.

Asshole.

He nods as if he's read my thoughts. "Don't try to entice The Beast, little July; you might bite off more than you can chew."

My neck heats. *I'm so damn embarrassed. And I thought he was empathetic?* Clearly, it was all an act. He pretended to confide in me, only to lull me into a false sense of safety. And then, he insulted me. Again.

I sidle away from him until I'm all but plastered against my door. "You're a jerk."

"And don't forget that."

The car pulls into the driveway and comes to a stop.

He pushes his door open and steps out.

I fumble around, trying to open mine, but he's there. He pulls my door open and holds out his hand. I ignore it, swing my feet out onto the ground, then stand up. He takes my arm and tugs me close, so I'm tucked into his side. Then, he guides me toward the door of the townhouse. As soon as we come to a stop, I try to pull away, but he tightens his hold. Not enough to hurt me, but just enough so I have no choice but to stand still, fuming.

"You'd better be on your best behavior, wife."

Like he has to remind me? I'm aware of how important this meeting with Arthur is to him. Also, the fact that he called me wife sends a thrill up my spine. *Dammit.* I shove it aside, focusing, instead, on how much I underestimated my new husband. How he could turn on the charm to get me to do what he wanted when really, he's nothing but a mean, surly, jerkosauraus at heart. And because I'm not going to let him think I'm yielding to his dominance… I set my jaw and tip up my chin. "And if I'm not?"

His gaze narrows, then he bends his knees and peers into my eyes. "I'm going to spank your arse so hard, you won't be able to sit without remembering the touch of my palm on your backside."

My knees turn to jelly, and it's a good thing he's holding me up.

32

Knox

Her lips part; her breath hitches. I know she's aroused by my words. *Good.* I'd rather she be turned on, than upset. And I know she was distressed by my earlier words. I push aside the regret that coils in my chest. There was a moment in the car earlier when I almost kissed her. And if I had, I wouldn't have been able to stop myself from pulling her across my lap and spanking her, then taking her right there in the car... And then... I'd be lost.

I needed to pull back. I needed to remind myself of all the reasons why I shouldn't consummate my marriage with my wife. *My. Wife. Fuck.* Every time I think of her in that vein, I want to thump my chest and declare to the word that she's mine. Then, I want to show her how I'll use her as the object of all my depraved fantasies when I fuck her every hole. How I'll tie her down and take her again and again, until she's so full of endorphins, that every time the high wears off, she'll want more.

And I'll give it to her. I'll soothe her fevered skin, and take care of her bruised behind, and ensure she's well rested before I fuck her again. I'll treat her like the princess she is. I'll ensure she never wants for anything. I'll...lose my heart to her. That's what'll happen. I'll make myself vulnerable to her. And somehow, that doesn't bother me anymore. The thought makes me reel.

I release her and take a step back, and she blinks in surprise. I see the question on her face, but before she can voice it, the door to Arthur's home opens. A member of his staff leads us into his study. I step inside and take in the people gathered there. Arthur's seated in an armchair, and Connor's in the chair next to him. They're in the midst of speaking with their heads bowed toward each other. Brody's seated on the couch opposite them, looking at his phone. Ryot's standing at the window, with his back to the room. He's the one who senses our presence and turns.

His gaze moves from me to my wife, then back to me, but there's no change in expression. He also doesn't seem inclined to let the others know of our presence. I sigh. He may have decided to be here, but he seems intent on ignoring everyone's presence.

Next to me, my wife shifts her weight from foot to foot. I put an arm around her, and she stills. I lead her into the room. Arthur and Connor look up at the same time. Arthur looks between us, and his mouth tightens. It's Connor who jumps up and walks over to us.

"Congratulations!" He grips my shoulder, before turning to my wife. "How did he convince you to marry him?"

Clearly, Arthur updated the troops on our nuptials. I am not surprised my grandfather knows about my wedding. He has eyes on all of us, as he's told us many times. His way of protecting his family, or so he claims. More like, he's a nosy bastard and needs to know everything.

My wife aims a dazzling smile at Connor. "He can be persuasive and charming, when he puts his mind to it."

Connor laughs, then bends and kisses her cheek.

A surge of possessiveness has me pulling her closer to my side.

Connor seems taken aback, then a sly smile curls his lips. He straightens and nods at me. "You did good."

Brody, having pocketed his phone, is the next to move toward us. "If you'd told us in advance, we'd have been there to help you celebrate the happy occasion." He holds out his hand, and I take it. "Not that I blame you for dodging the song and dance ceremony that Arthur would have insisted on." He lowers his voice. "Fair warning: Gramps isn't in a good mood." He turns to my wife, but I step in between them, so he can't touch her or kiss her cheek. Not that he's a threat, but it seems now that she's mine, I can't bear the thought of any other man — not even my own brothers — being close to her.

"What are you doing?" She tugs at her hand, but I don't release it.

Brody raises his eyebrow at me, but instead of calling me out on my proprietorial gesture he steps aside to reveal Arthur, who leans back in his chair and watches us approach.

I come to a stop in front of him, with my wife's hand clasped in mine.

He doesn't speak; the silence stretches. But damn if I'm going to break it. The old man needs me more than I need him. For a few more seconds, neither of us speaks. Behind me, one of my brothers clears his throat. From his position by the window Ryot watches the proceedings with a dispassionate eye. If Nathan or my uncle Quentin were here, they'd say something to defuse the tension, but both are traveling.

I hold my grandfather's gaze. His bushy eyebrows are drawn down. His expression is one of anger. But gone are the days when he could quell me with that look. Another few more seconds stretch out; then, just as things begin to get even more uncomfortable, my wife steps forward.

"Hello, Grandad. Or would you prefer I call you Arthur?" She bends and kisses his cheek, then straightens. "I know our wedding must come as a surprise, but I hope you'll understand that we were in love and decided to get married. And Knox here... Well, you know how he is once he makes up his mind." She chuckles and gives him a conspiratorial look, as if they're both in on some secret. "He couldn't wait. Once he realized I love him as much as he loves me" — she looks up at me with an adoring smile — "it felt best that we show our commitment to each other without waiting any longer."

I'm captured by the happiness in her eyes. I'm enthralled by the devotion in her features. I'm drawn to her in a way I've never been to anyone else before. My heart stutters in my chest. Without breaking the connection, I address my grandfather, "I hope you'll forgive us not inviting you to the wedding, but we really just wanted something intimate. Something without the press or anyone else, really, and as my wife said, we just wanted to get married right away." I take her left hand in mine, then bring it up to kiss my ring on her finger.

"You gave her your grandmother's ring?" Arthur's voice holds a trace of surprise.

I admit, I kissed the ring to draw his attention to it. If that's manipulative, well, it's for a worthy cause. "I did."

My wife's eyes round with shock. There's a question in them—one I'm not sure I can answer myself. I tear my gaze from hers and respond to my grandfather, "She's my wife. I want her to have it."

Arthur's brow furrows. The anger gives way to confusion. "Why did you agree to the alliance with the Whittingtons if you were in love with someone else?"

"It took me a while to acknowledge that the only woman I wanted to be my wife is June."

His gaze narrows. "Could have saved us all a lot of bother if you'd figured that out earlier."

I shrug. "What can I say?" I allow my expression to soften. "Sometimes, it's the threat of losing someone that makes you realize how much you need them. Thankfully, I realized I couldn't live without her before it was too late."

"You've put me in a pickle of a situation with the Whittingtons." Arthur leans back in his chair. "Toren Whittington is not going to be happy with this."

"It's not as if his sister wanted to go through with it either," I point out before adding, "Just between us, I think she has feelings for someone else."

"Hmm"—Arthur firms his lips, then nods toward June—"you love her?"

"I do."

My wife draws in a sharp breath. I sense the surprise emanating from her, combined with bewilderment. I'm sure she wants to ask me about it but instead, she stays quiet.

He turns to her. "Do you love him?"

My muscles bunch. The seconds tick by, then she nods before saying softly, "I do."

These declarations feel more significant than the ones we made a few hours ago at our wedding ceremony. My heart begins to race. My pulse rate spikes. A bead of sweat trickles down my spine, and I have to call on my reserves of strength to stay still and not give away my discomfort. *How did my life turn upside down this way?* The marriage was supposed to be a way to bind her to me, to ensure that I fulfill my grandfather's condition that I be married in order to stay on as CEO within the Davenport Group, and more importantly, secure the house in Cumbria. But already, it feels as real to me as my past as a Royal Marine. It feels as important as the oath I took to protect my country. It feels like my life has changed in a way I can't even begin to fathom.

I tighten my fingers around my wife's and nod at my grandfather. "I apologize you weren't invited to the wedding, but I'm sure, you're more concerned with the results than how I got there."

His jaw hardens, then to my surprise, he barks out a laugh. "Touché, young man. I'm glad to see you grew a pair and went after what you wanted." He looks between me and my wife. "In fact, to show my approval, I have a wedding gift for the two of you."

33

June

When you said you love me, did you mean it? is what I want to ask him. But one look at my husband's hard features, and I lose the resolve to do so. Knox's scarred features have never felt menacing to me. And his indigo eyes might be cold, but I've glimpsed the tenderness that hides there. His expression now, though, has nothing soft about it. If I asked him the question... I'm not sure I'd like the answer. Chances are, he said it to convince his grandfather of the veracity of our wedding, and if that's the case... I don't want to know. So, I settle for glancing down at the white cliffs of Dover which, from this height, feel like I'm looking at a picture postcard brought to life.

We're on our way to Paris in the Davenports' private jet because that was Arthur's gift to us. A trip to Paris for our honeymoon. I didn't realize what the gift was until we arrived at the private airport located less than an hour's drive from Arthur's place.

My husband hasn't spoken a word since we left his grandfather and brothers and drove there. I asked after my clothes, and he made a dismissive gesture and said he'd order everything we need. The look on his face was grim so, while I'd have preferred to get my own pajamas, I kept quiet. And now, he's back to being his brooding self because he hasn't said a word to me, not even when we boarded the plane.

I shoot him a sideways glance to find he's absorbed on his phone. Which reminds me— I pull out my own phone, which I've ignored all day, and forward emails that need Knox's attention. The rest, I send to Mary, who messaged me earlier to congratulate me and say she'll be covering for me until I return.

"You don't have to do that." He scowls.

"What do you mean?" I look up from my device to find he's staring at his. Apparently, he has eyes at the back of his head, and the sides, too.

"I already told you, you don't need a job. You're my wife," he explains in a patient voice that sets my teeth on edge.

"And I told you, I want to keep my job," I say slowly.

He blows out a breath. "We can park this discussion until we get back."

His voice rings with authority, and that part of me that wants to please him wants to agree right away. But the stubborn side of me won't let it go. "There is no discussion." I set my jaw. "I like my job and want to keep it."

I expect him to pull some line about being my boss, etc., but he simply nods. "Fine."

"Fine?" I stare. "You're okay with it?"

"Sure, it's your job for as long as you want it." His tone is sincere, but he hasn't raised his glance from his phone. How annoying. At least he's sitting next to me and didn't choose one of the other seats on this flight far away from me.

"I have to admit, Arthur's gift of this honeymoon trip caught me by surprise." I try, once more, to engage him in conversation.

He grunts in reply. Seems we went from being newly married to already being in a twenty-five-year-old relationship within hours.

I glance around the luxurious aircraft again, then frown at the approaching stewardess. She has a slim figure shown to advantage in her tight skirt. She ignores me and looks at my husband. "Can I get you anything else Mr. Davenport?" she simpers.

My husband doesn't look up from his phone.

"Anything at all?"

I begin to roll my eyes at the insinuation.

My husband shakes his head. "I'm good."

Does she give up? Of course, not. "We have some caviar, which I know is your personal favorite."

Implied in her words is that she knows about his tastes and that he's flown this jet with her on board. And the way she's eating him up with her eyes, anger squeezes my guts. I slide my arm through his and place my head on his shoulder. "He doesn't like caviar anymore."

"He doesn't?" She frowns.

"I —" Knox looks up from his phone. Then, to his credit, he looks from her to me and, wrapping his arm about my waist, pulls me even closer. "I don't. I have a special wedding night dinner planned for my wife, so I'd rather not spoil my appetite, thank you."

"Oh." She looks crestfallen, then recovers her composure. "May I take this opportunity to congratulate both of you on your wedding..." She lowers her head, then turns and leaves.

I begin to pull away, but Knox holds me in place. "Let me go," I mutter under my breath.

"Were you jealous? Is that what brought about this show of affection?"

"Why should I be jealous? And you're right, it was a show of affection. The operative word being *show*." I look to the side and out of the window again. We're still flying over the channel and the white caps of the waves are visible. It feels so bleak below, but the heat of his body against my side makes me feel secure. I hate that my body insists I can trust him, but my chattering mind doesn't know what to make of him yet.

He runs his fingers down the side of my lace-covered arm, and a shudder squeezes my lower belly. His scent surrounds me, and tucked under his armpit, I feel protected and distanced from everything outside this plane. I sense him looking down at me, and unable to stop myself, I turn toward him and tip up my chin. Our gazes meet, and the chemistry always simmering between us flares. My nipples harden; my stomach flip-flops. Every part of me is so tuned into him, and oh my god, those eyes of his are so blue, and his gaze so deep, it feels like I'm being drawn into them...into him.

"Knox," I whisper.

His nostrils flare. He lowers his gaze to my mouth, and then he bends his head and presses his mouth to mine. It's firm and authoritative, and the moment his lips touch mine, I feel any remaining resistance inside me dissolve. He slides his tongue over mine, and lust shoots through my veins. My head spins. My pussy clenches. I melt into him. He slides his arm down to grip my hip. The next moment, I gasp, for he's hauled me over the arm of the seat. He maneuvers me so I'm straddling him with my knee on either side of his waist. Thankfully, the skirt of my gown allows for such a position. He slides his palms down to grip my arse, and I gasp.

"There are people watching."

"I don't see anyone," he says without taking his gaze off my breasts. "You're so fucking sexy; it does my head in whenever I'm near you."

"Not as sexy as that stewardess though." I curse myself as soon as the words are out. I don't want to come across as needy or insecure but damn, if that wasn't a tell.

He scowls at me. "You're the most beautiful woman in the world, and let no one else tell you otherwise."

My heart melts. "Not that I believe you, but thanks."

His scowl intensifies. "Are you fishing for compliments? Because let me tell you, I've never had a problem controlling myself, until I met you. I keep telling myself I need to keep my distance from you, but one look at you, one whiff of your scent, a brush of my skin against yours, and everything goes out the window."

He squeezes my butt with enough force that pain streaks up my spine. And yet, I'm so turned on. Moisture pools between my legs. I look into his eyes, so dark they're like indigo pools you'd glimpse if you could look into the heart of a glacier. There's so much turmoil in them, I can't stop myself from cupping his cheek.

"Something's bothering you." I search his features. "Tell me what it is?"

Surprise flits across his features. Then just like that, he pulls down the mask I've often seen him wear when he wants to hide his feelings.

"Don't do that," I say in frustration. "Please don't disguise your emotions. I know you feel more than you let on. I know you're much more empathetic than you'd like to come across. I know you have feelings for me. It's why, when Arthur asked you if you love me, you said yes."

"Like I could say anything else. That would have defeated the purpose of this charade."

"Charade?" My heart turns into glass. "You're calling this marriage a charade?"

"Isn't it?" He arches an eyebrow.

Argh, I hate when he answers my questions with one of his. "Stop evading the question. Answer me, Knox. Is it as fake as you make it out to be? Because if it were, you wouldn't have gone against Arthur's plan and walked away from the arranged alliance he proposed and asked me to marry you."

"You think I'm in love with you, and that's why I asked you to marry me?" he asks in a derisive voice. And I hate it. And I hate the haughty expression he's managed to school his features into.

"What other reason would there be for you to do it?" I jut out my chin. "You could have paid anyone else to marry you, but you didn't. You could have gone ahead with the match Arthur proposed; instead, you decided it had to be me."

His gaze narrows. "Careful, you're overstepping."

There's that familiar hard edge to his tone. *Ooh, he's getting riled up.* My nerve-endings crackle. A shiver runs up my spine. "That's not overstepping"—I lean in until my lips are close to his—"this is." I dig my teeth into his lower lip until I draw blood. He doesn't even wince. But when I sit back and lick my lips, a dangerous look comes into his eyes. His nostrils flare. His left eyelid twitches and... *Oh shit, I might have crossed the line there.*

"Um, I think I'll move back to my seat now." I begin to sidle off, but his big fingers cup my backside so I can't move.

"Knox let me go," I demand.

"Too late. You wanted a rise out of me? You got it, baby." The next second, I yelp, for he's flipped me over on my front across his lap. The seat is wide enough that my entire torso fits across it. The handle digs into the middle of my thighs on one side and I grab the one on the other side. Then he slides my wedding dress up my thighs. Cool air kisses my butt. A second later, pain cracks across my behind.

34

Knox

She cries out, and the sound goes to my head. Or maybe that's the touch of my wife's curved arse under my palm. I fit my fingers into the perfect red print left by my hand on her butt cheek. "Fuck, you're so bloody sexy."

She gasps in reply, then clenches her arse cheeks, no doubt, bracing for the next blow. "Relax," I rub at the reddened skin, and she groans. The needy sound turns my cock into an instrument made of stone. My thigh muscles harden. I draw in a breath to calm myself. This was inevitable, being unable to hold back. My wanting to push her to the edge. My inflicting pain on her and enjoying every moment of it. But first, I need to make sure she's okay.

"Do you want me to stop?"

She instantly shakes her head, and the breath I wasn't aware I was holding rushes out. *Thank fuck.*

"I'm going to spank you for sassing me, and it's for your own good."

"How can it be for my own good?" She pouts at me over her shoulder. *So fucking cute.* I'm mesmerized by her lips, still swollen from my kiss. How her eyes widen as I raise my hand. "Face forward, baby; I don't want you to hurt yourself."

"But it's fine if you hurt me?"

"Only I have the right to hurt you; no one else, not even you. You're my property. My plaything."

She draws in a sharp breath.

"You're my fuck-toy. My whore. My slut."

She swallows.

"You're mine, baby—only mine—you feel me?"

Her entire body shudders, then she nods.

"Good, now face forward."

As soon as she does, I growl. "Count with me." I bring my palm down on her other arse cheek, then the first, then alternate between the two in rapid succession. She huffs but counts with me until I reach ten. I stop, then massage the tops of her thighs where the skin bears my mark.

She groans again. "Knox, please."

"Tell me how you feel, baby?"

"I—" She swallows. "I feel really aroused, if you want to know the truth."

"Good." I slip my fingers under her panties and brush up against her slit. She shudders. "Fuck baby, you're soaking." I scoop up some of the moisture and bring it to my mouth and suck on it. Sweet and tart with a taste of cherries. "Jesus, I could get used to your taste." I hear myself speak, and cold logic fills my head.

Continue along this path, and you'll want to make her your submissive. Keep touching her, and spanking her, and turning her on while you indulge your kinks, and you'll never be rid of her. But do I want to be? I understand this means becoming vulnerable to her. But not even that is enough to stop me from needing her. From wanting to bring her to climax over and over again. From wanting to worship every inch of her body and bury myself inside her. Maybe then, I'll find some solace from the scenes from my past haunting me? I pull her dress down her legs, then maneuver her body back into the seat.

She winces, and I allow myself a small smile.

"It's not funny; it hurts when I sit down."

"But it's a good hurt, right?"

She purses her lips, then reluctantly nods.

"It's turning you on even more, isn't it?"

She shoots me a look from under her heavy eyelids. "Doesn't mean I have to like it."

"Doesn't mean you don't need it."

Her lips twitch. "You're a master at turning my words against me, aren't you?"

"I'm your master, baby. Period."

She blinks slowly. "Which makes me your..."

"Slave. Submissive. Sex doll. Fuck-toy. Person I'd give my life to take care of. My wife. Mine." I hear my words, and they sound over-the-top. Also, it's all true. Best to be honest now and see what her response is. The more I touch her, the more I want her, and I'm not going to be able to control myself much longer. Yet, I want her to be on board with what I have in mind. And given I haven't prepared her more, I'm going to have to do my best to catch her up on what I want from her. "Does that bother you?"

She doesn't reply, just looks at me with those big brown eyes of hers that turn my heart to mush.

"July, does that bother you? My using those words with you?"

She shakes her head. "Why should it?"

"It doesn't strike me that you've had much sexual experience."

Her cheeks heat. "If you mean, have I been in a kinky relationship before, then the answer is no."

"But you're a virgin, aren't you?"

She seems taken aback by my question, then tips up her chin. "Does it matter?"

I stare. *No fucking way. I didn't really believe it when I said that.* "You're a virgin?" I cough.

"No big deal." The color on her cheeks deepens, but she doesn't glance away. "Besides, I've played enough sports growing up that I'm sure I don't have a hymen or anything."

"But you've never slept with anyone else before?"

She throws up her hands. "What's the problem? I don't understand."

And neither do I. I didn't think I cared about a woman being a virgin. It never mattered to me with any other woman I've been with. But she isn't any other woman. "You're my wife. Of course, it matters."

"Because now you get untouched goods?" she sneers. "You realize how misogynistic that is?"

I consider her words. "I understand why you think so, but I wouldn't call it misogynistic..."

"No? Then what would you call it?"

"Proprietary? Possessive? Protective?" I shake my head. "Actually, I'm not sure there's a word for it. There's something primal about it. I guess, I feel like this is a privilege, like it's something you treasured enough to save it, and since you're offering it to me, I shouldn't squander it or pretend it doesn't turn me on."

Her jaw drops. "Do you mean to say, if I'd had one single disappointing experience before this, you wouldn't consider fucking me?"

"Not at all. It wouldn't have stopped me if you weren't a virgin." I allow my lips to quirk. "And not only because when I fuck you, you'll forget any other man who may have come before me. But the discussion is moot because I'm your first." I peer into her features. "Do you have any idea how that makes me feel?"

She must hear the intensity in my voice for she swallows, then shakes her head slowly. "How does it make you feel?"

I reach for her hand, then twine my fingers through hers, before I lean in. *It makes me feel like I'm special, like I'm not the monster—the beast—I've made myself out to be.* "It makes me want to hide you away so you're unsullied by the universe."

She draws in a sharp breath.

"It makes me want to make love to you and give you so much pleasure, you'll never regret marrying me."

Her pupils dilate.

"It makes me want to push you down on your knees and fuck your mouth and feel my dick down your throat. It makes me want to"—I scan her features—"be the first to take you in every virgin orifice. It turns me into a possessive, over-protective, controlling, jealous monster who wants to tie you to our marital bed and never let you leave."

Also, I'm using your virginity as an excuse because I changed my mind about fucking you. The truth is, I'm dangerously close to falling for you, and that makes me want to make love to you. But I can never admit that to you.

She swallows. "I thought you said you wouldn't fuck me," she murmurs.

"Fuck that," I growl. "Nothing matters more than making love to my wife, not when I am the first to do so." *Not when I'm falling for her.*

No one else has had her before me, and that's such a fucking turn on. It's as if she's been waiting for me all this time, as if I'm worthy of her. It makes me feel so fucking hungry for her. It makes me want to own her in a way I haven't wanted anything else before. It makes me realize I should have never told her that I wouldn't fuck her. It makes it clear; I'm not abiding by that promise to myself either.

"Oh." She parts her sweet mouth in an 'O' that has me wishing I could turn my words into reality.

That's when the pilot announces we've commenced our descent into Paris.

35

June

Oh my god, his words are so filthy. And I should be disgusted. And I'm not. Since hearing them, my body seems to be running a fever. The wetness between my legs hasn't decreased at all. I soak in the tub of the massive bathroom that opens onto the equally beautiful room of the hotel we checked into.

It's a suite on the top floor of a beautiful heritage building from which I spotted the Eiffel Tower. My husband showed me the closet, stocked with everything I'd need. Apparently, he chose everything and ordered it while we were in the air. I'll never know how they were able to deliver everything so quickly. He ordered me to settle in and said he was heading to the gym.

I checked my phone, but for once, my inbox was empty. Seems Mary already forwarded the emails from my inbox to hers. I snapped a picture of the Eiffel Tower and messaged it to Zoey and Irene to let them know I was okay.

Then, I separately messaged Harper and Grace, bringing them up to date with what had happened in my life—specifically, my newly married status. My phone instantly started buzzing with messages and questions from both of them, but I tossed my phone aside and decided to take a bath.

After soaking for almost an hour, I dry myself, then step into the closet to pull on the lacy lingerie I find there. The silk chafes against my bottom, and a frisson of heat squeezes my belly. I turn around and take in the reddened fingerprints on my sore butt. My chest grows hot. My scalp tingles. That mark of ownership from him means so much to me. And when I look at the ring he placed on my finger, I feel complete.

My life finally has meaning. I was kidding myself by thinking I could take a stab at independence. It means nothing. It doesn't satisfy me the way serving at my master's pleasure does. The realization sends a burst of anticipation up my spine.

I reach for a lacy robe, then change my mind; the array of dresses is too tempting. Also, while I do want my husband to make love to me on my wedding night, perhaps changing into a robe so early in the evening seems presumptuous?

I step into a blue dress that reminds me of his eyes. It's simple, yet expensively cut, with a sweetheart neckline. The lacy sleeves that clasp at my wrists remind me of my wedding dress. It highlights my curves, so when I look at myself in the mirror, I almost blush at how it cinches my waist and accentuates my hips. But as he's told me, he likes the width of my hips and my hourglass figure. The dress hugs my throbbing arse cheeks, and I welcome the pain. It reminds me of the touch of his hands on my butt. I shiver. *I can't wait to find out what he does to me tonight. It's my wedding night. My first night with my husband, and I'm in Paris. Whoa, is this really happening to me?*

I walk over to the window and, once more, look out on the Eiffel Tower. The sun had set by the time we arrived in Paris, and it's all lit up and looks incredibly romantic. Exhaustion courses through me. Must be the result of the bath, which relaxed me to the point that I now feel sleepy. I settle on the chaise lounge by the window and lean back against the cushions.

The next thing I know, I'm being lifted and carried. I crack my eyelids open and glimpse his stern jaw. I'm held against his broad chest, and he feels so solid, so strong. I use the excuse of being half-asleep to cuddle into him. His arms tighten around me, and I sigh. "What time is it?"

"Eight p.m. You've been asleep for almost two hours." Then his forehead crinkles. "Are your eyes okay?"

"Huh?" I look at him questioningly.

"You're blinking your eyelids," he points out.

"I fell asleep wearing my contact lenses. I shouldn't have done that." I half laugh.

"Why do you wear contact lenses, when you can wear glasses?"

His tone is curious, a genuine question in his eyes.

I shrug. "I've always tended toward being heavy. And then I got teased for wearing glasses in high school. Once I started working and could afford to buy them, I switched to contact lenses." And then I discovered how expensive they are, so I only wear them on special occasions, like tonight. I wanted to look pretty for him tonight.

"Hmm"—he studies my face—"I prefer it when you wear your glasses."

I blink slowly. "You prefer that I wear my out-of-style glasses?"

"It's sexy." His lips quirk. "I find you sexy in whatever you wear, but especially with glasses on."

Heat flushes my cheeks. "You find my wearing glasses sexy?"

"Would you be more comfortable wearing them now?" He comes to a stop. "You *would be* more comfortable wearing them." It's a statement, not a question anymore.

"I guess you're right," I concede.

"Then you should swap out of your contact lenses." He walks into the ensuite, then sets me down on the counter next to the sink where I placed my contact lens supplies and eyeglasses. He watches me as I slide my contact lenses back in their case, then slip on my spectacles.

He scoops me up in his arms again.

I squeak, "Where are we going?"

"I ordered dinner, unless you'd prefer to go directly to bed?"

That sounds good, but before I can reply, my stomach growls loudly.

His lips twitch. "Dinner then."

He carries me out through the double doors near the window and onto a balcony, which has been set up with a table and two chairs. The table is set for dinner, complete with flowers and candles. There are also outdoor heaters, so the slight chill of the evening is minimized. He places me in one of the chairs and pushes it in. When he's satisfied, I'm comfortable, he walks around and sits in his chair.

I notice the damp hair that he's combed back and realize he showered. His chin is shadowed, the way it often is when he works late into the night in the office. I know a lot about this man and yet, very little. He's also wearing a black T-shirt which stretches across his chest and jeans which cling to his powerful thighs in a way that makes my pulse race.

"I like you in casual clothes," I murmur.

He pulls a phone from his pocket, and his fingers dance across the screen before he pockets it again. "And I like watching you sleep."

"Oh," — I swallow — "how long did you — "

"For a few minutes. Not that I haven't stalked you before."

My jaw drops. I suspected he watched me around the office but to hear him confess that is... *Whoa.* "What's brought about this bout of honesty?" I frown.

"Figured since we're here and married, and since I aim to stay married to you, it's time for me to be upfront."

I try to understand what he's implying, but the conclusion I draw doesn't make any sense. "You mean — "

"I don't believe in divorce, July."

I blow out a breath, "You mean, we're going to stay married, no matter what happens?"

If I'm being honest, it's a relief that he doesn't believe in divorce. It means... One way or another, he'll always be in my life. Goosebumps pop on my skin. My chest feels lighter, and I don't dare examine these sensations too closely.

He regards me closely. "I wanted to keep my distance from you, but it seems that's out of the question."

"What are you saying?"

The door to the suite opens; a uniformed member of the staff leads another, who rolls in a cart. He sets a dome-covered plate in front of each of us. Then whisks off the covers, one at a time.

"For madam, there's coconut ceviche with passion fruit caviar and avocado mousse." He turns to Knox. "Duck à l'Orange for you, Mr. Davenport. Enjoy." He bows, then leaves with the other guy who wheels out the cart with him.

The tropical scent of the coconut, accompanied by the sweeter notes of the passion fruit, teases my nostrils. I'm suddenly very hungry. I dig in and the sweet, delicate flavor is tinged with a subtle nuttiness that causes me to groan with a mouthgasm. I take another mouthful, and another. I'm halfway through the food before I look up and catch him watching me.

"What?"

"You have—" He reaches over, scoops some of the food from the corner of my mouth and brings it to his. He sucks on his thumb, and my entire body feels like it's about to burst into flames. I take another few mouthfuls, and with each, his blue eyes turn a shade of indigo that's almost black. Our gazes meet, and the desire I see in them sparks a heavy pulse between my legs. I point my fork in the direction of his plate. "You're not eating."

"I'm hungry for something else."

There's no mistaking what he's alluding to. An answering emptiness, having nothing to do with food, gnaws at my belly. Heat streaks through my veins. I'm so turned on, I might melt into a puddle right now. I place my fork down and swallow.

"What... What are you hungry for?" I'm proud that my voice comes out sounding steady; my insides are churning like I've swallowed a washing machine.

"What are you willing to offer me?"

I try to read his expression, but it's closed, except for his eyes. His attention is locked on me, reminiscent of a panther stalking through the undergrowth. Another shiver grips me. My panties are so wet, they stick to the insides of my thighs. Once again, it feels like I'm drawn into the vortex of his attention, like I'm being absorbed into *him*.

I rise to my feet as if in a dream. Then walk around to stand next to him. He pushes his chair back, and as if we've practiced this move, I step into the space between his massive thighs. With him seated, I'm a little above eye-level with him. It's how tall he is. His shoulders overwhelm the chair, and his arms dwarf those of the chair.

He reaches up and in a gesture that's already familiar to me, he removes my spectacles and places them out of reach and at one end of the table. Then he leans back in his chair. He watches me with a hint of curiosity that zips a ripple of anticipation through my nerve-endings. *Does he expect me to tap out? Does he think he can overwhelm me by putting me on the spot, so I'll sidle away and beg off?* I bet he'd be relieved if I did. For even though he seems to have decided that he wants me to be his wife, in every sense of the word, I sense hesitation in him, which I can't quite understand.

"Everything." I swallow. "I'll offer you anything you want."

"Careful." He looks me up and down, "I might take you at your word, and where would that leave you?"

"Satisfied and happy, and craving more. I'm not scared of what you can do to me. I want what you can do to me. I want you with every inch of my body. I want your fingers on me, your tongue in my mouth, your cock inside me, your invasion of every hole in my body, Sir."

I want him to realize I'm ready for him. I've been ready for him since I walked into his office and saw him as one with the shadows in his office. I've wanted to feel the intensity of his fucking since I looked at his scarred features and knew my world had changed. I know I've gotten through to him when he draws in a sharp breath. I know I've said the right thing when a vein pops at his temple. The intensity of his blue gaze makes me feel like I'm on show. Only for his gaze.

I put up my hair after my bath. Now, I pull the first pin from my messy bun. A strand of hair unfurls down to my shoulder.

His jaw tightens.

Then I pull out the second and third, and each time, another thick coil of hair unwinds and falls down to frame my neck. When I'm done, my hair hangs in a heavy curtain around my face.

The expression on his face is even more inscrutable, but his breathing is definitely shallow. It gives me the courage to turn around and present him with my back.

"Will you unzip me?" I clear my throat.

His fingers touch the nape of my neck, and the hair on my forearms rises. This is it. There's no turning back after this. I should feel scared perhaps, but instead, there's only a sense of anticipation. He's my husband. And I've wanted him from the moment I saw him. And this is my wedding night. And it feels right that he's the man who's going to take my virginity.

The r-r-ripping sound of the seams of the zipper parting fills the air. And when his fingertips brush up against the skin of my back, my toes curl. One side of my dress falls down my arm. The curve of my shoulder is exposed to the night air and while the outdoor heaters have warmed the air sufficiently, I can't stop the shiver that oscillates through me.

"You're cold?" His voice is low and hard, and oh my god, I could come from that dark timbre of his tone, surely. That's how close I am to going off, and he hasn't even begun to touch me.

"I'm fine." I shrug my other shoulder and the sleeve of my dress whispers down my arm. I begin to pull it off, but he stops me with a touch on my back. He holds me in place, and when he pushes aside my hair and presses a kiss to the small of my back, his touch is so tender, I shiver. He slides his hand around and flattens his big palm over my stomach. I've never had a flat tummy. Comes from having a plus-size figure. I always felt awkward about it with the couple of men I dated. But with Knox—from the beginning—I've felt small and delicate next to his much taller and broader size.

He slides his hand down to cup my pussy through my panties, and a moan slips from my mouth. He rubs his heel over my already wet pussy, and I gasp. "Knox, please."

In answer, he slips his fingers under the gusset of my panties, and when he brushes my slit, goosebumps pepper my skin. "You're so fucking responsive," he rumbles.

I try to turn to look at him, but he curls the fingers of his other hand around the nape of my neck and stops me. He releases his hold on my pussy and pushes the dishes out of the way.

What is he doing?

Before I can ask, he applies enough pressure that I find myself bending over the table. I push my cheek onto the surface. He kicks my legs apart, and there's a tearing sound as the dress splits up one side.

"My dress," I cry.

"I'll get you an entire closet full of them."

"But this one reminded me of my wedding dress," I protest.

"And I am your husband; that supersedes everything else."

The authority in his voice, once again, pushes all other thoughts from my head. I want to protest and tell him that buying me a new dress is not the same as wearing this one. But the words get lost somewhere between my brain and my mouth.

He must read my mind, for he bends over and places his mouth next to my ear. "I'll get this one mended for you, I promise." He licks around the shell of my ear, and I shiver. And when he bites down on my earlobe, the pain ignites an explosion that rolls over me like a gentle swell after the rain. The climax shudders through me like the tide coming in.

I come down from the orgasm to find he's looking at me with something like awe. "Did you orgasm?"

I blush. "Maybe..."

"It was beautiful," his voice is sincere, almost worshipful, and for some reason, that embarrasses me even more.

I squeeze my eyes shut. "I don't know what to say."

"Say nothing, just enjoy the first of many climaxes I intend to give you." Another hard kiss to the side of my mouth, then he rips my dress all the way down.

I wince at the sound, then cry as he tears off my panties. Bent over like this, I'm aware my large butt must be right in his face. It's stupid, but I can't stop myself from trying to cover my backside with my hand. Only, he grabs my wrist and wrenches my arm up and over my head. He does the same with the other arm, and suddenly, I'm pinned down. I'm at his disposal. At his pleasure. A keening need twists up from my belly. My knees grow weak. Good thing, I'm already bent over so the table can support me.

"So fucking gorgeous." He traces the cleavage between my arse cheeks, and I shudder. And when he slips two fingers inside me, my eyes roll back in my head. He begins to weave his fingers in and out of me, again and again. To my alarm, a familiar emptiness yawns in my core. It's like he's reopening that black hole inside of me, the one that formed when I orgasmed for the first time.

He picks up the pace, and when he stuffs a third finger inside me, I groan. I feel full and stretched, and yet, I already know I need more. "More, Knox. Please," I manage to choke out. My voice sounds needy and whiny, and when he twists his fingers inside of me to hit a spot deep inside that I never knew existed, my pussy clamps down on his digits. This time, the wave rises up from my toes, up my thighs, and curls around my core, before it grows larger and lighter, and bursts up my spine. I shudder and grab onto his hand with both of mine as my orgasm fills me. And when he pulls his fingers out, the sensations fade, leaving me empty and almost fulfilled, but still very needy inside.

Then I'm being pulled up, and he swings me up in his arms.

"Where are you taking me?"

36

Knox

"I'm going to fuck you, wife."

She wants me in all my kinky glory. In fact, she's wanted the unvarnished side of me from the beginning. She wants me as I am, proclivities and all. But I chose not to believe her. I chose not to accept her at face value. I was second guessing her. I was doing her a disservice. She deserves nothing less than my total belief in her. She deserves the maximum amount of pleasure I can give her.

She looks up at me from under heavy eyelashes. Her lips part. With her flushed cheeks and her thick hair mussed up around her face, she looks incredibly gorgeous. A siren who's bewitched me and who I can't stop wanting to bend to my will. I don't want to break her anymore; I enjoy and appreciate her sass too much for that. I simply want the privilege of making her mine. Perhaps, I subconsciously guessed she was a virgin, which is why I held back until our wedding night to make love to her. Old fashioned, maybe. And not how I viewed myself. But since she came into my life, so many preconceived notions of myself have gone out the window. All that's left is a man who is in thrall to his wife.

I place her on her feet at the foot of the bed, then peel off her dress. She steps out of it, and I drape it over a nearby chair. I walk over to the nightstand and flick on the bedside lamp. When I turn, it's to find she's covering her breasts with her arm.

I click my tongue. "Let me see you."

She tucks her elbows into her sides and allows me the honor of raking my gaze down her luscious breasts, her flared hips, the roll of her stomach, her thick thighs, which I can't wait to mark.

"Part your legs," I order.

When she obliges, I stare at the wetness that clings to her inner thighs.

The flush extends down her chest, and she shivers.

"Are you scared?" I walk over to stand in front of her.

She shakes her head. "More excited about what's to come."

I nod slowly. "And will you let me tie you up before I take you tonight?"

"T-tie me up?"

I search her face and find curiosity, and perhaps, a touch of trepidation, in her eyes.

"Do you trust me, July?" I murmur.

She blinks. "I wasn't sure I did, but"—she surveys my features—"I think I do." She nods. "In fact, I'm sure I do."

"Good girl."

Another quiver runs through her. I can taste the nervousness and the excitement that seeps from her pores, and it renders me almost immobile with need.

"Lay back, baby," I say through gritted teeth.

She instantly obliges.

"Show me your cunt," I growl.

And when she bends her knees and pushes her legs apart, baring her sweet pussy to my perusal, I groan. I reach for the tie I placed within easy reach on the nightstand while she was sleeping. Then I push my knee into the space between her thighs.

I lean over and, twisting her arms up and over her head, I knot it around both of her wrists. I didn't expect things to go this way, so I didn't come prepared, but that's okay. At the last minute, I got a special surprise for her, but other than that, I'll have to be resourceful when it comes to ensuring my wife has a wedding night she's going to remember for a long time.

I walk over to the closet and emerge with what I need. Her eyes round as I reach her again. Then, linking the tie in my hand to the one I looped around her wrists, I fasten it to the slat on the headboard. I tug on it to make sure it's not tight, but also, that it's secure enough to restrain her. Then, I step back and take in her body, "Okay?"

She nods. Her gaze is clear and, except for a hint of impatience in them, she doesn't show any other emotion.

"Good girl," I praise her again.

The flush on her cheeks deepens. Her chest rises and falls, and her breasts seem to swell. I lower myself until I'm planked over her, then wrap my lips around one erect nipple.

When I suck on it, she moans, then pushes her breast further into my mouth. I palm the other one and when I pluck on that nipple, her entire body jerks.

"Oh my god," she gasps.

"You mean 'oh my Knox,' don't you?" I smirk down into her face.

She huffs, "You're so corny."

"Say it, say my name," I order. I want to... *Need* to hear my name from her mouth.

"Knox," she whispers. "Oh. My. Knox."

A thrill spirals down my spine. Satisfaction presses in on my chest. "Good girl."

Then, I dive down between her legs and begin to eat her out. She writhes and groans and tries to pull away, but I hold onto her thighs. I lift her hips to give myself better access, then lick up her pussy lips. She whimpers, and when I throw her legs over my shoulders, she shudders. I stuff my tongue inside her weeping slit, she squeezes those thick thighs about my neck, and fuck, if I don't relish that. She can take my breath away... She does take my breath away. If I could go to my death between her legs, I'd die happy. And when I raise my head, she chases the feel of my tongue by raising her hips. I press little kisses to the inside of her thigh, all the way up to her pussy. And when I bite that little swollen nub of her clit, she gasps. Then thrusts up again.

"Ride my tongue, baby, just like that." I slide my tongue inside her, and she rolls her hips forward repeatedly. I lick inside her, and when I bring my hand down to grind into her cunt, she arches her back and cries out again. Little sounds emerge from her parted lips. Her body stiffens, and she's so close. I raise my head again, long enough to growl, "Come for me."

And she shatters. Her entire body jolts. Her thighs tremble. Moisture gushes out from between her pussy lips, and I lick it up. Only when the aftershocks abate, do I look up at her flushed features. She flutters her eyelids open, and her gaze meets mine. Her pupils are dilated, the black of her irises having expanded until there's only a golden circle around them. *Fuck.*

"You're gorgeous, you know that?"

She flushes. "I...came," she says in a slightly shocked voice.

"Did you like that, baby?" I smirk.

She nods again.

"Did you want to come harder next time?"

"I do," she breathes.

"Good girl."

I slap her pussy, and she cries out, "What was that for?"

"Just making sure you're primed for my penetration."

She swallows. The pulse at the base of her neck speeds up. Then she frowns. "You said that purposely, to make me wary about what's to come."

"Did I?" I chuckle.

The line between her eyebrows deepens. "I know you did."

"Or perhaps, I know that you need all the stimulation possible, so you can accommodate my girth?"

I crawl up her body and press my lips to hers. I kiss her deeply, drink from her and taste her cum mixed with that unique taste of her mouth. All the blood descends to my groin. I lower some of my weight onto her, pressing down into the wet flesh between her legs, and a trembling grips her. I make sure she can sense just how aroused I am when I fit my throbbing cock into the triangle between her legs. Even through my pants, I make sure she can feel the imprint of my swollen dick.

Her gaze widens, then she swallows. "Are you going to fuck me now?"

"I might," I murmur.

"But I *want* you to, fuck me." She writhes under me, trying to hump the ridge between my legs.

I chuckle. "You don't tell me what to do, baby." I sit back on my heels and pull her surprise out of my pocket. I sense the question in her eyes, but before she can ask it, I lean over and squeeze the nipple clamp I procured especially for her over one nipple.

She shudders. "Oh my god, that... That doesn't hurt as much as I thought it would."

"It boosts blood flow and heightens sensitivity to touch. Gives me the freedom to explore the rest of your body and make sure your climax is that much more memorable." I proceed to squeeze a second around her other nipple. When I pinch the clamp on the first, she throws her head back and groans.

I look down between her legs, and sure enough, moisture drips from her slit. I walk around to, once more stand, between her thighs, and before she can protest, I slide the special one I'd ordered for her around her clit.

"Jesus," she groans.

"Knox," I correct her. I can't wait to see the marks these are going to leave on her when I remove them. Just thinking of them turns my thigh muscles to granite. My balls tighten.

"Oh my God, Knox," she whines as she tries to squeeze her thighs together.

I grip her knees and hold them apart. "You're so pink, and so swollen, and so moist, wife."

I tighten the clit clamp by sliding the metal ring forward, and her entire body jolts. "You're a sadist. Next thing I know, you're going to go straight to anal, and without lube."

I look at her with longing. "Are you flirting with me, baby?"

She stares at me, then to my surprise, she chuckles. "I can't believe you said that. You're... You're—"

"A brute? A villain?" I smirk.

"All of them, but also"—her features soften—"you're my Sir. My master."

My heart stutters. This woman. She says the darnedest things that cut me off at my knees. I hold her gaze, and the air between us seems to ignite. Maintaining eye contact, I push back to stand next to the foot of the bed.

I unfasten one of my cuffs, then the other. I unbutton my shirt and shrug it off. I toss it aside, make quick work of my pants, and shove them off, along with my boxers, my shoes, and my socks. When I straighten, she's staring at my chest. More specifically, the scarred side of my torso. She rakes her gaze down the left side of my body to the scars that mar my thigh, and down to those on my leg.

"They're ugly. I'm ugly." The words are out before I can stop them. *I'm not looking for reassurance. I don't need reassurance... Except perhaps, I do? Perhaps, I want my new bride to assure me that she doesn't find me hideous?*

As she continues to take in my body, I resist the urge to turn the blemished side away from her. Instead, I angle my body to present her with a full-frontal view. She saw me at the gym in my shorts, but this is different.

This is the first time she's seen me without any clothes, in my full disfigured glory. And on our wedding night. It's a testament to how comfortable I've gotten with her that I didn't give a second thought to stripping down completely. I've never done so with any of the submissives I paid for at the club I frequented. This is a first for me, too. When there's no reaction from her, my guts tie themselves in knots. *Damn, I should have kept my clothes on. I—*

"You're beautiful, Knox Davenport," she says in that soft, sweet voice of hers. Instantly, my mind quietens. It's a balm to my senses, to that wounded part of me inside which made me believe that I'd never feel normal again. Something tightly wound inside of me unravels. My cock hardens further. And when she raises her gaze to stare at my very erect shaft, her eyes glaze over with lust.

I run my hand down my chest and grasp the base of my erect dick.

She swallows. "You said it's *big*?"

"It is." I squeeze my shaft from base to crown.

"It's not big." She sets her jaw.

"No?"

"It's a freakin' enormous penis."

"Thanks?" I allow myself another smirk, but she's too busy taking in the size of the organ I'm going to use to pleasure her.

"I... I don't think it will fit." Once again, she begins to close her legs. But I plant my knees between hers and force her to keep them apart.

"It will," I promise. Then. I grip the underside of her thighs and urge her to lock her ankles around my waist. "Hold on."

37

June

That's all the warning I get before he notches his dick at my opening, and, in one smooth move, he impales me. Pain lights up my nerve pathway. I open my mouth to cry out, but the sound sticks in my mouth.

"Are you okay?" He planks over me.

When I don't reply, he pushes up on one arm and cups my cheek. "Talk to me baby, is it too much for you?" He begins to withdraw, but I push my heels into his back.

"Don't stop," I gasp out. "Please."

He fills me up and stretches me, and it feels like too much. It feels like he's consuming me. Like he's splitting me in two and pinning me to the bed, and it feels so fucking perfect. He's finally giving in to his desire for me. He's wedged into me, pressing down on my inner walls, and it feels perfect. It feels like he's finally owning me. And filling me up in a way that leaves no doubt that we're finally joined. His cock throbs inside me, signaling his desire for me. Heat from his body pours over me, surrounds me, presses down on my chest. Combined with the bolts of pain zipping out from my nipples and my clit, it's overwhelming.

Tears knock behind my eyes. The sensations build inside me, and it feels so intense. I tug at my hands, wanting to touch him, and almost cry when I'm unable to do so.

He seems to sense my need for more contact, for he presses his forehead to mine. "You're so fucking tight. So hot. So wet. You feel like a dream, baby."

I make a sound deep in my throat.

He understands what I want, for he brushes his lips over mine. "You take me so beautifully." His praise fills a vacant space deep inside I hadn't realized existed. Warmth curls in my chest. My throat closes. A tear squeezes out from the corner of my eye, and he licks it up.

"You're crying," he murmurs.

"No." I shake my head. "It feels like a lot, is all."

It feels like I'm finally, utterly, completely yours. I'm your submissive. Only yours.

Only when I hear my words, do I realize I've said them aloud.

His shaft extends further inside me, and I feel like he's splitting me in two. Then, he closes his mouth over mine, and when his tongue mimics the intrusion of his dick, my belly flutters. Moisture pools in between my legs. I wrestle with the bindings around my wrists, wanting to touch him. Being unable to do so at will adds a layer of expectation which turns me on even more. He continues to kiss me, and when he sucks on my tongue, it feels like he's swallowing me up. I squirm under him, and his dick throbs inside me. He has me pinned in place, and I strain to get even closer to him.

Still kissing me, he pulls back, then propels his hips forward. This time, he sinks even deeper inside, and tendrils of sensation radiate out from where we're connected. His cock knocks against the clamp around my clit. Sparks flash out from where we're joined. He releases my mouth and peers deeply into my eyes. So deep. So blue. There are silver sparks deep inside, and again, I feel like I'm being absorbed into him.

He pulls back, and when he plunges inside me again, jolts of pleasure-pain spiral up my spine. My head spins. It feels like I'm caught in a tsunami of desire that threatens to turn my reality upside down.

"More, please," I gasp.

L. STEELE

His nostrils flare. His gaze narrows until being at the receiving end of
all that intensity is almost too much. Then he begins to drill into me. Each
time he thrusts inside me, the angle is such that he hits the clamp, which
pinches my clit tighter. The choke holds on the most sensitive parts of me,
and the way the ridges of his cock dig into the soft walls of my pussy have
me crying out, moaning, whimpering, and making noises I don't recognize.

He slides his hand down to pluck at the clamp on one of my nipples,
and heat crashes into my core. My pussy clenches down on his dick and he
groans, "Fuck, baby, you're killing me."

He pulls out, stays poised at the rim of my slit, then kicks his hips
forward again. He sinks so deep inside me, I swear, I can feel him in my
throat. For a second, we stay motionless. His gaze entwined with mine. His
dick brushing up against that part of me which no one else has touched.
It's so intimate, my climax begins to build in my core.

"Knox," I whisper, "please…" I'm not sure what I'm asking him for, but
it seems to spur him into action. He begins to fuck me with that single-
minded intensity I've always found irresistible about him. He doesn't avert
his gaze from mine. It's the single most erotic thing that has ever happened
to me. The fact that he's making love to me while looking deeply into my
eyes ignites my soul, draws sparks in my heart, and turns my entire body
into a cauldron of churning emotions.

Or maybe, that's the climax, building and building, until it seems to
engulf my entire body. And when he thrusts into me again with a grunt
and simultaneously reaches down and removes the clamp from my cunt,
then also from my nipples, the blood flows to those parts. The pins-and-
needles-like pain zips out to meet in my core, and the pleasure that follows
is unlike anything I've ever experienced.

It builds and builds, it fills me and flows over me, and it crashes into
me. I open my mouth to scream, and he places his lips over mine drawing
it in.

He reaches up to untie my wrists and I wrap my arms around his neck.
I hold onto him as the orgasm grips my body. It seems to go on and on, all
while he continues to fuck me. I'm aware of him grunting as he comes
inside me before darkness pulls me under.

When I open my eyes, he's still inside me and watching me with
concern. "How are you feeling?"

"I'm good." My voice comes out as a croak, and I spoil the effect by yawning. "Just very, very sleepy." I close my eyes and snuggle into his arms. I turn my cheek into the hard wall of his chest and yawn again.

"I'll be right back." He kisses the top of my head and pulls away to stand. I snuggle into the pillow, tracking his broad back, the sculpted musculature of his butt, and the powerful thighs that he uses to propel himself in the direction of the bathroom. The light comes on. I hear water running, the sound of the toilet flushing, then he walks out. The bathroom door is half open, and silhouetted against the light, he looks almost godly. With the breadth of his shoulders, those rippling abs, and the concave stomach, he's a Michelangelo statue come to life. Then my mind registers the fact that he's already erect, and his cock is much larger, much thicker, much more mesmerizing than any I've seen on any renaissance statue.

"You're staring," he murmurs as he draws closer.

"You're erect."

"It's a normal state with you."

He reaches the bed, then squeezes out something from a tube. When he touches it to my nipple, I sigh. "Aloe, to soothe the chafed skin." He does the same to my other nipple, then to my clit.

The slight burn on my skin fades away. A cool sensation takes its place. "That feels so good." He completes his ministrations, caps the tube, and sets it aside. Then he slides into bed and coaxes me to turn on my side so he can spoon me. "Thank you, wife." He kisses the top of my head.

"For what?" I yawn again, already half asleep.

"For making me feel whole again."

There's a tenderness in his voice I haven't heard before. A rawness I didn't think he was capable of. I begin to turn to see his face, but he stops me with his grip on my hip. "Go to sleep," he orders.

His cock is insistent at the small of my back, and when he wraps me in those big arms, I feel safe and secure...and warm...and so cherished. It feels incredible to have my Sir's complete attention, and his gratitude. It feels like I've finally come home. A place where I belong. I'm not only June, adopted daughter. I'm Knox's wife. I'm my Sir's submissive. My master's woman. And he's my husband. He's mine. I, too, feel complete in a way I hadn't realized I needed. I fall asleep with a smile on my face.

When I wake up next, it's to find his head between my legs, and his wicked tongue licking up my slit. He swipes his tongue up my pussy lips and liquid heat eases into my veins. I lower my head and grip his hair, and realize he untied me, at some point.

He peers up at me and his lips twitch. "Close your eyes."

His voice is bossy enough that I comply. Or maybe, it's because I feel deliciously warm and hedonistically sexy, and so very taken care of. To be the cynosure of his attention is the most amazing feeling in the world. To be the object of his attention, the crux of his intentness, the sole target of his concentration, makes my head spin. My chest grows warm, and my skin feels overly sensitive.

He continues to eat me out. He slips his tongue inside my slit while sliding his hands up to cup and massage my breasts. When he plucks at my nipples and bites down on my swollen cunt, I'm so turned on. I orgasm again.

This one is deep and slow, but no less intense. He crawls up my body and kisses me. I taste myself on his mouth, and it's so very decadent—this taste of me, and him, and everything it means. I wrap my arms and legs around him, and when he breaches me, I wince. He senses that little reaction and pauses. "I'm hurting you. I should have waited."

"No!" I cling to him. "I love it. It makes me feel close to you."

In the starlight that pours in through the windows, his eyes glitter. The silver sparks in their depths seem to catch fire. He balances himself on his arms and begins to plough into me. Each time he buries himself inside me, the bed moves up. The headboard crashes against the wall, and I can't stop the giggle that bubbles up. "We're *that* couple now," I gasp.

"I bought out the floor so no one can hear us."

"Oh." I stare back. Of course, he did. Then he drills into me again, and all thoughts vanish from my mind. If I thought he was deep inside me earlier, it's nothing compared to how thoroughly he penetrates me now. I feel like he's cleaving me in two. Like he's imprinting his cock inside my pussy, like he's leaving his mark on every cell of my body. Like I'm never going to be the same again. A bubble of happiness squeezes my chest. He owns me. He really does. I'll always have this moment when I felt so close to him. When it feels like we're two halves of a whole. Surely, he must have feelings for me for it to feel so incredible.

My heart hurts. My toes curl. My thigh muscles burn with the effort of holding him close. But he doesn't stop. Sweat tickles down his temple and plops on my cheek, and yet, he keeps going. He puts his entire body, mind, and soul behind each plunge into my body.

And I take it. I accept it. I welcome it. My breath catches in my chest. My throat feels raw.

"Come for me," he orders.

I shudder. Surely, I don't have the energy to come again. "I can't," I whisper.

"You can." He leans away from me, giving himself enough space to slap at my breast, I cry out. Goosebumps well up over my torso. A flash of pain sizzles up my nerve endings and arrows to my clit. It sets off a tsunami of pleasure which radiates out from my core.

"You will come for me," he snaps.

There's no mistaking the confidence in his voice. And it spurs me on. It ignites reserves of energy deep inside that I didn't know I had. And then, he slides his fingers under my butt, and when he brushes the forbidden hole between my arse-cheeks, I'm so shocked that I drop into myself completely. That's when he growls again, "Come. Right now."

38

Knox

Her entire body jolts. Her back curves. And with a cry, she orgasms. I watch her throw her head back and screw her eyes shut as she comes.

"Look at me," I command.

She slowly opens her eyelids, and I peer into her eyes as I fuck her through the tremors that grip her. I push my forehead into hers and allow myself to be drawn into the vortex that is her as I come inside her. Her body slumps under me and her eyelids flutter down. I stay there, reveling in the warmth of her pussy, the feeling of belonging, which is both new and also, so right. *She's home. She's mine. She's everything. And I'm hers.*

I pull out of her, conscious of my cum spilling down her thigh. I push it back inside of her, wanting her body to hold every drop of it. Then I ease myself onto my back and gather her in my arms as she sleeps. I tuck her head under my chin and hold her close.

I try to sleep but I can't. The sex was like nothing I've ever experienced. To say it was mind-blowing is putting it lightly. I wanted to get her to submit to me. Instead, it's as if my ribcage was cracked open, exposing my heart to her. It's like I'm the one who's been brought to my knees. I'll never be the same again. It can never be like this with anyone else.

She accepted and welcomed whatever I wanted to do with her; only, it's not enough. I want more. I want to test how long I can edge her. I want to tie her up and arouse her until she's screaming. I want to take her other virgin hole. I want to tie her up again and spank her until she's so turned on, she'll orgasm as soon as I finger her cunt. I want to...rouse her to fever pitch, then make her beg for my cock. And then, I want to refuse her until she's out of her mind with desire and spreading her thighs and parting her pussy lips and asking me to take her, to put her out of her misery. I want all of that and so much more. Damn. I want to explore every secret fetish, every kink I've dreamed of, with her.

I'm falling for her... I knew this would be the outcome the moment I first saw her. I knew, when I made love to her, it'd be like nothing I'd encountered before. I knew I'd be changed by it... And knowing I'm her first, that she's never been with anyone else before this and won't be after, is a thought that's headier than any aphrodisiac.

Consummating my wedding with my wife on our first night as husband and wife, with my wife being a virgin... If you'd painted this scenario for me, I'd have laughed. But that's how things worked out. And it feels right. And it's because of her. Because she's special...and dazzling...and beautiful...and unique... And I'm not worth the dirt under her feet. But I'm keeping her. I'm never letting go. I told her I wasn't going to consummate the marriage, but I did. We may have started out as an arrangement, but it means more to me than that. A strange fullness grips my chest. It's a sensation I'm unable to pin down.

"Hey—" She clears her throat. "Why are you frowning?"

I glance down to find her looking at me with sleepy eyes. She reaches up and traces the fold between my eyebrows. "You look so intense."

When I don't reply, she pushes her elbows into my chest and balances her chin on her palm. "Everything okay?"

"Why wouldn't it be?"

"You looked like you had a lot on your mind."

"I did," I admit.

"Care to share?"

These feelings inside me are too new. I need to make sense of them before I tell her.

L. STEELE

I find myself withdrawing from her and manage a smile. "Was wondering what to feed you for breakfast."

"This is a beautiful venue," She looks around the restaurant. It has a view of the Seine and the various bridges that crisscross it. In the distance is the Eiffel Tower which we visited earlier. She wanted to go, and I couldn't refuse her. She catches me watching her and flushes. "What? Is there something on my face?" She pulls up her phone and checks her appearance on the screen.

"You're good."

The wait staff places our food in front of us and retreats.

"You ordered for me again?" She glances down at her plate.

"Saffron-infused golden beetroot carpaccio with micro greens and aged balsamic pearls. " I nod toward her food.

"Ooh, that sounds and smells yummy." She glances at my plate. "What are you having?

"Grilled Portobello Mushroom Steaks with Truffle Risotto and Roasted Asparagus."

She pushes her glasses up her nose. She's not wearing her contact lenses today, and I'm so happy about that. Not only because it makes her sexier to look at, but also because she deserves to be comfortable in her own skin, always.

"It's vegan?" She peers at the food.

"It is." I nod. I opted for a dish she could eat, so I can do this. "Try it."

I scoop some of the food onto my fork and offer it to her.

She licks the morsels off the tines, and instantly, I'm hard again. *Fuck.* Throughout our sightseeing this morning, I found myself reaching for her, holding her hand, tucking strands of hair behind her ear. In short, behaving like a besotted husband on his honeymoon.

I have a feeling this is why Arthur gifted us this trip. He knew, the moment I had my wife alone in a hotel room, all bets were off.

Canny bastard wanted to make sure we'd consummate the marriage. It's well-known among the Davenports, the old man doesn't put merit on any of us being married—not unless it's also consummated. He stopped saying it to our faces though, and instead, found sneaky ways to ensure the deed was done so it'd increase his chances of a progeny. And I couldn't have refused the trip without arousing his suspicions, so here we were.

I set down my fork and rub my chin. "We never spoke about contraception. I'm sorry, I should have checked, but I got carried away." Very unlike me, again. "You're on the pill, aren't you?"

She shoots me a curious look.

"I saw it in your purse." I shrug. "And I'm clean. I can email the blood work to you."

She shakes her head. "I believe you. I'm clean, too. I mean, I would be, considering you're the first man I've slept with."

And the last, I think to myself. I shake my head. "It's unbelievable that you were a virgin, but just so you're aware, it wouldn't have made a difference if you hadn't been."

"No?"

I shake my head. "The pleasure I can give you would have far outweighed what anyone else could have."

She scoffs, "Ego much?"

"You know, it's a fact."

She narrows her gaze on me, then sighs. "I believe you, especially after the way you made me orgasm earlier."

I soften my gaze. "It's also you, baby. You're so sensitive to my touch."

"It's us," she says slowly. "I doubt I'd have that response to anyone else."

"It's us." I frown. She's right. I haven't felt this way with anyone else. It confirms to me what I felt before. What I have with my wife is singular. It's extraordinary, really. Unequalled by any other experience in my life. The rush I got from coming inside her beats the exhilaration of my first helo jump. And *that*, is saying something. *Fucking hell. I'm in love with her.* I lean back in my seat.

When Arthur asked me if I loved her... I wasn't lying when I said I did. It's why sex with her is so unique, so different, an almost spiritual experience. It's why I feel comfortable opening myself up to her. It's why I know I have to be vulnerable to her. It's why I want to share all of myself, including my proclivities, with her. Because I love her. I've been falling for her since the day I first saw her.

No wonder, I orchestrated events, so I'd marry her and find a way to keep her close to me. No wonder, I forgot about contraception in my need to take her. I want to bind her to me in the ultimate way possible. I subconsciously want her to have my child. Despite knowing she's using contraceptives. I want her enough to hope I'd impregnate her. I rub the back of my neck. *I'm well and truly fucked.*

She squirms around in her seat, then winces. "Are you okay?" I frown.

Her cheeks flush. "Uh, I'm sore."

"Sore?" Worry squeezes my chest. My guts churn. "Was I too rough with you? Did I not give you enough time to recover? I should have waited, before I fucked you again."

"What? No. What are you talking about? I wanted you to fuck me."

"And I listened to you; I shouldn't have."

I lean forward and survey her features. Flushed cheeks, over-bright eyes, and there are shadows under them too. Also, her cheekbones seem pronounced. "You seem tired. Did you sleep enough last night.?"

She hesitates. "I didn't, but I'm sure I'll make up for it over the next few nights."

"Don't count on it," I drawl.

She flushes, then laughs. And when her features light up and her eyes dance, I feel my heart stutter. That sensation in my chest grows bigger until it fills my torso and spreads to my extremities. I feel light and happy and exhilarated. I also feel... nervous. I'm in so much trouble.

I tear my gaze away from her face, refill her glass with water and slide it toward her. "Drink," I order.

She obeys, and satisfaction squeezes my chest. My blood begins to pump harder. The crotch of my pants tightens further. I berate my cock. *How can I be only thinking of myself right now?*

It's my fault she didn't get enough rest. My fault that I took her so quickly after her first time. What is wrong with me? I should have realized my needs, my kinks, my overblown sexual appetites would be too much for her. She's a delicate angel. And me? I don't deserve her. This is what I was afraid of—that I'd make demands and she'd never say no. She's a novice who's discovered her taste for kink, thanks to me. I've sullied her, as I knew I would. The fact that I'm in love with her has complicated things.

I thought I didn't need to hold back with her, but given how I took her again, when she was sore, and so soon after losing her virginity, proves otherwise. I should have stopped and given her space to recover but I didn't. I saw her wince and should have pulled back. Instead, I allowed my dick to lead me. That, and the fact I listened to her, shows me how wrong I am. She doesn't know what she wants. It's my job to protect her, even if it's from me. Because when it comes down to it, nothing changes the fact that she's this delicate angel, and I'm a beast who can only destroy her.

"Knox?" Her sweet voice interrupts my thoughts. "Are you okay?"

"You're not eating enough," I shoot back.

A line forms between her eyebrows. "What is it with you and food?" She tosses her head." Every time I turn around, you're trying to feed me."

"You're losing weight." I frown.

"Good," she huffs.

"It's not good. I like your curves the way they are, and don't want to see you withering away."

"Withering away?" She rolls her eyes, "You're exaggerating."

"I'm not." The anger lurches against the walls of my stomach. The burn extends from there to my chest, to the backs of my eyes. *I can't do this. I can't besmirch her. I can't dirty her. I can't control myself around her... Certainly not, when we're away in this romantic getaway, on our honeymoon. I need to get us back to London where I can hide behind the guise of work, at least.*

She must sense my thoughts, for she leans forward and touches my hand. I pull it away. Hurt flashes in her eyes, and that makes me feel worse. *Fucking hell, I have no tact. None at all. I'm not worthy of her. And if I value her in any way, if I want to stick to my marital vows of protecting her, I need to put distance between us.*

"Everything okay?" She frowns.

"It will be." *I'm* going to make sure it's okay. "Eat up; we need to get going."

39

June

"And that was the end of my honeymoon." I fix my lipstick in the mirror of the restroom.

"You're in the middle of a romantic lunch when he decides he has an emergency meeting. Next thing, you're both on the flight back to London?" Zoey frowns at me from the phone screen. I'm in the ladies' room on the executive floor, at the other end of the corridor from my boss, aka my husband's office.

In a way, it's a relief to be back and feel useful again as his assistant. Thankfully, he hasn't brought up his view that I shouldn't continue in this role, and I've accepted it as a sign to reprise my position. Though perhaps, if he'd mention it to me, it would've indicated he's thinking of me. I sigh. I'm trying to second guess him, and not succeeding.

I also took the initiative to move the person who'd been brought in to replace me to another position within the administrative team. She was only too happy to transition over. Not surprising, since I heard stories about how he treated her—and that assuaged my conscience about depriving someone of a job.

"He told me I could stay on in Paris." I cap my lipstick tube and drop it back in my handbag. "As if I'd have said yes. Staying on in the hotel room where we'd"—I was going to say, 'made love for the first time,' but it feels too personal to reveal that, so I settle for—"spent our wedding night without him?" I shake my head. "Seriously I don't know why he suddenly withdrew into himself and began acting like a dick, because"—I swallow—"because he's not one."

She stays silent. I glance down at the screen to find her features laced with worry.

"I know it sounds like I'm making excuses for him but really, I'm not. I saw another side of him once we got married."

"You mean, in the nearly forty-eight hours since you've been married?"

I hunch my shoulder. "I've worked closely with him more than a month now, and when you're someone's assistant and spend so much time with him on a daily basis, shadowing him to meetings and even to the gym, you do end up learning an awful lot about him."

She nods slowly. "I take your point. But I thought all you'd learned during that time was that he's a jerk."

"And he still is," I laugh. "But there's more to him. He broke things off with Priscilla. He went against his grandfather's wishes and put his inheritance at risk, but that didn't stop him from walking away from that arrangement. And he's been open-minded enough to admit to me when he was wrong. How many people do that?"

I shuffle my feet, wondering how to explain it to her without giving away any confidences.

"This might be oversimplifying things, but as soon as he put that ring on my finger, he seemed to change. And it was his grandmother's ring, too."

"He gave you his grandmother's ring?" she asks, surprised.

"Each of the Davenport brothers received a ring from their grandmother. She apparently loved wearing rings and had enough of them to will one to each of her sons and grandchildren."

"That, I did not expect." Zoey chews on her lower lip. "This wedding means something to him."

She notices me staring at her and holds up her hand. "Didn't mean it that way, but you have to admit, the sudden wedding seemed to hint he was in a rush to get things done. I wanted to think it was because he was so in love with you that he didn't want to go another day without making you, his wife. But hand on heart, I couldn't swear by it, especially when he used his money and his contacts as a reason to convince you. But the fact that he gave you his grandmother's ring? Yeah, that means something."

"He's surprised me a lot these last few days." I shift my weight from foot to foot. "I was sure we were reaching some kind of understanding. Then all of a sudden, he withdraws into himself and once more becomes the sullen, barely-grunting-in-response boss, who prefers to chew out everyone in meetings."

"Why are you at work? Now that you're his wife —"

"I should be staying home and spending time doing yoga and getting pedicures?" I scoff.

She sighs, "M-a-a-a-n, that sounds nice."

I make a gagging sound. "Can you imagine *me* doing that?"

She shakes her head. "You're the hardest-working person I know, so I didn't expect you to give it up right away. But perhaps —"

"Perhaps what?"

"Perhaps, once you've gotten used to your new position?" She raises her shoulder. "You *are* Mrs. Knox Davenport, and that does come with a lot of benefits."

I grip the edge of the sink. Hearing her refer to me as Mrs. Knox Davenport sends my stomach into a tailspin. I am his wife. But it all feels very new. And I haven't even thought about changing my surname. I'm sure he expects it, but I feel a certain loyalty toward Irene. She gave me an identity when I had none. *Am I going to cast it away like it didn't mean anything?*

"I'm sorry, I didn't mean to confuse you," Zoey says softly.

"You didn't and —"

The door to the restroom is pushed open. "There you are." Mary walks in. "That husband of yours has been driving his team up the wall. You'd best come rescue them."

"Gotta go, Zoey. I'll catch you again soon." I disconnect the call, then turn to Mary. "What's he been up to now?"

"He's acting like a bear with a sore head. It just so happened, I was filling in for the assistant of one of the other Vice Presidents, so I was in the sales meeting. And—" She shakes her head. "The boy certainly is all uptight. You can't tell he's just back from his honeymoon. Which is where I think he should still be, but what do I know?" She sniffs.

"Uh, you know how important work is for Knox."

"More than his marriage?" She shoots me a skeptical glance. "He had no business dragging you back so soon."

"Oh, no, I don't mind. Really. I like feeling useful."

She scoffs. "You need to accept your new position, young lady and make use of the benefits which come with it."

Her words are remarkably similar to what Zoey mentioned. A part of me recognizes I'm putting off the inevitable, but that workaholic part of me can't fathom what I'd do if I didn't come in to work. "You said he's in the meeting?"

"In the conference room. And you'd better get there before he fires the lot of them."

40

Knox

"Give me one reason why I should not fire the lot of you?" I widen my stance. A headache stabs behind my left eye, and I ignore it.

I didn't sleep well last night, and it has nothing to do with my not sleeping in the same bed as my wife. No way, can I miss not having her next to me in my bed when it's only one night that we spent together. And a few hours yesterday, where I listened to her soft breathing and even softer sighs, and the slide of sheets on her skin as she turned to face me.

We returned from Paris, and I buried myself in my home office without bothering to explain to her why I decided to return to London. Simply put, I'm confused about my feelings for her.

I needed to put distance between us, so I went straight into a meeting I'd scheduled on the flight back.

By the time I emerged from the meeting, she was asleep. In my bedroom, and in my bed. Seeing here there felt right.

It also intensified this feeling of panic gripping me. *I cannot give up control of my emotions. I cannot give up control of my life...* And it feels like I did just that in acknowledging my feelings for her.

I didn't dare slip into bed with her. So instead, I pulled up a chair and watched her sleep. Then, when it felt like I wouldn't be able to restrain myself from joining her, I marched back to my study and spent the rest of the night on the couch.

I made sure to come into the office early today, so I didn't have to see her.

But I knew she was back at her desk because she emailed to let me know. Then, she proceeded to take care of work and update me on various ongoing projects. I didn't reply to her. Didn't email or call her, like the coward I am.

All the pent-up anger at myself came to a head when I sat in on a sales meeting and realized our quarterly projections were way off. *Fuck.* People are not doing their jobs. And given my personal life is in chaos, no way, am I allowing my professional life to go down the toilet as well. I glare at the team gathered around the conference room table.

All of them avert their eyes. One of them shuffles their feet. Someone coughs. I scowl at my Vice President of Sales. He's sitting to my right. His eyes are ringed with dark circles. His hair is mussed like he's been running his hands through it. There's a stain on his collar, something that looks like spittle.

I've been unable to take my gaze off of it since I started this meeting. Now, I train my glare on him. "Do you have any excuse for why we're five percent below our projections for the last quarter?"

He shifts in his seat. "It's only five percent," he murmurs.

The way he responds infuriates me. This is not an insignificant amount. "It was an entire five percent." I scowl. "When we finalized the forecasts, did I or did I not tell you that if you didn't hit it, it would be your job at risk?"

He draws in a sharp breath. "I tried my best. My team and I? We worked nights; we pounded the pavement; we called in favors with media planners. We have several deals in the cooker; just couldn't close them by month-end. But we will. We did everything possible to hit the numbers."

"Not nearly enough, apparently." I look over the faces of the other team members, most of which are pale. One of them looks like he's about to cry. Another is clutching his stomach like he's about to puke.

My instinct warns me I should cool down, take a step back, try to get perspective. It's one of the things I was well known for when I was a Marine—the ability to be calm under pressure. To distance myself from a life and death situation so I could have an overhead view. It always helped me get in touch with my instinct and pick the best option.

Which is what I did when I married her. *So, why am I unable to come to grips with the depth of my feelings for her? And why the hell am I taking out my anger on my unsuspecting team?*

"You're the leader of this group, so I hold you personally responsible for not hitting your goals."

The Vice President swallows. More color fades from his cheeks, but he looks resigned. "The buck stops with me." He rises to his feet and gathers his phone and tablet. "I'll send you my resignation."

"That's not fair." One of the younger members of the team jumps to her feet. "He gave it everything. You have to realize he has a—"

"Sit down." My Vice President jerks his chin in her direction.

The woman firms her lip, then sinks down with a hateful look in my direction.

Great, now I've alienated the very team whose support I need to hit the numbers I've committed to Arthur. He confirmed me as the CEO of the Media Arm of the Davenport group—my reward for getting married. All the more reason for me to deliver on my forecasts. *Five percent is a margin of error too much. Five percent, either way, makes a difference in whether a bullet is lethal or not. I cannot not make the leader of this team pay for not having hit his estimates. It would set a precedent for my being weak. Only, this is not a life and death situation, is it?* I push the thought from my mind, fold my arms across my chest.

My Vice President nods in the direction of his team. "It's been a pleasure and an honor leading all of you." He turns to leave. That's when the door to the conference room bursts open.

My wife walks in. All eyes turn in her direction.

She reaches the head of the table, keeping enough distance between us that I can't touch her. My fingers tingle. I haven't seen her all morning, and now, I eat up her big brown eyes, her hair which she's piled on top of her head to show off the curve of her neck—which bears a mark.

My mark. Fuck. I have a recollection of biting down on the skin there when I took her for the third time that night in Paris. Satisfaction coils in my chest. Pride squeezes my ribcage. *Damn, I want to proclaim to the world that she's mine. Only, I'm not worthy of her.*

She glances around the team, then at my Vice President who's looking at her with bemusement.

"What happened?" she asks in a breathless tone.

The same team member who spoke up earlier nods in my VP's direction. "Mr. Davenport fired him because we missed the sales forecast by five percent."

"What?" She turns on me. "You can't do that."

I freeze. "Care to repeat that?" I ask slowly.

She blinks, then swallows hard. "You... You can't fire him."

"Are you telling me what I can and can't do with my team?" I lower my voice to a hush. The dominance in my tone is unmistakable. She winces, then nods slowly.

The rest of the team falls silent. They're following the exchange with great interest. The silence stretches. She swallows, and the sound is audible.

"You... You'll regret it if you let him go," she murmurs.

"And why is that?"

"He had a baby three months ago, yet he didn't take a day off. Instead of spending any time with his wife and newborn, he did his best to deliver on the numbers. Also, his child was unwell last night, and he and his wife spent the night in the emergency room. After which, he turned up for this meeting today." She tips up her chin. "He did try his best, and he and this team missed their goals by a very small percentage."

"Which is not the same as actually delivering," I remind her. "And a small percentage does not translate into a small amount of revenue."

"I'm sure they'll make up for it in the next quarter," she pleads.

There are nods around the table. I'm aware of the team looking at me with hope in their eyes. Even my Vice President is watching me carefully.

As for my wife? Her chin is set at that stubborn angle that tells me she's not going to give in on this. And I admit, I admire the fact that she held her own against me.

I scowl at my Vice President. "Is what she says true?"

He nods.

"Is your child, okay?"

He seems surprised, then nods again. "It was a virus, but you know kids," He half smiles. "The fever shot up and wasn't coming down at all. We took her to the hospital, and she's better now."

"I'm glad." I shift my weight to my right foot. "You may leave the room." I glance at the team gathered around the table. "You may all leave. On one condition."

They look at me with expectant expressions. "You need to deliver five percent *above* the projected numbers for next quarter."

"We will." My VP nods.

"Yes!" The girl who spoke earlier jumps to her feet. "You won't regret this, Mr. Davenport." They begin to file out, their steps hurried. They can't wait to get away from me. My wife turns to follow in their wake.

I call out, "Not you, Kelly Assistant."

41

June

I spin around and scowl at him. "Did you call me—" I notice the smirk on his features and bite the inside of my cheek. "That wasn't funny."

"Neither were you, challenging me in front of the team."

"'But I had to do it. You were in the wrong; you know that."

"Doesn't change the fact that you questioned my capabilities in front of others."

I curl my fingers into fists. "But I had to do it. If I hadn't, you'd have fired him and never forgiven yourself for it."

He inclines his head. "That might be true."

"You know it *is* true."

"It is," he concedes, "but what you did needs to be punished."

Excitement pinches at my nerve-endings. My belly flutters. Yes, I want to be punished. I need to be punished by him. But I don't say that aloud. Instead, I toss my head. "So, I prevented you from committing an error, and you're going to punish me for that."

He nods slowly. "You defied me. I can't let you get away with that." He looks me up and down. "I'll wager, you raced in here and confronted me because you wanted my attention."

Yes, I did, is what I think to myself. But outwardly, I scoff.

"Don't deny it. You were angry that I haven't spoken to you all day. And you were upset that I didn't spend last night in our bed."

He called it *our* bed. I shiver. *I really like the sound of that.* It means, he acknowledges that his place is by my side at night. And yes, I missed him, but I'm not going to admit to that. When I stay silent, he takes a step forward. "You were looking out for my emails all day, weren't you?"

"I was not." I tip up my chin.

"And you kept checking your phone to see if I'd messaged you," he says in that silky voice that feels like he's trailing a scarf across my skin. I shiver.

"What are you talking about?" I try to keep my voice noncommittal, but it comes out in a squeak.

"You could barely concentrate on your work because you kept looking at my office door, hoping to catch a glimpse of me."

Yes. It's true. I shake my head. "Your sense of importance is even more bloated than I thought."

His lips twist. Oh my god, that smile on his face is like that of a shark. It's mean and full of intent to punish. And so, so hot. *Why do I like this sadistic side of him? Why does it excite me so much that he's going to make me repent for what I did, no matter that I was in the right?* I take a step back, and his eyes gleam.

"You going to run, little July?" he asks in a silky voice that sparks a fountain of heat in my lower belly. "Are you?" He moves toward me, and I know I can't let him catch me. Yet, I want him to catch me. But not without a chase.

Without giving myself time to think, I spin around and race for the door. When I reach it, there's a click, and I realize he's locked it. I turn around to find he's prowling toward me at a leisurely pace. He has his phone in his hand. "I have access to the app that controls the security on this floor." He slides the device into the pocket of his slacks and continues to head in my direction.

"You're an asshole," I spit out, mainly to goad him further, and am rewarded by the flash of lust in his eyes. *Ooh, he knows I'm pushing him and is playing along.* He knows, at some point, I'm going to goad him over the edge and then... Then, I'm going to see that side of him he's been trying to hide since we got back from Paris. I sidle along the wall, away from him. He merely corrects his trajectory and continues walking toward me.

"How dare you try to punish me, when you're the one who's in the wrong?"

"Thought we established that doesn't matter. You go against me, you pay the price," he rumbles.

"And what about the fact that you didn't even speak to me on the way home from Paris."

"So, you did feel neglected." He smirks.

"I didn't say that."

"If that wasn't the case, why are you complaining?"

"Because..." I move around him in a circle, leaving enough space between us that he can't touch me...yet. He continues to turn with me, so it feels like he's in the center and I'm circling an orbit around him. He's the sun and I'm but a planet imprisoned by his gravitational pull. There's an illusion of freedom, in that I have my own orbit, but my path revolves around him. My life is him. I am him. The realization strikes me to the core. I falter. He jumps forward, arm out to righten me, but I find my balance again.

"You okay?" There's worry in his eyes.

"I'm not a weakling, Sir."

His eyes flash again. No doubt, it's in response to my using 'Sir'. It's one of the levers at my disposal. It's how I know he doesn't hold all the power in this relationship, either. That I can manipulate him, too... Not always, but sometimes. Like right now, when I need him to fuck me like I'm not just his wife but also his submissive.

"And you haven't caught me yet." I continue to wind my way around the room, moving to the other side of the table.

"Is that a challenge?" His chest seems to increase in size. His shoulders swell. He senses the thrill of the chase, and the predator in him can't help but feel called to give chase.

"Me, challenge you, Sir?" I flutter my eyelashes at him. I'm trying to be cute in the hope of riling him further. And I realize I've succeeded when his nostrils flare. He comes to a halt, and we eye each other across the width of the conference room table.

Then, because I have nothing to lose and because I really want to know, I ask, "Why did you cut short the honeymoon and return to London?"

"It was for an important meeting."

"Oh." It's almost an anticlimax that he tells me the truth without my having to coerce it out of him.

"In fact, we have another meeting coming up tonight." There's a look on his face I can't interpret.

"We?" I knit my eyebrows.

"You'll want to come to this one." He nods.

"Oh?" I cast my mind over what it could possibly be for. "I don't have anything on for this evening, and I don't recall putting any appointments in your calendar, either."

"It's not to do with the office."

"It's not?"

He shakes his head, slowly walking around the table. He approaches me without making any sudden moves, his gait casual. He's trying to look as benign as possible, which has about the same effect as a panther trying to fade into the undergrowth; meaning, he only succeeds in appearing more threatening.

"Stop." I throw up my hand.

I'm not surprised when he keeps coming.

"Don't come closer."

He bares his teeth. "You don't tell me what to do." Then, he swoops down on me.

I scream, then turn and dash forward, only to be yanked back when his big hands grab my waist. "Let me go!"

"No." He lifts me up like I weigh nothing, and flips me around, before plopping me onto the table. Before I can protest, he's planted himself between my legs. His movements are so confident, so dominant, a shiver squeezes my lower belly. He's so large, I'm forced to pry my legs wide apart. He grips the sides of my skirt-clad thighs and leans in. "Where were we?"

"I... I was trying to leave."

"And I chased you and caught you. You're mine now."

His bossy voice sends another shudder up my spine. I'm so turned on, I can feel moisture trickle out from my slit. And the possessiveness in his voice? Oh my god. I seem to be burning up from the inside. "Sir, please..." My voice emerges all breathy, and I sound as if I'm pleading. Only, I'm not sure what I want from him. The fact that he's holding me under his firm grasp makes me feel like he's controlling me, and I love it. I do. It also makes me want to push back a little. To test him. To see if I can be bratty enough that he'll want to punish me further. So, I reach down between his legs and grasp the tented fabric at his crotch.

His eyes snap blue fire. His lips curl in a snarl. Tension spools off of his body and saturates the air between us. It pushes down on my chest, and I feel faint with need.

"M-may I, Sir?"

"You haven't earned it yet."

Ugh, that menacing, unrelenting edge to his voice makes me faint with need. My pussy clenches in on itself and comes up empty.

"Please, please, Sir," I pant. "Please. I'll do anything you want, Sir. Anything."

"Hmm." He places his hand over mine and squeezes down. His cock becomes impossibly hard under our joint grasp.

"Do you want that, little July, hmm?"

"You know I do," I squeak.

"You'll have to earn it." He encircles my wrist with his fingers, and when he applies pressure, I release my hold on his cock.

"Tell me how," I pant. "Please sir, tell me what to do."

"Unzip me," he growls.

It doesn't even occur to me to disobey. I lower his zipper, and the r-r-ripping sound feels like someone's dragging broken glass over my nerve-endings. The hair on the back of my arms rises.

"Take it out," he commands.

I glance down to where the swollen head of his cock peeks out from the waistband of his boxers. And when I slide my fingers around the thick shaft, it jumps. The crown is almost purple, and the girth is so thick, my fingers don't even meet around it. I swallow. "You're so big." How did he fit that thing inside of me?

"Squeeze it from base to crown."

I follow his order and watch as precum glimmers at the slit. My mouth waters, and without waiting, I bend over, folding myself in half, and lick it up.

He groans, and a sense of power squeezes my chest. I look up at him. "May I, Sir?"

His grip on me tightens, then he steps back and lowers me to the floor. He shrugs off his jacket, folds it and drops it between us. He pushes down on my shoulder, and I slide down to place my knees on the cushion formed by his jacket. Oh, he was trying to make sure my knees don't hurt. His gesture is sweet, while the deliberateness of his movements leaves me in no doubt that he's in control. He threads his fingers through my hair and positions my head so my mouth is in front of his cock.

"Open."

I part my lips, and he places his cock at the rim of my lips. Then he takes my hand and places it on his thigh.

"Anytime you want to stop, tap my leg." His voice is serious, his gaze searching. He's concerned about my welfare. I realize now, no matter how much this man likes to play, he'll always put my safety first. And yes, he'll push me, like I do him—but he'll always place my needs front and center.

I nod, and some of the tension goes out his shoulders.

"Good girl. Now show your Master how much you want to please him."

42

Knox

Her pupils dilate, she looks up at me with those big brown eyes, and my heart stutters in my chest. The trust in them, the lust, the way she pants with her mouth open—all of it turns my groin to steel. I sense the need in her to please me, and it turns me on so much. That she stood up to me in front of my employees pleases me. She can go toe-to-toe with me when I'm wrong, and I like it. Only she can keep me in check... And I grant her that power. *Only her.*

She's stronger than I want to believe. Stronger than I've let myself believe. She's proven herself again, and that gives me the freedom to be myself. To let lose my propensities, my tendencies, my kinks, knowing she can take it. I don't want to stop myself. I don't want to pull away from her anymore. I can be me. That's the gift she's given me and now, I need to reward her. I may have started out chasing her and wanting to punish her but really, what I want to do is reward her for giving me the gift of freedom.

I tighten my grip on her hair, just enough to hold her in place without hurting her. Then I thrust forward and slide my cock inside her mouth. I hit the back of her throat, and she gags. Spittle drips from her mouth. She digs her fingers into my thigh but doesn't tap out. Her eyes grow impossibly large. Then she brings her free hand to my other thigh and grips it. I pull out and allow her to take a few deep breaths before she opens her mouth again. I punch my hips forward and my cock slides in between her teeth. This time, she takes me down her throat. She swallows, and the sucking motions sends a spurt of heat down to my feet and back up to my balls.

"Fuck, baby, you're so beautiful." I take in the tears that slide down her cheeks. Her mascara leaves a trail. Her cheeks are flushed. Her hair has long since come free from where she piled it on top of her head. She's falling apart, and I love the look. I adore the desire in her eyes. The longing in her gaze. The ardor in the way she tips up her chin so my dick slips further down. She gags, and this time, my balls draw up. *Fuck.* I pull out until I'm balanced on the rim of her mouth, then once again, I punch forward.

This time, I wrap my fingers around her throat, and the sensation of my shaft gliding down the column is too much. My balls draw up. "I'm coming." I empty myself with a low groan. My cum slides down her throat. When I pull out, a few drops cling to the corners of her mouth. I scoop them up and slip my fingers into her mouth. And when she licks them off, heat squeezes my groin again. I feel myself beginning to harden.

I grasp her under her armpits and coax her to her feet. And she looks so adorable, with the craving in her eyes and her mussed-up makeup and swollen lips. I close my mouth over hers. The taste of my cum combined with that of her lips forms an aphrodisiac; the kind I'll never be able to savor anywhere else.

"You're gorgeous," I whisper.

"Because I let you fuck my mouth?" Her voice is hoarse, her tone sassy, and when I look back, I'll know this is when I fell in love with her all over again.

"Please, don't stop," she gasps. "Please, Sir, use me any way you want. I'm your fuck toy. Your slut. Your whore. Just as long as you continue taking my holes anyway you want. That's all I want, Sir. To make you happy."

Pleasure flushes my chest. "Your words please me. I take it you want to be rewarded again, hmm?"

Color blooms on her cheeks. She draws in a sharp breath then lowers her chin, in a subservient gesture. "Are *you* flirting with me?" She lowers her gaze, and desire turns my balls to cannonballs. She's killing me, this woman. And I'm playing into her hands by upping my dominance, but it pleases me to please her, so I grant her her wish.

"Don't sass me." I slide my hands around her butt-cheeks and squeeze. She yelps.

"Remember our conversation on our wedding night?"

She glances at me from under her eyelids, and her gaze grows wary. I see the knowledge dawn, then the spark of alarm that ignites in her eyes.

"Exactly—" I smirk. "I'm going to take your other virgin hole, baby. But because I'm not completely heartless I'm going to use lube."

"And if I don't want you to?" She swallows. "What if I want you to take me as I am, the way you want to?"

My heart stutters in my chest. My thighs turn into columns of iron. As for my cock, the motherfucker is erect and so hard, I have to widen my stance to accommodate the girth.

"Are you sure, baby?"

She nods.

"It's going to hurt," I warn.

"I... I want it to." She looks at me with pleading in her eyes.

"I'm not sure if that's wise."

She frowns. "Why is that? Talk to me, Sir. Tell me what you're thinking."

The old me would have retreated back into my mind and refused to share my innermost thoughts. But I love her. She's, my wife. And if she's going to share my life, if I want to continue to have her as my submissive, it's important we communicate. And that goes both ways. I cup her cheek. "The last time, I thought you were ready for the full effect of my perversions, but I ended up hurting you."

"You mean the fact that I was sore when you took me that second time on our wedding night, and then I was uncomfortable all day the next day? That's why you cut our trip short and returned to London, right?"

I stiffen. She realized why I pulled back? She's more astute than I gave her credit for.

"And I wanted my husband to make love to me again. I knew I could weather the pain. Just as I know I can take whatever you choose to give me. Can't you see I *seek* the hurt you inflict on me? It fulfills my desire to be dominated. Giving you the power to hurt me physically is a way of expressing my dedication to you. When you hurt me, it arouses me. It makes me feel warm inside. It makes me feel like I belong to you. Like you've accepted me. Like I'm yours and you'll handle me as you please." She studies my face intently. "You should realize, I know my mind."

I nod. "And *you* should realize that it's my job to draw the limits. It's my role to protect you from everyone, including yourself. To protect you from reaching too far and taking on more than you can bear. You've placed your trust in me. I don't take that lightly."

"I love you, Sir." She tips up her chin and stares into my eyes. "And I know *you* know what's best for me. But you must know that I want to please you so much. And I know you'll be careful. I know you'll do your best to not take your responsibility lightly. I know that"—she reaches up and places her hand on where mine is flattened against her cheek—"you'll do everything to give me the orgasm I deserve."

I chuckle. She's so damn quick, thinking on her feet. She knows exactly what to say to defuse the tension and make me feel secure in my dominance. She knows me better than anyone else. And I... want to reward her for being so open to new experiences. My gut says she's ready for this. And it's my duty to ensure she not only enjoys this, but also has the most resounding orgasm ever.

"I'm going to make sure this is as pleasurable as I can make it—" She begins to speak but I shake my head. To my gratification, she stops speaking and trains those big brown eyes on me. "No matter what precautions I take, it will hurt a little, and while you crave the pain, as your master, it's up to me to decide on the threshold you can bear. And I'll tell you this much. I'm going to ensure the payoff will blow your mind. I'll make sure you have the most monstrous orgasm ever."

She parts her lips, and when her breathing grows choppy, I know she's ready for this.

"I'm going to make sure you're as prepared as I can get you to be."

I kiss her again, and she melts into me. I massage her gorgeous butt cheeks and pull her even closer, then unhook the back of her skirt. I lower the zipper and ease it down her hips, along with her panties. The clothes fall around her ankles. I lift her clear and place her on the table. I leave her heels on. I want to feel the stilettos dig into my back as I take her.

Then, I flatten my palm between her breasts and apply pressure. She lays back. I lift up her legs and fold them at the knee, balancing her stiletto clad feet at the edge of the table. When I stare down between her legs, she quivers.

"Knox," she whines.

"You're fucking soaked, baby." I indulge myself by staring at the streaks of moisture that glisten on her inner thighs. She's wet, but I can make her wetter to ensure this is as enjoyable for her as I can make it.

I pull up a chair and lower myself onto it, then I grip her thighs and bring her closer. And when I bend and lick my way up her pussy lips she cries out, "Oh, my Knox!"

"That's right, baby." I eat up her pussy like a man who was sentenced to a life of eternal hunger, despair, and loneliness, only to discover this sumptuous feast waiting for him. I slurp on her cunt like it's more succulent than any Michelin-starred dish I've ever tasted. Like it's made to order to fill the emptiness inside of me. I taste her like she's my very own starter, main course, and dessert rolled into one.

She writhes and tries to pull away, but I hold her in place. And when she digs her fingers into my hair and tugs on it, I revel in the pinpricks of pain chasing down my spine. My cock thickens further; my chest hurts. I want this woman so, so much. I lick around the rim of her slit and when I finally thrust inside, in the imitation of how I want to take her forbidden hole, she gasps.

I release my hold on her long enough to bring my hand down to her swollen clit. I pluck on it while I continue to stab my tongue inside her opening, and she moans and whimpers. When she pushes up against my mouth and tries to ride my tongue, I know she's ready. I rub the heel of my hand against her cunt and twist my tongue inside her melting hole. And when I slide my fingers down to her back hole, her entire body jolts.

Her back curves, her pussy squeezes down around my tongue, and she climaxes. She makes a strangled sound as she comes around my mouth. I lap up her cum, then scoop up the moisture and trail it down the cleavage between her butt cheeks to smear it around the rosette there.

"Knox, oh, Knox." She shudders as the aftershocks jolt through her. Her thighs tremble, the tension in her body bleeds away, and when I raise my head, it's to find her features relaxed.

I raise my fingers, spit on them, then slide two of them inside her back hole. They slip in easily. And when I breach the tight ring of muscle, a low whine emerges from her.

"That feels...better than I thought it would," she admits.

"Good Girl." Her tight channel squeezes around my knuckles. I wait there, allowing her to adjust to the size, then work in a third finger.

Her legs fall apart, allowing me further entry. "Oh my... Knox," she whines.

"That's right, baby, say my name again."

"Knox," she gasps as I manage to fit in a fourth finger into her tiny backside. Sparks of pleasure shudder up my arm. My cock extends. I am so fucking aroused, I have to take a breath and absorb the sensations coursing through my veins.

I curl my fingers inside her, and her entire body arches. "Oh...oh! That feels so—" she cries out as she comes. Throws up her hand, and I grip it. I clasp my fingers with hers as she holds on, as if I'm tethering her to this earth. When her eyelids finally flutter open, she looks at me with a dazed expression. "Was that... Did I—"

"That was hot, baby."

Her cheeks color. "I didn't think you could come from—"

"My fingers in your arse?" I smirk.

Her cheeks redden even more. "That sounds so dirty, and I shouldn't be turned on. I should not find this so arousing." She releases my hand and throws her arm over her eyes. "I'm so mortified."

I reach over and pull her arm away from her face. "Don't be. You're exquisite, you hear me? And you have no idea how incredible it feels to know I'm your first, in every way." I pull out my fingers, then reach over and pull a wet wipe from one of the packs scattered around the table. I wipe my fingers, toss it aside, then fit my cock to her forbidden hole. "Ready, baby?"

43

June

I nod slowly.

"You sure?" He bends over and peers into my eyes. "Do you want me to prep you further?"

"And make me come again?" It feels so intimate to do that. Makes me feel so very vulnerable. But also, I feel impatient. This entire experience has been so surprising. Who knew that part of me would be so sensitive?

"It's called the A-spot," he offers, almost as if he's reading my mind. Or perhaps, he sees the expression on my face and interprets it correctly?

"I promise you, it's going to feel good. And you're going to come so hard. You're going to love it."

I believe him because so far, he hasn't failed me. Also, I feel so, so turned on. And so limber. That orgasm definitely relaxed my muscles enough that I feel ready.

"Please, fuck me, I—" Even before the words are out of my mouth, he's pushed his big, thick cock inside my forbidden hole, and through the ring of muscle of my sphincter.

Pain pinches up my spine. I gasp, or try to, but nothing emerges from my mouth. Panic coils in my hind brain. I still seek the pain he can bestow on me, but... *Oh my god, this is like nothing I've ever felt before.* My master was right when he said he knew what my pain threshold was better than I do. *Oh god. Oh god. Nothing prepared me for his intrusion.*

He must see the shock in my eyes, for he cups my cheek. "Shh, baby, it will pass, I promise."

He kisses my mouth so tenderly, so softly, a sweetness I would have never suspected he harbored within him. The kind that seeps into my blood, calms my nerves, and coats my brain cells with a thick syrup of yearning. By the time he raises his head, I'm drugged with need. The burn where he penetrated me has eased up, to be replaced by a surge of pleasure that knifes through my insides. I moan, and he half smiles.

He kisses me again. This time, as he stabs his tongue into my mouth, he propels forward.

Suddenly, he's fully seated inside me. And it's uncomfortable, and huge, and yet it also feels right. He's filling me up in a completely unique way and it's... overwhelming. Sensations gather at the base of my spine. My heart knocks against my ribcage.

He stares into my eyes, twines his fingers through mine, and twists my arm up and over my head. He stays embedded in me, allowing me to adjust to his size. He leans enough of his weight on me that I'm not able to move, and yet, he's not too heavy so I know he's holding back. Sweat beads his forehead. The muscles in his jaw flex. It's only that, and the intensity of his gaze, that tells me he's not as calm as he seems.

I bring my free hand down between us and circle where he's seated in me. Instantly, his eyes flash. His lips part. And when the pulse at his temples kicks up, an answering beat thrums in my chest. Still holding my gaze, he pulls out, then thrusts inside me with enough force that the entire conference room table creaks.

"Oh!" I part my lips.

"Oh, indeed." He repeats the motion, and the table groans again. This time, he hits that spot deep inside me and I cry out. I squeeze down on his fingers and rub at the space where we're joined.

"Jesus, baby. You're going to send me over the edge."

"Good," I whisper. This pleases me so much. My heart seems to grow and fill my chest. I'm so happy. I feel so fulfilled to know I'm giving him this much pleasure.

He stares into my eyes, and it's so intimate. I feel the same sense of awe in him, see the surprise that it could feel this good, feel the shock that we fit so well together. Then, he slams into me again and again. He puts his entire weight behind it as he picks up speed. Each time he rams into me, he brushes against that spot.

Sparks zoom out from the point of contact to my extremities. My toes curl. At some point, I locked my ankles behind his back, and I feel his muscles flex with each thrust. It's animalistic and primal, and so very filthy and hot. So, so, hot. I push my breasts up and into his wide chest. And even through the layers of clothes we're wearing, I feel his pecs, the ridges between them, the coiled tension in his muscles. His breathing grows harsher, and the scent of him deepens. When he tilts his hips and plunges into me again, the angle is so intense, I cry out. A shudder rolls up my body. And the climax rears its head. It's going to overwhelm me, and I clutch at his fingers.

I'm going to lose myself. I'm going to shatter into a million tiny pieces. I'm going to dissolve into a puddle. I'm going to—" Knox," I beg, "please. Please. Please."

"Don't look away," he warns, then pushes into me again. At the same time, he releases my hand and slides it between us. He pinches my clit, and I scream "Knox."

"Give it to me, baby. Come with me. Now."

The orgasm burns through me. It incinerates everything in its path. It's a forest fire consuming me. Burning brighter. Higher. Still higher. Until it rears its head toward the skies and bursts into a fountain of light.

I'm dimly aware of his hoarse cry as he pours his release into me. Then, a warm darkness blankets me. I float for a while, feeling weightless, replete, and so, so spent.

I sense him pulling out of me. Hear the jingle of a belt and realize he's putting himself to rights. I doze off for a few moments and wake up in his lap. Still holding me, he rises from the chair. "Where are you taking me?" My words come out slurred. My throat feels like I've been screaming. Maybe I was. I can't remember.

He gathers me closer to his chest. "Shh, let me take care of you." He's already gathered up my skirt and my stilettos. The man is resourceful. He heads to the door and shoulders it open. He steps through, and when it shuts behind us, I rouse.

"Someone will see us —" I begin, but he cuts me off.

"I switched off all of the cameras. I also messaged Mary to tell everyone to stop what they were doing and go home at once. There's no one on this floor.

When did he — Oh, I must have dozed off for longer than I realized. That must be when he also switched off the cameras. I know he controls them via an app on his phone.

Then, another thought strikes me. "But everybody will know what we did."

"Does that bother you?"

"Umm — It does," I say honestly. Which is stupid because he's my husband. We're married, but doing this in the office, and especially when I stayed back in the conference room with him... People must have been speculating. I sigh. "I suppose it's inevitable they'll talk about us anyway."

"If I hear anyone has been gossiping about you, I'll fire them."

"Don't do that," I start. "I mean, it's normal for people to talk about us."

"Anyone makes you feel bad, they're gone."

I take in that uncompromising jaw of his, his chin with a hint of a dip in the center, that full lower lip... Then, because I can't stop myself, I reach up and place my palm against his gorgeous throat.

He flicks a glance down at me. "You okay?"

I nod. "I...like it when you get possessive."

His lips quirk. "What else do you like?"

"I like making you feel good."

"And I like that you like making me feel good." His features soften. "What else?"

"The orgasms." I chuckle. "Definitely, the orgasms."

"You like anal, huh?"

I slap at his chest. "I didn't say that."

He shoots me a look that says, 'remember how you came earlier?'

"Okay, I don't mind anal," I say reluctantly.

"Seemed to me, you enjoyed your first time, especially since you couldn't stop screaming my name."

I flush a little. "No need to look so happy."

He smirks, then reaching his office, he shoulders the door open. He walks across the floor to the ensuite and steps inside. He places my feet on the floor in front of the sink and places my skirt on the counter. He picks up a washcloth and wets it, then presses it between my legs, angled toward my sore backside.

"Oh, that feels good."

He urges me onto the counter next to the sink; then coaxes me to pick up my legs and place my heels at the edge of the counter. I don't feel self-conscious in exposing myself. Especially not when he flicks the washcloth into a bin, then reaches into a drawer and pulls out a tube of ointment. He proceeds to apply it around my slit and around my forbidden hole.

This time, I do feel embarrassed. "I can do it." I reach for the tube of ointment, but he brushes aside my hand.

He continues to smear the cooling ointment around my orifices, then caps it and drops it back in the drawer. He washes and dries his hands then turns to me. "How do you feel?"

"Good," I say with some bemusement. "A little tired, but good."

"Good." He bends and kisses my forehead, then pulls my panties from his pocket. I forgot about them, but my husband didn't. My heart melts a little more. If he'd left them behind on the conference room floor and someone else had found them, I'd have been so embarrassed. But he wouldn't let that happen.

He helps me down to the floor and goes down on one knee. I balance myself with one hand on his head and slide first one leg, then the other, into the underwear. He slides it up my thighs and smooths it over my hips. Then picks up the skirt and holds that out. I repeat the action, and he rises to his feet, tucking my blouse carefully inside the waistband of the skirt before pulling up the zipper. Then he slides the hook into place, once more smooths his palms over my cloth covered hips, and steps back. "All done."

"Thanks," I smile. "You're good at this."

"You sound surprised?"

I survey his features. "I guess, I am. I didn't expect you to be this... caring."

He tucks a strand of hair behind my ear. "You're mine, July. My wife. And I will always put your needs before mine. I will always take care of you. And when I push you out of your comfort zone, like I did earlier, I will make sure that I provide aftercare."

My heart turns to mush. I'm sure I have stars in my eyes. I love it when he talks with such possessiveness. I adore it when I am the recipient for his devotion. "I love you."

44

Knox

I love you too, wife. Of course, I love her. I know it. I've admitted it to myself. But saying it aloud? It feels like too much. Makes me feel like I've stripped off every defense between myself and the world and am standing naked before her. *Am I ready to do that? Am I ready to confess my feelings for her?*

My heart is willing, my soul has acquiesced, but my brain seems unable to form the three words she most wants to hear. Fear? Or perhaps, the fact that I'm getting used to how I feel for her? I know I need to tell her but when I clear my throat, I murmur, "As you wish."

Her gaze widens. "Did you quote from *The Princess Bride?*"

I pop a shoulder. "I'm not a complete neanderthal, contrary to how I often come across."

"Self-deprecating too." She chuckles. "My, my, Knox Davenport, there's more to you than meets the eye."

And you're all my eyes will ever want to see. Yours is the face I want to wake up to. Yours is the voice I want to hear every night when I go to sleep. You are my sun, the

*moon, and my stars. You are everything. The only thing that matters. It's always
been you. Only you.* And again, because I'm unable to voice my thoughts, I
content myself with reaching for her stilettos.

I go down on one knee and hold out a shoe. When she slips her foot
inside, I smooth a hand up her ankle, noting, with satisfaction, the goosebumps that pop on her skin, then hold out her other shoe. Once she's
wearing both, I straighten. "I'll get you your handbag so you can freshen
up."

"Oh." She turns to peer at her reflection. And like the coward I am, I
walk out of the bathroom and out of the office to her desk. I pull open the
bottom right-hand drawer, where I know she stores her bag, and return
with it.

By then, she's used my comb to smooth out her hair. She's also patted a
wet washcloth under her eyes and removed the mascara streaks, as well as
wiped her mouth. She drops the washcloth into the bin and accepts her
handbag. I watch as she refreshes her makeup, then draws her lipstick
over her mouth. She notices me following her actions in the mirror and
asks, "What?"

"I love watching you do that. It makes me feel closer to you, knowing
I'm the only one who gets this privilege."

"Privilege?" Her features soften.

"And it is one, to be your husband. I'll never take that gift lightly."

She holds my gaze for a few seconds. I sense the exact moment she
begins to realize what I said because she quirks one brow, then smirks.
Before she can point out the meaning of *As you wish*, I reach over and rub at
the corner of her mouth. "Your lipstick was awry."

"Thanks." She blushes, then scans herself with a critical look.

"You look good." I step up and wrap my arm about her waist, then
place my chin on her head. "You always look good, Mrs. Davenport."

"Thank you," she says softly. All the tension has faded from her
features, so I take that as a win.

"I have a surprise for you."

"You mean, the last one wasn't enough?" she asks jokingly.

"The last one was to pleasure your body. This one…" I hold her gaze in
the mirror. "This is for your soul."

"Where are we going?" She shoots me a sideways glance.

Once she had drunk the entire glass of juice, I'd poured for her from the refrigerator I kept in my office, I asked her if she wanted something to eat. She refused. I insisted she have an apple and watched her until she'd eaten it all. Then, she assumed we were heading home, but when I didn't take the turn-off to my place, she knew we were going somewhere else.

"It's a surprise." I do want to surprise her with what I'm about to do, but given how sensitive this is going to be, it might be best to give her some warning. "It's related to the conversation we had when I asked you to marry me."

She stills for a few seconds. I can tell when she connects the dots, for she turns to me. "You mean, tracking down my birth family?"

I glance at her sideways and find her looking at me wide-eyed.

"I assumed you'd want to meet her as soon as possible."

She pales further. "You found my birth mother?"

I nod slowly.

Tension radiates off of her.

"Hey, it's going to be okay." I reach out and place my hand over her joined ones.

I'm glad I asked my chauffeur to drive. This way, I can give my wife my full attention."

"We don't have to do this now." I scan her features. "We can postpone—"

"No." She turns to me. Her features are tense, but there's resolution in her eyes. "All my life, I've wondered about where I came from. I've wanted to find out who my biological family is, to find out why she... Did what she did. You know? And yes, it's difficult to think about it and to see her, but I want to... I need to do this."

"This is the address?" She looks from me to the house by the side of the road.

"That's the one, according to the adoption search specialist." We met her a few hours ago at her office. She gave us a brief summary of how she'd tracked down my wife's birth mother. She also gave us the name and the address. Her birth mother, apparently, lives alone and has never married. She also didn't have any other children. At least, none that the adoption search specialist was able to unearth. Turns out, she lives in Brighton, less than a two-hour drive from where we were.

My wife wanted to go see her right away. I asked her if she wanted to sleep on it, perhaps. Take a day to think about it. But July insisted. She called Irene on the way and told her what she was going to do. Irene was very supportive about it and told her she'd always be there for July, no matter what. My wife had tears in her eyes as she recounted the conversation to me. I was struck by how close she and Irene are. Irene is her adoptive mother, but their relationship is also one of best friends.

I never had a close relationship with my mother. She was the woman who gave birth to me, but I was one of a brood of boys. And my mother brought us up, more or less, on her own. My father was too focused on managing his relationship with Arthur, and keeping his role at the Davenport group, to play an active role in our upbringing. My mother worshipped the ground he walked on and spent all of her time trying to figure out how to get more of his attention. So, I never had the opportunity to get to know either of them well. My father's youngest brother Quentin became the most influential adult in my life. And when Q decided to join the Marines, he set an example that my brothers and I decided to follow. My wife is fortunate to have Irene in her life.

"You sure you don't want me to come in with you?"

She turns back to me. "I have to do this on my own."

I frown. *Is this another instance of her being stronger than I realized? Or is she overstretching herself? Like she thought she could handle me, and all that it involved, the night of our wedding? Or is she in a space where she's ready to do this on her own?*

She searches my features. "You don't believe I can?"

I rub my chin. "It's not that."

"Then, what is it?" She glances at the house, then back at me. "I've wanted to meet with my birth mother for so long. There are so many questions I want to ask of her. I've dreamed about this moment and built it up in my mind." She locks her hands together.

"This is going to be emotionally difficult for you, and I want to be there for you," I say softly.

She nods. "I know you do. But I want to do this on my own, so I can prove to myself that I can face the big question that's haunted me for most of my life." She reaches forward and grips my hand. "You understand what I'm saying, right? It's for my own self-esteem that I need to face this by myself."

45

June

The sound of a dog barking reaches me. I heard it as I walked up the garden path toward the house. I stare at the doorbell next to the pale blue door of what could be my birth mother's place. It's nice-looking, with a well-maintained garden and flowers lining the short walk to the doorstep. And the neighborhood seems like a typical middle class one. So, she's not struggling. I'm grateful for that. But it also raises the question: if she's a woman of some means, why didn't she try to track me before this?

Gosh, I have so many questions. About her. About my father. One of the big issues of not knowing where I come from is that I have no answer for the inevitable questions related to my medical history when I go to the doctor. I hope she'll be able to shed some light on this. I probably won't be able to ask about this in our first meeting, but hopefully, if we cultivate a relationship, I'll be able to get more information about this... I draw in a breath.

I've waited for this moment for so long, but now that it's here, I'm filled with trepidation.

Once I knock on the door, there's no going back. My past will no longer be what I'd imagined it to be. Once that door opens, everything will change. I'll know the truth of who I am. Where I come from and... I'm ready for it.

I raise my hand to ring the doorbell, then lower it. My stomach ties itself in knots, and I feel like I'm going to be sick. Instinct has me turning to glance over my shoulder to where the car is parked on the other side of the sidewalk.

My husband's leaning against the side of the car, and when our gazes meet, he nods at me. His expression is reassuring. Seeing his broad shoulders and his hewn-out-of-stone features sends a shiver down my spine. Guess I'll never be impervious to his charms. It also fills me with confidence to know he'll be at the car waiting for me.

He held my hand all the way here, and his presence filled me with confidence. It took the edge off what could've been a nerve-wracking few hours. And the fact that he remembered to contact the adoption search specialist and help me in tracking down my birth mother? Honestly, I'm so taken aback he remembered. Sure, he said it was one of the conditions for our getting married, but I didn't expect him to act on it so quickly. He must have realized how important it was to me to find her. He insisted on coming with me. And he didn't speak or ask any questions. I'm so grateful for that.

He wanted to come in with me...but I... I knew this was something I had to do on my own. My first meeting with my birth mother has to be just the two of us.

My husband wasn't happy, but he acquiesced. Still, having him there gave me the courage to get out of the car and walk to the door. And now, I'm here. *Oh god.* I swallow. He must sense my apprehension, for he places his fingers to his lips and blows me a kiss.

It's such a non-Knox thing to do, such a soft romantic gesture, that I can't help smiling. The tension inside me fades a little. I blow him a kiss back, then square my shoulders. I turn and ring the doorbell.

The dog starts barking more insistently. It's countered by a woman's voice saying something. The words are muffled. *Is it her voice? My birth mother's voice?* My heart begins to pound behind my ribcage. My palms grow sweaty. My stomach heaves, and I take a step back. *Ohgod. Ohgod.*

Ohgod. I can't do this. I can't. Then I hear his voice in my head: *You can, wife. You can.*

The confidence I've always felt from him reaches out to me, bridging the distance between us. I feel his presence, even though I know he's not standing next to me. I sense his watchful gaze on me from where he's standing beside the car.

I sense his strength supporting me. I sense...that he's with me. That he'll be there for me, no matter what happens inside this house. A calm descends on me. I firm my spine, square my shoulders, and when the door opens and I meet the gaze of the woman who I intuitively know is my birth mother, a resilience pours though my veins. I can see myself in her features. *Oh. God. Finally, after all these years, I'm seeing someone who looks like me.* It's surreal. It's also so grounding. Something clicks into place inside of me. I feel a little more complete than I was before I met her. I'm also surprised by how young she looks. I made up all kinds of images of my mother in my head, but nothing prepared me for the fact that she doesn't look that much older than me.

She searches my face, and her eyes light up. *She knows who I am.* The German Shepherd, whose collar she's holding onto, barks again. He pulls at her, and she must be taken aback by seeing me, for he breaks away and springs forward.

"Bruno no," she yells. But the mutt's excited. He's wagging his tail hard as he lunges toward me.

He's not attacking, but I instinctively step backward and lose my footing. Seeing the woman who's my birth mother must have weakened my sense of equilibrium, for I find myself stumbling back.

I throw my arms up to try to hold onto something and catch air. I keep falling, only instead of hitting the ground, firm hands descend on my waist. Then I'm righted. Heat flushes my skin, and I know it's him.

"Bruno, no! Get back." My birth mother grabs at Bruno's collar and wrenches him back. He whimpers and looks up at her innocently.

"I'm so sorry." She looks to my husband, who has his arm around me, then back to me. "He's normally better behaved. Bruno, sit."

To my surprise, the German Shephard parks his butt on the cement. He continues to wag his tail and look at me with melting brown eyes.

"It's my fault; sorry, he took me by surprise." I hold out my palm, and he sniffs it. Then he licks my fingers, and I smile. "He's adorable."

She looks at her dog. "He's a rescue, and from the day he arrived, he changed my life." Her features soften. Then she clears her throat and looks at me. "You're my daughter."

Her words hit me in the chest. I take another step back, or would, if not for my husband's grip on my shoulders stopping me. He must sense the turmoil in me, for he holds out his hand. "Knox Davenport, and this is my wife June Donnelly Davenport."

She buries her fingers in Bruno's fur and scratches behind his ears, crooning, "It's okay; it's okay." I can tell, it's as much to calm her nerves as it is for him. Slowly, she smiles and reaches out to shake my husband's hand. "Claire Gilbert."

So, that was my original surname? It doesn't feel familiar, at all. In fact, I don't feel anything for it. My mother's name, though... That was in the 'life story book' Irene once handed to me. She'd pieced it together, based on the file she'd received from social services. That book was part of my nighttime reading throughout my growing years. Every time I had questions, Irene would read it with me. She explained how I came to be with her, and that primal wound inside me would be filled, temporarily. Only, it never went away.

Now, I follow the woman who possibly has answers to so many of my questions. She leads us to the living room, which is an open plan, separated from the adjoining kitchen by a breakfast counter.

The decor is modern and comfortable. Wooden floors, deep sofas with cushions, a modern television hung on the wall above the fireplace. There are white and blue curtains at the windows of the living room, through which a backyard is visible. There are paintings—all abstracts—on the walls, but no photographs of family. One wall has a bookshelf overflowing with books, and there are more books in a stack next to it, pushed up against one wall.

There's no sign of dust anywhere. Everything is sparkling, and there's a vase full of flowers on one end of the breakfast bar. The scent of roses and lilies fills the air. It's not overpowering, but soothing. In fact, the entire space has a peaceful feeling about it. Some of the tension drains from my shoulders.

She walks straight through to the kitchen and begins to fill a pot with water. "I'm going to make us tea." She flicks the kettle on and busies herself with taking down cups from the shelves, then turns to look at us. "You will have some tea, won't you? Goodness, I should have checked first. I just assumed"—she shakes her head—"I'm sorry, I'm more thrown than I realized."

"Me too." I walk over to join her. "Why don't I make the tea?"

Standing so close to her, I realize, I'm a couple of inches taller than her, probably because I'm wearing stilettos. But our frame is similar. I'm not a slim person, and neither is my mother. She's not overweight either, and her figure is youthful and curvy, similar to mine. She wears her blonde hair piled on her head in a fashion I often prefer. And her eyes—her brown eyes—so like mine, gleam with intelligence. She's also wearing spectacles. I've always hated that I was short-sighted, but now it makes me feel a kinship with the woman who birthed me.

She looks well put together. And I... I'm not sure what I expected? That she'd be a sad, lonely person? Someone who spent her every waking moment thinking about the daughter she gave up? *Did she think of me at all?*

Perhaps, she sees some of my questions in my eyes, for her own grow watery. She sniffs, then blinks away her tears, and her lips curve in a gentle smile. "The teabags are in that shelf"—she gestures to the one above me on my right—"and the milk is in the fridge. If you need sugar—"

"I don't."

She looks at me with a hint of surprise and recognition. "I don't either. I have a sweet tooth, but when it comes to my tea, I prefer the natural bitter taste."

"Me too," I swallow. *This...this is what I've been looking for.* This feeling of being recognized. Of seeing myself in the face of another. Of being mirrored in some form. All my life, I've searched for this feeling of kinship. No matter, that I love Irene and my siblings, I've always felt something was missing. Despite the fact that I've resented my biological mother for giving me up, I've always known I needed to meet her face-to-face, in order to move on. Now that I'm here, though, all those questions have vanished. Everything I thought I wanted to ask her? All of that seems so unimportant.

My husband clears his throat. "Why don't I take Bruno for a walk while the two of you catch up."

"Thank you." She gazes at Knox with a grateful look on her features. "If you don't mind…" She disappears inside the house and re-emerges with a leash that she hands over to Knox. "There's a park at the end of the road."

"I'm sure I'll find it okay. Come on, boy." He hooks the leash onto Bruno's collar. The dog woofs and prances about, evidently sensing the outing and happy to follow him.

My husband leads him over to me. He kisses my forehead. "I'll be a phone call away, if you need anything." He surveys me closely. "You okay?"

"Yes." I lean up on tiptoes and, not caring that Claire is watching, I press my lips to his. "Thanks."

He kisses me back, then heads for the door.

"He's a good man," Claire says softly. "He obviously loves you very much."

"He does." *Even though he hasn't said it to me yet, I know he does.* I could see it in his features when he wanted to accompany me in here. I've seen it in his eyes when he makes love to me. And I knew it when he said, *As you wish. So, why hasn't he said the actual words yet?* Tears prick my eyes, and I realize I'm much more emotionally fragile than I thought.

My husband was right; I couldn't have done this on my own. Just knowing he's nearby gives me the strength to keep this conversation going. Never mind the fact that he hasn't come clean about his feelings which, along with the shock of meeting my birth mother, is making me feel too vulnerable. I clear my throat. "I'll uh—make the tea."

I hear her move away, then the scrape of a chair against the floor as she seats herself.

I'm conscious of her watching me as I pour the hot water onto the teabags, then retrieve the milk from the fridge. I pour a little milk into both cups, then take a spoon and stir the tea.

"Leave the teabag in," she instructs.

I stiffen, then turn slowly to look at her. "That's how I also take my tea," I whisper.

A teardrop rolls down her cheek. I hold back a sniffle and carry both cups over to the dining table. We sip our tea for a few seconds. I look up. "I—"

At the same moment she says, "I'm so sorry, June."

I bite the inside of my cheek.

"I really am sorry for what you must have gone through." She swallows.

I hook my fingers through the handle of the cup and raise it to my lips, "I haven't had a bad life. Far from it. Thanks to Irene—"

"Irene?"

"She adopted me when I was eleven. If not for her, I might not have turned out the way I did."

Claire's lips firm. She seems to digest what I said, then nods, "I'm glad, she turned out to be good people."

"Irene's the best." I feel compelled to share about my adoptive mother, perhaps, as a way of drawing a contrast between everything she did for me and Claire didn't? Honestly, I can't say, but I don't curb my instinct to speak. Not when I've waited so long to have this conversation with my birth mother. "After me, Irene also adopted Jillian and Ethan. She gave us a family. A home. A sense of identity. She's always encouraged us to find our own way. She ensured our past didn't hold us back."

Claire winces, then seems to compose herself. "I'd love to meet her," she says in a soft voice.

I look at her in surprise. "You would?" I certainly hadn't expected my birth mother to say that, and within minutes of meeting her, too.

"Why wouldn't I?" Claire half smiles.

"Just... I—," I try to form the words in my head. "Don't you feel threatened by her?"

"Why should I be?" Her smile turns sad. "She did everything I couldn't do for my daughter. I might have given birth to you, but she's the one who guided you through life. She made you the woman you are today."

Something clenched inside of me loosens. I didn't realize how conflicted I was about searching for my birth ties. In a way, it felt like I was being disloyal to Irene. While that wasn't my intention, I was never able to fully rid myself of that feeling.

"I wanted to find you...so many times," Claire admits.

"Why didn't you?" I cry. Some of the anger I thought I'd resolved bubbles up to the surface. "I thought about you every single day."

"So did I," she says softly. "I never forgot you, June. But I also didn't want to risk turning your life upside down. I convinced myself that you were better off wherever you were without me."

My thoughts ricochet around in my head. "I made up all these stories about you. I told myself you were a princess in a tower somewhere, and some villain was keeping you away from me. As I grew older, I was sure there was a reason you didn't search me out. I was angry with you one second, and the next, I would have given anything to see you." Emotions choke my throat, and I take another sip of tea to try and keep my tears at bay. *Gosh, I don't want to turn into a case of waterworks.*

"I am truly sorry for everything." She reaches out to place her hand on mine. I want to shake it off, but the warmth of her touch feels so right, I don't.

It's this contradiction in emotions that drives me crazy. This, wanting her to be in my life and loving her simply because she gave birth to me, and yet, always wanting to hold a grudge for how she cast me out of her life.

"Why did you do it? Why did you give me up?" The words burst out of me. "Why, Claire? Why?"

She winces, maybe because I called her by her given name. But what did she expect? Irene is my mother. And although this connection between Claire and me will always remain, I realize, I'm not ready to welcome her back into my life. Not without getting some understanding of the circumstances behind what led to her casting me out of her life.

"I was sixteen and pregnant. My family were devout Catholics. I went to a convent school for girls, where it was drilled into us that sex was a sin. I was rebellious. I couldn't accept what they told me. I always pushed boundaries."

Like me. I, too, was rebellious and hated restrictions being put on me, but I attributed that to being in the system and acting out to gain attention. But maybe, there's more to it. Maybe, it's part of my personality to test boundaries.

But maybe... That's because I secretly craved to be controlled. Which is why I'm so attracted to Knox. And his natural dominance invites me to put myself at his mercy. The relief that he'll recognize my needs and do what's right for me... Is something I appreciate even more now. It allows me to find a space where I can relax into myself. The limits he imposes on me, his commands, his orders—all of it gives me permission to let him take care of me. And that...is so incredibly freeing. I bring my attention back to what Claire's saying.

She leans back in her seat. "I always challenged authority and was often punished by my parents and teachers for it." She laughs without humor. "And once I hit puberty, I couldn't stay away from boys. I would sneak off on dates, which was forbidden by my parents, so I had to do it even more. And when I found myself pregnant. I knew my parents would disown me, so I never told them."

I frown. "What did you do?"

"I ran away from home. Being a minor, I was picked up by social services, and after I gave birth, relinquished all rights to you. It wasn't a decision I made easily, but I thought it was the best chance to give you a better start in life. I was sure you'd be adopted right away." She shakes her head. "I never imagined you'd be in foster care for so many years." She peers into my face. "You have to believe that what I did was done out of love. But I hoped you'd find me. I prayed you'd find your way to me."

"You did?" I rub at my temple. "You wanted me to find you?"

"I wanted to give the Council my address when I gave you up. I knew you'd get access to your records when you turned eighteen, and I hoped you'd find me then. Unfortunately, my mother found out what I'd done, and she removed any information that could be traced back to me. And I didn't find out for many years."

That's why the Council's file on me is so lean.

"But I thought of you every day." She takes another sip of tea and sets down her cup. "It's why, when the adoption search specialist reached out to me, I told her I'd be happy to meet you immediately."

"You were?" I swallow.

"I've been expecting you." She half smiles. "The adoption search specialist didn't give me more details about you, but I've been hoping you'd turn up on my doorstep. And when I saw your face, it was like I was looking at a younger version of myself."

Tears well up again, and I swallow them back. "And my father, what about him?"

Her features grow sad. "I'm embarrassed to admit this, but I didn't know him. I'd sneaked into a nightclub, met him there and had sex with him in the back alley." She rubs at her temple. "I never met him again. I didn't know his name or who he was so I couldn't tell him I was pregnant. I'm so sorry, June. I wish I had better news for you."

My chest tightens. I glance away. It's a lot to take in. I spent so much time thinking about my birth mother that my birth father was this shadowy figure who I hardly gave as much importance. And chances are, I'll never find him, even with the services of the best adoption search specialist in the country.

She reaches over and takes my hand in hers again. "You have no idea how many times I regretted my choices. How many times I questioned my actions. But looking at you today, at the woman you've become, at how beautiful you are and how intelligent and so full of promise, I don't regret anything."

I peer into her face, and the calmness and the love in her eyes are a soothing balm. That place inside of me yearning for my mother so much and for so long relaxes. I turn my palm over and grip hers. "It's so incredible, finally meeting someone whose features resemble mine. It's like I've finally found an anchor. A thread that connects me to this earth. Like I've found an explanation for my being here, you know?"

She nods, and a tear rolls down her cheek. "I'm so sorry for all the years we lost. So sorry for everything you went through. I wanted to go in search of you, but also, I wanted to believe you were happy. And I didn't want to intrude on your life. It had to be your choice to find me."

I suppose, I understand. But also, I don't. Maybe, a part of me will never be able to understand why this happened to me. But it is what it is. What I do know is that I'm lucky now to have two mothers: Irene and Claire. Now that I've met her and have the opportunity to get to know her, I'm not going to squander that. I choose to heal. I choose the positive side of life. I choose to be happy. That much is in my hands. I allow my tears to flow and smile through them.

"You were too young when I was born, and you didn't have a choice in relinquishing me. Neither did I." I turn my palm face up and clasp her fingers with mine. "I understand, you did what you thought was best. I forgive you."

46

Knox

I tuck my wife into my side. She has her hands locked together and has barely spoken a word since we left Claire's place.

An hour after I left, she messaged me and said she was ready to go. When I arrived to pick her up, she and Claire hugged.

Both women had tear-stained faces, but there seemed to be an understanding between them. The meeting, and whatever they spoke about during it, hopefully began the process of healing for both of them.

They promised to keep in touch, and June invited Claire to dinner at our place. She said she'd also invite Irene over. She'll call to confirm a date for some time soon. Then she patted Bruno, and we left.

Once inside the car, I open my arms, and she comes into my embrace willingly. She doesn't say anything, and I let her be. It was a long and emotionally testing day, and I know she needs time to recuperate. So, I hold her close, kiss the top of her head, and stare at the passing scenery. When the car eases to a stop in front of our apartment block, I look down to find she's fallen asleep. When the driver opens the door, I step out with her in my arms. She doesn't move as I carry her inside and to our private elevator, then up to our penthouse. I remove her shoes and her skirt and pull the covers over her. Then, not yet ready to sleep, I walk out into the living room and prepare to pour myself a drink.

When the security app on my phone signals there's someone at the door to the apartment, I stare at the face on the screen. *Ryot? What's he doing here?* He's the most silent of my brothers. He also doesn't want anything to do with the Davenport Group.

He's chosen to forge his own way and has made it clear to Arthur he doesn't want anything to do with the family fortune. So, to have him call is not an ordinary occurrence. It's the only reason I allow the elevator doors to open on my floor. He stands there with a scowl on his face.

"Ryot," I say by way of greeting.

He glares at me but stays silent. No surprise there. I gesture for him to come in. He stomps past me toward the floor-to-ceiling windows that cover one side of the living room, and stares at the lights of the city outside.

"Care for something to drink?"

He folds his arms across his chest.

"I take it, that's a 'no'?" I eye him warily. "What are you doing here?"

"You're an asshole," he says by way of greeting.

"Thanks?" I respond, half amused, half pissed-off. If it were any of my other brothers, I'd tell them to fuck off.

But with Ryot... Considering he never wastes his words, when he speaks, you listen.

"If you were in my place, you'd realize how lucky you are. If you saw what Michael's going through, you'd realize how fortunate you are to have everything."

"How is Michael?" Michael Sovrano is a friend of ours who lost his wife a few months ago. He went into a tailspin and dropped out of sight. "I heard from Connor that he decided to move back to Italy?"

Ryot nods, then lowers his chin. "I met him, briefly, before he left."

"You did?" *That's news to me.* "I didn't realize Michael had spoken to one of us before he left."

"He needed my help," he says simply.

Ryot, too, lost his wife. Like him, she served in the Marines, though in a different platoon. Her entire team was wiped out when they were in enemy territory. The grief was too much for him. He left the Marines shortly after.

"So, Michael's okay?"

Ryot grunts. "As okay as can be expected, considering."

"Hmm." I rub at my whiskered chin.

He widens his stance "But I'm here to talk about you and how absolutely asinine you are in not recognizing what you have."

"And what's that?"

"Have you told your wife that you love her?"

I fold my arms across my chest. It's a classic defensive position, but what-fucking-ever. "What's that got to do with anything?"

"You love her, but knowing what a wanker you are, I'll bet you haven't told her."

I draw myself up to my full height. "That's my personal business."

"No, that's all our business."

I growl, "I hate that we've always felt it's our right to get into each other's personal space."

His features soften a little. "It's all we had when our parents decided they had no time for us, or have you forgotten?"

I incline my head. "You're right. It was the only way we could put up a united front against Arthur," I say in recollection. "Gramps was always a mean ol' bastard. We knew, even then, the only way we could guard against his dictatorial ways was to stick close together."

Ryot's expression grows more vulnerable. "Of all of us, you and I are most alike."

It might be the fact that we're the ones who seek control the most, as well as the ones who rebelled the most. Which means, we had to stick up for each other and save each other from Arthur's wrath the most. But Ryot's right. I nod. "We have a bond that runs deeper than what we share with our other brothers…" I agree.

"It's why I know that you haven't told her you love her."

I rub the back of my neck. "I need a drink." I head toward the bar and pour myself a tumbler of Macallan. I toss it back. The alcohol burns its way down my throat and sets a fire in my belly.

"If you knew what I go through every single day." His voice reaches me. "If you knew how, every time I close my eyes, I see her face. What I'd give to speak to her one more time and tell her that I love her... You wouldn't be dicking around the way you are right now."

The hurt in his voice, the anguish of knowing he'll never again be able to tell his wife those three words, reaches out to me.

If anything were to happen to June... If I lost her, knowing I'd never told her about my true feelings for her, I'd never forgive myself. Ryot, and what happened to his wife, is a reminder I'm wasting time. I'm fighting with imaginary devils. My wife, clearly, is stronger than me—she had the courage to face her own. She wanted to do it on her own; that's how bold she is. Meanwhile, me? I've been dicking around, as my brother so eloquently put it.

I might be dominant, but when it comes to facing my own feelings, when it comes to telling her those three words, I haven't been able to do it.

I pour another splash of amber liquid into the glass and, holding it, turn to him. "How did you guess?" I murmur.

"That you haven't told her your true feelings?" He heads toward me and joins me at the bar, leaning a hip against it. "Because I know you well, brother. I know you're as stubborn as me. That you're as pig-headed as me. That you don't know a good thing when it smacks you in your face. Given how you hurried into the wedding, I had no doubt, you did it because you have feelings for her."

I level a disbelieving look at him. "Didn't it cross your mind that I did it to fulfill Arthur's condition and to keep my role as CEO?"

His lips twist. "You and I both know; Arthur doesn't have that much influence over us. Sure, our brothers might have kidded themselves with that, saying that's why they married their wives. But they also did it because they fell in love."

I stare at him, dumbfounded.

He gives me a look that conveys his opinion—*You knobhead.* He rolls his eyes and continues, "No matter, it took them a while to admit it. And it's not a big jump from there to conclude you did the same thing." He reaches for the bottle of Macallan and pours a little into a tumbler. "It's why I came here, to tell you not to squander the chance you've been given." He looks down into his glass.

I take in the hardness of his features. The lines around his eyes. The grey at his temples, which wasn't there before. He's suffered since his wife's death. And clearly, he's been working out even more, for he's become a behemoth.

"Thanks," I murmur.

He raises his glass. "I know you'll do the right thing. You—"

"Knox?" My wife's voice reaches me from the doorway.

47

June

Ryot nods in my direction, then turns to my husband. A look I can't decipher passes between them. Then, Ryot jerks his head, and walks past me, toward the elevator.

"Everything okay?" My husband walks over to me.

"I woke up and thought I heard voices." It's why I changed into a pair of yoga pants and a sweatshirt before I came to investigate.

The elevator doors swish shut behind me.

"He decided to drop in with some brotherly advice." My husband tucks a strand of hair behind my ear. "You hungry? You want something to eat?"

"I'm not really hungry," I demur.

"You need to eat something." He leads me into the kitchen.

"Brotherly advice, you say?" I lean a hip against the island and watch him pull the ingredients for a sandwich from the fridge. He's wearing his pants and a button-down but has lost the jacket and tie. He's also barefoot, and his hair is mussed. With the shadow of a beard on his chin, he's so sexy. So delightfully rumpled. My pussy clenches. I grip the edge of the counter to stop myself from doing something stupid like walking over and wrapping my arms about his waist and pressing my nose into his back and drawing in his heady masculine smell. *Give the man some space, will ya?*

"Mm-hmm." He cuts open a couple of avocados, dices them and adds them onto two of the bread slices. He slathers on peanut butter and jelly, then proceeds to crush some potato crisps and sprinkle them on top. He places fresh slices on top, slides one of the resulting sandwiches onto a plate, and offers it to me.

"Umm, I'm not sure—" I begin but he cuts me off.

"Don't mock it until you try it." He pours orange juice into two glasses and places them between us. Then, he grabs a stool, picks up his sandwich, and bites into it. He chews, then swallows. "Delicious."

I slip onto another stool and take a small bite. "Not bad," I concede.

"It's bloody good." He takes another giant bite from his sandwich, washing it down with the juice.

I follow his example, finding I'm hungrier than I realized. Before I'm halfway done with the sandwich, he's finished his. I place the sandwich down and take a small sip of the juice.

"When did you learn to make this combination?"

"It was late one evening, when I was still in high school. I got home at midnight felt hungry and raided the refrigerator, and by the time I'd started assembling the sandwich, Ryot had joined me. I found whatever was available and decided to throw it together. Ryot was the first to taste it, and when he polished it off, I realized I had a hit on my hands."

"The two of you are close."

"We used to be closer. But after his wife died, he withdrew into himself. Good thing, he's found a new assignment. Might help take his mind off the past."

"Assignment?" I pick up my sandwich again and take another bite. It really does taste better than what I expected.

"He's joining Quentin's security agency. Apparently, he's been allocated to a very confidential detail."

"That's good, right?"

I nod. "I hope it helps keep his mind occupied and gives him a chance to re-discover his spirit."

"You're a good brother," I offer.

He rolls his shoulders. "If I were, I wouldn't've agreed to marry Priscilla in the first place. Not when I realized there was history between her and Tyler, and it would hurt him."

"But you didn't go through with it, did you?"

He shakes his head.

I hold up my hands. "I maintain, you all seem to have each other's backs."

The skin around his eyes crinkles. "You insist on seeing the good in me, don't you?"

I blush a little, then flutter my eyelashes, "Of course, I do. I'm your wife."

Our gazes meet, hold. That chemistry between us, always fluttering beneath the surface, intensifies. My nipples harden, and my scalp tightens. A thick pulse kicks up between my legs.

He must sense my arousal for his gaze darkens. Then, he seems to collect himself and nods in the direction of my plate. "Eat."

I obediently pick up my sandwich and nibble on it.

"How do you feel about having met Claire?" he asks.

I swallow past the lump in my throat, place the sandwich back on the plate, and stare at the crumbs there. "It was what I expected, but also... Not. I built it up in my head more than I realized. And then to meet her..." I shake my head. "I felt an instant connection, but it also put things in perspective."

"How's that?"

"It made me realize how much I already have. With Irene and my siblings, and with you." I hold his gaze. "I thought I was alone, but I wasn't. I already had a family with Irene. And now I have two families. And a third, which is even more important, with you."

His expression softens. And when I slide off my stool and walk around the island to him, he opens his arms. I step in between his legs and slide my arms about his neck. "Thank you for taking me to see her."

"It wasn't too sudden, was it?" He searches my features. "I was worried that, perhaps, I should have forewarned you more."

"I was ready to meet her. And it was never going to get easier. In fact, it was good you didn't give me too much advance notice. I might have gotten cold feet." I laugh a little. "So, you're good."

His stares at me.

"What?"

"I love your laughter, baby."

I find myself flushing and glance away.

He notches his knuckles under my chin and gently turns my chin in his direction. "No, don't hide from me. I love nothing more than gazing into your eyes." He cups my cheek. "I love your eyes, you know that?" He bends and kisses my eyelids. "And your cute little upturned nose." He kisses the tip of my nose.

"It's not upturned."

"It is." He smiles. "And your stubborn chin." He presses his lips there, "And the way you blush so prettily." He kisses me first, on one cheek, then the other. "And your smile. I adore your smile." He presses a kiss to the corner of my mouth, then the other.

"And how you taste." He brushes his lips over mine, and when I part my lips, he swipes his tongue across the seam of my mouth. A moan spills from my lips, and he swallows it up. He continues to kiss me for a few seconds more, then pulls back slightly. "What I'm trying to say is that I love *you*."

48

Knox

I watch her closely as I say the words and am rewarded by her eyes widening in surprise. But she also looks wary. I frown. Not the response I expected.

"I love you, my June. I think I knew I would the moment I saw you. I knew, subconsciously, that I loved you when I proposed to you. It's why I couldn't go through with the arrangement Arthur had proposed. I knew it when I placed my grandmothers' ring on your finger. I was sure about it when I consummated our wedding. And I was sure about it, when I saw you stumble at your birth mother's place earlier. When her dog lunged toward you, and you slipped? I swear, my heart almost punched out of my chest."

Understanding comes into her eyes. "How did you get behind me so quickly? You were at the car, and then—"

"My feet didn't touch the ground." I half laugh. "I know you wanted to go in there on your own. And I know I agreed. But my instinct—that side of me I can't switch off from having been a Marine—couldn't relax." I firm my lips. "I didn't take my gaze off of you as you walked toward the house. And when I saw the dog barking and straining to break free—" I shake my head. "My instincts screamed at me to move closer to you. So, when Bruno jumped toward you, I was halfway up the path to the door. I raced forward. The next thing I knew, I was standing behind you. And not a second too late." I shudder.

"If anything had happened to you, baby, I never would've forgiven myself. I was already berating myself for having brought you there without preparing you more. And then, you wanted to meet her alone, and I agreed. And I just knew, while I respected your decision, I also wanted to be there with you. So, I followed my instinct, and thank god for that."

She stays silent and my heart begins to race. *Why isn't she responding? Why isn't she saying something. Does she not believe me?* "June?" I search her features. "Talk to me baby. What is it?"

"Despite my telling you I could handle it; you decided you were going to accompany me in there?" She frowns.

I blow out a breath. "I do trust you, June. I do. And I was ready to let you go in there and deal with your devils on your own, but"—I shake my head—"call it a Marine's instinct. As you walked up that garden path, something in me insisted I prepare to follow you. And when I saw the way that dog was acting, I knew I had to move closer, just in case you needed me. And you did. If you hadn't started to fall, I would have stayed back. I'm not going to apologize for being there."

"You won't?" The fold between her eyebrows deepens.

"I'll always do what's best for you, even if it means, sometimes, going against what you want." I peer into her face. "I'm sorry if that upsets you, but you need to trust my judgement too. I am your Master, and that means I'll do everything in my power to take care of you. I am duty-bound to keep you safe, and I'll do that, even at the cost of pissing you off."

She glances away. My heart sinks. I'm being honest with her. I'll never lie to her. "June, say something," I plead.

She hunches her shoulders. "I understand what you did, I suppose. And in the end, it worked out because you were there when I needed you most. You were right."

"I was?" Hope has a chokehold on my heart. Warmth floods my skin.

"As it turned out, I was so relieved to have you there. Your presence gave me the strength to face all of the images from my past that came flooding back. I couldn't have done it without you."

"I love you." I cup her cheek. "I do, July. I love you so much."

"You... You love me?" She swallows, as if hearing me for the first time.

I plant my hands on her hips and draw her closer. "I love you. I wish I'd had the balls to tell you so earlier, but I hope you' realize how much I mean it." I hold her gaze. "I want you with me, in my life, by my side, through thick and thin, for better or worse, through sickness and in health. Through all the ups and downs of life. I need you, July. Only you. It was always you. There's no one else but you."

"Oh, Knox. I have waited so long to hear those words from you."

I bend and kiss her forehead, then her eyelids, then her nose. I press my lips to hers and whisper, "I love you. I have loved you from the second I laid eyes on you. I had a sneaky feeling you were going to be my downfall. And when I realized how you had the gumption to challenge me, I knew you were going to be my undoing. I knew I was going to be powerless when it came to you. I knew I'd met my ruin, so I had to find a way to resist my emotions."

"Of course, you did," she says dryly.

"You're my kryptonite, baby. I knew you'd put a chink in my armor, and that would change my future forever." I half smile. "I also knew it was inevitable, but that didn't stop me from putting up a fight. And then what Ryot told me earlier—"

"I knew there was a reason he was here," she says, almost triumphantly.

"There was. He came by to kick my arse into gear, and to tell me I needed to man up and tell you how I felt."

"He told you that?" she asks in wonder.

"Not that politely, but yeah, that was the gist of the conversation. But I have to say, even if he hadn't come by, I'd have told you my feelings. What he said simply confirmed to me that I was doing the right thing. I knew I couldn't wait any longer. I knew I had to do it right now."

I bend and push my forehead into hers.

"I love you, July. I'll never stop loving you. I promise to take care of you, and look after you, and protect you. I promise to always keep you happy. When I say I want to spend my life with you, I'm serious. I want to be with you, July. I want to wake up next to you and fall asleep with you in my arms. I want to wipe your tears and see you smile and do everything in my power to keep you happy. I love you. I love you. I love you." I swallow. "And I can't imagine anything better than breathing the same air as you." I take in her features and sweat pools in my armpits. Shit. Why isn't she saying anything? "July?" I narrow my gaze. "Say something."

She stays quiet a few seconds more, then a big smile curves her lips. "I feel the same way."

49

June

I glance across the front seat of the Jaguar and take in my husband's thick fingers on the wheel of the car. He's dressed in a black T-shirt that stretches across his broad chest. The short sleeves mean his arms are bare, and when he turns off the highway, the veins in his forearms flex. My thighs clench. My clit begins to throb. Damn, this man is a walking, talking sex-on-legs. Just looking at him sends my hormones into high drive.

When I woke up this morning, it was to find him already dressed and waiting by my bedside with a cup of coffee. The heady scent of caffeine and the headier sight of my man watching me with love in his eyes made me want to throw my arms around him and pull him back under the covers. Only, he offered me the coffee, then told me to get dressed so we could resume our honeymoon. Then he'd kissed me, informing me that he'd already packed my bag and all I had to do was wake up and get dressed in the clothes he'd set out for me.

In that moment, he switched from doting husband to demanding master. Both sides of which, I like. I love it when he looks into my eyes and tells me he loves me. I adore it when he bends me over and spanks me, then uses my mouth and my pussy any which way he wants. I polished off my coffee, then got dressed in the pink lacy underwear, jeans, and plaid shirt he chose for me. Finally, I pulled on socks and low-heeled boots.

Now, I run my hand down the soft fabric of the jeans. It's one of those brands that, even though the jeans are brand new, the material feels like it was washed enough times to stretch easily when I pulled it on. He touched these clothes when he picked them out for me. He was thinking of me when he did it. He imagined how I'd look. He planned for the trip ahead when he chose the shearling aviator jacket to go with it.

And when I look at myself in the mirror, I feel like I'm seeing a different side of me. A confident woman who's smartly dressed yet, who seems relaxed enough to indicate she's going on holiday. I turn from the mirror in our closet to find him waiting for me by the door. He holds out his hand, and I take it. He slings my bag over his shoulder, grabs his own, then leads me to the car.

The sun's rays slant through the windows, and I can't bring myself to tear my gaze away from his strong features. I'll never get over how gorgeous he is. With his scarred visage and his thick eyelashes, and the concentration with which he focuses ahead, I feel that tingling start all over again in my belly.

"You're staring," he drawls.

I flush, then begin to look away, when he reaches over and weaves his fingers through mine. "I like it. I like it a lot when my wife looks at me like she wants me to fuck her."

"You do?" I begin to smile.

"However"—he lowers his voice to a hush—"I get to decide when that happens."

"You mean, I need to earn it?" My scalp tingles. A rush of heat erupts between my legs, and I squeeze my thighs together.

"Lower your zipper and pull down your jeans and panties," he commands.

His bossy voice shoots a thrill of anticipation up my spine. I hasten to obey him. When I've pulled down my jeans and underwear to mid-thigh, I flick him a sideways glance to find he's looking straight ahead as if he hasn't just ordered me to undress myself in a moving vehicle. The car's windows are tinted, and we're moving fast enough that passing vehicles can't see what I'm doing, but it does add to the illicit feel of the scene.

"Slide your legs apart."

I do.

"Stuff your fingers inside your cunt," he growls.

Oh god. Hearing him talk filthy in that dark voice makes my pulse race. Excitement buzzes through my body like electricity. I touch my throbbing clit, and a moan bleeds from my lips. I'm not surprised to find I'm already wet. So very wet. *God.* I slide two fingers inside myself with no resistance, then add a third. I lean my head back against my seat and groan.

"Pretend they're my fingers," he orders. "Pretend I'm fucking you with my thick fingers. Weave them in and out of you like you're riding them."

I oblige and begin to skewer my fingers in and out of my slit. Each time I pull my fingers out, the sucking sound my pussy makes when it releases its hold feels so loud in the silence. It sounds so obscene, my cheeks flush. I begin to slow down my movements, but he notices right away.

"Don't stop. Keep going," he says in his hard voice.

I swallow; my nerve-endings tighten. I speed up, spread my thighs wider, and tilt my hips up to give myself better access.

"That's it, baby. Just like that." His encouragement is like a lit match to gasoline. Arousal crowds my mind. Desire thickens my blood. A craving presses down on my chest and sweat beads my forehead. "Oh, Knox," I gasp.

"I'm here, baby. You're doing so well," he croons.

His approval spurts liquid heat through my veins. A familiar trembling twists up my legs, my thighs, coils in my belly, and grows tighter and tighter. I grit my teeth to stop myself from coming. I can't—not until he lets me. *I can't. I can't.* My skin feels like it's on the verge of catching fire. My toes curl. I shudder and gasp knowing my orgasm is not far, then plunge my fingers in and out of myself, in and out.

"Squeeze your clit," he orders.

With just enough brain power left to follow his directions, I pinch the swollen nub. Sensations zip out to meet the coming orgasm, intensifying it, turning it into a wave that grows bigger, and higher, and fills the horizon and —

"Come," he snaps.

With a cry, I allow the wave to crash over me. I arch my back, push my head into the seat, and continue to fuck myself as lightning sweeps over me. And when it finally recedes, I slump. My eyelids flutter down. I sense him wrapping his fingers around my wrist and bringing my hand to his mouth. He licks at my fingertips. "So sweet."

He sucks on them, and unbelievably, my clit throbs in response. Desire squeezes my lower belly, and a pressure begins to build all over again behind my pussy. I manage to crack my eyes open and look sideways to take in the way the skin stretches across his knuckles where he's squeezing the wheel. He locks the fingers of his other hand with mine and, turning my palm over, kisses it.

"Put yourself to rights," he releases my hand long enough for me to pull up my panties, then my jeans and zip them.

Then he takes my palm and places it on his thigh. Contentment is a syrupy thickness that infiltrates my veins and relaxes my muscles. All too soon, he turns down a smaller country road and keeps driving until we reach a pair of tall gates. There must be a camera somewhere tracking us, for the gates open and we drive through, up a driveway lined with trees on both sides which opens into a circular courtyard with a fountain in the center. He parks in front of the doors to the house, in front of which stands a couple.

"We're here." He puts the car in park and turns to me. "Ready to see the place that's the second most important thing in the world to me?"

I nod slowly, and before I can ask who or what is the first, his features grow tender. He tugs me close and leans in until his breath fans my lips. "You're the first. You're the most important thing in the world to me, baby."

Then he kisses me gently, tenderly, in a way he's never kissed me before. It's the kiss of a husband. The kiss of a man reaffirming his commitment. The kiss of someone who's in love. *He's in love with me. My master loves me. My husband adores me.* He communicates all of that with the meeting of our lips. And when he pulls away, my head spins with the sensations that crowd my mind. He pushes his door open, comes around, and gets mine. Then he bends and hauls me up in his arms.

"Knox," I protest.

He laughs. "Welcome to Cumbria, baby."

50

Knox

Her cheeks flush, and she flicks a glance toward the couple who live on the grounds and keep this place in working condition all year around. They smile at both of us, not put out at all by my affectionate display. I messaged ahead to let them know I'd be bringing my wife with me.

"This is Earnest and Agatha the caretakers and this is my wife June," I introduce them.

"Welcome back, Mr. Davenport. A pleasure Mrs. Davenport." Earnest nods. "I'll get the bags."

"Lovely to meet you, Mrs. Davenport." Agatha holds out her hand.

"It's June," my wife protests in her sweet voice.

Agatha's features soften. "June." She nods.

"Lovely to meet you too." My wife squeezes her hand then releases it.

"We are so happy to see the both of you," Agatha turns to me. "The place is ready for you. The fridge and the pantry are stocked. We've ensured you'll have the supplies you requested."

"Thanks, Agatha."

I walk past her and follow Earnest, who's gone ahead with the bags.

The Cumbria home was inherited by Arthur from his grandfather. He never used it, but my grandmother loved it. She came here often with her children, my father, and his brothers. Probably to get away from Arthur's overbearing presence, is my personal theory about that. After her death, it wasn't used much. Until I needed a place to recuperate. Now, I carry my wife over the threshold and into the grand hallway.

"Wow," She takes in the branching staircase that sweeps up to divide into two on the second floor. High above us, the stained glass set into the roof of the house lets in jeweled hues of sunlight. In the center of the space is a table with a vase in which blue and pink flowers are arranged.

"Those flowers— They're forget-me-nots and dahlias. The same flowers I had in my wedding bouquet." She looks up at me. "You had this done for me?"

I take in her gorgeous, precious features. "I'll do anything for you, wife; you know that don't you?"

She sniffs. "You're spoiling me."

"I'm giving you everything you deserve, baby." I bend and kiss her forehead. And when she tips up her chin, I oblige her with a kiss. A meeting of lips and tongue and breath sweeps through me, turning my heart to putty and my cock to titanium. I soften the kiss and pull back.

She pouts. "I want more."

"That was a husband's kiss. But you'll have to earn your Master's, baby."

"Oh." Her breathing grows choppy. Her pupils dilate. "What do you want me to do, Sir?"

My pulse rate accelerates. The blood pumps in my veins. The need radiates out from my groin and entwines with the love in my chest. "Everything, sweet girl. I want you to do everything."

She swallows. "Please, show me how to please you, Sir."

"So eager, hmm?" I allow my lips to twitch.

She nods. "I'll do anything you want, Sir. Anything."

I allow myself a small smile. "Such a willing little slut you are, wife."

"I am." She reaches up and winds her hand around my neck. "I revel in being your slut. I love being your wife. I love you so much, Sir."

"I love you, wife." I press another kiss to her lips, sweet, tender, and so soft. Her lips, her curves, the way she melts into me and parts her mouth so I can sweep my tongue inside and drink of her taste causes goosebumps to pop on my skin. My cock stabs into the crotch of my pants, eager to be released... But not yet. I pull back and press my forehead into hers. "You drive me crazy."

"I'm glad, Sir," she says shyly.

I stare into her eyes and find myself being drawn into the love I see shining there. "I don't deserve you. I'm going to do everything in my power to always keep you happy, darling. Your smile means everything to me."

"And my tears?" She tips up her chin.

"Your tears mean even more."

She shudders, then pushes her chest into mine so I can feel the outline of her breasts and her hardened nipples. "They're yours, Sir. Everything I am is for you."

I hold her close, then take the stairs two at a time. When I reach the landing, I turn toward the end of the corridor. The double doors to our bedroom are open and I walk through it.

Earnest, who's placed our bags inside the closet, turns and walks back toward us. "Enjoy your stay, Mr. & Mrs. Davenport." He smiles, then leaves the room, closing the door behind him.

I reach the large floor-to-ceiling windows and lower her to her feet. Together we glance out at the view. The place is on a cliff which gives way to a golden strip of beach. Beyond that is the sea.

"Whoa" — she leans forward and takes in the scene — "this is incredible."

"You can see the beach on this side, and if you walk to the other side, you can see the national park."

"It's amazing!" She looks up at me, her eyes wide with anticipation.

I wrap my arm about her waist and pull her close. "What do you want to see first?"

"I want to explore the beach, and then the park, but—" She looks at the scenery over her shoulder, then back at me. "Would it be greedy if I said that, first, I want to explore how I can serve my master?"

My thigh muscles bunch. The blood pumping in my veins threatens to drown out every other voice of reason that I try to follow, telling me that I need to take it slow. That I needed to romance her, court her, make this experience beautiful for her, and it will be. Unbelievably beautiful. But the need to be her master in this moment outweighs everything else. To please her. To bring her so much pain, and even more pleasure, so she'll never forget this evening. To have her here in a place that means so much to me, when she herself means more than the world, is the biggest gift I could ever receive.

"Are you sure about this?" I cup her cheek. "I thought you'd want to be romanced first."

"I do." She smiles a secret feminine smile that sends a flame of lust shooting up my spine. "I want to be romanced in a way a submissive is by her Sir. By her master. By the one person in the world who gets her need for every filthy depraved thing that he can do to her. To have you, the man I love and trust most in the world, also take me to the dark side. To have you touch that part of me that wants to be owned and made to bend. To have you push me to the edge of my limitations, to reveal that part of me I can only share with you, is the greatest gift you can give me, husband."

51

June

His gaze widens, those blue eyes I know so well turn into polar flares. Need leaps off of his body. The very air between us is saturated with a dense, thick, syrupy lust that threatens to knock my knees together and squeeze every last bit of moisture from my pussy. Then he schools his features into an expression of disdain. A curtain seems to drop in front of his eyes, blocking off the fierce passion that swirls below. His lips thin, and his jaw hardens. The very air about him turns from warm savannah to an arctic breeze. In seconds, he's changed from passionate, loving husband to cold-hearted, sadistic master. I know both. Love one and revere the other. He continues to glare at me, and the force of his gaze is too much.

I'm not worth this attention. I haven't earned his recognition in this encounter yet. I lower my eyes; then, because it only seems correct, I lower myself to my knees. I keep my head lowered, my fingers locked together in front of me, as I looked down at his sneakers. I've come a long way from the first time I kneeled at his feet and took in his polished Italian dress shoes. Today, instead of wearing a suit, he's wearing jeans and a T-shirt.

We're both dressed in informal clothes. But we're married, and he's my master in every way, and I—I live to serve him. To please him. So, he'll reward me with the most delicious orgasms only he can bestow on me.

"You will stay in this position until I'm ready for you." Without a second's pause, he walks away. My knees dig into the wooden floor. There isn't even a rug under me. It's not particularly comfortable. In fact, as the seconds pass, my knees begin to hurt. I shift my weight from side to side, but it doesn't get easier. The sun's rays' slant through the window. Sweat breaks out on my forehead. I wipe it away, hear him moving around behind me. I hear the sound of a zipper and realize he's unpacking the suitcases. Then, his footsteps thud across the floor. Is he putting away our clothes? This continues for a few minutes, and the entire time, the discomfort in my knees grows.

"You okay?" he calls out.

I nod.

"If you'd rather stand..."

He's testing me. He thinks I'm going to give in and admit I can't do this. But I can. He's pushing my limits, and I can take it. I can.

"Whatever you wish, Sir," I say without turning around.

I sense satisfaction radiating off of him. He goes back to whatever he's doing.

I stay kneeling, trying to ignore the way the bones in my knees are digging into the floor. I have to keep moving around to try to ease the pain. My thigh muscles tighten. A bead of sweat trickles down my spine. I keep my gaze trained on the floor in front of me. *I can do this. I can.* Footsteps approach. He walks around to stand in front of me. Once more, I see his sneakers. Then he reaches down and cups my cheek. "You can stand up now."

Relief rushes through my body. I try to straighten my legs, but my legs have gone to sleep. I begin to topple over, but he catches me and scoops me up in his arms. I sigh in relief to have the weight taken off my legs. I turn my head into his chest and draw in lungfuls of my Sir. That scent of rich tobacco and leather, laced with sandalwood, washes over me.

My heart calms, and my pussy stutters like it's been struck. *Damn, I do hope he'll do that. And I also don't want him to.* It's a shock to my system when he spanks me in that tender spot and yet, the rush of sensations that follow it turn me into a horny, mindless slave whose only desire is to gratify her master. He reaches the bed and lays me down. He stands near my feet, pulls off my low-heeled boots and socks, and drops them on the floor. Then, he sits down on the bed next to me and reaches for the zipper on my jeans. He pulls it down, and I raise my hips and allow him to slide them off my legs. Next, he reaches for a hand towel and dips it in a bowl of water I hadn't noticed on the nightstand—it's next to a wooden box I'm also seeing for the first time. So, this is what he was doing earlier when I heard him walking about the room? I don't see our bags by the door anymore, so maybe, he did that, too.

He presses the wet towel to my knee. The slight throbbing there recedes, and I sigh. He does the same with my other knee. His head is bent, and he's focused on what he's doing. I have his complete attention, and a thrill courses through me. This is what I love. This is what I've wanted since I first met him. And now, I have him, and it's incredible. All those years I bounced around from foster home to foster home and felt unwelcome. And the fact that I was given up for adoption meant there was a part of me that felt rejected. And now, having him so tuned into my needs fills that emptiness inside of me. It makes me feel loved, cherished, and so very needed.

He looks up to meet my eyes. "Does it hurt?"

I shake my head.

"Good girl." He drops the wet cloth on the bedside table, then places his big hand on my naked thigh. "You realize, I did it because I know how much it means to you to be punished. I know how important it is for you to explore this sexual intensity, this emotional connection you feel toward me. I know what it means to give yourself completely to me. You're asking for the freedom to explore your own identity."

I swallow.

"To go places you cannot go yourself. To have experiences you cannot ask for. You're depending on me, your master, to lead you into the place beyond any resistance you might encounter."

A soft moan spills from my lips. His words cut me to the core. *How have I been seen this easily? How can he look at me and know what I want?* It's more intimate than the sex we've had. More personal than even being married to him. This, him telling me what I want, is tender and erotic, and it's unconditional. This is unconditional love. The liberty to reveal myself to him completely and not feel judged feels like I've been set free.

His support makes me feel safe enough to explore the depths of my own perversity. This is what I sensed when I first saw him in his office. As he helps me open up my body to him, my mind and heart follow. I've never been this vulnerable to anyone else... And yet, in that, there's also a strength. A faith. A trust that my master recognizes what I want, and he'll give it to me. When he decides the time is right.

The feelings course through my legs and my chest to coalesce in my lower belly. Every part of me feels like it's waking up. My blood thrums in my veins. My pulse thuds at my ankles, my wrists, and in the hollow at the base of my throat. Emotions squeeze my chest and well up my throat. It's so intense, a tear squeezes out from the corner of my eye. "Sir. Please, sir," I whisper.

His lips twitch, then he bends and kisses my forehead. So soft. So tender. I feel like I've been reborn and that he's touching me for the first time.

"Move over to the center of the bed." He straightens, and I wriggle over toward the middle. "Show me your wrists."

I extend my arms as he's asked.

He reaches down and pulls off his belt, and the sound of the leather against the fabric of his jeans sets off sensations across my nerve-endings. Then, he knots it around my wrists, testing it before he pulls my arms up and ties me to the headboard. He tugs on it and the pull sends a shiver down my spine. My toes curl. My thighs shiver. He hasn't even started, and I'm already so aroused. He slides off the bed, walks into the closet and returns with three scarves. He uses them to tie one of my ankles to the side of the bed, then the other, so I'm spreadeagled. Then he moves over to straddle my waist without putting any weight on me. "I'm going to blind-fold you."

52

Knox

"B-blindfold?" Her gaze grows wide. There's a lick of fear and of excitement in them.

"How do you feel about that?"

She casts her eyes down. "I feel...nervous, but also I want to explore how it feels."

"That's very good, baby." I lean in and kiss her forehead. "Any time you want me to stop, you simply have to say so, and I will.

"Okay," she says in a soft voice.

"You ready to find out your limits?"

She nods, a firm jerk of her chin. There's no hesitation in her expression, and that makes me so happy. A flutter ripples through my chest. This woman is beautiful and brave and trusts me so much. I will not let her down. I am going to ensure she has the most incredible experience of her life. "Close your eyes, baby."

Her eyelids flutter down. I wrap the scarf over them and tie it behind her head. I tug to make sure it's not too tight, and she shivers. The edginess that jumps off of her is laced with excitement. Because I can't help myself, I press my lips to hers. Her mouth clings to mine, but before I'm tempted to deepen the kiss, I pull back. *This is all about her. Only about her. I want to cherish her, and love her, and make her feel incredible. She's the most beautiful woman on this earth, and I want her to feel so very spoiled.*

I kiss her forehead, then gently slide my palm down her cheek to her chin, then trail my finger down her neck to the dip between her breasts. I hook my finger into the neckline of her shirt. Then I grip the lapels and tug. The buttons spring off and fall to the bed. She gasps and pulls on her bindings, which strain. Her chest rises and falls, anticipation thrumming in the air between us. I wait until she subsides, then ease the two sides of her shirt apart. Her nipples are hard and poke through her bra. The areolas are dark and outlined against the silk.

Lust squeezes my guts. I bend and close my mouth around one of her breasts through the fabric. A moan slips from her lips. It urges me to palm her other breast. I squeeze it, then bite down on the nipple of the first one. She cries out, tries to pull away, but I don't let her. I lean some of my weight on her, and she pants.

"So sweet. So fucking addictive," I praise her.

Goosebump pepper the space between her breasts. She's so responsive. *My woman. My wife. My submissive. Mine.* I reach over to the wooden box on the nightstand, open it, extract a pair of scissors, and proceed to cut through her bra.

She flinches.

I cut off the straps, pull off the scraps of pink lace, and toss them aside.

"Did you cut off my bra?" she gasps.

"Not only." I reach down and slip the blade of the scissor under the side of her panties. She flinches. I cut it off, then do the same to the other side. I slide the remnants of her underwear off her.

Another shiver grips her. I cup her cheek and press a kiss to her cheek. "Okay, baby?"

She nods.

"Good girl."

Her chest rises and falls. The air is thick with anticipation and lust. Her nipples are so tight, when I pinch one of them, she jolts.

"Oh, Sir. Please. Sir. Please," she whines.

"You don't get to set the pace, you understand that?"

She stills, then nods slowly, "Yes, Sir. Whatever you want, Sir."

"Who do you belong to?"

"You, Sir."

"Who do your tits belong to?"

She swallows. "Only you, Sir."

I slide my hand down to cover the mound between her thighs. "Who owns your cunt."

"You, Sir," she whispers. "Only you."

"That's right." I pinch her clit, and she cries out. I tweak it with enough force that her entire body jerks. Then release it and, before she's able to recuperate, I bend and lick the swollen bud.

She whimpers. The sound is so erotic, it goes straight to my head. My cock extends, pre-cum trickling from the crown. I have to squeeze the base of my shaft to stop myself from coming.

I place the scissors back in the box.

I slide off the bed and proceed to peel off my T-shirt. Divesting myself off my shoes, socks, and jeans, along with my underwear, I grab the vibrator.

I look in her direction to find she's calmed down. Her shoulders are relaxed.

When I switch on the vibrator a quiver grips her. I push one knee then the other into the space between her knees. When I touch the vibrator to her pussy, she cries out and arches her body. I raise it, then hold it to her clit again.

She writhes and moans and curses. "What are you doing?"

"Do you want me to stop?" I ask as I raise the vibrator.

She swallows, then shakes her head.

"Then stay still and take it. You know you can."

I touch the vibrator to the entrance of her slit and a long low moan emerges from her. Her legs tremble, but she doesn't move away. Instead, she stays still, or as still as her quivering body allows her. I drag the vibrator up her pussy lips, and she huffs. And when I touch it again to her slit, she groans.

I slide the vibrator down to her melting entrance. I breach it, only to pull back, and she groans. "Oh Sir, please, please, please Sir." She pushes her pelvis up, chasing the head of the vibrator, and I allow myself a small smile.

"Hush now, behave yourself."

She draws in a sharp breath, then relaxes her body.

"Good girl."

Her lips part. The pulse at the base of her throat kicks up.

I allow the vibrator to breach her slit, and she groans.

"You okay, darling?"

She nods.

"Do you want me to stop?"

She shakes her head.

"I need you to tell me so, baby."

"I... I don't want you to stop, Sir." Her chin trembles, but her voice is firm.

"That's good, baby." I press another kiss to her mouth, then slip the vibrator deeper inside her. Her entire body bucks. She presses her full breasts into my chest, and it's my turn to groan. I pull the vibrator to the rim of her entrance, then squeeze her breast. I tweak her nipple, and she writhes again. She thrashes her head from side to side, and her panting grows louder. I push the vibrator inside her pussy, all the way in, until it hits her cervix. She cries out, and a trembling grips her. She arches her back again, and when I pull it out of her again, she gasps. "I'm so close," she chokes out.

I drag the vibrator up her lower belly, over her stomach, and touch it to her nipple. She whimpers, and a flush crawls up her chest, then her throat. I press the vibrator to her other nipple, and she shivers.

"Sir," she pleads, "please sir."

I bring the vibrator to her clit and hold it there. She pants, and when she opens her mouth again, I place my tongue between her lips. She bites down on it, and my entire body seems to catch fire. *Fuck.* I swipe my tongue across her teeth and kiss her deeply. All the while, I keep the vibrator pressed to her cunt. She shivers and shudders and arches into me, and she's so close. I can smell the sugary scent of her arousal, and something inside me snaps. I switch off the vibrator and toss it aside then position my cock at her slit.

53

June

The head of his monster dick teases my pussy, and that yearning which has grown and grown inside of me swells until it seems to extend to every part of my body. I want him, I need him. I have to feel him inside of me. I tilt my pelvis up until his cock breaches my slit, and the sensations from the point of contact zip out under my skin. *Finally. Finally. He's going to fuck me.* Only he doesn't.

He clicks his tongue. "No topping from the bottom, baby."

He pulls out, his weight slides off me, and I cry out, "Sir, no!"

"What did you say?" He slaps my pussy, and pain spirals out from the contact. Only, the pleasure that follows in its wake turns my thighs to jelly. My eyes roll back in my head. A buzzing sound reaches me, and I realize, he's turned on that hated vibrator again. Yes, it makes me feel good, but that's the problem. It makes me feel too good. *So good...it almost feels like a punishment.*

I only realize I've spoken the words aloud when he growls, "You have to pay, baby. You realize that, don't you?"

I nod miserably.

Not looking forward to this. *Ohgod, ohgod, ohgod!* The breath whooshes out of me as he uses his free hand to scoop up my cum from my cunt and smear it around my forbidden entrance. Then, he breaches me there with the vibrator, and I cry out. More out of surprise than anything because, strangely, it doesn't hurt too much.

He keeps the vibrator there, allowing me to adjust to its size. He begins to rub at my swollen clit with his fingers. My climax builds almost at once. He tweaks my clit, and I want to cry out, but the sensations building inside me block my throat. All that emerges is a puff of air from my mouth as I moan and whimper and try to pull away, all the while aching for more. *More. More.* The word seems to be etched into my brain. It's on a repeating loop, like a mantra I'm chanting. I try to tug my hands free so I can hold onto him, try to wrap my legs about him to pull him close, but can't. I have to settle for being spreadeagled and open, at his disposal.

He grinds the heel of his palm into my cunt, relentless in the pursuit of the pleasure that fills me, and expands, and heats my blood. And when he slaps my pussy again, I orgasm.

It's quick and sharp, and it's accompanied by blinding sparks that crash behind my eyes. By the time it ebbs, I'm shivering, and mewling, and trembling so hard, he grips my hip to keep me in place. I'm so relaxed, the vibrator slips in further. I huff, adjusting to the sensation of being filled in this way. He holds it there, the vibrations pushing up against my inner walls. I feel it in my innermost space, in my pussy, up my spine, in my breasts. And when he, once again, pushes his cock into my slit, I moan.

I'm so spent, I don't think I can orgasm again. Only, he takes off my blindfold, and the sight of those sapphire eyes flashing with desire, his cheeks flushed with need, and his mouth parted as he fixes me with that fierce gaze, tells me I'm wrong. My master knows exactly how to manipulate my body. He knows what I want better than I do.

He thrusts forward and impales my cunt, and I open my mouth in a silent scream. Too much. Too full. He's taken me in both my holes and the sensation is unlike anything I've ever experienced. He holds my gaze, pinning me down with his cock in my pussy and the vibrator in my forbidden channel. I shudder and whimper and feel so completely taken. So completely under his power. So completely at his disposal.

The emotions churn in my chest. My belly twists in on itself. He stays there allowing me to adjust to the intrusions, and just as the sensations ebb, he begins to move. He holds the vibrator in place as he pulls out and stays poised at the rim of my pussy. Then he plunges forward and impales me again. He hits that spot deep inside. Instantly, I feel the tendrils of a new orgasm wrap around me and begin to squeeze.

"Oh, Sir," I moan.

"Stay with me." He pulls out again, and this time when he impales me, my entire body moves forward. Without missing a beat, he continues to fuck me with the vibrator, easing it out when he's inside me. And sliding it back in when he slams his cock into me.

Liquid heat spurts up and through me. It's too much. I open my mouth to cry out, and he's there. He places his mouth on mine and absorbs the sounds. Then reaches up and releases first, one of my hands, then the other. I wrap them around his shoulders and hold on as he fucks me in both of my holes. He sets a punishing pace, throwing his entire body into how he plunges his cock inside of me, fucking each of my holes in a steady rhythm. A tinge of pain, and a whole lot of pleasure rockets through my veins. And the way he kisses me, it's too much.

All the sensations coalesce in my core and build up until it reaches my chest. And when he tears his mouth from mine and growls, "Come," I instantly shatter. The world goes dark. I'm dimly aware of his low groan as he comes inside me. Of the warmth of his release filling me. Of him continuing to fuck me with his dick and the vibrator until a second orgasm builds in my lower belly. *NO way. Again?*

My eyelids flutter open, but before I can protest, the climax washes over me, gentler than the first, but even more intense, for he's kissing me again, and looking into my eyes. And it's so profound. So *everything*. I'm filled with him, and surrounded by him, and weighed down by him. I'm subsumed by him. I'm his, in every sense of the word. And then the blackness overpowers me.

When I open my eyes, he's holding me in his arms. I'm laid out on top of him, while he's on his back. It's quiet because he switched off the vibrator,

which is no longer inside me. He also untied the bindings around my
ankles. My cheek is pressed into his chest, and I can hear the boom-boom-
boom of his heart as it bangs into his ribcage. It's so reassuring to know
I'm not the only one affected by what happened. I turn my face into his
chest and kiss him. I taste the salt of sweat on his skin, smell the scent of
sex that clings to his pores, and shiver in response.

His arms around me tighten. "Cold?"

I shake my head. "Overwhelmed."

He dips his head and kisses the top of mine. "You were incredible. You
allowed me to push you at every stage and matched me step-for-step. You
never backed down and opened yourself up completely. You humble me,
baby."

Tears prick the backs of my eyes. It's silly wanting to cry, but his praise
is so incredible. It fills me, heals me, and swells my heart with so much
warmth, I'm sure it's going to burst. I press my lips to his chest again, as
the tears drip down my cheeks.

"Hey." He flips me over on my back. Balancing his weight on his arms,
he looks at me closely. "Did I hurt you? Did I push you beyond your
limits?" Worry shadows his eyes.

"No." I swallow down the emotions bubbling inside me. I have this
ridiculous urge to cry, which is strange. Why should I feel so undone? But
it's like he's given me permission to allow things I bottled up inside to be
unleashed.

"It's okay." He cups my cheek and kisses my forehead, my eyelids, my
nose, my mouth. "It's okay to let it all out."

More tears flow down my face, and I don't try to stop them. I allow
myself to be held by my husband and soothed by my master as I cry for
things I didn't dare acknowledge until now. About how the very act of
being given up by my mother left me with a primal wound I've spent my
entire life trying to come to terms with.

How with every foster family I was bundled off to I tried to fit in, and
in doing so, never felt free to be myself. How I could never give myself
permission to stay in the moment. How abandoned I felt all through my
childhood, until Irene adopted me; and how, even after that, I carried the
burden of feeling like I had to be grateful to her. How despite her best
efforts in trying to give me a home, it felt like a part of me was missing.

How lost I felt, like I was always searching for something. How I never found the space to mourn everything I'd lost. How that loss hit me anew when I met my birth mother, and that brought all of my grief to the fore again. How, in his arms, I have the space to let go, for the first time in my life. How the relief of submitting to him completely means I'm in a vulnerable enough space for the dam to break open.

I sob silently, then with more abandon, as he holds me. As he pulls me in and rolls onto his back, stroking my head and murmuring encouraging words. And when I'm done crying and spent, he rocks me to sleep.

When I open my eyes again, it's morning and he's still holding me. I look up into his face, take in the growth of whiskers on his jaw, his slightly parted lips, the scars on his cheek which only add to his vulnerability. His long lashes graze his cheeks as he slumbers. I reach up and touch his scarred cheek, tracing the curve of the puckered flesh up to his temple.

His eyelids flutter, and his bright blue eyes stare down at me. He's awake instantly—thanks to his military training. His arms around me tighten, then one side of his lips hitches up. "Good morning, wife."

EPILOGUE

Three months later

June

"Do I look okay?" I glance sideways at my husband.

A month ago, we'd moved into a gorgeous townhouse in Primrose Hill. It's the same area where Quentin and Nathan have their homes. As do Sinclair and Summer Sterling. It's nice to be surrounded by friends and family, and this place feels much more like home. As for my apartment I'd offered it to a charity that works with adoptive families, so they could rent it out to those most-in-need.

Without waiting for my husband's response, I turn toward my reflection in the mirror. The dress I'm wearing falls below my knees. Its sleeves flow down my arms to wrap around my wrists. The neckline is modest, the color dark pink. It sets off the flush on my cheeks and the deep rose lipstick I've painted across my mouth. I fuss with my hair, then turn and take in my silhouette. "I feel like I'm already showing. I can't be, can I?" I groan.

"You look perfect." My husband steps up and wraps his arm about my thickening waist.

Yes, I was on birth control. But apparently, that was no match for my husband's super sperm. I'd never tell him that because that would only go to his head. I have a sneaky suspicion I became pregnant that first night at the Cumbria home. Or it might have been the next night, or the night after that, or during the next few days, when we proceeded to christen every single surface in that house. And quite a few objects in that space were used, as well, in some interesting ways. Good thing, it's our place and no one else in the family is interested in using it. Because, I have to tell you, it wouldn't be hygienic for them to use that house after our activities. We were there for a week, and it was an amazing break. We returned reluctantly, and only because there were a spate of emergencies Knox was unable to manage remotely.

When I showed Knox the results of the pregnancy test a month ago, he turned so white, I was sure he'd faint. Then he'd whooped, and scooped me up, and proceeded to kiss me until I was breathless.

And since then, he hasn't let me out of his sight. I'd already decided to leave my job at Davenport industries by then, so becoming pregnant simply spurred me to accelerate my decision. I decided to join forces with my adoption search specialist and expand the services we could offer to both adopters and adoptees.

As Knox's wife, I have a monthly allowance from the Davenport family trust fund. Apparently, I'm a beneficiary because I married into the family. At first, it didn't feel right to accept it, until Knox pointed out I'm entitled to it, and I can use the money to further my own causes. Which is when I approached my adoption search specialist and asked if I could become a partner with her. Turns out, she was looking for someone to bring in fresh equity, and I'm that person.

We're formulating our roles and responsibilities, but it's so exciting. For the first time in my life, I have a sense that I'm building something of my own. We're also building our family.

Knox bends and presses his cheek against mine, "You look gorgeous."

"You're biased."

"And rightly so. You make me feel like the luckiest man alive."

My heart flutters. My pussy melts. Pregnancy has only enhanced my sexual appetite, and Knox has no problem keeping up with me. Much to my disappointment, anything kinky is out.

He also refuses to let me do anything—not complaining about that. Which means, I get the full benefit of him loving me with his wicked tongue, and his clever fingers, and that very big, very thick, very active part of him which, even now, prods me above the curve of my butt.

"Hmm, someone's up."

"Someone hasn't gone down since the day I saw your beautiful face." He slides his hand around and flattens his palm over my belly. "And the thought of you growing big with my baby is the ultimate aphrodisiac."

I place my palm over his and lean back into his broad chest.

"You look like you're mine." He pulls me in close and tucks my head under his chin. "You're glowing, baby."

"I've never felt this happy." I look into his deep blue eyes in the mirror.

He's not that good at showing his emotions, but he hasn't shut me out since the day he told me he loves me. I sense he's learning to be more open and vulnerable with me, and while it doesn't come easily, I know he's trying his best.

"I've never felt this content." His azure gaze lights up with silver embers. His smile is tender, and his expression is soft. I'm not surprised. I've known all along that behind that strong, unemotional, unfeeling façade he likes to project, he's someone who, perhaps, feels too deeply. Someone who cares too much. Someone who, once he admits his feelings, will do anything for the people he's chosen as his own. "I'm so incredibly lucky to have found you." I turn in his arms and tip up my chin.

"I thank the universe every day for bringing you into my life. I'm not religious, but you make me believe in a higher power. Surely, that's the only reason I met you. You make me a better man, baby." He cups my cheek.

"You make me believe in a better future. You make me believe that surviving everything I did, all that I saw as a Marine, which showed me the depths that the human race can fall to—All of it's worth it, because it led me to you. You make me believe in hope, and *that* is a priceless gift. *You* are my priceless gift. My future. Everything in my life has led me to this moment when I'm holding you in my arms, my wife. My role as your husband is the most important one in my life. And as the father of your child, I swear, I'll always put the two of you before myself. I'll lay down my life to protect both of you. I'll ensure you both never want for anything. Your security is my priority. Your happiness is my goal. Your needs are my primary concern. And if anything threatens that, I'll burn down the world if it affects you."

Tears trickle down my cheeks, and a look of horror filters into his eyes. "Baby, don't cry."

"Sorry, it's these pregnancy hormones." I sniff. "And your words were so beautiful, so heartfelt. I"—I shake my head—"I can't believe how lucky I am."

"I'm the one who's lucky." He lowers his head and brushes his lips over mine. "It's *my* job to make sure the two of you are always happy. You leave all the worrying to me, baby. You focus on yourself and our child."

"Oh, Knox." I rise up on my tiptoes, and he meets me halfway. He presses his lips to mine, and the kiss is tender, and heartfelt, and filled with love and passion and desire. With it, is this growing feeling of being cherished. This confidence that I am the center of his world. This trust that I, and our child, will always be safe with him. This conviction that I'm blessed. That my baby and I are both blessed that we're his.

He slides his big palms down my back to cup my behind. I fretted that I was piling on the pounds on my backside in the last month, thanks to the pregnancy, but he reassured me that he loves it, no matter what. He relished having more of me to hold. And when he squeezes my butt, a pulse of eager energy flutters through my veins.

My already sensitive nipples seem to turn into hard points of desire. And the delicious friction from pushing my breasts into his hard chest lights liquid fire in my veins. A moan wells up my throat.

His breathing grows choppy. I feel the thick column of his arousal stabbing into my stomach. "Jesus, baby, you're so sexy." He nibbles on my lower lip, and that fire turns into a tsunami of desire.

"Knox," I groan.

"I know, baby." He whispers tiny kisses up my cheek to the corner of my eye, then kisses the tip of my nose. "I want to carry you off to bed and make sweet love to you all night long."

"Do it." I dig my fingers into his strong, muscle-bound forearms. "Please, Sir. Please."

It's his turn to groan, "Hearing you beg turns my world upside down. It makes me forget everything but being buried inside you."

"And I want you in me. I want you on top of me. I want to be crushed under your weight. I want to be surrounded by you, wallowing in your scent." I laugh a little. "Did I just say that?"

He quirks a smile. "You did, and it fucking turns me on. I—"

There's a knock on the door, "Knox? June? You guys ready? Everyone's here and waiting for you." It's Zoey.

In honor of my pregnancy-cum-housewarming, Arthur agreed to shift the venue of the weekly family and friend's lunch to our place this Sunday. It seemed like a promising idea, especially as it gave me the perfect excuse to invite Irene and my siblings, and also Claire, to our place. It feels like a good, neutral way to have the two of them meet without putting too much pressure on them to have to converse with each other. I told them about it in advance, so it wouldn't be a surprise, and they both agreed it was an excellent idea. But now, the thought of them meeting fills me with trepidation. It feels like a collision of both of my worlds... Of all of my worlds.

Everyone important to me under one roof, which didn't happen, even for my wedding, so it feels symbolic. A start of something new and significant, in more ways than one. It's why I'm delaying the inevitable, wanting to spend more time with him. But my husband knows my stalling tactics, for he steps back. I underestimated just how much he can read my mind, for he looks deep into my eyes and says, "I'm with you, every step of the way. When you feel like everything is out of control, simply look at me and know, I'm there with you. I'll always be there in your corner, rooting for you. I'm your wingman, baby."

Once again, emotions choke my throat. But something lighter, frothier, bubbles in my heart. Hope and happiness and excitement. Yes, excitement that the future will bring what's best for me, and no matter what happens, I can handle it because he's with me. "I love you, Knox."

"I love you too, Duchess."

My cheeks redden. It seems like such a long time ago when I was so upset that he insisted on calling me by names which weren't my own, that I threw out a few ridiculous ones for him to use. "You don't have to call me that."

"I want to, for you are the center of my universe. My queen. And I'll do anything to keep you happy."

"Oh, Knox." Those frothy emotions in my throat extend to the rest of my body, until it feels like I'm floating on air.

"Are you happy?" he asks tenderly.

"Very." My lips curve.

"Good." He grins back at me. "Ready to face the hordes?"

"I can't tell you how happy I am to see you settled down." Arthur beams between me and my husband. "Of course, I take credit for it."

Knox sneers. "Have you forgotten, if you'd had your way, you'd have married me off to someone else?"

Arthur's smile grows even wider. "I pushed you to marry Toren's sister, knowing it would push you to acknowledge your feelings for June."

When I risk a look at my husband's features, he seems taken aback. "Let me get this right, you set me up in a possible arranged marriage to someone else so that—"

"—you got a kick in the pants to acknowledge how much in love you were with your wife." Arthur glances at me and his features soften. "And I don't blame you. June is a one in a million—"

My heart swells in my chest.

"When I saw the two of you in your office, I knew she was the one for you. But like my other grandsons, you were, clearly, too pig-headed to realize the woman you wanted was right in front of your eyes." He turns his gaze on Knox. "I didn't want you to lose your chance at your own happy ending."

My husband's jaw hardens. "Goddamn meddling old man, you orchestrated that sequence of events?" His navy irises turn glacial. He looks pissed off. And I admit, he looks hot. I love my husband's 'angry face,' but this is his grandfather.

Arthur welcomed me warmly into the family. I hadn't realized that by marrying Knox, I was also marrying his entire family. His grandfather, uncle, and brothers are all up in each other's business in a way I love. It's what I missed growing up. I slip my arm around my husband's waist. He looks down at me, and the cold in his eyes melts away.

He pulls me in closer, then turns to his grandfather. "You were right in what you did."

"I was?" Arthur seems surprised.

"It gave me the incentive I needed to get my life back on track. If it weren't for you, I wouldn't have married the love of my life. And to think, I didn't suspect a thing?" Knox chuckles.

"Of course, I hoped it'd bring Tyler and Priscilla together, as well. Unfortunately, I haven't succeeded in that regard"—Arthur sighs—"yet."

I ran into Priscilla at a coffee shop in Primrose Hill when she came to meet a friend. What could have been an awkward meeting turned out to be a pleasant encounter. We got to talking and decided to stay in touch. She says she's over Tyler, but I'm not so sure. In fact, I suspect that the engagement Arthur masterminded might yet bear fruit for them. But that's really Priscilla's story to tell. I stay silent.

Arthur looks past us, and his expression brightens. "On the other hand, there are others who need my help."

"What are you up to now, Gramps?" my husband mutters under his breath in a pitch only I can hear.

"Ryot, my boy—" Arthur beckons to him. Ryot prowls over, a groove between his eyebrows. He's not happy at having caught his grandfather's attention.

"—are you sure about this assignment?" Arthur asks in a voice that's supposed to be casual, but there's no mistaking the undertone of interest.

Out of the corner of my eye, I catch Irene and Claire deep in conversation. I introduced them, and to my amazement, they embraced; and then, it was out of my hands. They started talking and haven't stopped for the last fifteen minutes.

My siblings, too, were swept up by the crowd. Nathan's wife Skylar took them under her wing. She made sure they had enough to eat and drink, and when Tiny arrived with Arthur, they made a beeline for the Great Dane. It's wonderful to hear the house echoing with good natured ribbing between the Davenport brothers, and the sounds of Tiny's barking, interspersed with the excited laughter of my siblings, as well as of Summer and Sinclair's son, who's happily toddling around under Summer's watchful eye.

So, I'm only half listening when Ryot replies, "I told you about it out of courtesy. Your opinion about it doesn't matter to me in the least."

Arthur harrumphs, "Either way, you should know I approve."

Excuse me? Did he just say he approved? I whip my head around in time to see Ryot's gaze narrow.

My husband, too, is staring at his grandfather. "You okay, Grandad? You want to sit down, perhaps?" He flags down one of the passing wait-staff we've hired to cater for the evening. He takes a glass of water from his tray and hands it over to Arthur, who waves it aside impatiently.

"I don't need to sit down. I'm not thirsty. I feel just fine."

Knox, Ryot, and I look at him warily.

"Oh, for heaven's sake, why is it so surprising that I approve of Ryot striking out on his own?"

"Probably because you've made it very clear how much you want your grandsons to join the Davenport Group and grow its reach and influence?" Knox says wryly.

"And I do believe in that. I have no doubt that Ryot will, one day, join the family business."

Ryot's eyebrows draw down.

"But meanwhile, he's doing what he thinks is best for him. And if that's becoming a bodyguard for a princess, so be it."

Ryot firms his jaw. "I shouldn't be surprised you know about it already, but I am. How did you—"

Arthur waves his hand. "There's little that happens that I don't get to know about." His eyes gleam. "Besides, connections with the Royal Family are always useful, don't you think?"

My husband groans. "So that's why you're on board. You think Ryot's assignment will help forge closer relations with royalty. In fact—" He does a double take, then shakes his head. "Nope, that can't be it."

Ryot's frown deepens.

Arthur watches my husband with interest. "Go on then, spit it out, boy."

"Nope. I don't believe it. In fact, I'm quite sure, not even you could be that devious"—he rubs his chin—"could you?" He narrows his gaze on Arthur, whose features take on an innocent veneer. And that convinces me, my husband is onto something.

Ryot glares at my husband. Something passes between them, and he scoffs. "No fucking way, am I falling for that."

"For what?" I look between Ryot and my husband. "What is it? Will someone explain it to me?"

Ryot continues to scowl at Knox, then he turns to me. "Your husband suspects, as do I, that Arthur thinks my becoming a bodyguard for a princess means there's every possibility I'll fall for her and marry her, thus fulfilling his aspirations for his grandsons, but"—he nods at Arthur—"you can put away your machinations. I'm not falling for that."

For someone who prefers not to speak too much, Ryot sure isn't holding back his opinion. He must be wary that Arthur will try to get him settled down next.

Arthur schools his expressions into one of virtue, which comes off as anything but. "Surely, you can't be accusing me of being that devious."

Ryot sneers, "You *are* that devious. And if it weren't for the fact I know this assignment is genuine, I'd suspect you of manipulating it so Quentin's security company got it. But not even you could have predicted I'd be joining him, so—" He rolls his shoulders. "So, for what it's worth, I'm glad you think it's important to give me your assent, but I wasn't asking for it. And I couldn't care less what you think of it. And it would've satisfied me to no end if you were pissed off, which is what I was aiming for, but what-fucking-ever." He turns to Knox. "I came, only because you called me and I'm truly happy for the both of you." He turns to me, and his features soften.

"I know my brother loves you and I can tell you're good for him. I wish the two of you the absolute best, and—" His phone buzzes. He pulls it out, and whoever he reads on the screen has him setting his jaw. A change comes over him. He becomes even more distant; his stance grows stiffer. When he looks up, his gaze is already remote.

"You have to go," Knox says with resignation.

"I do." He nods at Knox. "Wishing you the best, brother. I'm confident you're going to make an amazing father." Then, he half bows in my direction. "Any time the two of you need anything, I'm at your disposal." Then, without another glance in Arthur's direction, he turns and leaves.

Knox turns to Arthur. "There's someone here I think you'll want to meet."

Arthur arches an eyebrow, and the gesture is so Knox-like, I stare. Damn, if Knox doesn't get some of his surliness from this old man. Only, I sense the tenderness in Knox, while Arthur... Not sure if he has a soft bone in his entire body.

"Who would that be?" Arthur asks with curiosity.

Laughter rings out, and Arthur pales. "Is that?" He swallows.

Knox nods. "Imelda's here." Then he shuffles his feet. "I apologize for not warning you she was within earshot of our conversation in my office. I didn't realize how much it would impact your relationship. But, having found my own happily ever after, I want you to have the same. Of course, knowing how much of a stubborn, old codger you are, I figured I needed to do my bit to bring the two of you face-to-face."

Arthur swallows. He looks genuinely moved by Knox's gesture. "You don't have to apologize. You didn't do anything wrong. I was the one who was too stubborn to acknowledge my emotions."

"Sounds familiar," Knox murmurs.

"I'm glad you found a woman to make you face up to your feelings. And when I realized I'd lost Imelda, it was a shock. Enough to make me see the error of my ways." He rubs the back of his neck. "I guess I owe her an apology."

"She's right there." Knox looks past him. "And she's noticed you. You'd better go to her before she decides to leave."

Arthur squares his shoulders. "Wish me luck." He turns and walks toward Imelda. Imelda sees him coming, pivots, and heads toward the door. Arthur hurries his pace. "Imelda, wait."

They disappear into the hallway. "You think they'll be okay?" I ask.

Knox pulls me closer. "That's in Arthur's hands."

"And Ryot? Do you think Arthur—"

"Manipulated things so Ryot got put on the bodyguard detail with the Princess?" Knox grunts. "I wouldn't put it past him. Either way, Arthur would be ecstatic if Ryot and the Princess fell in love. But will Ryot see it that way?"

TO FIND OUT WHAT HAPPENS NEXT READ RYOT AND PRINCESS AURELIA'S STORY IN THE UNPLANNED WEDDING

READ AN EXCERPT FROM RYOT & AURELIA'S STORY

Aurelia

"Another espresso martini," I flutter my eyelashes at the bartender.

The man's gaze widens, his Adam's apple moves as he swallows. "Coming right up," his actions speed up. He pours the liquids into the mixer, then proceeds to shake it, adding enough oomph to his actions that I want to giggle. But I manage to swallow down my mirth. Men are so predictable. I'm going to use it to my advantage. He slides my martini across the counter.

"Thank you," I say in a soft voice.

He sighs, "anytime."

I stifle another chuckle, snatch up the martini and raising it to my lips down it in one gulp.

"Whoa," His eyes bug out. "That was quick."

"I was thirsty." I smile and notice with satisfaction when his color rises. "How much do I owe you."

"It's on the house."

I arch an eyebrow, "I insist." I don't accept favors from anyone.

When he hesitates, I dig into my purse, pull out a few notes and place it on the counter.

"Can I call you sometime?" He murmurs, not taking his gaze off my face. "You won't regret it, I promise."

"Thanks, but no thanks. My boyfriend won't like that."

"You and I both know that's a lie, doll." A new voice interjects.

I glance sideways to find a man of medium height with thick shoulders and an even thicker waistline leaning against the bar. Catching my eye, he winks at me, a look of satisfaction on his wide features. Ugh.

Narrow eyes, a crooked nose and combined with his stout features and an ox-like neck, not to mention the gut hanging over his belt give the impression that he might have spent all his time at the gym once upon a time but now he's allowed himself to go to seed. He leers at me, I stiffen.

I draw myself to my full height, tuck my handbag under my arm and sniff. "Goodbye."

I sail past him and I'm sure I've made it and begin to relax when a heavy hand descends on my shoulder. "Now just a minute, I haven't finished talking to you, I —" the man begins to say, but I turn on him, "Let go of me!" I tug at his hold and must take him by surprise for I pull out of his grasp.

His features twist. I sense the intent in his eyes a second before his features twist. He reaches for me, but I evade him. Then bring up my knee and bury it in his groin. I sense rather than hear the sound of the crunch with satisfaction. The man cries out. I pull back, and when he begins to clutch at his center I pivot and elbow my way through the crowd of people milling around the bar counter and in the direction of the exit. Only my progress is slow.

I sense rather than hear my aggressor gain on me, and when I turn and look my suspicion is confirmed. The man limps in my direction, an angry look on his face. Oh no! Adrenaline spikes my blood. Fear squeezes my guts. I turn and plunge forward, trying to shove people out of the way. This is when I wish I was taller.

My five feet four inches puts me at a disadvantage. "Please let me through," I shove at the woman standing in front of me. She moves aside but then I'm faced with someone else. "Excuse me."

I shoulder my way through only to crash into something so hard, and so wide I'm sure I've smashed into a wall. Only it's warm and covered with cloth that smells of fabric conditioner and below that I can scent the unmistakable muskiness of man laced with something spicy which makes my mouth water. Then the thing turns and I'm at eye-level with corrugated slabs of muscle that stretch a black T-shirt so worn with age there are tiny rips in the cloth through which I can make out flashes of skin. The heat from this expanse of chest reaches out to me and crashes into me and curls itself around me. I swallow.

My mouth goes dry. My throat feels like it's clogged with emotions I cannot identify. My head spins. What's happening to me? Why am I reacting like this? I'm not going to faint. I'm not. I draw in a sharp breath and that spicy scent intensifies. I sway and grab at his arm to steady myself. His skin is warm, the muscles under the surface turn to stone. It feels like I'm holding onto a pillar of strength. A very live, very vital column of living flesh. The hair on the nape of my neck rises. I risk a glance behind me to find my pursuer is almost on me. Argh!

I hook my arm through that of the man I'm holding onto, then for good measure, I push my cheek into that expanse of steel that passes of his chest and sigh, "Where were you, darling? I looked everywhere for you."

The chest under my cheek grows harder if that's possible. I sense the surprise which courses through the man's body. He grows so still that but for the warmth which pours off him in waves I'd have sworn he'd turned to granite. I'm sure he's going to push me away, but instead he wraps his big arm around my shoulders and tucks me into his side. I fit so well against him.

The massive bulk of his body is comforting, and the scent of his very male presence is so very arousing, I melt into his side.

For a few seconds I allow myself to wallow in his nearness. Then I sneak a glance to the side to find my antagonist from the bar standing in front of me. He looks from me to the man next to me, then back at me. He seems confused. Taking advantage of his uncertainty, I pat the chest of the giant I'm leaning against. Muscles jump under my palm. Oh god, he feels so huge. So well built. I resist the urge to massage the skin under his T-shirt and tip up my chin. "This is my husband, and I warn you, he can get mean when he's angry so if you value your life, I suggest you leave."

Something suspiciously like a chuckle reaches me, I could have sworn it came from the giant, but the tension radiating off of his body indicates otherwise. I keep my gaze firmly on my adversary who scowls between us again. He opens his mind as if to say something, but then the giant rumbles from above me, "You heard my wife. Best be off, or I'll have to rearrange your features."

My wife. He said my wife. My insides melt. And that voice? Oh my god, it's like butter poured over dark chocolate with a bite of whiskey to it. My entire body seems to catch fire. I shiver. He must feel it because he pulls me closer. And I'm too shocked at my response and too bemused at how familiar it feels to be held against him. I dumbly stare at my antagonist who's gone pale. He swallows, then turns and walks off. The crowds close in behind him.

Once again, we're surrounded by the hum of voices, and the sound of the music over the speakers. None of which penetrates this strange thrum of awareness that encompasses the two of us. We could be alone on our own deserted island among this sea of humanity. Then something crashes behind the bar. It cuts through the haze in my head. I push away and he lets me. I turn to face him, standing almost toe to toe in that throng.

"Thank you," I swallow. Then because an imp of mischief pushes me on, I murmur, "husband."

I raise my gaze to his, and further up, and up. I have to tilt my head all the way back and when I meet his eyes I gasp. A deep green, so green they're almost black, but for those silver flares in them which highlight those emerald depths. So verdant it feels like I'm peering into the depths of a lush forest, so intense I'm sure I'm gazing into a swell of the Northern Lights that's going to swoop down from the heavens and sweep me away.

I gulp, take another step back and stumble. He shoots out his arm and wraps his thick fingers around my bicep. Instantly sensations shoot out from the point of contact. His eyes turn almost black, the silver sparks crackling and turning almost gold, which is how I know that he's experiencing the same level of awareness I am.

Then he releases me, and I miss his touch. "Thank you, wife."

His voice is pitched low and has an edge of harshness which grates over my nerve-endings. I shiver again. Try to tear my gaze away from his, but it feels like I've fallen down a rabbit-hole and there's no end in sight. My stomach bottoms out. My knees turn hollow. I sway toward him but stop myself before I crash into him again. I take in that high intelligent forehead, that thick dark hair which must definitely be silky to the touch, the straight nose, those high cheekbones which seem sharp enough to cut through glass, and then that mouth. Oh god, that mouth with the pouty lower lip that invites me to dig my teeth in and suck on it. Goosebumps pop on my arms. My stomach feels so heavy, and there's a hollowness in the place my heart should be. I'll probably never see him again anyway. It's that thought which pushes me lean up on tip toe.

I grab at the front of his T-shirt and tug. I must take him by surprise for he lowers his head enough that I can press my mouth to his. For a few seconds it's like I'm kissing a stone, then suddenly he comes to life. He fits his big hand to the back of my neck, the other to my hip. He draws me in close enough that my chest brushes his, then he tilts his head and deepens the kiss.

Ryot

Soft. And sweet. Like honey, powdered sugar, and candy. Her taste pours through my veins and lights up my blood. My heart begins to thud in my chest. My pulse rate heightens. I swipe my tongue over her's and the taste of her intensifies. I haul her closer and her scent—like honeysuckle and strawberries—invades my senses. My mouth waters. The blood drains to my lower belly. Fire zips down my spine. This. Her. Here. I've been waiting for this moment for so long. I've been waiting for her forever, and I hadn't been aware. I need her. I want her. I have yearned for her. She is the antidote to my past. She is the reason I'm alive. She is why I was awarded a fresh lease of life when I knew I shouldn't have been spared at war. But now I realize why I was given a second chance. I feel like I'd been drowning since the day my wife was killed on mission, two years ago. I felt guilty I'd made it back safe. I'd shut down since. Locked myself off. Never noticed another woman... until now.

I firm my grip around the nape of her neck, she shivers.

I flatten my hand across her back and her entire being shudders. So responsive. So pliant. She was made for me. Sensations course through my veins. I haul her closer and when she whimpers a fierceness grips me. She's mine. Mine. Mine. Mine. I growl deep in my throat and am rewarded when she melts further into me. She throws her arms around my neck and arches into my embrace. I allow myself to drink of her, to revel in her closeness, am aware she must be aware of how I'm responding to her but am unable to stop myself. I need her too much. I need her more than anyone I've ever met before and—I tear my mouth from hers. What's wrong with me?

Why am I thinking like this? I stare down into her shining eyes. It's like I'm looking into the heart of the very earth. The kind that'd provide me with a safe space. A place where I could call home. I shake my head to clear it.

What bizarre thoughts are these? I've never felt this moved before. This touched in a way that makes me feel vulnerable like I've exposed all my deepest secrets to another. I cannot allow myself to feel this way. I release her so suddenly she gasps. Her eyes round with surprise. The color rises on her cheeks.

The next moment she pushes past me and stepping between two groups of people she heads for the door. For a few seconds I watch her retreat, then as if I'm connected to her, I stalk after her. I muscle my way through the crowd, and those in front of me move aside as if sensing the angry mood, I am in. Good thing too. I'm not sure why I'm so affected by her. I'm not sure why I feel like she means something to me already when I just met her.

She heads out of the bar and into the hallway.

Instead of continuing on to the main exit that leads out onto the sidewalk, she pauses. So, do I. She stays still for a second, another as if making up her mind. Then she looks at me over her shoulder. There's a challenge in her eyes. Eh? What is she up to? What is she — she turns and heads up the corridor. Only when my feet hit the floor do I realize I'm following her. I'd been kidding myself earlier by thinking I could let her go. I take in the sway of her hips under the dress she's wearing. It clings to her curves and reaches halfway down her thighs. Combined with the three-inch heels she's wearing; her shapely ankles and the flow of her calves pulse a thrill of anticipation under my skin. Sweat pools under my armpits. I raise my gaze in time to catch her gathering her hair over a shoulder.

The creamy expanse of her back bared by the V-back of her dress has me entranced. She passes the line of women waiting for the Ladies', past the Gents' until she reaches the door that must open out onto the back alley. When she steps through, I'm right behind her. The door slams shut. The sound echoes around the empty space. It sends a shudder of something through her—anticipation, fear? A mixture of both? She pauses. And when I place my hand on her shoulder, she shivers.

When I run my hand down the expanse of skin revealed by the plunging back neckline of the dress, she sighs. I slide my hand down the arch of her back. I want her so much. I could push her up against the wall and she wouldn't resist. But something makes me stop. A sixth sense... that instinct that had saved my life so many times when I was on a tour of duty. Something about the softness of the fabric of her dress, about the fit which proclaims it's not a charity shop buy. The sleek leather of her heels which indicates it's a comfortable fit that wouldn't hurt her feet, the kind that only money—lots of money—can buy.

The thick waterfall of her hair with its strands of fiery auburn and copper and mahogany proclaims loudly that it's been tended to by masterful hands. And that skin of hers—I swallow. That gossamer fine, satiny plush, buttery smooth skin of hers. One touch and it'd stop the devil himself in his tracks. And I'm only human. I pull her up against me and she gasps.

I lower my head and drag my whiskered chin up the side of her neck. She shudders. And when I bite down on the lobe of her ear she whines. The sound cuts through the haze in my mind. I raise my head and look around the empty alley. There are dumpsters opposite us lined up like sentinels. A dog barks in the distance. The faint sound of voices, a muffled crash as something breaks reaches us through the door at our back. I wince. Then twist her around to face me. She looks up into my face.

"Come home with me," I growl.

Her gaze widens, then she shakes her head, "I can't."

"Why not? You want this. So do I." I frown. "Unless I read your signals wrong."

She blinks rapidly.

"Did I? Is that what this is? Didn't take you for a tease."

"I'm not a tease." She sets her jaw. "And I do want you. But I can't wait." She jumps up and I catch her. She wraps her legs around my waist. "Here," She pants. "Right here."

I hesitate.

She rises up throwing her arms about my neck and holds on. "I want you." Her lips tremble. "Please."

Her soft whisper infiltrates my resolve. I turn and press her into the wall near the door we'd come through. She must sense the evidence of my need for her lips part. Then she's raising her chin, I low mine. Our mouths clash. The kiss is everything the earlier one had promised and more, so much more. Her taste permeates my senses, her scent fills my nostrils, the feel of her in my arms is heaven. I tilt my head and drink from her, feel the barrenness in my chest absorb the sensations and come to life.

Once again, I feel this... meeting is not trivial. It's meant to be much more. More than a chance getting together. More than a fumbling encounter in the alleyway. I pull back and chest heaving stare into her flushed features. Her eyelids flutter open, and she looks back with dilated pupils. Her fiery red strands have fallen over her forehead, and something in the angle at which she's staring at me sends a ripple of awareness up my spine. "Have I met you before?" I frown.

She startles, then panic filters into her eyes. "Of course not," she half laughs. The sound is feeble, and a flash of guilt laces her features. She pushes against my chest, and I let her down and take a step back. I steady her until she finds her footing, then stay in place until she's put her clothes to right.

"You know what? Forget it," she tosses her head, "I don't think I want you after all."

I allow a small smirk to curl my features and am rewarded by her glower.

"That's not what I read on your features earlier, Princess," I scoff.

An expression of alarm comes over her.

"What's wrong, you—" I grunt for she's kneed me in the groin. Bloody hell. It's not that it's painful as much as she's taken me by surprise. She darts past me and by the time I recover and hurry after her she's reached the mouth of the alley. I run after her, turn the corner to find she's racing up the sidewalk. Past the entrance to the bar. I run toward her then pause when a limousine draws to a halt in front of her.

She steps into the vehicle and shuts the door. A limousine? And based on my experience in the Marines I can tell that it has been reinforced with bullet proof armor. I frown. Who is this mystery woman? One who looks like an angel and smells like heaven yet has the presence of mind to pretend I was her husband to get rid of unwanted attention, but kisses like a siren. She's so full of contradictions, so full of life, so enticing that surely, I won't be able to forget her. The car drives past. The window lowers and her gaze meets mine. Despite the darkness, there's enough light from the street lamps to light up her features. Her eyes sparkle like smoky quartz, like the richness of Tiger's Eye and Topaz. Something so precious, so unique. My heart skips a beat. Then she's gone and the taillights disappear up the road and into the distance.

Silence for a second. Another. The wind blows. Scraps of paper caught in the whirlwind dance in circles. Like my life. Like this emptiness left behind. I shove my hand into the pocket of my jeans. It's not like me to give into such fanciful thinking. Whoever she was is gone. Good riddance. I'll never see her again. Never feel the press of those gorgeous lips against mine. Good thing too. I don't have time for such distractions. I've sworn never to allow myself to be this susceptible again. Will never allow myself to feel for another. Not after what I've been through. And yet—the way she'd felt in my arms. The way she'd molded herself to me. Those curves of hers which had felt so right. So vital. So, everything. I shake my head. She's gone. Time for me to move onto and put her out of my mind. My phone buzzes. I pull it out of my pocket and bark, "What?"

"Be ready to report for your assignment at oh-nine-hundred, hours," my uncle's voice snaps.

It's as if I'm back in the Marines and he's my commander. Only I'm not and neither is he. If he'd been he'd be asking me to turn up for duty at a god-forsaken hour. Nine a.m, would have been the middle of the day for me. As it is, I'd have been up and trained for a few hours before I'd shower and be at the place I'm expected to be.

"I haven't said I'm accepting the task."

He laughs, "cut the crap, both of us know you are. Besides it's not like you have other options."

"Not like joining a brand-new security agency which hasn't yet built its reputation is," I remind him.

"My reputation precedes me," he says softly. Only a fool would take Quentin Davenport at face value. His tone masks an edge of steel. I can almost picture the harsh set to his features which resemble mine. Q was the first to join the Marines. It set an example for me and my brothers to follow. And all of us expect the youngest, Connor joined the armed forces. Each of us retired after giving our best years to the service. None of us regretted it, either. Though, dealing with the guilt of living while so many of others didn't, is one I'm not sure I'll be over anytime soon either.

"You're not going to join the Davenport group, at least you're smart enough to not make *that* mistake," he admits.

Q like my older brothers Nathan and Knox had given it a shot, but while both had stayed on as CEO of group companies, Q had resigned his role. He'd agreed to stay on the board, but channeled his efforts into setting up his security agency.

When I'd heard about it, it'd felt like a viable alternative to riding a desk—a possibility which had as much appeal as being trapped in an almost airless container by my enemies. I squeeze my fingers around my phone.

"I haven't forgiven you," I snap.

"I don't expect you to," he blows out a breath. "But you need a goal, a focus to keep you going, and I need good men. And you don't want your training to go to waste. If there's one thing I know about you Ryot Davenport, it's that you want to continue to protect those in need. But do you have the guts to accept this challenge? Do you have the courage to rise above your past and move on? Do you—" he hesitates, "—do you have the fortitude to not just survive but live once again?"

To find out what happens next read Ryot & Aurelia's story in *The Reluctant Wife*

Scan this QR code to get the book

How to scan a QR code?

1. Open the camera app on your phone or tablet.
2. Point the camera at the QR code.
3. Tap the banner that appears on your phone or tablet.
4. Follow the instructions on the screen to finish signing in.

READ THE BONUS EPILOGUE FROM *THE UNPLANNED WEDDING KNOX &*
JUNE'S STORY

June

"It's a boy." The nurse places the crying child on my chest.

The skin-to-skin contact sends a surge of emotions so intense through my chest, I draw in a sharp breath. I take in his red features, his tiny eyes, his little nose, rose-bud mouth, screwed up features, and feel a love so immense, so deep, so bountiful, it crashes over me, swallows me, and pushes out the tears I didn't manage to shed through the eight-hour labor.

I pushed through the night when the urge built and became too much, and felt like an earthquake was splintering my insides. He's a big boy. No surprise there. But now, here he is. My flesh and bone. My son. Born of me. From me. And in his features, I see myself reflected—as well as my husband—and the tears flow down my cheeks.

I hold him close, draw in a deep breath of his scent—a fresh baby fragrance that smells like me and my husband, but is also so unique. It's his, my child's. It belongs to him, an identity already crafted and his because he's mine and Knox's. And he'll always know the both of us. From the moment he drew his first breath, he was loved. From his first cry, he was cherished. I kiss the top of his little head, marveling at the full head of hair he has.

My tears slide down my cheeks and drip onto him, and I can't help but wonder if this is how my mother felt when she gave birth to me. Did she hold me and feel this kind of love pour through her? Did she touch my little fingers and wonder how it was possible that a little human had emerged from her? Did she consider how she'd gone from being alone to never being alone because there was someone who reflected her? Someone carrying a little piece of her heart around with them. Did she look into my face and see herself, the way I do with my son? Was the pain of childbirth forgotten in the thrill of holding new life in her arms? Knowing she'd never be the same again? Knowing her future had changed? Knowing...

She'd never be able to keep me. Feeling so helpless, so completely in over her head. So vulnerable and responsible for another...because of which, she had to make the decision she did. I wonder how difficult it must have been for her. How heartbreaking. And what strength it must have taken to put my needs before her desires. Tears well up in my eyes as I think about teenaged Claire and the opportunity she never really had. It's not something I'd ever wish anyone to experience. For the first time, I wonder if the pain of loss she experienced was just as bad as my feelings of abandonment.

I take in my son's face again, unable to look away. I'm drawn to him so powerfully, in a way I never will be to anyone else. Not even my Sir. My husband. And that's humbling. To be gifted with not only one love, but two.

A love for the man who gave me the space to come to terms with my past. The man who allowed me to explore the different facets of myself with no judgement. The man responsible for giving me my son.

And then, this little being who's completely turned my world upside down in a way I never would have believed, and he only just arrived. What a privilege to be his mother and feel grounded. There's someone I have a flesh and blood connection to, who I will unconditionally love, who'll love me back.

Yes, Claire does love me too... But this up-swell of emotions I feel for my son feels new and unique. It anchors me so much.

"Are you okay, baby?" My husband wraps his arms about me and our son. He anchors me, too. But in a distinct way. His love fills my body and heart and soul. And my son—his very presence threads the needle of my existence. He helps reinforce my identity in a manner that completes me. And it's not only because I am a mother. No, it's because I see my son, and I see myself reflected in him. And that mirroring of myself validates me in a way I've missed all my life.

"Darling?" My husband cups my cheek. "What is it?"

I sniffle, then shake my head. "A little overwhelmed by everything," I concede.

"Understandable. Take your time. You've been through a mentally and physically taxing few hours. What you did..." His throat moves as he swallows. "I don't think I'd have the strength and fortitude to give birth. You're the most incredible woman in the world, you know that?"

My son chooses this moment to open his mouth and cry. "Oh, there, there." I rock him, following an age-old instinct that seems to take over from somewhere inside of me. The same instinct that had me pushing and channeling all the women who came before me who gave birth. The same instinct that had me pulling on reserves of energy inside me that I was sure I didn't have. It's that same instinct which has my son moving his legs and using his arms to push upward in tiny movements toward my breast.

"Oh, he wants to feed."

I maneuver him toward my nipple, and he tries to latch on but fails. Tries again; fails again. He begins to cry but continues to reach for my nipple.

"Here, why don't you change the angle?" The lactation expert on standby steps up. She helps me change how I've positioned him, and within seconds, my son's latched onto my breast. He begins to suck, and the sensation turns my heart into one melting puddle of goo. Tears squeeze out from my eyes. I'm unable to stop them. I feel more than overwhelmed. I feel like my world has tilted off its axis. And I love it.

"Oh, honey, you're crying?" my husband exclaims.

"It's these hormones. I'm good, really; more than good." I take in my child suckling at my breast, then glance up at him. "I feel so good, I think I'm going to burst."

His features soften. Those blue eyes I once thought as cold as the North Pole now burn with emotions. Looking into his eyes now makes me feel like I'm about to dive into a tropical lagoon.

"Me too." He bends and kisses my forehead, then glances at the baby who's fallen asleep at my breast with his mouth open.

"Do you want to hold him?

He swallows, then nods.

I hand our boy to him, and he places our son on his bare chest. The sight of my husband with his rippled abs, huge shoulders and biceps — which are twice the size of the baby he's holding in his hands — placing the newborn against his chest and looking down at him with such open adoration, brings on a fresh wave of tears. I'm not ashamed to say my chest squeezes and my pussy clenches.

Or perhaps, that's the afterbirth? My womb contracts, confirming what I guessed.

I groan, and my husband looks at me in alarm.

The doctor steps up. "All right, Mr. Davenport, if you'll hand the baby over to the nurse, we can assist your wife with delivering the placenta."

My husband pales. Throughout the delivery, I was too focused on the actual birth process to notice his reactions. Now, I swallow down a chuckle, realizing the event has changed him in ways I can't wait to discover.

Knox hands our boy to a nurse who whisks him away to the other side of the room, to clean him and weigh him. Then, he reaches over and slips his hand into mine. I squeeze his fingers and get ready to push again.

Knox

"He's beautiful." Ryot glances from the baby in my arms, to my face, then back to the child.

We're in the nursery adjoining our bedroom at home. My wife is asleep inside, and when the baby began to fuss, I came over to take care of him. I moved my home office to the room opposite the nursery, and hooked up a feed to the baby-cam up on one of my monitors, so I can keep an eye on the baby while I work.

I especially love watching my wife and our son together as she feeds him and sings to him. No, I don't get that much work done. Many times, I delegate projects I'm working on to my new VP of Finance—who I chose from the shortlist my wife had drawn up—and walk over to join her.

"Thank god, he has her features," Ryot quips, and I laugh.

"You can say that again." I can't take my gaze off of my sleeping son. It's been three days since we brought him back from the hospital. My grandfather, as well as all of my brothers, except Connor, have visited us. Connor is away on another of his research expeditions but video-called to congratulate us. Ryot is the last to visit us.

He was content to sit in silence and watch as I rocked the boy back to sleep. I didn't expected him to say much, as is his habit. His features grew soft when he saw my son, and he hasn't taken his gaze off of the baby since walking in here.

"Would you like to hold him?" I ask in a casual tone. Having lost his wife not that long ago, it must be difficult for him to see me all settled in and nesting with my wife and son. I didn't expect him to come by, either, considering how fresh his wounds are, so I was surprised when he turned up.

And when he holds out his arms, I'm glad he does. Seeing how much I've already changed, just going through the experience of my wife giving birth and taking care of my new son, I know first-hand how life-affirming it is to hold a newborn in your hands.

I slide the baby into his arms, and he holds his nephew close. His features soften further, his gaze riveted by the little fella. The baby stirs, and he rocks the child like he's done it many times before.

"You're going to make an amazing father some day," I comment.

He stiffens, continues to soothe his nephew, but doesn't respond.

I'm content to sit there watching my brother and my son for a few minutes. I should probably keep quiet and allow him to soak up this closeness with his nephew but because I know he's embarking on a new assignment with Quentin's security firm, and because I don't know when I'll see him next, I reach over and grip his shoulder. "I want this for you Ryot. This happiness, this closeness, this peace that comes with having a family. I hope you get it too brother."

The tendons on his throat flex, then he nods. I allow myself to squeeze his shoulder, hoping he feels all the comfort I'm offering him. This seems to be the best way to indicate to him that I empathize with what he's going through. I hope I'm never in his position, faced with such loss. I was lucky to walk away from my time as a Marine without losing a spouse. I lost brothers-in-arms, yes, I spent time behind enemy lines, and yes, I bear the scars on my face and my body, but I walked away with the rest of me intact. And the wounds I carried internally are on the way to healing, thanks to my wife.

"I hope you find love again, brother," I say slowly.

He draws in a sharp breath, then gently hands the child to me. He bends, kisses his nephew's forehead, then straightens. "I cannot go through that kind of loss again. I won't do it," he declares.

"But—"I begin, but he shakes his head.

"Let it be, brother. I'm happy for everything you have. Seeing you and your family thrive is more than enough for me. I'm not going to have that; I've accepted it."

"Have you?" I place the sleeping baby in his crib, then stand up and stretch.

"I'm happy with my lot. Besides, my new job doesn't give me time to mull over the past, or the future. I have to be on guard and stay focused. I have no time for anything that will take my attention away from the task at hand."

He heads for the door, and I call out. "Ryot?"

He pauses.

"Watch out. Love finds you when you least expect it."

To find out what happens next read Ryot and Princess Aurelia's story in the reluctant Wife

Want to be the first to find out when L. Steele's next book is out? Sign up for her newsletter

Read Summer & Sinclair Sterling's story in The Billionaire's Fake Wife

Read an excerpt from Summer & Sinclair's story

Summer

"Slap, slap, kiss, kiss."

"Huh?" I stare up at the bartender.

"Aka, there's a thin line between love and hate." He shakes out the crimson liquid into my glass.

"Nah." I snort. "Why would she allow him to control her, and after he insulted her?"

"It's the chemistry between them." He lowers his head. "You have to admit that, when the man is arrogant and the woman resists, it's a challenge to both of them, to see who blinks first, huh?"

"Why?" I wave my hand in the air. "Because they hate each other?"

"Because," he chuckles, "the girl in school whose braids I pulled and teased mercilessly, is the one who I—"

"Proposed to?" I huff.

His face lights up. "You get it now?"

Yeah. No. A headache begins to pound at my temples. This crash course in pop psychology is not why I came to my favorite bar in Islington, to meet my best friend, who is—I glance at the face of my phone—thirty minutes late.

I inhale the drink, and his eyebrows rise.

"What?" I glower up at the bartender. "I can barely taste the alcohol. Besides, it's free drinks at happy hour for women, right?"

"Which ends in precisely—" he holds up five fingers— "minutes."

"Oh! Yay!" I mock fist pump. "Time enough for one more, at least."

A hiccough swells my throat and I swallow it back, nod.

One has to do what one has to do... when everything else in the world is going to shit.

A hot sensation stabs behind my eyes; my chest tightens. Is this what people call growing up?

The bartender tips his mixing flask, strains out a fresh batch of the ruby red liquid onto the glass in front of me.

"Salut." I nod my thanks, then toss it back. It hits my stomach and tendrils of fire crawl up my spine, I cough.

My head spins. Warmth sears my chest, spreads to my extremities. I can't feel my fingers or toes. Good. Almost there. "Top me up."

"You sure?"

"Yes." I square my shoulders and reach for the drink.

"No. She's had enough."

"What the—?" I pivot on the bar stool.

Indigo eyes bore into me.

Fathomless. Black at the bottom, the intensity in their depths grips me. He swoops out his arm, grabs the glass and holds it up. Thick fingers dwarf the glass. Tapered at the edges. The nails short and buff. *All the better to grab you with.* I gulp.

"Like what you see?"

I flush, peer up into his face.

Hard cheekbones, hollows under them, and a tiny scar that slashes at his left eyebrow. *How did he get that?* Not that I care. My gaze slides to his mouth. Thin upper lip, a lower lip that is full and cushioned. Pouty with a hint of bad boy. *Oh!* My toes curl. My thighs clench.

The corner of his mouth kicks up. *Asshole.*

Bet he thinks life is one big smug-fest. I glower, reach for my glass, and he holds it up and out of my reach.

I scowl. "Gimme that."

He shakes his head.

"That's my drink."

"Not anymore." He shoves my glass at the bartender. "Water for her. Get me a whiskey, neat."

I splutter, then reach for my drink again. The barstool tips in his direction. This is when I fall against him, and my breasts slam into his hard chest, sculpted planes with layers upon layers of muscle that ripple and writhe as he turns aside, flattens himself against the bar. The floor rises up to meet me.

What the actual hell?

I twist my torso at the last second and my butt connects with the surface. *Ow!*

The breath rushes out of me. My hair swirls around my face. I scramble for purchase, and my knee connects with his leg.

"Watch it." He steps around, stands in front of me.

"You stepped aside?" I splutter. "You let me fall?"

"Hmph."

I tilt my chin back, all the way back, look up the expanse of muscled thigh that stretches the silken material of his suit. *What is he wearing? Could any suit fit a man with such precision?* Hand crafted on Saville Row, no doubt. I glance at the bulge that tents the fabric between his legs. *Oh!* I blink.

Look away, look away. I hold out my arm. He'll help me up at least, won't he?

He glances at my palm, then turns away. *No, he didn't do that, no way.*

A glass of amber liquid appears in front of him. He lifts the tumbler to his sculpted mouth.

His throat moves, strong tendons flexing. He tilts his head back, and the column of his neck moves as he swallows. Dark hair covers his chin — it's a discordant chord in that clean-cut profile, I shiver. He would scrape that rough skin down my core. He'd mark my inner thighs, lick my core, thrust his tongue inside my melting channel and drink from my pussy. *Oh! God.* Goosebumps rise on my skin.

No one has the right to look this beautiful, this achingly gorgeous. Too magnificent for his own good. Anger coils in my chest.

"Arrogant wanker."

"I'll take that under advisement."

"You're a jerk, you know that?"

He presses his lips together. The grooves on either side of his mouth deepen. Clearly the man has never laughed a single day in his life. Bet that stick up his arse is uncomfortable. I chuckle.

He runs his gaze down my features, my chest, down to my toes, then yawns.

The hell! I will not let him provoke me. Will not. "Like what you see?" I jut out my chin.

"Sorry, you're not my type." He slides a hand into the pocket of those perfectly cut pants, stretching it across that heavy bulge.

Heat curls low in my belly.

Not fair, that he could afford a wardrobe that clearly shouts his status and what amounts to the economy of a small third-world country. A hot feeling stabs in my chest.

He reeks of privilege, of taking his status in life for granted.

While I've had to fight every inch of the way. Hell, I am still battling to hold onto the last of my equilibrium.

"Last chance—" I wiggle my fingers from where I am sprawled out on the floor at his feet, "—to redeem yourself..."

"You have me there." He places the glass on the counter, then bends and holds out his hand. The hint of discolored steel at his wrist catches my attention. Huh?

He wears a cheap-ass watch?

That's got to bring down the net worth of his presence by more than 1000% percent. Weird.

I reach up and he straightens.

I lurch back.

"Oops, I changed my mind." His lips curl.

A hot burning sensation claws at my stomach. I am not a violent person, honestly. But Smirky Pants here, he needs to be taught a lesson.

I swipe out my legs, kicking his out from under him.

Sinclair

My knees give way, and I hurtle toward the ground.

What the—? I twist around, thrust out my arms. My palms hit the floor. The impact jostles up my elbows. I firm my biceps and come to a halt planked above her.

A huffing sound fills my ear.

I turn to find my whippet, Max, panting with his mouth open. I scowl and he flattens his ears.

All of my businesses are dog-friendly. Before you draw conclusions about me being the caring sort or some such shit—it attracts footfall.

Max scrutinizes the girl, then glances at me. *Huh?* He hates women, but not her, apparently.

I straighten and my nose grazes hers.

My arms are on either side of her head. Her chest heaves. The fabric of her dress stretches across her gorgeous breasts. My fingers tingle; my palms ache to cup those tits, squeeze those hard nipples outlined against the—hold on, what is she wearing? A tunic shirt in a sparkly pink... and are those shoulder pads she has on?

I glance up, and a squeak escapes her lips.

Pink hair surrounds her face. *Pink? Who dyes their hair that color past the age of eighteen?*

I stare at her face. *How old is she?* Un-furrowed forehead, dark eyelashes that flutter against pale cheeks. Tiny nose, and that mouth—luscious, tempting. A whiff of her scent, cherries and caramel, assails my senses. My mouth waters. *What the hell?*

She opens her eyes and our eyelashes brush. Her gaze widens. Green, like the leaves of the evergreens, flickers of gold sparkling in their depths. "What?" She glowers. "You're demonstrating the plank position?"

"Actually," I lower my weight onto her, the ridge of my hardness thrusting into the softness between her legs, "I was thinking of something else, altogether."

She gulps and her pupils dilate. *Ah, so she feels it, too?*

I drop my head toward her, closer, closer.

Color floods the creamy expanse of her neck. Her eyelids flutter down. She tilts her chin up.

I push up and off of her.

"That... Sweetheart, is an emphatic 'no thank you' to whatever you are offering."

Her eyelids spring open and pink stains her cheeks. Adorable. Such a range of emotions across those gorgeous features in a few seconds. What else is hidden under that exquisite exterior of hers?

She scrambles up, eyes blazing.

Ah! The little bird is trying to spread her wings? My dick twitches. My groin hardens, *Why does her anger turn me on so, huh?*

She steps forward, thrusts a finger in my chest.

My heart begins to thud.

She peers up from under those hooded eyelashes. "Wake up and taste the wasabi, asshole."

"What does that even mean?"

She makes a sound deep in her throat. My dick twitches. My pulse speeds up.

She pivots, grabs a half-full beer mug sitting on the bar counter.

I growl, "Oh, no, you don't."

She turns, swings it at me. The smell of hops envelops the space.

I stare down at the beer-splattered shirt, the lapels of my camel colored jacket deepening to a dull brown. Anger squeezes my guts.

I fist my fingers at my side, broaden my stance.

She snickers.

I tip my chin up. "You're going to regret that."

The smile fades from her face. "Umm." She places the now empty mug on the bar.

I take a step forward and she skitters back. "It's only clothes." She gulps. "They'll wash."

I glare at her and she swallows, wiggles her fingers in the air. "I should have known that you wouldn't have a sense of humor."

I thrust out my jaw. "That's a ten-thousand-pound suit you destroyed."

She blanches, then straightens her shoulders. "Must have been some hot date you were trying to impress, huh?"

"Actually," I flick some of the offending liquid from my lapels, "it's you I was after."

"Me?" She frowns.

"We need to speak."

She glances toward the bartender who's on the other side of the bar. "I don't know you." She chews on her lower lip, biting off some of the hot pink. How would she look, with that pouty mouth fastened on my cock?

The blood rushes to my groin so quickly that my head spins. My pulse rate ratchets up. Focus, focus on the task you came here for.

"This will take only a few seconds." I take a step forward.

She moves aside.

I frown. "You want to hear this, I promise."

"Go to hell." She pivots and darts forward.

I let her go, a step, another, because... I can? Besides it's fun to create the illusion of freedom first; makes the hunt so much more entertaining, huh?

I swoop forward, loop an arm around her waist, and yank her toward me.

She yelps. "Release me."

Good thing the bar is not yet full. It's too early for the usual officegoers to stop by. And the staff...? Well they are well aware of who cuts their paychecks.

I spin her around and against the bar, then release her. "You will listen to me."

She swallows; she glances left to right.

Not letting you go yet, little Bird. I move into her space, crowd her.

She tips her chin up. "Whatever you're selling, I'm not interested."

I allow my lips to curl. "You don't fool me."

A flush steals up her throat, sears her cheeks. So tiny, so innocent. Such a good little liar. I narrow my gaze. "Every action has its consequences."

"Are you daft?" She blinks.

"This pretense of yours?" I thrust my face into hers, growling, "It's not working."

She blinks, then color suffuses her cheeks. "You're certifiably mad —"

"Getting tired of your insults."

"It's true, everything I said." She scrapes back the hair from her face.

Her fingernails are painted... You guessed it, pink.

"And here's something else. You are a selfish, egotistical jackass."

I smirk. "You're beginning to repeat your insults and I haven't even kissed you yet."

"Don't you dare." She gulps.

I tilt my head. "Is that a challenge?"

"It's a..." she scans the crowded space, then turns to me. Her lips firm, "...a warning. You're delusional, you jackass." She inhales a deep breath before she speaks, "Your ego is bigger than the size of a black hole." She snickers. "Bet it's to compensate for your lack of balls."

A-n-d, that's it. I've had enough of her mouth that threatens to never stop spewing words. How many insults can one tiny woman hurl my way? Answer: too many to count.

"You—"

I lower my chin, touch my lips to hers.

Heat, sweetness, the honey of her essence explodes on my palate. My dick twitches. I tilt my head, deepen the kiss, reaching for that something more... more... of whatever scent she's wearing on her skin, infused with that breath of hers that crowds my senses, rushes down my spine. My groin hardens; my cock lengthens. I thrust my tongue between those infuriating lips.

She makes a sound deep in her throat and my heart begins to pound.

So innocent, yet so crafty. Beautiful and feisty. The kind of complication I don't need in my life.

I prefer the straight and narrow. Gray and black, that's how I choose to define my world. She, with her flashes of color—pink hair and lips that threaten to drive me to the edge of distraction—is exactly what I hate.

Give me a female who has her priorities set in life. To pleasure me, get me off, then walk away before her emotions engage. Yeah. That's what I prefer.

Not this... this bundle of craziness who flings her arms around my shoulders, thrusts her breasts up and into my chest, tips up her chin, opens her mouth, and invites me to take and take.

Does she have no self-preservation? Does she think I am going to fall for her wide-eyed appeal? She has another thing coming.

I tear my mouth away and she protests.

She twines her leg with mine, pushes up her hips, so that melting softness between her thighs cradles my aching hardness.

I glare into her face and she holds my gaze.

Trains her green eyes on me. Her cheeks flush a bright red. Her lips fall open and a moan bleeds into the air. The blood rushes to my dick, which instantly thickens. *Fuck.*

Time to put distance between myself and the situation.

It's how I prefer to manage things. Stay in control, always. Cut out anything that threatens to impinge on my equilibrium. Shut it down or buy them off. Reduce it to a transaction. That I understand.

The power of money, to be able to buy and sell—numbers, logic. That's what's worked for me so far.

"How much?"

Her forehead furrows.

"Whatever it is, I can afford it."

Her jaw slackens. "You think... you—"

"A million?"

"What?"

"Pounds, dollars... You name the currency, and it will be in your account."

Her jaw slackens. "You're offering me money?"

"For your time, and for you to fall in line with my plan."

She reddens. "You think I am for sale?"

"Everyone is."

"Not me."

Here we go again. "Is that a challenge?"

Color fades from her face. "Get away from me."

"Are you shy, is that what this is?" I frown. "You can write your price down on a piece of paper if you prefer." I glance up, notice the bartender watching us. I jerk my chin toward the napkins. He grabs one, then offers it to her.

She glowers at him. "Did you buy him, too?"

"What do you think?"

She glances around. "I think everyone here is ignoring us."

"It's what I'd expect."

"Why is that?"

I wave the tissue in front of her face. "Why do you think?"

"You own the place?"

"As I am going to own you."

She sets her jaw. "Let me leave and you won't regret this."

A chuckle bubbles up. I swallow it away. This is no laughing matter. I never smile during a transaction. Especially not when I am negotiating a new acquisition. And that's all she is. The final piece in the puzzle I am building.

"No one threatens me."

"You're right."

"Huh?"

"I'd rather act on my instinct."

Her lips twist, her gaze narrows. All of my senses scream a warning.

No, she wouldn't, no way—pain slices through my middle and sparks explode behind my eyes.

Read Sinclair and Summer's enemies to lovers, marriage of convenience romance in The Billionaire's Fake Wife here

read Liam and Isla's fake relationship romance in The Proposal where Tiny first makes an appearance, click here

Read an excerpt from The Proposal

Liam

"Where is she?"

The receptionist gazes at me cow-eyed. Her lips move, but no words emerge. She clears her throat, glances sideways at the door to the side and behind her, then back at me.

"So, I take it she's in there?" I brush past her, and she jumps to her feet.

"Sir, y-y-you can't go in there."

"Watch me." I glare at her.

She stammers, then gulps. Sweat beads her forehead. She shuffles back, and I stalk past her.

Really, is there no one who can stand up to me? All of this scraping of chairs and fawning over me? It's enough to drive a man to boredom. I need a challenge. So, when my ex-wife-to-be texted me to say she was calling off our wedding, I was pissed. But when she let it slip that her wedding planner was right—that she needs to marry for love, and not for some family obligation, rage gripped me. I squeezed my phone so hard the screen cracked. I almost hurled the device across the room. When I got a hold of myself, for the first time in a long time, a shiver of something like excitement passed through me. *Finally, fuck.*

That familiar pulse of adrenaline pulses through my veins. It's a sensation I was familiar with in the early days of building my business.

After my father died and I took charge of the group of companies he'd run, I was filled with a sense of purpose; a one-directional focus to prove myself and nurture his legacy. To make my group of companies the leader, in its own right. To make so much money and amass so much power, I'd be a force to be reckoned with.

I tackled each business meeting with a zeal that none of my opponents were able to withstand. But with each passing year—as I crossed the benchmarks I'd set myself, as my bottom line grew healthier, my cash reserves engorged, and the people working for me began treating me with the kind of respect normally reserved for larger-than-life icons—some of that enthusiasm waned. Oh, I still wake up ready to give my best to my job every day, but the zest that once fired me up faded, leaving a sense of purposelessness behind.

The one thing that has kept me going is to lock down my legacy. To ensure the business I've built will finally be transferred to my name. For which my father informed me I would need to marry. Which is why, after much research, I tracked down Lila Kumar, wooed her, and proposed to her. And then, her meddling wedding planner came along and turned all of my plans upside down.

Now, that same sense of purpose grips me. That laser focus I've been lacking envelops me and fills my being. All of my senses sharpen as I shove the door of her office open and stalk in.

The scent envelops me first. The lush notes of violets and peaches. Evocative and fruity. Complex, yet with a core of mystery that begs to be unraveled. Huh? I'm not the kind to be affected by the scent of a woman, but this... Her scent... It's always chafed at my nerve endings. The hair on my forearms straightens.

My guts tie themselves up in knots, and my heart pounds in my chest. It's not comfortable. The kind of feeling I got the first time I went white-water rafting. A combination of nervousness and excitement as I faced my first rapids. A sensation that had since ebbed. One I'd been chasing ever since, pushing myself to take on extreme sports. One I hadn't thought I'd find in the office of a wedding planner.

My feet thud on the wooden floor, and I get a good look at the space which is one-fourth the size of my own office. In the far corner is a bookcase packed with books. On the opposite side is a comfortable settee packed with cushions women seem to like so much. There's a colorful patchwork quilt thrown over it, and behind that, a window that looks onto the back of the adjacent office building. On the coffee table in front of the settee is a bowl with crystal-like objects that reflect the light from the floor lamps. There are paintings on the wall that depict scenes from beaches. No doubt, the kind she'd point to and sell the idea of a honeymoon to gullible brides. I suppose the entire space would appeal to women. With its mood lighting and homey feel, the space invites you to kick back, relax and pour out your problems. A ruse I'm not going to fall for.

"You!" I stab my finger in the direction of the woman seated behind the antique desk straight ahead. "Call Lila, right now, and tell her she needs to go through with the wedding. Tell her she can't back out. Tell her I'm the right choice for her."

She peers up at me from behind large, black horn-rimmed glasses perched on her nose. "No."

I blink. "Excuse me?"

She leans back in her chair. "I'm not going to do that."

"Why the hell not?"

"Are you the right choice for her?

"Of course, I am." I glare at her.

Some of the color fades from her cheeks. She taps her pen on the table, then juts out her chin. "What makes you think you're the right choice of husband for her?"

"What makes you think I'm not."

"Do you love her?"

"That's no one's problem except mine and hers."

"You don't love her."

"What does that have to do with anything?"

"Excuse me?" She pushes the glasses further up her nose. "Are you seriously asking what loving the woman you're going to marry has to do with actually marrying her?" Her voice pulses with fury.

"Yes, exactly. Why don't you explain it to me?" The sarcasm in my tone is impossible to miss.

She stares at me from behind those large glasses that should make her look owlish and studious, but only add an edge of what I can only describe as quirky-sexiness. The few times I've met her before, she's gotten on my nerves so much, I couldn't wait to get the hell away from her. Now, giving her the full benefit of my attention, I realize, she's actually quite striking. And the addition of those spectacles? Fuck me—I never thought I had a weakness for women wearing glasses. Maybe I was wrong. Or maybe it's specifically this woman wearing glasses... Preferably only glasses and nothing else.

Hmm. Interesting. This reaction to her. It's unwarranted and not something I planned for. I widen my stance, mainly to accommodate the thickness between my legs. An inconvenience... which perhaps I can use to my benefit? I drag my thumb under my lower lip.

Her gaze drops to my mouth, and if I'm not mistaken, her breath hitches. *Very interesting.* Has she always reacted to me like that in the past? Nope, I would've noticed. We've always tried to have as little as possible to do with each other. Like I said, interesting. And unusual.

"First," —she drums her fingers on the table— "are you going to answer my question?"

I tilt my head, the makings of an idea buzzing through my synapses. I need a little time to flesh things out though. It's the only reason I deign to answer her question which, let's face it, I have no obligation to respond to. But for the moment, it's in my interest to humor her and buy myself a little time.

"Lila and I are well-matched in every way. We come from good families—"

"You mean rich families?"

"That, too. Our families move in the same circles."

"Don't you mean boring country clubs?" she says in a voice that drips with distaste.

I frown. "Among other places. We have the pedigree, the bloodline, our backgrounds are congruent, and we'd be able to fold into an arrangement of coexistence with the least amount of disruption on either side."

"Sounds like you're arranging a merger."

"A takeover, but what-fucking-ever." I raise a shoulder.

Her scowl deepens. "This is how you approached the upcoming wedding... And you wonder why Lila left you?"

"I gave her the biggest ring money could buy—"

"You didn't make an appearance at the engagement party."

"I signed off on all the costs related to the upcoming nuptials—"

"Your own engagement party. You didn't come to it. You left her alone to face her family and friends." Her tone rises. Her cheeks are flushed. You'd think she was talking about her own wedding, not that of her friend. In fact, it's more entertaining to talk to her than discuss business matters with my employees. *How interesting.*

"You also didn't show up for most of the rehearsals." She glowers.

"I did show up for the last one."

"Not that it made any difference. You were either checking your watch and indicating that it was time for you to leave, or you were glowering at the plans being discussed."

"I still agreed to that god-awful wedding cake, didn't I?

"On the other hand, it's probably good you didn't come for the previous rehearsals. If you had, Lila and I might have had this conversation earlier—"

"Aha!" I straighten. "So, you confess that it's because of you Lila walked away from this wedding."

She tips her head back. "Hardly. It's because of you."

"So you say, but your guilt is written large on your face."

"Guilt?" Her features flush. The color brings out the dewy hue of her skin, and the blue of her eyes deepens until they remind me of forget-me-nots. No, more like the royal blue of the ink that spilled onto my paper the first time I attempted to write with a fountain pen.

"The only person here who should feel guilty is you, for attempting to coerce an innocent, young woman into an arrangement that would have trapped her for life."

Anger thuds at my temples. My pulse begins to race. "I never have to coerce women. And what you call being trapped is what most women call security. But clearly, you wouldn't know that, considering" —I wave my hand in the air— "you prefer to run your kitchen-table business which, no doubt, barely makes ends meet."

She loosens her grip on her pencil, and it falls to the table with a clatter. Sparks flash deep in her eyes.

You know what I said earlier about the royal blue? Strike that. There are flickers of silver hidden in the depths of her gaze. Flickers that blaze when she's upset. How would it be to push her over the edge? To be at the receiving end of all that passion, that fervor, that ardor... that absolute avidness of existence when she's one with the moment? How would it feel to rein in her spirit, absorb it, drink from it, revel in it, and use it to spark color into my life?

"Kitchen-table business?" She makes a growling sound under her breath. "You dare come into my office and insult my enterprise? The company I have grown all by myself—"

"And outside of your assistant" —I nod toward the door I came through— "you're the sole employee, I take it?"

Her color deepens. "I work with a group of vendors—"

I scoff, "None of whom you could hold accountable when they don't deliver."

"—who have been carefully vetted to ensure that they always deliver," she says at the same time. "Anyway, why do you care, since you don't have a wedding to go to?"

"That's where you're wrong." I peel back my lips. "I'm not going to be labeled as the joke of the century. After all, the media labelled it 'the wedding of the century'." I make air quotes with my fingers.

It was Isla's idea to build up the wedding with the media. She also wanted to invite influencers from all walks of life to attend, but I have no interest in turning my nuptials into a circus. So, I vetoed the idea of journalists attending in person. I have, however, agreed to the event being recorded by professionals and exclusive clips being shared with the media and the influencers. This way, we'll get the necessary PR coverage, without the media being physically present.

In all fairness, the publicity generated by the upcoming nuptials has already been beneficial. It's not like I'll ever tell her, but Isla was right to feed the public's interest in the upcoming event. Apparently, not even the most hard-nosed investors can resist the warm, fuzzy feelings that a marriage invokes. And this can only help with the IPO I have planned for the most important company in my portfolio. "I have a lot riding on this wedding."

"Too bad you don't have a bride."

"Ah," —I smirk— "but I do."

She scowls. "No, you don't. Lila—"

"I'm not talking about her."

"Then who are you talking about?"

"You."

To find out what happens next read Liam and Isla's fake relationship romance in The Proposal where Tiny first makes an appearance

read Michael and Karma's forced marriage romance in Mafia King

Read JJ and Lena's ex-boyfriend's father, age-gap romance

Read Knight and Penny's, best friend's brother romance in The Wrong Wife

Read Dr. Weston Kincaid and Amelie's forced proximity, one-bed Christmas Romance in The Billionaire's Fake Wife

MARRIAGE OF CONVENIENCE
BILLIONAIRE ROMANCE FROM L. STEELE

The Billionaire's Fake Wife - Sinclair and Summer's story that started this universe... with a plot twist you won't see coming!

The Billionaire's Secret - Victoria and Saint's story. Saint is maybe the most alphahole of them all!

Marrying the Billionaire Single Dad - Damian and Julia's story, watch out for the plot twist!

The Proposal - Liam and Isla's story. What's a wedding planner to do when you tell the bride not to go through with the wedding and the groom demands you take her place and give him a heir? And yes plot twist!

CHRISTMAS ROMANCE BOOKS BY L. STEELE FOR YOU

Want to find out how Dr. Weston Kincaid and Amelie met? Read *The Billionaire's Christmas Bride*

Want even more Christmas Romance books? *Read A very Mafia Christmas, Christian and Aurora's story*

Read a marriage of convenience billionaire Christmas romance, Hunter and Zara's story - *The Christmas One Night Stand*

ABOUT THE AUTHOR

Hello, I'm L. Steele.

I write romance stories with strong powerful men who meet their match in sassy, curvy, spitfire women.

I love to push myself with each book on both the spice and the angst so I can deliver well rounded, multidimensional characters.

I enjoy trading trivia with my husband, watching lots and lots of movies, and walking nature trails. I live in London.

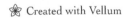 Created with Vellum

Made in the USA
Monee, IL
04 October 2024

67234696R00216